# THE HAMMER OF GOD

GINA MIANI

To Dick and Nikki —
Go Army!
To great friends —
today and always —

12/14

Copyright © 2014 GINA MIANI DETWILER

All rights reserved.

ISBN: 1500385131
ISBN-13: 978-1500385132

This book is a work of fiction. Names, places and events are used fictionally. Any resemblance to persons living or dead is coincidental.

www.ginamiani.com

*For my daughters*
*Danielle, Dominique and Samantha*
*Battle Swans all*

# CONTENTS

# FRANCIA, CIRCA 700 AD

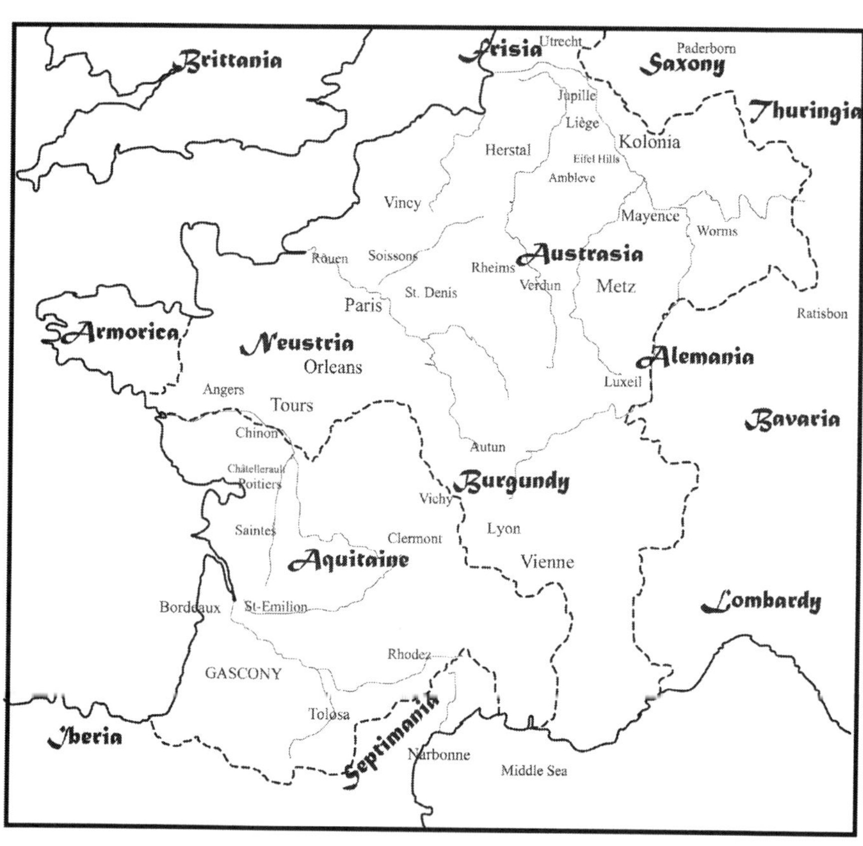

## AUTHOR'S NOTE

Writing about the "Dark Ages" is a lot like putting together a 500-piece puzzle with 400 pieces missing. Though most of the places and events in this book are portrayed as accurately as possible given the available source material, this is a work of imagination and should be read as such.

Gina Miani
August, 2014

*History is not a long dark tunnel.*
*It is a mirror.*
*And the people we see there are,*
*for better or worse,*
*ourselves.*

# DECEMBER, 731

## Invasion

## Tolosa
## The Aquitaine

ON A COLD afternoon three days before the celebration of the birth of the Christian God, the forward guard of a massive new Arab army emerged from an obscure pass of the central Pyrenees Mountains and entered the Duchy of the Aquitaine.

No one saw it coming.

The leader was Abd 'ar-Rayman, the newly crowned Emir of an-Andalus, the former Gothic kingdom of Iberia. He rode at the front of the column on a white Andalusian, wearing a long shirt of scaled mail under his white *qaba*, the metal cone of a helmet protruding from his turban. A curved, single-edged sword hung at his side. He was an aristocrat of his kind, a proud and fearless warrior, a would-be king.

The Arabs usually crossed the mountains through the low hills nearer the coast into Septimania, which lay along the southern Aquitainian border. The coastline and the western foothills of the Pyrenees were heavily patrolled by scouts, but the central ranges were steep and forbidding, crisscrossed by trails no wider than goat tracks, largely ignored. Rayman had chosen that path, despite its obvious treacheries. He wanted his arrival to be a complete surprise.

More troops would arrive soon at the port of Narbonne as well. Then the real invasion could begin. Eudo, the Duke of Aquitaine, would be in his palace in Bordeaux, enjoying his Christmas feast, oblivious to his own imminent destruction. The same would hold true for Othman-ben-abi-Nêssa, the Arab governor of Septimania. This pleased Rayman very much. Othman—in power now in Septimania for eight years—was an old woman in Rayman's eyes: a dealmaker, a compromiser, a weakling. Othman had made a peace treaty with the Aquitainian duke; Othman had married the man's Christian daughter and was living in sin and filth in an Aquitainian palace in Tolosa. Yet Rayman's father had refused to depose him.

Now his father was dead, and Rayman was named Emir by the Caliph Hashim in Mauritania. And just in time, too, for the new year would be the one hundredth anniversary of the death of Mohamet—a propitious year for the capitulation of Gaul. Rayman believed firmly that Allah had planned it this way; in His great wisdom, He had kept his father alive until the fateful year had come, when the real warrior of Mohamet, Rayman himself, would be ready to fulfill the prophesy. For 'Abd ar-Rayman was a man well aware of his destiny, as were all great men. He was the Chosen One, sent by Allah to deliver Islam into the heathen plains of the north. Once the Aquitaine was subdued, he would set his sights on the even greater kingdom of Francia and its ruler, Charles Martel, the one they called *The Hammer.*

Before long he entered Tolosa and marched down the wide Roman boulevard with fifty of his finest warriors. He felt like spitting when he saw the palace. The lazy beast Othman had been living the life of luxury while Rayman's father had waited in vain for him to liberate Gaul. What a fool he had been, to have trusted such a man!

A feast was in progress, attended by Muslims and Christians, drinking, dancing, laughing together. Rayman spat this time for real.

Suddenly the room fell silent, everyone turning to stare at him. Rayman's gaze roamed about and landed on the big, brown man at the head table, seated before a large tureen of soup, his Christian bride beside him.

Rayman crossed the hall to stand before him. Othman was drinking wine—a great sin. He stared at the stranger before him, bleary-eyed, forcing a smile.

"Othman-ben-abi-Nêssa?" said 'Abd ar-Rayman softly.

"Yes, and who are you?" said Othman, his speech slightly slurred.

"I am 'Abd ar-Rayman."

Othman's eyes grew to huge circles. He rose to his feet, his movement clumsy, a fine sweat breaking out on his forehead. "We are honored, young Rayman," he said. "We were not expecting you. Your father … "

"My father is dead. I am Emir now," said Rayman, his voice still soft, almost gentle. He glanced around at the lavish hall, the sumptuously laden tables, the flagons of wine. "You have made a nice life for yourself here, haven't you Othman-ben-abi-Nêssa? What would the Caliph say if he could see you now? Do you imagine my father sent you here to fill your belly and empty your seed in Christian filth? Do you?"

Othman's mouth worked furiously. "I was sent to settle Gaul, that I have done."

"You were sent to *conquer* Gaul," said Rayman, the softness in his voice giving way to a subtle menace. "And you have failed, Othman-ben-abi-

Nêssa, you have failed. You must pay for this failure. Where is Duke Eudo?"

"In ... Bordeaux, Emir—" said Othman, his lip quivering. He reached up to wipe his brow. Beside him, the woman stared at Rayman, her eyes like daggers, though he did not think she understood a word that was said.

"His army is with him?"

"Yes, Emir."

"Hmmm." Rayman was silent a moment, thinking. Then he smiled, quite pleasantly, and even Othman seemed to relax. "I would like to meet this Eudo for myself. But I think I must bring him a gift. A special gift, something he will not forget." He focused upon the twisted gold band around Othman's neck. "What is that you wear?"

"A ... a torc, Emir."

"Where did it come from?"

"It was a wedding gift—from Duke Eudo."

"Ah. Perfect. I will take it."

Othman put his hands to his throat as if to remove the ornament.

"Never mind. I will get it myself." With that, 'Abd ar-Rayman drew his curved sword and swung it with such force the blade seemed to sing before colliding with Othman's thick neck. The head, completely severed in a single stroke, twisted and soared in the air, suspended for a moment before it fell again, landing in the silver tureen and sending up a tidal wave of fish soup. Othman's body twitched and lurched, shooting up fountains of blood. The woman shot to her feet, screaming. It was the only sound, save the falling bodies of the other women in the hall who took the opportunity to faint dead away.

Rayman reached out and delicately plucked the torc from the headless neck. He held it up for all to see. "Othman is dead," he said. "I am your governor now. And things will be different from now on." He pulled the severed head of Othman from the soup and impaled it on the spear of a nearby warrior, who lifted it high, like a banner.

Then he looked at the screaming infidel woman, his eyes falling to her nearly exposed bosom. He moved to her, leaning far over the table so his face was inches from hers. She stopped screaming and stared at him with pulsing hatred.

"Yes," said Rayman softly, "I can see why Othman wanted a treaty."

She curled her lips and spat—a globe of saliva hit him right between the eyes. He jumped back, gasping. "Take her away!" he shouted. "Send her to Hashim. She will make a nice present for the Caliph, this Christian whore!"

Three Arab warriors jumped the table and grabbed her, pinning her arms behind her back. She started screaming again, kicking and shrieking and hurling curses upon his head as they dragged her away. Rayman wiped his face, turned to the guests in the hall. He smiled, composed and triumphant.

"Now," he said pleasantly, "we go to Bordeaux."

# Part One

## The Sword

# 1

## Metz
## March, 707 AD

IT RAINED THE day of the funeral, but then it always rained in Metz in the spring. A great crowd had gathered at the church, not so much to mourn the deceased as to escape the Moselle, which had overflowed its banks and flooded the town.

After the Mass, servants carried the body to the burial plot on a south-facing hill, a sword on the chest, bowls of nuts and pitchers of wine at the feet to nourish the soul on its journey. The carcass of a stag was placed beside the body as well, for the Old Franks believed the stag would lead the soul to Paradise.

Once the burial was done, the feast began, a feast that might last for several days.

By the second day of feasting the servants shuffled, exhausted, about the smoke-filled kitchen while Einhard, the chief seneschal for Pipin Herstal, shouted for more food.

"Where's the meat?" he wailed, his bony shoulders sloping. Sweaty clumps of hair fell into his eyes. No one answered. No one seemed to be listening. "The butcher should have delivered a carcass hours ago!"

He strode up to the cook, who dangled a squirming rat in front of his nose. Einhard gasped. The cook, sweating and bloated, laughed and dropped the rat in a pot of stew.

"They're too drunk to notice the difference."

Dogs ambled through the kitchen, taking whatever scraps they could find. Weary servant girls came and went, tossing empty pitchers in a heap and picking up filled ones. Einhard sat on a beer barrel and sighed deeply.

*Just for a moment,* he thought. He had not slept in days. And there seemed no end in sight.

"We need more beer." Einhard looked up to see a plump, sullen-faced girl waving an empty pitcher in the air as if she meant to club him with it.

"Here!" Einhard said, rising in order to push the barrel toward her. "It's the last one—"

Before he could finish the outside doors burst open, letting in a blast of cold, rain-washed air. A boy stood in the portal, his face stricken.

"Attack! Attack! Soldiers at the gate!"

He was joined by more voices, screams of alarm from the courtyard. There was a moment of stunned silence, then the kitchen exploded in a frenzy of motion. Shrieking servants ran to the door, colliding and running again, dogs yapping at their heels. Einhard was nearly trampled. He struggled to his feet, rubbing his wounded skull.

Attack? Was it possible that Metz was under attack? Metz, the seat of Roman princes and Queen Brunhilde herself? Pipin Herstal's capital?

Well, what better time to attack a palace than when the occupants are drinking themselves to oblivion at a funeral?

Einhard was almost glad. *At least it will put an end to this wretched feast.* So he grabbed a poker from the fire and followed the stream of people into the courtyard.

The rain cast the lunatic scene in shades of gray, blurred by the smoke from the kitchen that seemed to sizzle in the sodden air. People ran in all directions, women corralling children into shelters, guards fumbling for spears. Einhard could see no sign of imminent danger. He yelled at the kitchen servants to get back to work.

And then he saw them. Horses, huge, black horses galloping into the courtyard. They had long manes, powerful bodies and thick, feathered fetlocks, the most beautiful and terrifying creatures he had ever seen. Their riders were armed but helmetless, longhaired. They wore leather tunics and braccos, the baggy, cross-gartered leggings favored by peasants; their weapons were sheathed.

There were only a half dozen of them. The palace guards watched them, wary, making no move to intervene. Children peeked out from shelters, wide-eyed at the sight. Even the dogs grew quiet.

The horsemen gathered in a cluster, apparently conferring. Then one of them broke away and trotted toward Einhard. The other servants dove for cover, deserting him. Einhard stepped back, raising the poker, which shook in his hands. He closed his eyes, bracing himself.

"What are you planning to do with that? Build a fire or bash some heads?"

The voice was young and amused. Einhard opened one eye to see the rider seated calmly, watching him, a half smile on his face. Behind him the other riders began to laugh.

Einhard opened the other eye and stared, blinking. He saw a tall man with long blond hair wet from the rain, a face made of broken planes like an unfinished sculpture, young and old at the same time. He lowered the poker, still staring, feeling as though he had seen this face somewhere before.

And then he saw the eyes, eyes not quite blue, the color of a frozen lake on a white winter day. The eyes, at least, had not changed.

"Charles?"

"Hello, Einhard."

He said it as if ten years had not passed since the last time they had seen each other. As if he had not left a boy and returned a man. The ghost of that boy was still there, in the eyes, though the face was harder, sharper, older than his nineteen years.

"Good to see you again, old man."

Einhard could not bring himself to speak. Charles had been nine years old when he went to the Abbey of Saint-Denis to attend school and eventually take orders. It was the fate of most "extra" sons from noble families. Einhard had hoped he would be safer there, away from Pipin's scheming wife and her brutish sons. But five years later Charles disappeared from the abbey, and no one had heard from him since.

Einhard swallowed, searching for his lost voice. "Charles, is that really you? Good Lord, boy, where have you been?"

He sounded like an old nurse, nagging and fretful. The boy's disappearance had been a stone in his soul. Could it be that the boy was still alive? And more than that, a warrior with his own retinue? Einhard blinked, wondering if this were not some strange, cruel dream.

Charles tossed a leg over the horse's neck and slid from the saddle. Einhard inhaled, gazing up at him. The small boy he once knew was now taller than any man he had ever seen. So like his beautiful but unlucky mother.

*Ah, Alpaide. If only you could witness this.*

"I heard Drogo was dead," Charles said. "What did he die of?"

"What? What did you ask? Drogo? Oh yes. Your brother. *Half* brother. He's dead, yes. Some sort of stomach ailment, turned septic. Bad mead the doctors said. Too much mead, I would say. Good lord. I cannot think. You've come back. But tell me, where have you been all this time?"

"Here and there. I'll explain later. But right now I'm going in to see him." He turned toward his men, most of whom had dismounted. "Rodolf!" A skinny boy with rusty hair rushed forward to take the reins of the giant horse, which stamped its huge hooves, sending up a spray of rainwater and mud. Einhard stepped back, gasping. Charles was walking toward the doors, signaling to his friends to follow.

"Wait!" Einhard shouted, running after him. "You are going in there—*now?* No, no, Charles. This is not the best day—"

"Today is perfect."

"But—what are you planning to do?"

The question was left unanswered. His friends had joined him. Einhard gasped, running in front of them, holding up his hands, as if he could slow their momentum with some magic incantation.

"Wait! Give me a moment! Let me tell him you are here—"

Einhard raced as fast as his spindly legs would carry him, charging through the doors first.

Pipin Herstal, Leader of the Franks, sat at the high table, staring into space. He was nearing sixty, a bear of a man, all muscle and beard. His wife Plectruda sat beside him, her red hair neatly spun around her imperious head, her face a mask, her green eyes dull, unfocused. Drogo had been their eldest son, a dedicated if undisciplined soldier, the one on whom they had pinned all their hopes. The other son, Grimoald, was dutiful but otherwise unspectacular.

Einhard sprinted to his master's side. "My lord, listen to me—"

"Go away and get me more wine!" Pipin growled, his voice soaked in wine and grief. He shoved his empty cup into Einhard's chest. "More wine—" But he could say nothing more. For then Charles came into the room.

All eyes turned to him, all movement stopped.

"My lord, please listen …" Einhard pleaded, but Pipin did not seem able to hear. He set his cup down, his mouth falling open, his eyes flattening with bright, hot anger.

"What is the meaning of this?" he bellowed. He raised a hand to summon his guards but something—Einhard never knew what—made him stop, his hand floating in mid-air, as if caught in a web.

Charles came to the center of the room, his formidable companions forming a protective cordon around him. Pipin's guards surrounded them, alert but curiously inert, as was their master. Drogo's widow Anstrude shrieked in fear, pulling her two young sons close to her. Grimoald's mouth opened then closed again.

Einhard's gaze went first to Plectruda, who was staring at Charles with frozen eyes, perhaps the only one in the room to recognize him.

Charles drew his sword. The guards twitched, watching their master, who gave them no command. Even the dogs had stopped foraging to watch.

"Who are you?" Pipin demanded. "How dare you come here on the day of my son's funeral—?"

Charles ignored him, touched the sword tip to the floor and bent to one knee, both hands on the hilt.

"I, Charles, give my solemn oath of loyalty and subjugation to the King of the Franks and to Pipin Herstal, the Mayor of the Palaces of Austrasia, Neustria and Burgundy. I promise to serve them faithfully, to the best of my ability, may God have mercy on my soul."

Pipin stared, riveted, understanding slowly dawning on his reddened face. "Charles?" he whispered, "is that you?"

Charles did not answer. His companions knelt with him, bowing their heads as well. The entire company looked from Pipin to the man on his knees in utter amazement. A woman fainted. A dog whimpered. A boy—Drogo's son Arnulf—laughed.

Einhard saw a look of incomprehensible joy cross his master's face; he was certain that Pipin would jump over the table in a single bound and run to greet this lost son.

But the moment passed. Instead, Pipin moved around the table, limping as if the act of walking gave him pain, and stepped down from the dais. He shuffled toward Charles and covered his hands with his own, speaking the words of acceptance of the oath, though his voice was barely audible. Einhard could see that his hands were shaking.

"Charles." Pipin stood back, dropping his hands. He could hardly do more than whisper. "My son … rise."

Charles stood, sheathing his sword. The crowd of mourners now cheered, clapping and whistling, as if some horrible disaster had just been averted. Einhard saw Grimoald's face cloud with anger. Plectruda stood silently and left the room, trailed by her women.

"Come and sit," Pipin beckoned. His voice was still weak, worn down, and yet his face was painted with a lopsided smile. "Einhard, bring more wine! Bring food! Come and eat, all of you, drink, and tell us your tales!" Everyone began talking at once.

"No," Charles said. The room hushed again. "We've traveled a long way and we're tired. I need to settle my men first. I'll come and see you—when all this is over." Charles nodded to his men, turned and left the hall. Two hundred people watched him go, staring like gaping corpses, as if he had blasted the hall with Greek fire. Pipin was left to stand alone in the center of the room, gazing at the empty door, wondering perhaps if what he had witnessed had really happened or had been a moment's fantasy, a dream conjured by his drunken, grieving mind.

Einhard did not stop to wonder. He found his feet, rushing out to find Charles once more in the courtyard, mounting his black horse. The others were mounting as well, ignoring the cowering peasants and bewildered guards who watched from a safe distance. The misty air swirled around them, making the giant horses appear as mythical creatures from some dark and malevolent age. Yet now Einhard felt light as air, and he bounded up to the stamping horse with no more fear than a child racing to his favorite toy.

"Charles, wait! You must stay awhile—"

"I'll come back tomorrow."

"But where will you go?"

"To the fort."

"On the river? But it's a ruin!"

"It will do."

"Nonsense! Why won't you stay here? There is plenty of room—"

"No," Charles said. "I won't stay in this house." He swung his horse away, signaling to his men.

"But what can I do?" Einhard stumbled after him.

Charles smiled down at him as he rode away. "Bring us beer," he said. "And blankets. And oil. And whatever food you can find."

"Yes! Yes, I will!" Einhard shouted to the retreating figure of the boy he supposed he never knew.

# 2

## Dorestad
## Southern Frisia
## August, 709

"CHARLES! WE'VE BEEN sitting here all day! What in the name of Odin are we doing?"

Lothar glared down, jaw clenched, his long blond hair whipping across his handsome face in the hot breeze. He stood with legs spread, arms folded in ropy muscle over his bare chest. Charles sat on a rock by a small stream, skipping stones. The others lounged along the grassy bank, sheltered by the trees, gazing at the two of them. The horses grazed nearby, tails swishing and muscles quivering to fend off flies.

"We're waiting for nightfall," Charles said.

"Then what?"

"Then we are going to take that fortress."

Charles pointed through the trees to the walls of Dorestad, a middling town situated at the high bend of the Crooked Rhine. It was one of many fortresses the Romans had built along this winding river to keep the unconquered tribes out of Roman territory. It had been fought over by Franks and Frisians for centuries and was currently under Frisian control.

"That town has a mint," Charles said. "A Merovingian mint. I think we should go and see."

"It's a Roman fortress," Lothar retorted. "It's got a garrison, a guard tower! There are a hundred men guarding the walls!"

"Not that many. I see only ten or so at a time and they change only four times a day—"

"Charles, be serious—"

"Oh, I am."

There was a steel edge in his voice. They had spent a long, muggy, fruitless summer chasing shadows across Frisia. The Frisians, the pagan people to the north, had once again rebelled against Frankish suzerainty, withholding tribute and attacking Frankish missionaries. Pipin retaliated swiftly, laying siege to the capital of Utrecht. But the Frisian king Radbod had not risen to the bait, firmly entrenched behind his walls. The siege was going nowhere.

Meanwhile Charles' brother Grimoald, in an effort to keep Charles away from the main fighting, had sent him on pointless scouting missions along the frontier, searching out patrols and raiders, of which there were none. For two years Grimoald had tried to starve Charles of men and booty, wanting no competitors for Pipin Herstal's affections or his rule.

The men had grown frustrated, then resigned. Some of them had already left, went back to their own homesteads, realizing there was no plunder to be had that year. Others reluctantly joined with Grimoald's forces on the front. Charles had less than thirty men left. He knew he could not hold onto them much longer if he didn't give them some action soon.

And now this small but valuable fortress beckoned him.

"I suspect many of its defenders have been sent to Utrecht," Charles said. "There can only be a handful left."

Lothar made a sound like a laugh in his throat. "You remember what Andrius used to say: *fifty men with walls is worth a thousand without.*"

He remembered. The old Greek had been a veteran of sieges, having fought for the Empire against Bulgars and Khazers before forsaking his sword for the life of a monk. He was supposed to have been teaching the boys Greek, but he taught them many other things as well.

"It can be done," Charles said.

"How?"

"I'm not sure yet."

Lothar sighed. "I'm going to take a nap. Let me know when you have a plan."

When he told his men of his plan, they laughed.

Only Milo looked intrigued. Like Charles, he had been a schoolboy at the Abbey of Saint-Denis. The other boys called him "Bishop" because he was the only one who learned to read the Bible and never fell asleep in Mass. He was smaller than the rest, dark-eyed, with the angular look of a jackal. "It is how Gideon defeated the Midianites—that's what gave you the idea, right Charles? And here I thought you weren't paying attention during bible lessons." His smile gleamed. "It's an old trick, but it might work. These Frisians are a jumpy lot, given to superstition. The question is, what if it *doesn't* work?"

"Then we need to be able to run faster than they can," Charles said. "We could make it over the river, and they would not follow us there." He spoke with a confidence he did not really feel, but he knew he had to give these men hope, an assurance that his plan would work. It was one of many such moments he would face in his life; it was a time of testing for him.

He let out a cautious breath. "Okay, listen to me. Gather up all the kindling you can find: twigs, dried brush, cattails, cottonseeds, lint from the blankets, grass, whatever will burn quickly. It is the end of summer; this meadow will burn hot all by itself. All we need to do is get it started. We'll use all the oil we have left for that."

*Fire is a poor man's weapon.* Another of Andrius' favorite sayings. *And we are poor men today.*

"What about the gate?" Lothar said, his voice betraying a newfound excitement at the prospect of killing Frisians. Lothar was a killer by nature. He had been found as a small boy in the abbey forests, half-dead from a grievous wound delivered by a wild boar. The monks had nursed him back to health, only to discover that the boy was more savage than the animal that had nearly killed him. Lothar routinely beat up other boys, played vicious tricks on the monks, and eventually took to killing dozens of the cats that roamed the abbey grounds, nailing the carcasses to the abbot's door in the night. The abbot wanted to send him to Britannia as a ship's slave to be rid of him. Andrius intervened. But it was Charles, in the end, who stopped the cat killings, and Charles who turned Lothar's violent energies into a storied career as a warrior.

"Rodolf got close enough to get a good look. It's old and rotting. We can break it down, given the time. Gerold, cut down a tree. But do it quietly."

"That I can do." The big Rhinelander rose, shouldering his long-handled axe. He was very broad, top-heavy like the axe he carried, bald but for a knot of red hair that sprouted absurdly from the top of his head.

"Goon, you need to keep the horses quiet," Charles said, turning to a hulking man with a misshapen face as impregnable as a rock. His real name was Gunther. He had been left on the abbey steps as a baby, his mother no doubt believing his deformity the result of some unforgiven sin. He'd grown up in the stables and had more affection for horses than men.

"Fire will spook them," he grumbled.

Charles thought about this. "Can you make them lie down?"

"Lie down? Yes. They won't like it."

"Do it. As soon as it's dark. Now, get to work."

There was no more discussion. Once the darkness fell, the men crept out of the woods and began gathering kindling, working quickly, feeling their way. Gunther brought the horses down, one by one, managing to keep them from making too much noise. Soon all twelve were on their sides, their riders half-lying on top of them, patting their necks and whispering softly.

Charles watched the walls, sweat trickling down the back of his neck. Despite the cool breeze the air felt thick and fetid, buoyed by his own anxiety. The breeze was good, he told himself; the fire would burn brighter and spread faster.

But the longer he sat, waiting, the more the doubts in his mind grew. Was this sheer lunacy, for a few men to try and take a fortress by pure deception? Yet it had worked for Gideon. Andrius had taught him to always do the unexpected. And never overlook the genius of God Almighty when it comes to planning a battle. Andrius had been attracted to Christianity because of the deeds of the mighty warrior David and the tales of his amazing victories over the Philistines. Yahweh was a God of war as much as a God of peace.

Milo crouched beside him. "You look nervous. Fear not, Charles. God is with you."

"How do you know?"

Milo shrugged. "I just do. Why do you think I stay with you?" He paused, following Charles' gaze to the walls of Dorestad. "Wait until the watch changes. That's what Gideon did. The new watch will not have adjusted to the darkness."

Charles sent his young groom Rodolf to spy on the town, to watch for the changing of the guard. The rest of them waited, silent, at the edge of the tree line. They'd built a shelter of grass and twigs to hide their fire. They would not be able to light the torches until the last minute. Gideon had used clay pots to hide his fires. Gideon had also used trumpets to make a tremendous noise, but Charles had to hope that the men's voices alone would do the trick.

Gerold returned with his log, so big it took six men to carry it. Charles calculated: twelve riders, six men on the battering ram. That left only ten spear-carriers. Not nearly enough. They would have to be fast, get inside before the Frisians knew what hit them. Or they would be dead.

At last Rodolf came running back from his watch, staying low to the grass, whispering that the time had come.

Charles called to Ragnor. *Are you ready?* The Saxon archer nodded to him, grinning, flexing the muscles of his bare chest. The Saxons were notorious enemies of the Franks, but Ragnor had deserted his own people over a dispute with his chieftain concerning a certain woman. Ragnor often had trouble keeping his hands off other men's women. Charles had taken him in, because he was the only one among them who knew how to shoot a bow.

"Light the torches," Charles said.

The Frisian guards on the wall stared into the night in horror. A ring of fire had risen from nowhere, encircling the meadow. Then there was a noise, like a thousand souls drowning in the pit of hell. Shapes appeared, black shapes against the leaping flames, coming toward them. Balls of fire burst in the night air. One soldier was struck and fell, engulfed in flame. The rest abandoned their posts and ran, screaming in fear.

The noise awoke the chieftain of the town, who had been sleeping peacefully in his small cell inside the city wall. He jumped up and ran outside to see what was the matter. What he saw was amazing to him: the courtyard was filled with people running in every direction, complete chaos. He grabbed a boy darting past him, headed for the safety of the inner wall.

"What's happened?" the chieftain bellowed.

"Demons!" the boy said, twisting away from him and continuing his flight.

Just then there was another horrific noise, the sound of the great wooden gate being pounded from the outside. The chieftain saw the gate bulge, straining against the pressure, and screamed for help, rushing toward it. Some men turned to follow him. But just as they reached the gate the wood splintered and exploded in front of them, and the men of Dorestad were greeted by what would be their last vision on earth, gigantic black horses bursting upon them.

Charles felt bones crunch under his horse's hooves; he heard guttural screams mingling with the shrieks of the frightened animals. He charged forward through the gate and his men followed him, throwing their torches and then javelins and francas. Fires erupted everywhere, causing the already panicked Frisians to scatter in terror. From the corner of his vision Charles saw his foot soldiers rush in at his flanks, fanning out, impaling men with their spears. He cried out an order and jumped from the horse; his riders followed his lead, drawing their swords as more Frisian warriors poured into the courtyard from the inner walls.

Lothar was there, in front of him, a sword in each hand. He would always be there. Charles kept his back to him and gave himself over to his sword, reverting to his most ancient instinct. They fought like two halves of the same body, each sensing the other's movement before he'd moved at all. The others formed similar circles, backs together, each man a protective barrier for the man beside him. They had fought this way for years, ever since leaving the abbey to roam the wild lands of the north, hiring themselves out to local seigniors who'd had enough of Frisian and Saxon raiders. They had learned to fight on horseback, because for them speed meant survival. They had been night fighters, skirmishers, learning war as they went. The Frisians, still too frightened and disorganized at the surprise night attack, could do little against them. Too many were already dead; too many had fled in panic. They had no leader. Their fate was sealed.

It was over quickly, the courtyard rife with bodies, none of them Franks. Charles took a quick count. He had not lost a single man, though several had serious spear wounds and might be dead in a few days. It had worked, the mad plan. He felt exultant, exhausted. Relieved.

Charles ordered the prisoners bound together to prevent any of them escaping. Milo reported that the town, enclosed beyond the inner wall, was secured.

"Now what?" Lothar asked, still breathless from the rapture of battle. "Kill them?"

Charles shook his head, taking the first full breath he had managed all day. "Not yet. Milo will want to convert them first. Find the mint. And send a message to Pipin. Tell him we have a town for him."

Pipin Herstal came with a hundred men to the gates of Dorestad, walking as he always did, for he abhorred riding any kind of animal and insisted that litters were for old people and women. Charles had burned the bodies of the dead Frisians, but he had mounted the heads on spears outside the walls as a warning to any who would challenge him, and also to show Pipin the extent of his victory. Pipin picked his way through the gruesome display as the newly-repaired gates opened for him. Charles, watching from the wall, did not go down to meet him.

"Have Milo take him to the Roman house," Charles told Lothar, referring to the house of the former overlord of Dorestad, now a prisoner. "Give him food and wine. I'll see him there later."

Lothar grinned, madness in his eyes. "Perhaps you should greet him with a dagger in that case."

Pipin Herstal paced about the large reception room, cradling a goblet of wine. He could hear commotion outside, the arrival of horsemen, the shouts of soldiers. *Charles*, he thought. *Finally*. He had been waiting for nearly five hours.

He was angry, though it was a vague, abstracted anger, a frustration that had settled deep in his bones. The problem was bigger than this one show of insolence. Charles had disobeyed orders, had acted without permission or consent, yet had pulled off an almost miraculous victory and taken a significant Frisian town from right under Radbod's nose. He had done what Pipin himself had not done, and what Grimoald would never have done. Pipin had not even believed the messenger at first, not until the boy brought forth a sack containing several Frisian armbands that could only have been taken from dead Frisians.

He heard the scuffling of boots and soft voices in the atrium, then Charles appeared. Pipin stopped, his breath catching. The sight of this son of his always took him off-guard, the tall body, the long hair, the spectral eyes. *Alpaide,* he thought. Charles' mother. Since returning to his service, Charles had not mentioned her once. Yet she was always there, between them. A looming shadow, a question unasked and unanswered.

Charles was dressed in his peasant clothes, as usual, and had made no effort to wash before coming to see his father. Pipin felt affronted, as he usually did around this man.

"Well," he said, watching his son move to the wine table and pour wine into a cup. "I've been here all day! Will you tell me now what happened here? You disobeyed orders."

He was never sure how to speak to this man. As a vassal? Or a son? He always felt as though Charles were the one in control of the conversation.

"I had no choice," Charles replied. "I could not support my men by being Grimoald's messenger boy."

"You were supposed to be patrolling—"

"I was. And I found this." Charles turned, his eyes resting on his father. Pipin looked away.

"You know what I am talking about … "

"Let me ask you a question, Pipin. If you had been in my place, what would you have done?"

Pipin sighed, slumping into a chair. "How did you do it?" he asked, his voice emptied of anger, merely curious now.

Charles told him. Pipin listened, his eyes wide with amazement. He did not know what to say for a long time. He drank his wine.

"Why did you not send me word? I would have sent help … "

"I did not have time for that. I couldn't stay in those woods without risk of exposure. I saw an opportunity. I took it."

"What if you had failed?"

Charles smiled, a thing without warmth or humor. "But I didn't."

Pipin shook his head, as if he were enormously tired. "And the mint? How much money did you find?"

"About fifty pounds of silver. The locals had been hoarding it. I doubt even Radbod knew about it."

"Fifty?" Pipin's eyebrows lifted slightly. It was more than he would have guessed. "I suppose you will want to distribute that to your men."

"Half of it. The rest is yours."

"Is that to placate me?"

"No. It is the rules of division. *Your* rules. I'm not your enemy, Pipin."

Pipin looked away. He knew his son was laughing at him, throwing in his face not only his amazing victory but also Pipin's ultimate failure. Charles, Pipin realized with sudden dread, was not afraid of him at all. Pipin felt unnerved at the thought. He was a man who liked to intimidate people, and Charles was a man wholly incapable of being intimidated.

*So what hold do I have over him?* Then he remembered.

Pipin leaned forward in his chair.

"Sit down, boy. Will you please? You make me nervous, lurking there in the corner like that. There is something I need to discuss with you. I was going to wait until this wretched war was over, but this is as good a time as any."

Charles hesitated, then walked to a chair near his father and sat. Pipin saw the sudden wary look in his son's eyes and smiled.

"I've arranged a marriage for you," he said in a cheerful voice. "With the Duke of Rouen's daughter, Rotruda. It is an excellent match. She is quite lovely. You should be very pleased."

Pipin drank from his cup, gazing intently at Charles' face; he could see the lines of his son's jaw tighten slightly, his eyes narrow. Pipin smiled to himself.

After a long moment, Charles said: "Rouen is a Neustrian duchy. Shouldn't you be giving this marriage to Grimoald?"

Pipin set down his cup. "I have decided to give this alliance to you, Charles. You need to shore up Neustrian support. The Neustrians don't care much for your—tactics. Or the company you keep. Riff raff, Saxons. Peasant girls. You are the son of the Leader of the Franks. Time you learned to act like it. We can announce the banns at the Autumn Assembly—"

"No." Charles rose and headed to the door, as if that ended the discussion.

Pipin blinked. "What did you say?"

"I'm not going to marry her."

Pipin shot to his feet, exploding. "You think you can disobey me again?"

"I am not your first born son," Charles said, turning on him. "I cannot marry before Grimoald. Besides, you are a fool to make a marriage alliance with Rouen. He will never be your friend, Pipin. You cannot marry your way into the good graces of the Neustrians. They hate us, hate all Austrasians. They only look for a way to take power from us."

"Nonsense! The duke would not give his only daughter to a family he hates! The decision is made, Charles. I will make another marriage for Grimoald, and then you will be free to marry the Lady Rotruda." He paused, rising, moving toward Charles, his voice lowered, threatening. "You are sworn to me, Charles. You are my son—"

"A bastard son," Charles said.

"God in heaven! Are you still so blind?" Pipin's voice crested with anger and something else—a long suppressed suffering. "After these two years when I have had you at my side, treated you as my son, even though you refuse to live in my house? Why did you come back in the first place? Was it only to drive me to madness for whatever pain you think I have caused you? It was your mother that was to blame, not me!"

The last statement blundered out of him; Pipin wished he had not spoken. He whirled away, back to his chair, sitting heavily. Charles stayed in the doorway, unmoving a long time. Then he spoke in a different voice.

"How's your siege going, Pipin?"

Pipin made a noise in his throat. "It isn't going, if you must know," he said sourly. "Utrecht is buttoned up like a virgin. And Radbod won't come out and fight."

"He can't hold out forever."

"No, but he can hold out long enough to make me lose my patience," Pipin nearly shouted. "Which I have already lost."

"I might have a solution."

Pipin looked up, his face a silent question.

"Send me three hundred men. I can take more fortresses along the Crooked Rhine. Radbod won't stand for it. He will have to come out and fight."

Pipin gazed at his son a long time before speaking. "I can give you a hundred men only, maybe two hundred. No more."

"Two hundred then."

"You think you can take the Crooked Rhine with two hundred men?"

"I know I can. Make sure Radbod knows his towns are falling. He will come out."

Pipin threw back his head and laughed. It was not a happy sound. "All right," he said, his voice breaking with exertion. "We will do it your way. I will send you two hundred men, and you will take Ravenswall and as many other fortresses as you can manage. If Radbod does take the bait, I will crush him." Pipin pushed himself to his feet as if the effort caused him pain. "But Charles, one way or another, you *will* marry the Lady Rotruda."

They stared at each other.

"You are sworn to me Charles. You will marry whomever I say you will marry. Or you will have no place in my army. Do you understand?"

Charles, after a long moment, nodded.

# 3

CHARLES TOOK RAVENSWALL easily, along with several more towns along the Crooked Rhine, establishing new strongholds for the Franks. As he had predicted, King Radbod was infuriated at the loss of his fortresses and marched out from his walls at Utrecht. Pipin was waiting for him; by the end of the long, bloody day Radbod had surrendered.

Charles rode into Utrecht a few days later with some of his men to see what had happened. Pipin was deep in negotiations with the Frisian king and the other Austrasian nobles, but Charles was not invited to the meeting.

"He knows you won this damned war for him, and he can't stand it," Lothar told him as they slouched around a fire pit outside the city walls, chewing on dried meat sticks. "So he's leaving you out of the talks, as if you had nothing to do with it! He wants the glory for himself. And for that pustule your brother."

Charles laughed. "I got what I wanted. Besides half the spoils." He tried to sound indifferent, but they could all hear the taut frustration in his voice.

"And you've given your brother even more reason to hate you," Lothar added tersely. "That will come back to bite you."

"Grimoald does not have very sharp teeth these days," Milo said with a snort. "I think now Charles' future is secured. Grimoald will have to spend his days prowling the whorehouses, his favorite sport." They all laughed at that.

"Who the devil is that?" Gerold said, standing up and pointing.

They all turned. A company of black-cloaked men riding donkeys was shuffling up the hill, toward the gate.

"Monks," Lothar scowled.

Charles rose, drawing his sword, the others followed his lead. The group of monks stopped in their tracks when they saw the warriors approach.

"What's your business?" said Charles.

One of the company dismounted from his donkey and came to meet him. The monk appeared quite old, though there was an inherent vigor about him. He looked at Charles with lively gray eyes.

"You must be Charles," he said with a cautious smile and a slight bow. "I am Willibrord, apostle to the Frisians. Your father summoned me."

"What for?"

"I believe he wanted me to be present for the surrender of the king."

Charles understood. Safe passage for Frankish missionaries was paramount on Pipin's agenda. He was about to send them on their way when another voice stopped him, this one higher, with a musical lilt.

"Lord Charles?" The new monk had dismounted and was walking toward him, smiling. He was very tall, rail thin like Willibrord but younger, with peculiar amber eyes. His tonsure betrayed the fact that he was rapidly losing his hair. He smiled with genuine warmth.

"I'm not a lord," Charles said, regarding him with interest. There was something about the man's face that drew him, though he could not fathom what it was.

"My apologies. I am Winfrith of Wessex."

"What is an English monk doing here in Frisia?"

"It has always been my ambition to join Willibrord on his adventures in Frisia," Winfrith said, coloring a little under the weight of Charles' icy gaze.

"Good luck to you then," Charles said, turning away.

"Actually, I have wanted to meet you—to give you my thanks. We have heard of your action in Dorestad. It was quite … remarkable. Your victory here will open the way for these poor pagans to come to Christ."

Charles scoffed a little. "Your job will be harder than ours was," he said. To his surprise, Winfrith laughed.

"You may be right about that. But it has always been my belief that you can conquer the land, but never the people. The Frisians will not bend their knees to the Franks until they learn to bend their knees to Christ."

Charles, unexpectedly, smiled.

"I will try to remember that."

Winfrith inclined his head and turned away, following Willibrord through the gates. Charles watched him go.

"When was the last time you heard a word of thanks from a priest?" Lothar said. "He won't last long in that company, I'm sure of it."

The negotiations with Radbod went on for several days. In the end, Pipin got what he wanted: safe passage for his missionaries, a large portion of Radbod's treasure paid to ransom the city and the Frisian captains, and relinquishment of Dorestad as well as the mint. But there was another surprise as well, one that Pipin relished sharing with his younger son: he had made a marriage alliance for Grimoald with Radbod's youngest daughter Theudesinda. The marriage would be sealed at once in the presence of the Benedictine missionary Willibrord and the Frisian king. They waited only for the girl herself to be fetched from her safe house outside the city.

But Charles did not wait. As soon as he heard this news, he took his treasure, divided it among his men, and released them for the winter. He left Frisia without speaking to Pipin again.

# 4

## Paris
## June, 711

ROTRUDA, PRINCESS OF Rouen, stood before her little audience flush with joy, arms spread so that the silky fabric of her sleeves spread like angels' wings. Her ladies gasped and cooed, breaking into applause. Rotruda curtsied like a queen, careful not to smile too much so as not to crack the powder on her face.

She was dressed in bridal blue, the silk overtunic with plunging neckline and gold-belted girdle strangling her waist, enhancing the high, round breasts, the full hips, the long, arched slope of her neck. Her golden hair hung in silken plaits around her face, shimmering beneath the white veil crowned in tiny flowers. Her skin, bathed in milk all winter to retain its baby softness, glowed like alabaster, setting off the rare, blue-violet color of her eyes. She wore only one piece of jewelry, a thick gold torc around her neck studded with garnets, an enormous ornament she looked much too fragile to carry, yet she carried it well.

"Do you think he will be pleased?" she asked, certain of their reaction. The women babbled anew, full of superlatives.

"If only your mother could see you," said her old nurse Fredda wistfully. Rotruda felt tears press to her eyes at the mention of her mother.

"I believe she can see me," Rotruda said. She prayed to her mother every day, as if she were one of the saints. She had prayed that one day she would be Charles' wife. And that day had come.

She first saw him at the Autumn Assembly three years before. He was so tall; she had never seen a man as tall as him. He had a way of moving through a crowd that made the crowd disappear, for no one could see anyone but him. Rotruda watched him striding through the courtyard with his strange menagerie of friends or standing insolently at the back of the courtroom while the speeches and petitions were made, his eyes like ice, as if he did not see anything at all, or he saw everything at once and found nothing to interest him.

He never came to the feasts, which she found curious, as did everyone else. She had made inquiries and learned he lived with an unmarried woman somewhere on the outskirts of Metz, and that he had made his own headquarters at a ford by the river where he trained and housed his men. His behavior seemed to drive everyone crazy, especially Pipin Herstal. But Rotruda was fascinated. She wondered about this woman of his and learned that she was of common birth; she knew that this girl could be no more than a diversion to him, someone to keep his bed warm. No woman could match Rotruda's beauty or grace and breeding.

But she knew as well that, though she was of high birth and great beauty, she was still a child. Charles never noticed her. He had no idea she existed. But once, walking through the courtyard with her nurse, she had caught the eye of one of his warriors, a wildly handsome, blond-headed man with brilliant blue eyes. They stared at each other a moment too long, and she saw him say something to Charles, who lifted his gaze to glance at her for a brief moment before turning away again. She had replayed that glance over and over in her mind, for time had stopped, the world had ceased to exist, and all she had seen were his eyes, that all-seeing insolence, the rough-hewn face young yet somehow ancient, slightly cruel, alluringly dangerous. She feared it and loved it at once, and she knew with a quiet certainty that she would marry this man and no one else.

She told her father of her choice, but he would not hear of it. The bastard Charles, a rude, unmannered Austrasian, whose allegiance to his own father was clearly in question? But even the duke could see that of the two of Pipin's sons, Charles was the one gaining power and popularity, attracting leudes to his service like moths to a flame. Charles would rule one day, everyone knew it. He had no choice but to give his consent.

There was a knock at the door and one of her ladies rushed in, panting.

"The Lady Plectruda to see you," she whispered. Rotruda took a breath, clutching her nurse, who pushed her into a stuffed chair and shooed the others out of the room. Plectruda, the wife of Pipin Herstal.

"What does she want with me? I had heard she wanted this marriage for her son Grimoald. Perhaps she is angry—"

"Nonsense. She only wants to wish you well on your wedding day," Fredda said in her thick, Germanic accent. "She wants to take your measure. Any woman at court is a rival, no doubt. Here now, you are every bit the noble lady she is, the daughter of a duke, same as her. Remember that." She went to the door and opened it, bowing.

As soon as the door opened, it seemed to Rotruda that a spray of spangled light exploded in the room. Then she saw that it was only the reflection of the morning sun upon Plectruda's jeweled gown. The woman was a vision of moving color, her eyes emerald green, her red hair floating suspended on her head, barely covered by a veil, giving her an exaggerated sense of height. She had a strong, imperialistic beauty, the most formidable woman Rotruda had ever set eyes on.

"Rotruda, my dear!" the older woman said in her deep, honeyed voice, moving over the rushes soundlessly as if her feet never touched the floor. "You are lovely." She took the girl's hands, pulling her to her feet, her lips brushing Rotruda's cheeks like gentle puffs of air.

"My lady, how kind of you to visit me," Rotruda murmured, curtsying deeply. "Please sit awhile." She indicated a chair and Plectruda slid into it. Rotruda avoided the stuffed chair and sat on a round wooden stool so as not to wrinkle her gown, holding her hands together in her lap to keep them from shaking.

Plectruda smiled, looking her over. Rotruda could not gauge the look, assessing if not quite approving. She saw flecks of gold in the green eyes, making them look even more like precious gems.

"You look nervous, and I am ashamed to be the cause of that. Please forgive me." Plectruda smiled without showing her teeth. "I don't want to upset you on this most important day. But I thought it would be good if we got acquainted, so you would be able to look upon at least one friendly face in the crowd on the day you meet the man who will be your husband."

Rotruda shivered a little, looking down at her lap. "I do thank you for your kindness."

Plectruda smiled at her unease. "Surely there are things you wish to know about this man you are about to marry? You do not know him well, do you?"

"No." She had met him only once, in fact, at the announcement of the banns at the Autumn Assembly two years before, right after Pipin had won the war against the Frisians. Their meeting had been brief and formal. He had taken her hand when the banns were announced, had said the proper words, but had left right after the ceremony and disappeared from Metz altogether a day later, leaving the nobles fuming.

"I know what he did at the banns," Plectruda said. "So like Charles, always riding off to fight some war or other, never paying much attention to the little people, least of all his future bride. It's his way, though I'm sure I don't understand it."

"Perhaps it was … " Rotruda looked out the window, searching for the words. "I had heard … that he had a woman—"

"A commoner," Plectruda said quickly, "of no consequence."

"But … he put off the wedding for almost two years—"

"Oh! Well. I'm sure that had to do with other things. Wars and such. You know how these men are, my dear. It is something you will have to learn to accept. They are gone more than they are present."

"What happened to her?" Rotruda looked into Plectruda's eyes for the first time, but the older woman looked away, smoothing out her skirt.

"Who? The woman? Oh well … she died, I think."

"How?"

"I really don't know," Plectruda's gaze wandered around the room. "But it's a common occurrence among the lower people. You need not be concerned about that. It's all in the past. Besides, you have grown up in two years—you have become even more beautiful. Once he sees you today, no other woman will ever disturb his dreams again. You are a vision, truly. Charles does not know how lucky he is. How could he *not* fall in love with you?"

Rotruda blushed. She did not want to tell Plectruda how desperately she wanted her words to be true.

"That is not to say," the older woman went on, "that Charles is—an easy man."

Rotruda frowned slightly. "What do you mean?"

"I don't mean to frighten you, dear girl. It's just that my stepson spends all his time playing war with his friends, you see. He has little experience with gentlewomen." She smiled. "Pipin was much the same at his age. Hardheaded, I called it. Hard-hearted too. But Pipin softened. Charles will too. Give him time."

"I will give him the rest of my life," Rotruda said, her hands moving to cover her heart, as if giving an oath.

"Of course you will," Plectruda said, smiling her strange, stilted smile. "Of course you will."

"What else do you know about him? I mean … what does he like for dinner? So I can know what to have prepared for him—"

Plectruda's expression changed, her smile faded. "I don't know, as Charles has never dined with us."

Rotruda sat straighter, her shoulders tensing. "Never?"

"As I said, he is not an easy man. He doesn't like me, that much you probably already know. I suppose that has to do with his mother. My husband had to have her—well, it was an ugly business, but it could not be helped at the time. The woman was an adulteress after all. She'd gotten herself pregnant. And we have laws, they must be followed. Well, Charles blames *me* for that. But I can assure you, I had nothing to do with it."

"Of course … " Rotruda's hands moved back to her lap; she flexed her fingers, watching them curl and straighten. "Is he … kind?"

A trace of pity crossed Plectruda's carefully composed face. "Kind? That is not a word I would ascribe to him." She saw the sudden, swift fear that crossed the younger woman's face. She went on hurriedly: "I do not believe he is a brutal man, though, so rest assured you are perfectly safe. He is not much given to passion of any sort."

Plectruda stood, making the ladies on the perimeter of the room jump to attention. She let out a fluttering laugh, as if she had just remembered something important she had to attend to. "Well, I can see you are very busy. I will leave you now." She took Rotruda's hands in her own, drawing her to her feet. She said in a softer voice, "I know you must be frightened … about tonight. It is something we all had to face once in our lives. Be of good courage; don't cry out, whatever you do. Men do not like that. I will send my doctor to you in the morning, to help you—recover."

The words chilled Rotruda. She blanched, feeling slightly dizzy. Plectruda gripped her hands harder and said in a louder voice: "I know we will be great friends. If there is anything you need, don't hesitate to call on me." She kissed the shaking girl on both cheeks and then exited in a glittering flurry. Rotruda stood still watching her go, sick to her stomach with fear. She wondered if that was not Plectruda's intention, after all.

# 5

SHE WAS TAKEN to the church in a covered litter, peasants choking the wide boulevard, screaming and throwing flowers, calling her name. She waved back, pushing aside the curtains to see better, thrilled by this unexpected reception.

It wasn't until she saw him, standing beside her before the altar, that she remembered her fear. He wore a rich tunica of deep blue, a garment that looked wonderful and yet unnatural to him. He smiled at her, but his eyes were vacant, like shards of glass. She had the impression he was looking right through her, not into her soul but beyond it, as if she had no soul. She felt a shiver, a blackness at the edge of her vision; she clutched the rail of the altar, longing to feel something solid under her hand, something real.

She barely knew what happened next, the murmuring of vows, the low chanting of the monks, the droning prayers. She felt vaporous, insubstantial, as if she didn't exist at all, as if his presence consumed them both, leaving her with nothing. It went on a long time. She understood little of the priests' words, but she said the words she had been told to say as she had practiced them over and over in her room every night for two years. She heard her own voice but hardly recognized it, as if someone outside herself held the strings to her body, her lips, making her say and do all the right things while inside she was screaming in panic.

It seemed an eternity until it was all over. She never once looked at Charles, not until the end, when he took the veil from her face and looked down at her. She closed her eyes, felt his mouth on hers, his kiss so light it seemed like only a thought in her mind. Yet it lingered there a moment, longer than she had expected, his mouth warm and dry. She had thought of this moment for so long, waiting for it, anticipating her own reaction, but now all she could think of were Plectruda's words: *he is not much given to passion of any sort.* Then it was over, and she turned to face the crowd of onlookers as if surfacing from a dream.

It was better once she got outside. Hordes of people thronged her, vying for her attention. Plectruda parted the crowd to kiss her, followed by Pipin himself, dressed in a long brown tunica trimmed in beaver fur. He greeted her with what warmth he could muster. He hardly looked at Charles.

Another man came forward with Pipin, like him but younger, less bulky, much less forceful. Grimoald. She bowed to him, smiling and offering her hand, which he took but did not kiss. Beside him was a pale, unfriendly woman Rotruda knew to be Theudesinda, Grimoald's Frisian wife. She was very tall, broad-shouldered and extremely thin. She did not speak. She looked resentful, the scowl on her face marring her chiseled beauty. Rotruda knew that the marriage had not been successful; she suspected Theudesinda was terribly unhappy. She pitied her.

She met Hugo and Arnulf, the teenage sons of the dead Drogo, who seemed in awe of her and bowed continually. Another boy stood near them, about five years old, with a mop of tousled brown hair and a soft, malleable face. Theodoald, someone told her, Grimoald's son by his favored mistress. It was said Plectruda doted on this boy, though he was bastard born, favoring him over her own legitimate grandsons. Rotruda wondered why; the boy did not seem especially handsome or intelligent to her.

But then the crowds parted and a prancing chestnut horse was brought to her, led by a groom. Rotruda squealed with delight. Charles was beside her.

"Do you ride?" he asked.

"Of course! Oh thank you! She's beautiful! What's her name?"

"They call her Delilah."

Rotruda laughed. "How perfect."

Charles helped her into the saddle and mounted another horse beside her, not his black horse, she saw.

"Where is your own horse?" she asked him.

"We don't put mares and stallions together."

She nodded, feeling foolish that she hadn't thought of that. They rode together down the road to the palace of Paris, while crowds of people screamed her name and threw flowers. The warriors followed them, and she saw for herself how large Charles' retinue really was. Yet the crowds of this Neustrian city were there only for her. She was a princess in their eyes, beautiful, enchanted, utterly adored. It is all she ever wanted. Yet somehow it still did not seem to be quite enough.

When they arrived at the palace courtyard, Charles helped her down from the saddle and led her to the main doors. She saw his friends standing in a line, bowing to her as she passed. She was caught by the sight of the beautiful one with the blue eyes she had seen at the Autumn Assembly, wearing a plain leather tunic with no crest. He watched her intently as she passed, his face full of unmasked tension. She smiled at him, her eyelashes fluttering a little. Then she looked away, aware of the heat in her cheeks.

"Who was that man?" she whispered to Ani, her maid, who giggled.

"That's Lothar, Charles' best friend," she said conspiratorially. "Isn't he the handsomest? But so fierce. They say he has killed over two hundred men!"

"What family is he from?"

"No family. A wilding!"

Rotruda frowned. "So he is not noble?"

"No, but who cares? All the girls are after him, even just for a toss. They say he is most obliging!" She giggled again.

Charles pulled her away from the girl and steered her into the hall. The king himself sat on an elaborate moveable throne in the center of the room. Dagobert IV. Rotruda had never seen the king before. The Merovingians, the formal rulers of Francia, usually did not stray far from their stronghold in Rheims, as they were prone to die easily. Dagobert, like most of his predecessors, was frail and sickly and light in the head. He was twelve years old, his pale face scarred by acne, his large brown eyes watery and unfocused. His hair was long and oily, for it was forbidden to cut the hair or the beard of a Frankish king.

Rotruda curtsied low before him. He said nothing, looking at her abstractedly, as if his gaze could not quite reach her.

"The king is pleased to meet you," said the Bishop of Rheims, Rigobert, who stood close to him, ever watchful. "And he congratulates you on your wedding day. To you as well, Charles. He hopes this new alliance will bear the fruit of healing for the provinces of Francia."

"Thank you, Your Majesty," Charles said.

The young king gazed at Rotruda, then his arm shot out to grab at her, clutching her veil in his spindly hand. Rotruda gasped, as did everyone watching. Charles pulled his wife away while the bishop put a gentle hand on the king's wrists, disengaging him.

"His Majesty thinks the lady is very lovely," the bishop sputtered, pressing the king's arm to the chair once more. "His Majesty is tired now and wishes to retire. His Majesty will take his dinner in his apartments, and tomorrow he will ride through the streets to greet the people." Everyone clapped approvingly, relieved. The king was lifted and hurried quickly away.

"The king does not seem … very well," she whispered to Charles, pressing her hands together to stop them shaking.

"All Merovings die young. It is their only redeeming quality."

She turned to see who had spoken and caught the glimmering gaze of the one called Lothar, standing behind them.

"Oh," she said in a soft voice. "How very sad." Charles introduced them. She felt Lothar's eyes on her like a caress, the look she had longed to see in her husband's eyes.

"Don't feel too sorry for the Merovings," Lothar continued. "They nearly broke this kingdom with their foolish war making, brother against brother—"

"That's enough," Charles said. Lothar fell silent. *He really was the most beautiful man*, Rotruda thought. *Too bad he is not a nobleman.*

Charles led her into the main hall. The music was playing, and people began to applaud as she made her way to the dais. She blushed, smiling, thrilled.

She was seated in her place of honor, Charles beside her, Pipin and Plectruda and Grimoald sitting grimly on one side, Charles' nephews Hugo and Arnulf, cheerful and winsome, on the other. She saw her father, seated at the far end of the table, his face dour. He refused to look at her.

The party went on endlessly, each guest in turn coming before her, laying gifts at her feet, whispering words of praise and blessing, bowing to her, fawning over her. She lost herself in their attention, forgetting momentarily about the man who sat at her side. She felt like a little girl trapped in a grown up body, playing at being a lady of import, a queen even, as she had often imagined in her own room at home. Home … it was far away from her now.

And then she remembered what would happen next.

The night.

She felt a sharp sting of panic. It was not the act itself she feared, though, it was being alone with him. Alone, where in his eyes she felt the fearful invisibility of her soul.

Late in the evening she was taken to her room by the maids who set about preparing her for her first night with her new husband. They laid her in the bed wearing a thin white shift of expensive silk, her hair loose and free, artfully arranged on the pillow. They stood about a moment admiring their handiwork. She felt like a virgin on the altar, prepared for the sacrifice.

It was a long time before he arrived, thankfully alone, but by then she had worked herself into such a panic she could not move, could not speak. He, on the other hand, did not treat the matter with any importance, and this made her feel calmer. He gave her a cup of mead and sat beside her on the bed as she drank; it was sweet and strong, it made her cheeks hot.

He told her that the mead was drunk originally because the pagan Franks thought women were ruled by the moon—their monthly cycles coincided with the moon's phases—and were therefore dangerous and unpredictable, like the moon goddess. The honey would chase away those moon spirits and allow the husband and wife to have union without fear of demonic intervention. This was why the Franks called the wedding night the "honey-moon." She laughed at this and drank more of the mead, relaxing. In truth the drink was highly intoxicating; it made her feel at once languid and euphoric, a kind of love potion. When he finally reached for her, she was no longer afraid.

She felt his hands on her face, her throat; how amazingly soft, she thought, for such rough hands. She lay still, watching them slide down her body, fingers curled under the silky fabric of her shift, gliding over her breasts, her belly, her thighs. She closed her eyes—the fingers probed deeper. She shivered and flushed, the heat raging now in her cheeks, her body opening to him with a will of its own, unfolding like a flower, lifting. She felt a shimmering release, like the rush of water against her face, cascading down her skin, in her belly, hard and fast, a pleasure so complete it was not to be endured. She felt her body arc and shudder, felt her breath in the space between her lips—she lay still.

She didn't know the distance of time between that moment and the next, when she felt the weight of him, the cool metal shock of his naked skin. His arms encircled her, gathering, lifting her to him, so that she felt she was floating above the bed and he was holding her there, pressed beneath him. She was aware of a growing pressure between her legs, a pressure that turned violently to pain. She stifled a cry, remembering Plectruda's warning; she felt his arms tighten around her, a gesture of reassurance and, unbelievably, compassion.

She had known he was a skillful lover, but it was that careless, thoughtless perfection of his—his hallmark in all things—which left her curiously empty afterward. He made love not with the passion of an artist, but with the precision of a good craftsman who likes a job well done. He had not been moved to give her more.

He stayed with her that night, and in the morning presented her with the *morgangabe*, the gift the groom bestows upon the wife the morning after their first night together, to express his gratitude at finding her a virgin. The gift was a silver necklace of very fine, rounded links, an unusual choice. Rotruda was thrilled; she put it on, vowing never to take it off.

He stayed in Paris for two weeks. She hardly ever saw him during the day; he seemed to take no notice of her, leaving her to her handmaidens who fussed over her like a flock of bossy geese.

He came to her room most nights. He did not talk much. Her fears proved unfounded—it was he who seemed to disappear whenever they were alone. Sometimes she wondered, in the darkness after he left her—for he never again stayed with her the entire night— if he had really been there at all.

She tried to draw him into conversation, asking him about his life, his plans, the horses that seemed his only real interest. His answers were short and neutral. She wanted him to teach her how to do things for him, things to give him pleasure in bed, but he seemed uninterested in being pleased. He treated her like a pampered child, or a favored pet, which she supposed was how he saw her.

There was only one thing that would bring them together: a child. Perhaps if she got pregnant, he would look upon her differently, as someone more useful to him. And that would make him love her.

"Charles," she said to him one night when he came into the room. "How long are we staying here?" She knew he did not intend to make Paris his home, though he had spent his time there shoring up his Neustrian alliances.

"Do you want to leave?"

He had taken off his shirt and picked up a cup of wine. She stared at his body, the hardened cords of muscle, the numerous, sinister scars that told a story she would never hear.

"I only wondered … if we would be going back to your home—in Metz."

He sat in a chair, stretching out his long legs cat-like on the rush rug. "You can live there if you want." He said this as if he did not care what she did. She swallowed hard.

"I want to live wherever you live," she said in a small voice. Weren't they married? Wasn't it common for a man and his wife to live together? How very strange he was.

"All right. Lothar will take you Metz. He's going for the Spring Assembly."

"But … " She looked at him, confused. "Aren't you going too?"

"Not for awhile. I'm leaving tomorrow."

"Where are you going?"

"South. To Iberia."

"Where is that?"

"Far away."

"Why do you need to go there?"

"There's been an invasion. The Berbers have attacked. I want to see what's going on."

"Berbers?"

"From Mauritania."

She did not know what that was, but she was afraid to ask. Her heart pounded. This is not how she envisioned married life. He would send her to Metz, while he went off to some godforsaken place a thousand miles away? And he had never thought to tell her this before?

"Does your father know you are going there?" she asked.

"I sent him a message."

She was silent a moment. "I will go with you."

"No," he said firmly. "You will not. You can stay here or go to Metz with Lothar."

She felt a wave of apprehension. "Why isn't he going with you?"

"I need him in charge of my men."

"And when will you be back?"

"Before winter, perhaps."

She sighed. "It's a long time."

"You have your women, don't you? Plectruda will be there. You can live at the palace until I return."

She looked up at him, surprised. "Really? You would allow that?"

"If it makes you happy, Rotruda."

She smiled when he said her name. She could not remember him ever saying it aloud. She took off her robe and went to him, straddling him boldly, her hands on his chest. His skin was very warm; he smelled of horses and grass and smoke and wind. She loved the smell. She put her face to his chest and kissed him there; he put a hand on the back of her head, his body tensing, awakening to her. She looked at him. His eyes were smoky, torn, his hand entangled in her hair. She kissed him.

"Come to bed," she said.

# 6

## Metz
## April, 713

PIPIN STARED AT the scroll in his hands.

"Damn," he said softly. Then he coughed. "Damn, damn, damn."

"My lord," Einhard said, rushing to his side. In the past few months his master had gotten old very suddenly, the flesh of his once massive arms sagging like empty sacks on his bones, his cheeks sunken into his skull. His abundant hair had gone gray; his beard, too, was gray and straggly—he no longer tended it as carefully as he used to. He was nearly seventy, ancient by most standards, yet he had never looked his age, not until now. He coughed again, a loose, phlegmy sound, dangerous.

Plectruda glanced up from her sewing loop. "What's the matter?"

"It's from Willibrord," Pipin said. "Those damned pagans are at it again. They've raided a mission and killed seven of his monks—" He spit up a wad of phlegm. Einhard tried to wipe his beard with a cloth; Pipin waved him away with a low growl.

"But we have a treaty!" Grimoald said. The three of them often spent the evenings together in Pipin's sitting room. Theudesinda was not there. She made no secret of the fact that she did not care for her husband, or any of the Franks, for that matter. It had been four years since the victory in Frisia, and now the Frisians were up to their old tricks again.

Pipin crumbled the parchment into a brittle ball. "I should have known Radbod wouldn't hold to any treaty. Monks dead! Impaled, their bodies cut open—" He stopped, his head falling back on the chair. "I have had enough of this." His words seemed to convey his whole world of feeling.

"Does that mean we are going to Frisia again?" Grimoald said anxiously. "Because of a bunch of foolish monks who should know better than to venture to that wild land in the first place?"

"Yes, we are going back. What choice do we have? Radbod has broken the treaty. This cannot go unanswered. Einhard, my cup is empty!" Pipin shouted this last, though the effort cost him, and he fell into a fit of coughing. Einhard hurried to replace the cup.

"Husband," said Plectruda, leaning toward him, her eyes for the first time betraying a hint of concern, "I think it would be best if Grimoald went alone. The alliance is really his, after all."

"Yes, Father," Grimoald agreed. "You must not go to Frisia this year. I can handle this."

Pipin shook his head. "No you can't. Radbod will pay no attention unless I go myself."

"But you are not well—"

"Nonsense. I've had worse colds than this. It will pass. Always does." He drank his wine, trying to stifle the need to cough.

"So," said Plectruda, returning her attention to her sewing, "I suppose you will insist on Charles going with you."

"Ha! He's the only one that can deal with these idiot pagans. He's practically one himself, after all." Pipin laughed, the laugh turning into another cough.

"Father—" Grimoald said in a halting tone. "Father—I don't think you should—take him with you, I mean."

Pipin peered at his son with narrowed eyes. "Why not?"

Grimoald sat up, leaned in and spoke in a harsh whisper. "Father, listen to me. There's something wrong with him, something … I don't know what it is, but something definitely wrong. He's not natural. He hates you, he hates me, he's only looking for a way to destroy us both … to take the kingdom from us—"

Pipin's face shuttered to a standstill. "You are talking about a son of mine—"

"A son of yours? He's nothing like you! Father, listen to me … think about what he has done since coming back. His followers become more numerous every year! He's trying to steal your power; he's been doing it for years. He's draining you of your strength; he's draining me as well. He has put a curse on us. He is the devil—"

"Shut up," Pipin said, his voice deadly flat. "Get out."

Grimoald stood, trembling. He looked at his mother; she did not meet his eyes. He set down his cup, turned stiffly and left the room.

There was silence. Then Pipin coughed, a globule of phlegm dribbling onto his tunic. Einhard was at his side to wipe it away.

"The devil … " Pipin mumbled, pushing Einhard away feebly. "Rot."

"Husband," Plectruda said, "you should go to bed. You need rest."

"Don't tell me what I need," he snapped. The coughing erupted once more. When Einhard came to him this time, he did not resist.

"I'm going to bed," he declared when he could speak again. Einhard helped him to his feet and directed him to the door.

"Did you hear what he said?" Pipin said as Einhard sat him on the bed and began removing his boots and garters. "Did you?"

"I heard," Einhard said quietly.

"Well? What do you think of it?"

Einhard stood him up and began to remove his tunic. "It's our nature, my lord, there is nothing very sinister about it. Charles, you see, is not ordinary, and that frightens people. So they attribute his abilities to the devil or God or luck or magic, and they feel better because of it. They are forgiven their mere … humanity."

Pipin stared into the face of his servant. In his linen shirt and leggings he looked even thinner, his flesh loose and flaky, exposing ridges of brittle bone. Einhard could scarcely believe that this was the same man who'd vanquished the Neustrians at Tertry, who pounded the Alemanni and thrashed the Saxons time and again.

"Yes," Pipin said in a broken voice, "perhaps it is true … to be forgiven … " He closed his eyes and fell into the bed.

Einhard sighed, lifting his master's feet onto the stuffed mattress and pulling the coverings to his chin. He saw the old man shiver, and he shivered himself, in sympathy.

He did not want to tell him that he believed Grimoald had a point. It pressed on Pipin like a physical weight, this constant, silent battle with his son, because it was a battle like so many others that Charles himself refused to fight. It was hard to watch a man suffer as Pipin suffered, even if the man deserved to suffer a little, as Pipin surely did. What he needed was mercy, but he needed it from the one man on earth incapable of granting it.

Then one afternoon a few days later, Charles offered it after all.

Pipin was in his study in the middle of an altercation with his doctor over a cup of foul-smelling liquid the man insisted he drink. The cup was suffering serious damage in the exchange.

"It's absinthe," the doctor said. "It will reduce the fever … it's good for you!"

"Wormwood!" Pipin shouted, shoving the cup back in his chest. "Drink it yourself if it's so damned good for you."

Einhard stifled a chuckle. *He must be feeling better*, he thought. "There is no fever as yet," he said to the doctor, "but we will keep it on hand, just in case." Pipin looked at him gratefully. The doctor straightened, harrumphed, set down the cup.

"I cannot be blamed if something happens because you refuse to follow my prescription," he pronounced.

Just then a steward entered and bowed. "Your son to see you, my lord."

"All right, all right." Pipin growled. "Let him in. And you, out you go. Just looking at you and your damned potions makes me sick. Out!"

The doctor hesitated. Pipin made a move as if he were going to leap at the man's throat—he jumped and danced for the door. Pipin sat back heavily in his chair, laughing. Einhard laughed too.

The door opened. Neither man noticed. They were expecting Grimoald—Grimoald was the only son who ever came to see him.

Einhard looked up first, saw that it was Charles in the doorway. His mouth hung open. "Huh, my lord," he said, nudging his master.

Pipin glanced up. He stood suddenly, his body as straight as a young man's. Einhard thought he had a sudden impulse to move toward his son, to grasp his arm in greeting. But the desk was in the way. Why was there always some immovable piece of furniture between them?

"What are you doing here?" Pipin said, his voice suddenly clear and sharp.

"I wanted to talk to you," Charles said. He was dressed in his peasant garb, as usual, the black cross-gartered braccos; his long hair hung loosely around his shoulders the way his father detested. He stood still a moment, waiting. Pipin stared at him, his fists pressed into the desk. Einhard saw something like hope in his face, hope that perhaps at last Charles had come to him not as a soldier, but as a son, that the time for punishment was over.

But Charles wanted to talk about horses.

For years he had been developing his band of riders into a permanent detachment of the main army. Now he wanted to expand its role still further, to create a real cavalry capable of maneuvering on a larger scale. He told Pipin about the Greeks, the Romans, and especially, the Arabs. In two years the Arabs had virtually wiped out the Gothic kingdom on the Iberian Peninsula, due in large part to their expansive mounted forces. The Franks needed such a cavalry, he said, in order to *survive*. The methods of warfare were changing, and they must change with it, or they would perish. The Arabs, he said, would come north. They would come to conquer Francia; the Franks needed to be ready for that.

Charles spoke for a long time, detailing, outlining, summarizing. He spoke with more energy, more conviction, more passion than he ever had before.

Einhard watched from his corner, enthralled. At last, Charles had broken his silence, laying before his father his ideas, his vision, his plans for the future. Einhard looked hopefully to his master, expecting to see joy in his face, believing he would welcome this offering as the gesture of peace he had long desired.

But he saw, to his horror, that Pipin was not pleased. He had heard only the insult to his own military prowess, his capability as a warleader. He was mortally offended. His expression became stony. Einhard's momentary hope faded. He shut his eyes.

"No," Pipin said when Charles was through. "Do you want to know why? I'll tell you why. Mounted warfare is a thing of the past, not the future! It is suitable only for savages, not civilized men. What do we need horses for? Do Saxons fight on horseback? Do Frisians? Do the Germans? No, they don't."

"The Arabs do," said Charles.

"Arabs!" Pipin scoffed. "The Arabs are in Iberia, and there they will stay. You may not have noticed, but there is rather a large set of mountains between Iberia and the Aquitaine. The Arabs will be content with Iberia—they will never come here, never."

Charles did not respond to that. Instead he said, "And what about the Lombards? They have a cavalry as large as the Emperor's, and their new king Liutprand is a very ambitious man. He is out for conquest."

"He won't come here either," Pipin spat out. "The Lombards don't want Francia, they want Italy! If Liutprand goes anywhere it will be south, to Rome. No one wants Francia, don't you understand? Not the Arabs, not the Lombards, not the Romans—they couldn't stand the weather! No, I will not hear any more talk about horses. You may use them for your … excursions, if you wish. I do admit their usefulness for patrols and foraging and small surprise attacks. But that is as far as it goes."

He had moved to the window, stared into the bright, open sky. He could not turn around, could not look at his son. "I am going to Frisia soon."

"I heard."

"I won't be needing you this time." He paused, but Charles did not respond. "This is Grimoald's alliance, it is up to him to have … victory." Another silence. "You will do the recruitment. Our ranks are getting low again; we need more men. There are several of the nobles who have not been doing their share. You will make them see the error of their ways."

Charles' face was carefully neutral, but Einhard saw in the set of his body that something had changed, hardened. Finally, he said: "As you wish."

Pipin still did not turn around. "Go away now. I'm tired. Tired to death."

Charles stared at the hunched, sagging figure of his father at the window, glanced once at Einhard without expression, then turned and left the room. The door slammed between them for the last time.

# 7

## Liège
## April, 714

GRIMOALD PRAYED.

He prayed for his father, still suffering from a nagging cold that had sunk into his chest. He prayed for the war in Frisia, which was going poorly, some would say disastrously. He had been praying every morning for a week in the homely, airless Church of Saint-Lambert, a church he himself had dedicated. He prayed for guidance.

The Frisians, once again, were unrepentant. And without Charles, much of the army did not even show up to fight. Grimoald and his father had spent a long summer in Frisia with nothing to show for their efforts. Pipin retreated for the winter to the Abbey of Jupille-on-the-Meuse, planning to resume his fruitless offensive in the spring. His health had not improved, made worse by the cold weather and relentless rain. Grimoald wanted to give up this fight. But Pipin would not give up. Now spring had come, and the war would resume, with Pipin in no shape to lead an army, and Grimoald wanting nothing more than to go home.

He heard the mains doors open behind him, the monks arriving for morning offices, swinging their incense thuribles. He did not look up, stayed bent over his folded hands. His knees ached from kneeling for so long. Saint-Lambert himself looked down upon him from his pedestal behind the altar, one hand lifted, two fingers extended in benediction.

They were singing, the monks. Chanting their toneless hymns, haunting and beautiful. The sound filled the windowless chapel, swirling in the air with the incense, the stifling smoke of guttered candles. The music filled him; he raised his eyes, saw the old saint looking at him sadly.

He felt a searing pain sweep his body. He could not breathe. He thought at first it was the Holy Spirit, burning into his heart like a flaming arrow. In the next moment he realized it was a *real* arrow.

He rose up, trying to scream, without the breath to make a sound. He gestured wildly, stumbling to the feet of the saint. His guards rushed forward, swords drawn, searching for the culprit. Shouting filled the sanctuary. The monks froze, dropping their thuribles, their song broken. They began to flee, all was chaos. Grimoald grabbed hold of one of his men, shaking him as he crumbled to the floor, screaming with his last breath a single name.

# 8

## Jupille-on-the-Meuse
## August, 714

"HOW IS HE?" Charles asked, swinging down from his horse. Lothar and the other guards had fanned out, keeping watch. The abbey looked deserted, but they all knew that in these uncertain times there were enemies around every corner.

"He lingers." Einhard's face was drawn and pale. Pipin's illness had clearly taken its toll on the old servant.

"What took you so long?" Arnulf demanded. He and Einhard had come to greet Charles in the courtyard before the stone church, the cloister lined with fruit trees that bent over the walkways like tired old men, providing ample shade from the late summer sun.

"I had some business to take care of. Did they catch the assassin?"

"A Frisian," Arnulf scoffed, taking hold of the horse's bridle. "They killed him before he could confess, naturally. Idiots. Probably hired by Theudesinda. She hated him. And she has lots of brothers. But that has not stopped Plectruda from making accusations."

Charles looked at him, questioning.

Einhard cleared his throat. "There is talk of a plot."

"An *Austrasian* plot," Arnulf added. "His sword-bearer claims that Grimoald screamed *your* name before dying."

"*My* name?"

"Some say it was his way of accusing you of his death. Or at least of the conspiracy of it. It's not hard for anyone to believe, is it? You had more cause than anyone. You've spent much time in Frisia, you could have hired the assassin. And with Pipin on his death bed—"

"Is that what *you* believe?" Charles asked his nephew.

"Of course not! It's all rot. But it's *plausible* rot, that's the point. It's something Plectruda can sell. And you know she will."

Charles nodded, understanding. "Where is he?"

"In the guest house," Einhard said. "He drifts in and out of consciousness. Plectruda guards him day and night."

"Your men have been arriving daily," said Arnulf. "They have made camp outside the walls."

"Fine. I will need some messengers close at hand. Is your brother here?"

"Of course. I'll send him to you. He's been with the monks, praying day and night. God only knows for what."

Charles smiled grimly. "We are going to need all the prayers we can get," he said.

"What about your father?" Einhard asked nervously.

"Tell him I'm here," Charles said. "If he wants to talk to me, he can send for me."

Pipin lingered into the autumn, much to the dismay of the nobles who hovered about the abbey, impatient for him to die and be done with it. But death did not come easily to the Pipinid family; even the weakest of them had proved tremendously hard to kill. Though wasted and skeletal, unable to rise from his bed, unable to speak without convulsions of blood-laced coughing, hardly able to breathe without excruciating pain, Pipin Herstal stubbornly refused to die, clinging to a febrile rage that had become the source and succor of his life.

He made no public announcement of his successor. Rather, he had his choice inscribed in a sealed scroll and kept in the possession of his faithful chancellor Norbert, with instructions that it should not be opened until after his death. Once this was done he seemed to become calmer, more at peace with his fate. He lay in his bed, staring up at the beams overhead, a strange, half-smile on his parched, drawn face. When he thought of the scroll and its contents he would laugh suddenly, horribly, the laughter bubbling blood to his lips. His attendants would shake their heads, supposing this a sign of madness brought on by the fever.

Early in December, he asked to see Charles.

Charles entered his sick room, rank with the smell of herbs and urine and death, and stood by the bed. Pipin appeared to be asleep. Charles waited until his father became aware of his presence. Pipin opened his eyes finally, looked up into the gray ones, blinking. He seemed remarkably lucid, despite his condition, as if he had just awoken from a protracted nap.

"Did you kill my son?" he asked in a raspy voice.

"No," Charles said. "I was in the south, recruiting, as you told me to do. I have plenty of witnesses."

"Your leudes do not make good witnesses," Pipin said. "You could have hired an assassin."

"I could have," Charles said. "But do you really think I cared enough about Grimoald to go through the trouble of having him killed? Especially when I would be so easily implicated?"

Pipin made a gurgling sound. "Your arrogance knows no bounds. Do you want to know whom I chose as my successor?"

Charles shrugged. "It doesn't matter who you choose, Pipin."

The sick man's eyes came to life, blazing with anger. "Still you insult me! You have insulted me from the first moment you set foot in my palace."

"I only did what I had to do," Charles said. "You would have done the same. Didn't you help in the assassination of the Neustrian mayor Ebroin? So that you could make a deal with his successor?"

Pipin stared at his son, aghast. "How dare you accuse me of such a conspiracy! I am Pipin of Herstal, Prince of the Franks! I do not need to murder anyone!"

"It was convenient for you, though, since he had beaten you in battle and was close to uniting all of Francia under his banner—"

"Shut up!" Pipin fell into a fit of coughing.

Charles took a breath. "I am not here to fight with you, Pipin. I have served you faithfully. I have enriched your treasure and enlarged your territory. I married the woman you wanted me to marry. I have done everything you ever asked of me."

"You … never … sat at my table," Pipin said, his voice barely a whisper. "You never … " he didn't finish the sentence.

"I did the best I could," Charles said with a sigh.

"This is because of your mother, isn't it? You blame me for her death."

Charles froze, gazing at the dying man, his eyes suddenly bright, hard. "You killed her."

"Yes," he sighed, "I suppose I did. Now I am repaid. My sons are dead. That is God's retribution on me, I am sure of it. But I will have my own revenge—" He rose up suddenly, throwing the blankets aside, hurling himself at his son. A flash of metal caught Charles' eye. Before he could react the knife slashed across his chest. He felt the hot burn, looked down and saw blood seeping through his leather jerkin. If not for the leather, the blade would have slashed right through his heart. He grabbed the knife from his father's hand, stumbling backward, clutching at his chest at the same time. Pipin was raving at him, screaming, flailing like a madman. Guards and servants rushed into the room, grabbing hold of him, trying to settle him back into the bed.

Plectruda stood in the doorway, stony faced, staring at the blood on Charles' tunic, the knife in his hand. He caught her gaze, noticed for the first time the knife had jewels embedded in the handle. He tossed it to her.

"Yours, I believe."

Plectruda raised her arm to shield herself; the knife fell on the floor at her feet, exactly where he had aimed it. Then he turned and left the room. He never saw his father again.

That same day Pipin lapsed into a coma, and on the sixteenth of December, in the early evening, Pipin Herstal, Mayor of the Palaces of Austrasia, Neustria and Burgundy, Leader of the Franks, died.

# 9

THE NOBLES NEARLY overran Chancellor Norbert, who stood in the apse of the church clutching the sealed scroll to his chest. It was rumored he even slept with it. Pipin lay dead in the abbey chapel. Plectruda stayed with him, mourning. She did not need to hear the scroll read. She knew what it said.

Unable to do else, Norbert broke the seal and read the contents aloud. A frozen hush fell over the room, a collection of mouths dropping in unison like flies on a flame. Einhard, who stood among them, felt his knees go weak. He closed his eyes and moaned softly.

He took the news to Charles, who had been waiting for him in the camp outside the walls, surrounded by his followers. The weather had fallen chill suddenly, a light snow covered the ground, the tents, the bedrolls, the men who had gathered around the fire to hear the news. Einhard could not help but feel it was a sign of things to come, of a long, cold winter ahead.

"Theodoald," Einhard said, his voice barely a whisper. "He's chosen Grimoald's bastard son Theodoald to be his heir, with Plectruda as regent."

There was no sound, all of them too shocked to respond.

"It's over," Einhard said, in despair.

"On the contrary," Charles said in the silence, "it is just beginning."

They gathered in the tent, nine of them: Charles, Einhard, Gunther, Lothar, Gerold, Milo, Arnulf, Hugo and Ragnor. The rest waited outside, listening at the tent flaps.

"He's given it all to a child, a child!" Lothar ranted. "With that green-eyed gorgon as regent! He's thrown away the kingdom purely out of spite!"

"To a boy as much a bastard as Charles too! Amazing! He had two legitimate grandsons he could have chosen— it doesn't make any sense!" said Gerold, exasperated.

"She knows Hugo and I are loyal to Charles," Arnulf said. "Plectruda needed someone she could control." Hugo nodded, closed his eyes and prayed, his lips moving. Arnulf nudged him.

"You mean to say that this is all Plectruda's doing?" Gerold blurted, disgusted. "Women! Vipers, all of them, starting with Eve herself!"

"She hates Charles, everyone knows it," Arnulf said. "She hates us too. She hates everyone except that brat. We shouldn't be so surprised, should we? Anyway, what can she do, an old woman like that? She won't last long."

"But the nobles will support her," Milo said, more soberly. "They think they can control her, whereas they know they cannot control Charles. We're going to have to act fast if we intend to fight this."

"We will not fight," Charles said.

They all stopped talking and stared at him.

"Are you off your head?" Lothar bellowed. "We've got to get back to Metz, seize the treasure and the army before that bitch—"

"No," said Charles.

"Charles!" Lothar rounded on him, livid. "Listen to me. We are not simply talking about the rule now, we are talking about your *life*. Plectruda has been waiting to sink her fangs into you for years, and now she has the power—"

"She won't kill me," Charles interrupted. "She knows if she does, she would be dead herself within a week. But she can have me thrown in jail, awaiting a trial that will never take place. She could never get a conviction, she has no proof, and anyway she knows I would get enough jurors to swear to my innocence. But she could keep me in jail a very long time, until her rule is secure. That would suit her very well."

Lothar stared at him, incredulous. "And you are going to let her do it?"

"Yes."

They all seemed to shout at once. Charles rose, finally, moving them to silence.

"Listen to me, all of you," he said. "Milo is right—the Austrasian magnates will support Pipin's decision. They have to; it is the law. But there is something else to consider—there is revolt in the wind. My scouts inform me that the Neustrians have already nominated their own mayor, Raginfrid of Angers. They are making plans with Frisia and probably Burgundy to rebel against Plectruda and seize control of the kingdom. That means we will be fighting not only Austrasia but Neustria, Frisia, Burgundy and perhaps even the Aquitaine as well. It's too much. We can't do it."

"We understand all that," Milo said, "but there is no point in making a sacrifice of yourself, is there? You can escape, hide out and raise a new force. Most of the army would follow you."

Everyone agreed. But Charles shook his head.

"No," he said. They began to protest again; he motioned them to be still. "It won't work, don't you see? As long as I am free, I am a threat. I will be giving them a common enemy. Raginfrid has probably made a pact with Plectruda to get rid of me. But once I am out of the way, he will have no further use for her. And he certainly will not want to share power with an old woman and a child. He will turn against her, and that is what we want. Let Raginfrid take care of Plectruda, let the Austrasian stronghold fall into chaos, as we know it will. Then we make our move."

"What good will that do us if you are in prison!" Gerold shouted, mouth frothing.

Charles took a breath. "We will deal with that when the time comes," he said. "Most likely she'll send me to Kolonia—it's the only place with a decent Roman prison. In the meantime, you will go into hiding. You all must disappear entirely—we can't have her thinking that a rescue might be attempted. Stay hidden and wait for instructions."

"How are you going to get word to us? Plectruda will have you surrounded by guards!" Arnulf said.

"I have my ways," Charles said. "Do you not think I have planned for this? Trust me. Do as I say."

They all began shouting again, but Charles would discuss it no more. He sent them away, with orders they be well out of reach by morning. Reluctantly they went, filing slowly out of the tent, informing the others of the news. Only Einhard and Lothar remained. Lothar took hold of Charles' wineskin and drained it, threw it down.

"You could have prevented this," he said, turning on Charles. "All you had to do was go to him. Humble yourself a little. But no, you couldn't do that. Now you will have to fight."

"I would have had to fight anyway," Charles said. "Do you think Plectruda would have allowed me to rule, even if Pipin wanted it so? She would have found another way to get what she wanted. So we will play her game for the time being."

Lothar turned away again, folding his arms over his chest. In the ensuing silence Charles heard a low, sobbing sound and noticed Einhard, sitting in a darkened corner of the tent, his shoulders hunched and trembling slightly.

"Einhard," he said.

Einhard did not turn to look at him. "Did you know the name Pipin means 'Father'?" he murmured. "I know you never thought of him as your father, but I often thought of him as mine … " He bowed his head, brushing his cheeks as if fearful Charles would see his tears.

Charles said softly: "Listen, old man, you are going to have to help me now, like you did when I was young, remember? Are you prepared to do that again?"

Einhard turned to him, his eyes brightening, hopeful. "Yes … "

"Good. You must stay with Plectruda, keep her trust. You will go to her now and tell her that you were wrong about me, that you believe I *did* kill Grimoald—"

"No, I can't—"

"Yes. You can. You have to be very convincing. She must believe you are hers absolutely, or you will be of no use to me at all. You are our only source of information, the only one who will have access to the palace. Without you we will have no idea of her plans. Can you do this for me now?"

Einhard's mouth still trembled, but his eyes continued to brighten, dry now, focusing on the man before him. "Yes," he said softly. "I can."

Charles nodded. "Go now."

Einhard rose unsteadily and moved to the tent flaps, then stopped and turned back, his face once more clouded with grief. "Charles … you mustn't blame him. It wasn't that he didn't love you, you know. Because I believe he did, in his own way. The problem was: you could never love him."

Einhard turned with a sigh and left the tent.

"You too," Charles said to Lothar, rising to face him. "Go before the moon rises. You'll need cover of darkness. I want you well away by morning. Take them to the Eifel hills. They won't look for you there. Take this." He unbuckled his sword belt and held it out. Lothar did not take it, his hands pressed tightly to his sides, as if restrained by some invisible force. Finally, he reached out, grasped the sword by the scabbard. Charles let go. He smiled.

"What about Rotruda?" Lothar asked then. "What about your son, Carloman?"

"I sent Rotruda and the boy to Rouen. She will stay with her father for the time being." He paused. "She's pregnant."

"What? God in heaven." Lothar sighed. "You think she will be safe there? Rouen is in the midst of the enemy! Carloman—he will be used as a pawn. Who knows whose side her father is on? If Raginfrid—"

"Her father will protect her," Charles said, his voice taut and reedy, a band about to snap. "She will be safe. Stay away from Neustria, Lothar. The Neustrians will not harm Rotruda, but they will have no qualms about killing you." He paused, took a breath. "You'd better go." He put a hand around the back of his friend's neck. "We will see each other again."

Lothar grabbed the arm that held him, the sword still pressed to his chest. They stood there a long moment, the silence passing between them, the things never spoken but always known. Then Lothar breathed, turning away, slipping quietly out of the tent.

Gunther appeared in the opening, silent.

"What is it?" Charles said finally.

The giant man cleared his throat. "I could … take care of him," he said bluntly. "The boy. And the old woman. The army is loyal to you—"

Charles' eyes closed, his head dropped, chin to his chest. After a moment he looked up.

"No, Goon. If I am ever to lead this kingdom, it must not begin with murder."

Gunther shook his head. "What if you never get out?"

Charles smiled, a gleam of mischief returning to his pale eyes. "I do not foresee any difficulty in getting out of Plectruda's prison when the time comes."

Gunther nodded. Then he straightened, drew his sword and held it before him in salute. Charles nodded to him. Gunther turned and left the tent.

In the darkness, when Plectruda's soldiers came for him, he was alone.

# 10

CHARLES WENT TO prison, and Francia fell apart.

As he had predicted, Neustria rose up against Austrasia, declaring its own king, Chilperic II, and moving against Pipin's Neustrian strongholds. Three months after Pipin's death Count Raginfrid of Angers and his Frisian allies fell upon the Austrasian army in the forest of Guise near Compiegne, fifty miles north of Paris. The House of Pipin was completely routed—Plectruda and her grandson fled to Metz. But that proved no safe haven, and on the advice of the counts she moved immediately north, to the stout Roman walls of Kolonia, where she might reorganize her army and put up a credible defense.

At the same time the German provinces of Bavaria, Alemannia and Thuringia, seeing the collapse of Pipin's strongholds, seized the opportunity to declare independence and withhold tribute, turning a deaf ear to Plectruda's pleas for help. The Saxons too saw the time was ripe for invasion; they pressed south over the Rhine into Austrasian territory looting and burning as they went, unchecked by anyone.

And in that year as well, the Arabs crossed the Pyrenees and invaded Gaul, taking all of the southern coast of Septimania from the Goths and threatening the Aquitaine.

Charles learned all these bits of news as he sat in his cell in Deutz, the Roman castrum across the river from Kolonia. Einhard sent messages through Leutgar, one of Charles' young spies, who had managed to get himself hired as a prison guard. Leutgar smuggled in food from Einhard as well, for Charles suspected that Plectruda would try to have him poisoned. Charles could do little but wait.

It was an agony, the waiting. There were times when he thought he might go mad, might die in that miserable cell, times when he wanted to die. He spent his days walking its length, pausing at the walls to push hard against them, throwing his weight into the effort to keep his strength up and to keep warm for the cell had no brazier. The guards were wary of him, knowing his reputation as a warrior. They also knew he had fearsome and loyal friends who would no doubt make a rescue attempt, and so the watches were doubled on Charles day and night, and the whole castrum was shut down tight.

One day in late winter, Leutgar came with a written message. From his wife.

> *You have another son. I have given him the name Pipin, in honor of your father. I hope that does not displease you. I am well. Carloman is well. Pipin is—very small. He came much too early. It was a difficult time, but he is thriving. He is very strong and healthy, praise be to God. I pray for you every day. I have written numerous letters to Plectruda and the other nobles, begging for your release. So far I have heard nothing. But I will not give up—*

Charles rerolled the scroll and handed it back to the scout.

"Do you have a message to send back to her?" Leutgar asked.

"Yes. Tell her to stop sending letters. I want them all to forget I am here."

"Yes." Leutgar nodded. "Is it time yet?"

"No."

"Soon?"

"Perhaps."

From the tiny window Charles watched the sun trail across the sky, the rains turn the courtyard to mud, the seasons pass. He watched the coming and going of the guards, knew their every movement, could predict to the minute when they would pass on the walls, when the guard changed outside his door. His hair and beard grew long, his body grew thin. He fought the dark despair in his soul.

The captain of the garrison, a man named Willem, came to see him one day in late September. Willem had long gray hair and a weather-beaten face, though he did not seem very old. He stood in the doorway, looking at his prisoner with guarded eyes.

"Do you want to get out of here?" he asked casually. Charles did not answer. "You've been here almost a year now. It is clear your men are not coming for you. Reports are they have been found and ... disbanded. Killed. Those left have crossed the border into Saxony and Frisia. They are not coming."

"Why do you tell me all this?" Charles asked.

"Well, I might be able to help you."

"Help me with what?"

"Perhaps I could arrange it so that we—lose track of you."

Charles looked at the jailor, his clear eyes intently focused now. "Why would you want to do that?"

Willem's gaze shifted, his tone became more conciliatory.

"Look, Charles, you and I both know you don't belong here. Plectruda doesn't care about you anymore. She has much bigger problems now. This war is lost. We are sitting ducks here, just waiting for the Neustrians to come. I want to go home. We all want to go home."

"Where is home?"

"Mayence," the captain said. "We want to get out before it is too late. I may never see my wife and children again—"

"Your wife? What is her name?"

Willem hesitated, his eyes shifting. "It's Mildreth—"

"You're a liar," Charles said flatly. "You have no wife. Plectruda sent you, didn't she?"

Willem looked at him. "How did you know?" he said after a moment.

"I've had lots of time here, nothing to do but think. To wonder what Plectruda would do with me. She doesn't like holding me here any more than you do. She needs an excuse to kill me. She tried poisoning my food but that didn't work—"

"How—?"

"Never mind that. The best way to kill me without bringing suspicion on herself is to get me to try to escape. It was a tactic my father used often enough, a convenient way to get rid of one's enemies without dealing with a tiresome inquiry."

Willem lowered his gaze, shame-faced. "I told her it wouldn't work."

"I do not blame you for trying," Charles said.

Willem regarded him a long moment. "Must be hard for you. To have won battles for Pipin, then to be treated like this. To be disinherited by your own father. Jailed by your stepmother. Must be worse than anything. What did you do to make him so mad?"

Charles closed his eyes, leaning back against the wall. "I told him the truth," he said.

"Ha! Well. Doesn't seem fair, anyway."

"Whoever said life was fair?" Charles' voice sounded almost forlorn. "Tell me something … why is Plectruda in such a hurry to be rid of me now?"

Willem shrugged. "Because of the council, I suppose."

"Council?"

"They are all coming within the month, all the nobles. For a war council."

Charles looked interested. "You know this for sure?"

"Yes. I heard it from one of her guards."

"Thank you, Willem. You've been very helpful."

The council met in early November, on a cold, windy night. The guards of the castrum at Deutz gathered around a barrel fire in the courtyard, huddled close to keep it from going out in the bitter wind. There were few men on the walls, even less in the courtyard. Willem had been forced to send thirty men to the palace. That left him less than twenty. He envied those men who were inside the palace, out of the weather that night. He had given his men mead to drink to keep their spirits up. He was not supposed to allow them to drink, especially when they were on duty, but it was cold, and the men were bored and miserable, and without the mead they would likely turn on each other.

Suddenly, out of nowhere, a burning arrow hurtled into the huddled group of men. Willem shot to his feet as the men jumped away. *Was it the mead?* He wondered. How much had he drunk? He stared at the arrow, not five paces from where he stood, trying to make sense of it.

Then another arrow fell, this one landing right at the captain's feet. He screamed involuntarily, leaping away. The men scrambled for their spears, gazing about in fear.

Willem drew his sword. He looked up to the top of the wall. Instead of his sentries, he saw two men, one—nearly naked—lighting another arrow from a torch the other one held. In the flickering light Willem could make out wild yellow hair and naked, painted torso.

"Christ in Heaven," he gasped. "Saxons."

At the word "Saxons" the men scattered, running for what little cover they could find along the walls. Willem found himself alone.

"Open this gate, Captain, or you will not live to see another dawn." The voice boomed down on him like the voice of God. It was the other man who spoke, though all Willem could see was a hooded mantel.

"Who are you? Identify yourself!" Willem shouted, standing straight despite his fear.

"The first two were warning shots. Ragnor never misses, unless he means to."

*Ragnor* … the name was familiar. One of Charles' infamous band of warriors. *The Plague*, they were called. Because of the havoc they wreaked on their enemies. Willem had heard stories—many stories. So the hooded man could only be …

"Do you know who I am now?"

"I know who you are, Lothar the Lawless!" Willem shouted. "But I will not open the gates for you—"

Before he could finish the sentence, a burning arrow slammed into one of the guards huddled against the wall. The man pitched forward, rolling on the ground, screaming, engulfed in flame. Willem turned away, his hands over his ears to shut out the terrible noise.

"Open the gate, Captain! Or more will die!"

"I will! Stop shooting!" Willem pleaded. He saw the Saxon lower his bow. He sighed, shouting to his men to open the gate.

"Throw down your weapons, all of you," said Lothar. "And come out to the fire where we can see you. On your knees."

Willem threw down his own sword. The others joined him by the fire, dropping their spears and falling to their knees. The screams of the dying man began to subside.

The gates creaked open and soon men on black horses filled the courtyard, leading three more horses by the reins. Lothar came down the wall steps to join them, still carrying the torch. Ragnor stayed on the wall with his bow.

"You know who we are here for," Lothar said to Willem. "Release him to us, and you will most likely live, though I won't guarantee it. I've had a miserable time getting here and I would really like to kill someone, I don't care who."

Willem swallowed hard. "North tower," he said.

"I know where he is. Stay here. Don't move a muscle or Ragnor might get the wrong idea."

It had taken every ounce of restraint Lothar had in his body to not kill all of them. But Charles had insisted he enter the castrum without undue bloodshed. Deutz's walls were rather easy to scale; the crumbled outer stones made natural footholds. Ragnor and Lothar had managed to kill the sentries and scramble up without detection. It was Ragnor's idea to use the flaming arrows; he always liked to make a strong first impression.

Still, Lothar had hoped for some resistance, for the guards to put up a fight. Charles' message had said they would not fight, that there was no fight in them. Most had already run, the best of them had been sent to the palace to guard Plectruda's brat. Those who were left did not care about Plectruda's brat, or about Charles, and they certainly would not risk their lives for either one. Yet Lothar could not help but be disappointed. The months of waiting while Charles sat in jail had only sharpened his anger. Someone, he thought, would have to pay.

He crossed the courtyard to the north tower, Gunther staying close to make sure he didn't kill anyone unnecessarily. They passed through the main door and took the steps two at a time until they reached the landing at the top. A guard stood with his spear upraised.

"Stop!" he shouted, but he got no further, for Lothar drew his scramsax with his free hand and thrust it into the man's gut. The man gurgled and crumpled, sliding off the blade as he made his way to the floor.

"Lothar," Gunther said warningly.

"Shut up." Lothar sheathed the weapon and pulled the key from around the dead man's neck. "Stay here. Watch for others." He bounded up the narrow stairs alone.

Charles had watched the scene of Lothar's arrival from his tiny tower window. He stood in the center of his cell, waiting. Presently he heard the scuffle on the stairs, the scrape of the heavy door opening. The light of a torch appeared, followed by the familiar form of his friend. Charles moved into his small circle of light.

Lothar saw him then, gasped, taking in the long hair and beard, the ragged clothes, the withered body.

"God, Charles, you look like a Meroving!"

They gazed at each other a long moment.

"We'd better go," Charles said, his voice dusty with disuse. "Plectruda may still have spies about."

They descended to the lower landing where Gunther stood watch. He stared at Charles but said nothing, his expression unreadable.

"Goon," Charles said.

Gunther nodded once, turned and led the way to the courtyard.

Rodolf was the only one to come forward, leading Epone by the reins. Charles greeted him with a weak smile, then put a hand on the horse's muzzle. Epone shoved his nose in Charles' chest, the first one to greet him properly. The men seemed to take comfort in this; they began moving toward him as well.

"Great mad beast," Gunther said. "I'll be glad to be rid of him." Charles continued to stroke Epone's nose, talking to him softly.

"Here," Lothar said. Charles turned to see his friend holding out his sword, still in its scabbard. Charles sighed, took it, buckled it on. Then he pulled himself into the saddle. The men cheered, elation and relief overcoming them. Charles turned to the captain of the prison.

"Let them all out," he said.

"What?" Willem's eyes widened in alarm.

"All the prisoners you have here. Let them go free."

"But Plectruda—"

"Plectruda will have your head for your failure here. All of you will be hunted men the rest of your lives. But you have a choice. You can come with us. We offer you no sanctuary, no comfort. We don't even promise you life. But we can give you a chance to live as free men, to decide your own fate."

The wind howled mournfully in answer. Willem shook his head. "Open them," he said. The guards obeyed, and soon the courtyard was filled with prisoners, more than fifty of them, ragged and filthy as Charles was, some old, some young, all of them wasted and dead-eyed. Charles cleared his throat and told them the same thing he had told the guards, offering them the chance to join him. They did not speak, but they nodded and bent their knees to him.

Charles turned to Willem. "You have been my jailor these past months," he said. "Will you accept me as your lord now?"

Willem looked from Charles to the men he had commanded. He bit his lip, his fists clenching and unclenching. Then he fell to his knees. The rest followed.

Charles took a breath.

*So it begins.*

# 11

## The Eifel Hills
## Central Austrasia

THEY HEADED SOUTH, to the Eifel Hills, following the ancient aqueduct that had been built by the Romans to supply water to Kolonia. The low mountains surrounded a long, jagged, crescent-shaped lake, clear and still and brilliantly blue. To Charles it seemed like paradise, a Garden of Eden well hidden inside the encircling mountains. After eleven months in a prison cell, it was all he could do but lift his face to the sky and breathe.

There were more men encamped in these hills than there had been in Jupille the night of his arrest. Throughout the year they had come, men seeking refuge from the war, men disgusted with the Austrasian leadership, men who had nowhere else to go. Gerold and Milo had brought men from their own provinces. Arnulf was there as well, though his brother Hugo had elected to stay in Paris, seeking sanctuary at the parish cathedral.

They celebrated Charles' return with what they had of beer and mead and the few casks of wine they were able to purloin from local monasteries. But for weeks after Charles hardly spoke at all. He swam in the cold water of the lake, not caring that his fingers and toes turned blue. He rode Epone up and down the hills, enjoying the warm pressure of the horse between his weakened legs. He ate boar and fish and rabbit, adding meat to his own bones. He slept under the stars, as if he never wanted to see a roof again. He seemed engrossed in the sky and the grass and the water, mesmerized by the light, the chill of the breeze, the dazzling color of the world after the long darkness of prison, the endless gray. He had not realized until he was released how nearly he had died in that cell, how the dank stone walls had almost crushed his soul. *I will never put a man in a prison,* he thought. *Kinder to kill him than put him in a cage.*

The men had built shelters and were busy cutting heath to store for feed for the animals. There were a few women in the valley as well: wives, mistresses and widows needing protection. They tended gardens and gathered berries and skinned and cooked the food. The woods ran with wild pigs, the lake teemed with fish. The camp was more like a village, a settlement, a town.

Winter on the lake was cold and still, settling deep into men's bones. Very little moved in the mountains, and when it snowed it seemed as though the whole valley had been lifted into the heavens, and the sun made the lake so brilliant it was hard to look at. Charles loved that winter, the bracing air, the utter quiet. There was no war, no enemy, no world beyond that valley, nothing past those mountains that enclosed them. He could forget completely about what had happened, and what was to come.

"He won't even talk to me," Lothar said, pacing before the central fire pit. Arnulf sat on a log, picking the meat off a pork rib.

"He just needs time. I think prison was worse than he expected."

"How much time will it take? He's got to know that if Raginfrid wins this war he will face something far worse than prison."

"He knows," Arnulf said. "Leave him be, will you? In the meantime, you need to train all these men you've brought with you. What a rabble. Not sure they are worth it, but we need every warm body we can get, as long as we can put a weapon in their hands and point them in the right direction."

"I know it," said Lothar darkly. But he was glad, at least, for something to do. He took a particular pleasure in training new men; it allowed him to be almost unreservedly brutal, his only real release. Charles had taken no interest in the training, and Lothar was beginning to think it had been a waste of time to rescue him; he was about as much use as Plectruda's bungling guards. *Give him time*, Arnulf had said. And he would do that, for the moment. But he would not give Charles forever.

"In the spring," Lothar said. "We must move in the spring."

Spring came unexpectedly early. March brought a soft wind and welcoming sun. Women began clearing patches of ground for gardens. Men were repairing roofs with new thatch. The ice on the lake broke up enough to make fishing possible, and soon bass and pike sizzled on cooking fires.

Charles walked along the lake one sunny, early morning and came upon a woman sitting on a rock overlooking the water. Her dark brown hair was unbound and wet. She was wrapped in a towel, as if she had just come from bathing in the lake. He stopped; they looked at each other. He had seen her before, had wondered who she was but had never gone to speak to her. Now there seemed to be no words necessary. She got up slowly, letting the towel fall away. She walked to him, sliding her bare arms over his shoulders, lifting her face to meet his mouth.

They found a patch of grass between some rocks and lay down, their bodies ground together in dirt and sweat and murmurs and soft laughter. She told him her name was Adele. Her husband, an Austrasian freeman called to fight by his seignior, had been killed in the first battle against the Neustrians, who had swept over the countryside destroying everything in their wake. Her farm near Liège had been burned, her children killed. She had been raped repeatedly and left for dead. It was an all too familiar story. She had buried her children and wandered into the hills, not knowing where she was going or what she would do. One day, while begging at a monastery, she spied a band of thieves breaking into the cellar to steal beer. She followed them back to the camp. She was soon discovered, but after telling her tale, and proving she could carry her own weight, the men decided to let her stay.

He brought her to the hut he had built, and she cooked for him and mended his clothes and slept with him in the dark, chill nights. She was not quite beautiful, but there was solace and peace in her sharp face and soft body, and he found himself drawn to her by their mutual loss, their inability to love anything in the world.

In early May two men arrived in Charles' camp. Guards apprehended them, took their weapons and brought them to Charles, who knew them well. One was Sigebald, Bishop of Metz, the other Peppo, Bishop of Verdun. They had both been loyal to Pipin and, like many bishops, had their own retinues.

Charles invited them to sit by his fire. Adele brought them beer. Peppo eyed her with disapproval.

"How did you find me?" Charles asked them.

"Einhard told us," Sigebald said. He was a big, stout man with a very full red beard and a huge metal crucifix around his neck that clanged annoyingly against his armor. He liked to wear full plate armor rather than leather or mail, despite the fact that it was extremely heavy and prone to rust. But he liked the *Romanness* of it, the fact that real plate armor was rare and expensive and intimidating.

"Did you hurt him?" Charles asked.

"Of course not, what do you take us for? We are men of the Church!"

"Forgive me if I don't find that a recommendation," Charles said.

"I see you are staying warm in the nights," Peppo said, eyeing Adele who had gone back into the hut. He was not as big as Sigebald but still imposing, with a dark, pointed beard and small calculating eyes.

"Why did you come here?" Charles asked, his voice betraying some small annoyance.

Peppo looked at his companion, who took a long swallow of beer before speaking.

"We have an offer for you Charles. We want to help you."

"And how many men did you bring with you?"

The two bishops exchanged glances.

Charles shook his head. "That's what I thought."

"You have to understand," Peppo said, leaning in close. "There are many that would come to you, Charles, but you need to … *do* something. Show them you are alive and willing to fight."

"What would you like me to do? I have barely two hundred men here. If the nobles are not willing to commit, I cannot attack Raginfrid."

"The nobles are confused," Sigebald offered apologetically. "They don't know who to follow. It is all chaos, Charles. Plectruda has lost control. The Saxons have overrun the northern frontier. Even Bavaria is in revolt."

Charles nodded. "And the Aquitaine?"

Peppo sighed. "So far Eudo has stayed out of it. He's got his hands full with Arabs right now. They've taken all of Septimania. Cut him off from the coast! They are raiding farther north as well."

Charles sighed. "I tried to tell Pipin that would happen. He wouldn't listen."

Sigebald shook his head. "Well, a year ago I wouldn't have listened to you either. Such is the fate of prophets. That's why you need to take back this kingdom. What are you waiting for? Plectruda cannot launch even a minor attack against that Neustrian birdbrain Raginfrid. This is a war of clowns and fools, Charles. You need to get in there and stop all this nonsense."

"I don't have enough men to attack Raginfrid—"

"Not Raginfrid! Just listen for a minute." Peppo put down his cup, clearing his throat. "The Frisians are on the move now; they will meet up with Raginfrid for a full assault on Kolonia. So you have an opportunity. Head west, to the river, and you will find the Frisians moving south. There are only about five hundred of them. If you take them out, it will deny Raginfrid his reinforcements. And then you will see the nobles flock to you."

"Five hundred," Charles said. "Too many."

"You've been outnumbered before!"

"These men are not fully trained. I have too few horses, too few weapons—"

"Charles, we're talking about *Frisians* here, not the whole Neustrian army!" Peppo said, annoyed. "You can handle this alone. Just make a good show of it. Once you have defeated the Frisians, we will all be able to join you against Raginfrid. I can promise it."

Charles said nothing for a time, staring at the fire.

"What's the matter with you?" Sigebald said, irritated with his silence. "You can do this, Charles! Easily! It's only Frisians, after all. What could possibly go wrong?"

"That," Charles said slowly, "is what I would like to know."

Late that night, as he lay beside her in the hut, Charles told Adele what the bishops had said, though he didn't have to, she had heard it all. She was silent a long time.

"How do you know they are telling you the truth?"

"I *don't* know," Charles said. "But I don't think they would come here if they were not truly desperate."

"Of course they are desperate. You are their only hope. The only one with a legitimate claim to the rule. And the men will follow you into hell, if necessary." She paused, looking at him. "What is it you fear, Charles?"

He closed his eyes. "I don't know … if I can do this again. If I even want to."

She curled her body around him, stroking him idly. "I will pray for you."

# 12

CHARLES STOOD AT the edge of the trees on the ridgeline and watched them come. They were moving slowly, without caution or haste; he thought he heard some sort of chanting, though he could not be sure.

He recognized the Frisians by their golden hair, braided in elaborate knots on their heads. They were bare-chested, as usual, their bodies pierced and tattooed, their arms bedecked with golden bands. They had fanned out along the stream's edge, stopping to fill skins and rest, completely unaware of the presence of a warband on the ridge above them.

"We should move now," Lothar said, coming up beside him. "While they suspect nothing."

Charles hesitated. "We should reconnoiter first, make sure there are no more in the area."

"We don't have time for that," Lothar retorted. "They're here now. They will see us before too long. If we are fast enough we will be in and out before they know what hit them."

*Speed was everything.*

Charles sighed, nodding. "All right. We'll go in with the horses first. We need to scatter them. We cannot let them form a shield wall." They would be powerless against a shield wall, which could only be broken by one of greater numbers, and he did not have the numbers today.

*Speed was everything.*

He felt the blood pulse in his temple, a familiar rhythm, the start of a battle. Every instinct he had told him to wait. Was that only his fear talking? The nameless doubts he had carried with him from his prison cell? He looked around at the eager, impatient faces watching him; he knew that hesitation would not be tolerated.

He turned and looked over at his men, crouched along the tree line, invisible to the enemy army frolicking at the grassy bank. He watched their eyes, the nervous energy, the unacknowledged fear. He saw Willem, his former jailor, leading his cluster of guards and prisoners. Charles thought how strange it was that this man, who once had control over his life and death, was now at his mercy; how a man's fortunes rested on the smallest of circumstances. Willem had been sullen for a while, but he did not look sullen anymore. He almost smiled when Charles' gaze passed over him. This was far better than watching over a stable of criminals, no doubt, overcome with boredom and despair.

Lothar was at his side, as always, along with the nearly identical brothers Frido and Herne, and the others Charles had chosen for his bodyguard. Lothar had trained most of them personally. They hated him; he had spent the winter trying hard to kill them, but they respected him and they trusted him now. Lothar was the ultimate warrior in their eyes; he could not be killed. They felt safe with him, though they did not feel safe *from* him.

Charles glanced at Ragnor, who led the small posse of archers, mostly older boys mounted on fleet steppe ponies they had stolen in raids. Ragnor was grinning, as he always was, flexing his bow more to show off his muscles than for any other reason. His archers had all taken to dressing like mad Saxon horse archers, half-naked and streaked with war paint.

Gunther, to his right, sat motionless on his big horse, along with the other horsemen. He would lead the charge. There was no expression on his face, but he had the sort of face that didn't invite expression. Its distortion was horror enough to make the most hardened warrior cower in fear.

Gerold and Milo were on the flanks with their hardscrabble foot warriors. They would not run, no matter how hot it got. They would contain the fighting, keep the Frisians hemmed in.

He turned to Rodolf, who was holding his horse patiently. He mounted the stallion and took the reins. "Stay with the extra horses. Bring them in if we lose any down there."

"Lord, I want to fight."

"No, boy, not this time."

"I'm good with a spear."

"I know you are, but not this time. I need you with the horses."

Rodolf turned away, dejected.

Charles drew his sword, studying the edge. The sword had belonged to Andrius; it had been the old Greek's pride and joy, the sword that had accompanied him into many a battle. He remembered the night his teacher had given it to him. He was fourteen years old when Andrius told him to meet him in the chapel at midnight. Charles had found him kneeling at the low altar, praying. He knew the monk was aware of his presence; like every old warrior there was no small sound he missed.

Suddenly, Andrius spoke aloud: "I am going to die soon." He had not been sick, so far as anyone could tell.

"I want you to have this." He had risen and turned then, lifted the sword he was leaning on as he prayed, lifting it so the blade rose up and then fell softly in his hands. It glinted in the candlelight. He had always taken exquisite care of that sword, despite the fact that the abbot strongly disapproved of him keeping it.

Charles was astonished. "Why me?" he asked.

Andrius shrugged. "You are the only one tall enough for it." He laughed. "I think you know the reason. You are Pipin's son. I believe— you will need it one day." He beckoned Charles to come to him and take the sword. Charles held it, surprised at its weight and perfect balance.

"It's a good blade, well-cared for. Saved my life many times, as it will yours." He paused, and Charles saw a strange mist in his eyes. "You have a hard road ahead of you, Charles. You need to be prepared. I have tried to prepare you, as best I could. I fear it was not enough. God forgive me." He crossed himself. "Life is full of storms. They must never take you off-guard. You must always look for them, on the horizon. If you look, you will see. Most men don't look. That is their downfall. But you … promise me, you will never fail to look."

"I promise," Charles said, not quite knowing what he was promising, but sensing something important in the words.

Andrius nodded, seeming to smile. "Good. Now go to bed."

The next morning, the old Greek was gone. Vanished. The monks supposed he had gone to the hermitage, as he often did, to pray or fast. But Charles knew he would not come back. Like a dog that goes off alone to die, Andrius had taken his own road home.

Now Charles looked at the sword, a sword that had killed more men than he could count, a thing of violent beauty, a warrior's only friend. The hilt was shaped oddly, with three tongues, two curling outward, the center one standing straight. Like a flower, or a flame. He held the sword in the air, staring at it, waiting. Everyone was silent, watching him. Behind them the sun crept higher, blades of light breaking through the tree line, falling upon the shining steel, reflecting back to him. He took a breath.

*Now.*

He raised the sword and swung it forward.

Gunther and the horsemen surged from the trees, kicking up dirt, charging in a black mass down the slope toward the unsuspecting Frisians. They scattered in confusion, the sight of those black beasts always terrifying to them. Gerold and Milo charged from both flanks as the Frisians scrambled about, grabbing for their long spears. Charles followed down the center with Lothar and the Bodyguard, covered by Ragnor and his flying archers, and the air was filled with the screams of men, the shattering of swords, the pounding of hooves, the hymn of his life.

The Frisians struggled to regroup but were blinded by the sun, which had cleared the trees and shone directly in their eyes. The horsemen plowed into them, throwing their short javelins and francas, thrusting with spears. Ragnor and his archers seemed to be everywhere, their arrows spitting as if from the sun itself. The ground was growing red with flowing death, and the sounds were no longer screams but grunts and moans and the sinister cadence of dying men. Charles screamed more orders, slashing with the sword as he spun Epone in circles, his heart beating to the rhythm of this dance, a dance as natural to him as breathing.

"More coming!"

Charles turned from the fight as Leutgar charged toward him on horseback. He was shouting and pointing. Charles could see nothing, so he broke away, rode toward the hill for a better view. What he saw made his heart sink. An army had emerged from the tree line at the far end of the ridge and was streaming down the hill toward the battle. But it was not a Frisian army; it was Neustrian. He could see the banners clearly. *Damn.* He cursed himself for not reconnoitering.

He rushed back down into the fighting, "Retreat!" he shouted at Lothar. Lothar turned on him, his face savage, speckled with blood.

"Are you mad?"

"Now, Lothar! Pull them back!"

Lothar would not listen. Charles screamed again. The word was passed: *Neustrians! Turn back now! Run!*

Gunther was the first to react, bellowing to the horsemen to retreat. Finally Charles' small army turned from the battle and began a long, hectic scramble up the slope. The Neustrians started to pursue but abandoned the chase once Charles' men were well out of the way in the woods. Charles could hear their braying victory cries echoing even through the trees. The sound burned into his soul.

The warriors returned to their camp, dejected and angry. Lothar was beside himself with fury. There would be no offensive against Raginfrid now.

"How many did we lose?" Charles asked Milo.

"Seven or so, I think," Milo said. He paused. "You did the right thing. It could have been much worse. Your friend Willem died today."

Charles looked at him. "The jailor?"

Milo nodded.

"We'll go back for them," Charles said. He felt completely exhausted, spent. He wanted to sleep, to forget this day ever happened.

"We'll have to wait until they have moved on."

*Yes*, Charles thought dismally. *Until they move on. To Kolonia.*

A few weeks later a message arrived from Sigebald: Raginfrid had marched on Kolonia. The Austrasians had put up a paltry defense; Plectruda had surrendered the city and the whole of Pipin's treasure to the invaders. The Austrasian king was shorn and sent to a monastery. Kolonia, and all of Austrasia, belonged to the Neustrians.

It was bitter gall in Charles' gut. He had never lost a battle, never retreated in the face of a greater force, and the knowledge burrowed inside of him like a rampant tumor. He knew the men were angry that they had been forced to abandon a fight they had been winning. He suspected they might not trust him as once they had. But at least they were alive. They could try again. Charles' pride was wounded, but his resolve was reborn.

# 13

## Ambléve
## September, 716

THE NEUSTRIAN ARMY moved languidly along the western road from Kolonia, a wide plain dotted by farms and pastures, which gave way, eventually, to low, forested hills. After a summer spent gorging on the fruits of Pipin's treasure in Kolonia, Raginfrid, the new Mayor of Francia, was going home, to the green pastures of Angers with the scent of the sea. He had less than a thousand men with him, as many had to be left behind to guard the city. Many had also deserted, but it did not matter anymore. Raginfrid had secured the kingdom, all of Francia belonged to him now.

He was not in a great hurry. The weather was very fine, dry and cool; there was plenty to eat and even more to drink. He had pilfered much of the palace of Kolonia's furniture and wanted, it seemed, to use it all on the march. Once complete his tent was so comfortable that he slept in most days, and so the army got a late start on the day's march. He was a genial commander, well liked by his soldiers, though he lacked a certain discipline. His men were boisterous, singing songs and telling jokes as they traveled. They were pleased with their booty and looking forward to spending it on wine and pretty girls and small farms in Neustria.

At the center of the column fifty guards surrounded the wagons carrying the pilfered treasure of Kolonia, as well as the king in his litter. Raginfrid stayed close to them, for these were two things he could not afford to lose.

The road began to curve to the southwest, skirting the low hills with their pockets of pine woods. The air grew humid as the days went on, rife with swift, savage thunderstorms. The army slowed.

Five days after leaving Kolonia, they passed to the east of the town of Malmedy, on the western edge of the Eifel hills. The Roman road led south between layers of hills and blanketed forests toward Ambléve. As the army made its way down one of these hills it came upon a wide, rocky stream. Raginfrid called for a halt and consulted with his captains.

"There are too many rocks. We'll have to carry the wagons across," said one of them, an older man with a large scar that ran the whole length of his face. He did not sound pleased with the prospect. It would take the rest of the day.

"What else can we do?" Raginfrid asked, annoyed.

"There is a bridge downriver," said the captain.

"How far?"

"Ten leagues, maybe more."

"Ah! Too far." Raginfrid shook his head dismissively. "We'll carry the wagons across. We'll be over and into the trees before the day is done. Besides," he added, sniffing the air knowingly, "I think it is going to rain."

At his command, all the captains began organizing parties to carry the wagons over the stream. It would have helped if Raginfrid had emptied them first, but he was nervous about exposing the cargo to too many prying eyes. The progress was slow, the men strained to their limit. By the time they finished the sky was streaked with dark, ominous clouds. Raginfrid, already on the other side of the river with the wagons and the king's litter, told his men to rest and take some food while the rest of the army began crossing.

Raginfrid dismounted and demanded a chair and food be brought to him. While his servants scrambled to pull a chair from the wagon the scar-faced captain rode up to him again.

"My lord. This is not a good place to stop, in the middle of this crossing. We must put some men on guard and send out scouts—"

He got no farther. Raginfrid stared, aghast, as the captain gasped, lurched, and fell from his horse. There was an arrow in his back. He opened his mouth to scream, but then he saw more men, his captains, falling from their saddles, picked off one by one. Archers. His bodyguards moved in around him, drawing their swords.

"Dismount!" Raginfrid screamed. "Get down! Who is shooting?"

"Saxons!" came a cry from somewhere.

Raginfrid looked up to the ridgeline above the stream. He saw a dozen figures standing there, longhaired and bare-chested, firing their missiles almost nonstop. Saxons? How could this be? They were much too far south for Saxons—

"Get them!" he screamed at his men. The men on the other side of the stream grabbed spears and charged up the hill. At once the archers retreated. The air emptied of arrows. Raginfrid breathed a sigh of relief. Saxons, he thought. They had come for the treasure. But they would not get close enough—

Thunder boomed over his head, making him nearly jump out of his skin. He would remember that sound as the voice of God pronouncing judgment upon him that day, for at that moment an army appeared, an army cloaked in black, riding over the ridge in a molten mass. It made a sound like nothing human as it bore down upon the Neustrians struggling up the hill.

Raginfrid knew that this was not a Saxon attack. It was Charles, the Bastard.

Raginfrid spun around, his heart thumping madly. There was nothing he could do for his soldiers, he saw that. He needed, above all, to secure the king. He ran to the king's litter.

Just at that moment, as if sealing his fate, the heavens opened, and the rain came down. It didn't just fall, it plummeted, not in individual drops but in a great soaking curtain, as if a celestial bucket had been dumped on its side.

Raginfrid made his way through the drenching rain to the king, who sat shivering in his litter, his face as pale as death.

"Your Majesty," he shouted, "you must get on a horse!"

"The king does not ride," said the king, his voice quivering.

"The king will ride today," Raginfrid said savagely. He hauled the king from the litter, screaming for a spare horse. He could see almost nothing in the pelting rain, but he got the king mounted and managed to mount his own horse, calling for his bodyguards and racing away from the battle. His wagons, however, his precious cargo, Pipin's treasure, had to be left behind. But the treasure was not nearly so important as the king. As long as he had the king, he was still the ruler of Francia, and he could try again to get his stolen treasure back.

Charles raced across the stream in the sheeting rain to see the wagons standing, unguarded, and the king's litter empty. Lothar followed him and swore loudly. Raginfrid had deserted the field of battle, leaving his troops to die, but he had gotten away with the king.

"We can catch him," Lothar shouted. "Give me ten men—"

"No," Charles said. "Let him go. We have the treasure. It's enough for today."

As the rain abated the men began to cheer their victory. The hillside was littered with bodies, most of them Neustrian. Charles' guards gathered at the stream, rounding up prisoners. Charles turned his horse, surveying the field, as Sigebald rode up to him, smiling with great satisfaction.

"Well now, that is how it's done," said the bishop. "Though you did have a bit of help from God. See how useful I am to you? Prayer has more power than the sword, Charles, even yours. Where's Raginfrid?"

"Gone," Charles said.

"Ran, did he? Spineless toad. Took the king, I suppose?"

"Yes."

Sigebald sighed. "Well, you can't have everything can you? But you've recovered Pipin's treasure, thanks be to God. I don't have to tell you that after that debacle in the spring I've had a difficult time persuading the nobles to trust in you."

"You don't have to tell me."

"Well, the tables have turned, eh? Now onto Kolonia."

"One thing at a time, Bishop," Charles said. "We've got all these prisoners to deal with first." But he didn't try to hide his relief.

It had been absurdly easy, in the end. Raginfrid's scouting parties had stayed in front, had never bothered to look behind. Charles had been able to track them for miles, waiting for them to come upon a vulnerable place. A stream bed, where the army would be divided and Raginfrid would be preoccupied with his precious loot. It had been like a gift from heaven. Charles had pushed his men hard all that summer, training them in Roman-style maneuvers like feigned retreats and dressed charges, forcing them to work as a team, something most of them had never done before. He had promised them victory. And he had delivered.

In the lingering drizzle the men looted the bodies and began the grisly work of burying the dead. The Neustrian captives did most of the digging, and by late afternoon they lay in drenched heaps by the side of the stream, too exhausted to think of escaping, which was more or less the point.

Charles' men gave them food, dried meatsticks and pieces of hard bread, and they drank the water of the stream, which held a faint taste of blood. Then he spoke to them.

"I'm not going to hold you prisoner," he said to their astonishment. "I don't need prisoners or slaves. I need fighting men. If you wish to fight for me, you will give me your oath. Any man who doesn't wish to give his oath can fight for his freedom—to the death—in single combat against my best warriors. I give you your choice."

The prisoners stared at him in mute shock for a long time. They looked around at each other. No one made a sound. Then one of them stood. He was quite young, with a long, stern face. Charles noted the crest on his tunic: the House of Lyon. He was a nobleman. Yet he had not run with Raginfrid and the other nobles. He had stayed and fought to the end.

"You wish to fight?" Charles asked him.

The young man nodded.

"What's your name?"

"Rogan. Of Lyon."

"Rogan. Son of Richomer."

Rogan looked surprised. "You know my father?"

"I knew of him," Charles said. "How old are you?"

"Twenty."

Charles smiled. "It is a young age to die."

"I would die before I'd follow an Austrasian."

"You consider Raginfrid a worthy commander? He led you into a trap here and then deserted you."

"His responsibility is to the king, not to me," Rogan retorted, lifting his chin in defiance.

"So you would follow him again?"

Something changed in Rogan's face, his eyes flickered, his jaw clenched. "I am a son of Lyon. I do not forsake my family or my family's honor, no matter what idiot is in charge."

Charles laughed out loud. "Then you should have your chance to redeem your family's honor." He turned and motioned to Lothar, who stood with the other guards watching the exchange. Lothar came forward, his eyes bright with anticipation. He drew his sword. Charles put a hand on his arm. "Teach him a lesson," he said softly, "But don't kill him."

"Why not?" Lothar snapped.

Charles shrugged. "I like him. I want to keep him. And we are going to need him if we want to win over this enemy."

"Why bother? Just kill them all."

"No," Charles said. "We need these men on our side." Lothar made a noise of displeasure. "Stay your hand, Lothar, or I will stay it for you."

He turned back to the young nobleman, spreading one arm in invitation.

"Rogan of Lyon. Meet Lothar, Captain of my bodyguard."

The prisoners still on the ground between them scrambled away forming a circle, surrounded by Charles' men. They began shouting words of encouragement to Rogan, the only one to stand up and fight. Rogan was given his sword; he held it high in two hands, the blade trembling only slightly. He waited for Lothar to come to him, his chin still lifted, his eyes hard and focused.

Lothar tore off his mail shirt and stood bare-chested before his opponent, showing off his lean, muscular body. Charles' men hooted and cheered at the sight. Rogan stood his ground, undaunted. Lothar circled Rogan with the slow, hungry gait of a rabid wolf, his sword low. Rogan countered him with lithe, rhythmic steps, his sword up and at the ready, fully prepared for a strike. Lothar continued to circle, just out of reach, until Rogan grew impatient and struck first, slashing downward with a breathless grunt. Lothar blocked the blow easily, and the next one, toying with his opponent as a lion plays with its food before squashing it to death.

Then Lothar made a strike, but it was only a feint, forcing Rogan off his stance. Lothar laughed.

Rogan, seeing that Lothar was mocking him, grew vexed, pressing his attack harder. Lothar encouraged his anger, taunting him between strikes, disparaging his entire family, especially his father Richomer, who had fallen against Pipin Herstal. Steel rang against steel, echoing in the rain-dense air, the audience growing more vocal, insistent.

Finally Rogan struck out hard, his sword slicing down upon Lothar's head. Lothar countered the blow but staggered back, off-balance. Rogan saw his moment, gripped the hilt in both hands and lunged for Lothar's exposed torso.

Then Lothar did something quite unbelievable, something Rogan would try to recreate in his mind for years afterward. He realized in hindsight that Lothar had never actually lost his balance at all. As Rogan's sword thrust forward, Lothar leapt into the air, kicking the blade out of Rogan's hand with his foot. Rogan was flung backward at the impact, and before he knew it he was lying on the ground with the tip of a sword pressed against his throat. He said in a frayed whisper, "Kill me then."

Lothar held his sword a long moment, his eyes burning with the desire to thrust it through that smooth white neck. But he said, "Not today whelp," and stepped back, withdrawing the blade. The crowd moaned in disappointment. "But I will give you one piece of advice: keep your head, or you will lose it for good." He glanced at Charles then stalked away, scowling.

Rogan, still on the ground, felt a shadow over him. He looked up to see Charles the Bastard gazing down at him.

"Get up, Rogan of Lyon."

Rogan drew himself to his feet, ignoring the mud streaming down his face, the unbearable humiliation. The clear eyes bore into him, appraising him, though there was no scorn in them.

"Why didn't he kill me?" Rogan whispered in a hollow voice.

"I've had enough killing for one day," Charles said. "I know your family has a long history of hatred for mine. But I am not my father, nor are you yours. This can end today, Rogan. It can end for all time. We don't need to live by rules set down by dead men. We make our own rules. We are free men. We can choose our destiny. So make your choice, Rogan of Lyon. Swear oath to me and you can live."

Rogan was too astonished to speak. He glanced around at the faces of his fellow warriors, saw no anger or outrage, only questions, uncertainty. This was new ground. No victor on any field had ever offered such terms to a defeated enemy before. They gave him no answer and no comfort. He felt Charles' presence before him, silent and waiting. He knew he had to make a decision.

He thought of his father, an enemy of Pipin Herstal to the very end. Richomer had given his life in trying to restore the Merovingian monarchy, in toppling Pipin Herstal from power. Had he ever imagined that his own son would be standing in the presence of Pipin's son, even considering the idea of an alliance? Of swearing oath to an Austrasian? No, Rogan thought finally, he would not.

He turned abruptly and walked to where his sword still lay in the mud. He picked it up and swung it around. A dozen of Charles' guards moved in quickly, drawing their weapons. Charles held up a hand to stay them.

Rogan held the sword aloft rigidly for a long moment. Then he moved toward Charles, the sword dipping slowly as he did, the tip sliding toward the mud. Rogan sank with it, on both knees, his hands gripping the hilt tightly as if it alone held him upright.

Then Rogan of Lyon heard himself say the words he never would have dreamed he would say, the oath of loyalty and subjugation to an Austrasian warlord, the bastard son of Pipin Herstal.

Charles waited until he was done, then stepped toward him and laid his own hand on Rogan's trembling knuckles, murmuring the words of acceptance. The sultry air seemed to lighten, allowing Rogan to breathe again, to lift his face to his new lord and sigh audibly.

"On your feet," Charles said. Rogan stood, his hands dropping to his sides. He stepped back. Charles pulled the sword from the mud and handed it to him, hilt first. Rogan looked up at him, surprised.

"You are in command of these men now," Charles said, indicating the prisoners surrounding them.

Rogan shook his head. "No," he said. "I can't do that."

"Yes you can. And you will. You are mine now, you answer to me. You will do as I tell you, and you will not fail. Do you understand?"

Rogan nodded slowly, swallowing hard. To his surprise, the men cheered.

"Now," Charles said when the cheering had died down. "We go to Kolonia."

# 14

## Kolonia

LEUTGAR RODE HARD to Charles' camp. Behind him, the city of Kolonia sprawled just out of reach, the mighty Rhine churning in the distance. Charles met the scout as he slid from the animal, panting hard but thankfully unhurt. It was a habit of city rulers to send messengers back to their own camps with daggers in their guts and just enough life in their bodies to deliver their message.

"Plectruda refuses to surrender the city," said Leutgar. "The captain is called Warrick—Raginfrid's man. He is holding the gate."

"Warrick," Charles said grimly. "I think I need to speak to him."

Charles took a few of his captains, including Rogan of Lyon, and rode directly to the gates of the city that same day. They carried no weapons and no banner but a white flag on a standard, held high. The guards on the walls looked down curiously, some of them laughing at the spectacle.

"I want to speak to the one called Warrick," Charles shouted.

"Who are you?" demanded the guard on the wall.

"I am Charles, son of Pipin," said Charles.

The pronouncement of the name created general commotion. Spears appeared. Charles' men grew nervous; he raised a hand to calm them.

An older man with a gruff beard appeared. He wore no helmet or mantel. He carried only a short sword. But he looked down at Charles with steely eyes.

"I am Warrick. What do you want?" he shouted.

"Open the gates," Charles said.

"I will not. This city belongs to the Mayor of Francia, Raginfrid of Angers and his agent, Plectruda. You are a criminal, an escaped criminal. I should kill you where you stand."

"I have defeated Raginfrid at Ambléve," Charles said. "He ran from the field like the coward he is."

Warrick scoffed at the news. "You are lying!" he growled.

"He doesn't lie," said Rogan, riding forward. "I am Rogan, son of Richomer. I can attest to the fact that Charles defeated the Neustrians at Ambléve and took back the treasure as well as three hundred prisoners, including me."

"You are a prisoner?" Warrick said, incredulous.

"Not anymore," Rogan said in a clear voice. "I have given my oath to Charles, son of Pipin. I urge you, noble captain, to do the same."

Warrick's mouth worked, clearly astounded. The guards on the walls looked at each other and then at their captain.

"No matter," Warrick shouted. "We will not open the gates to you. Try and break them down, if you dare."

Charles did not respond. Instead, he kicked his horse and broke ranks, trotting along the wall, shouting up to the men guarding it.

"Are there no Austrasians among you? Have you all surrendered to Raginfrid, as Plectruda has done? Do you want to serve her and her whelp and their Neustrian allies all your lives? Do you think she will protect you? I will attack this city, tomorrow, and if I have to break down these gates to do it, I will. But if I must do that, I am warning you, it will not go well for you."

The words echoed off the wall, chilling the very air. There was no response from inside; even Warrick was silent. Charles turned his horse and trotted back to his captains.

"We attack in the morning," he said.

The gates were still closed when Charles rode up to them the next morning, along with his entire army. The city seemed deserted. There were no sentries on the wall, no movement from within. An eerie silence, borne on the cold wind, filled the space between the army and the gate, which looked rather impregnable in the full light of day. Charles took a breath then spoke to his captains.

"Follow me. Slow. Stay in line." The order was passed down. Charles nudged Epone forward; the horse pranced, working the bit, wanting to run. Charles kept a tight rein, his knees locked on the horse's flank. The rest of the horsemen followed in dressed lines, as if they were going on parade. The foot soldiers brought up the rear. They advanced on the gate with aching slowness, falling into a steady rhythm of hooves and marching feet.

Just before the gate they stopped. There was no sound but the banners snapping in the wind. Charles waited, his breath shallow, his chest tightening. He had no idea how he was going to break down the gate. He had no siege weapons, no battering rams. Yet the silence from within gave him slim hope. He drew his sword, screaming from its sheath, and raised the point in the air. Epone danced in a circle, snorting.

The horsemen followed suit; the foot soldiers raised their spears, preparing for a charge. But before Charles could shout the order there was a piercing screech like a pig being speared. It took a moment for him to realize it was the sound of the huge winches of the gate starting to turn.

Charles held his sword still aloft, watching the gates creak open. But no enemy army appeared; no soldiers came crashing through the opening. He lowered his sword. There would be no attack. Did this mean Warrick and Plectruda had surrendered? He doubted it. He nudged Epone forward, still holding tight to the reins. His army followed him.

And so it was that Charles entered Kolonia. The main road was choked with people, soldiers and citizens alike, staring at him as he passed, silent. A man pushed through the crowd and knelt. Others began kneeling as well. Charles was astonished. *Who are they kneeling to?* he wondered. *There is no king here.*

As he neared the palace he saw the Neustrians lined up, Warrick in front, swords and spears drawn as if prepared for battle. Yet not one of them moved. Charles' guards fanned out around him, forming a protective shell. He drew up to the Neustrian captain and stopped.

"They opened the gates to you, Bastard," said Warrick. "But you will set foot in the palace over my dead body."

Charles sighed. "Very well." All at once Warrick was staggering backward, several arrows in his chest. Everyone turned to see Ragnor's archers lowering their bows. They gasped, watching the Neustrian captain die.

"You have two choices," Charles said to the remaining soldiers. "You can join your captain, or join me." The Neustrians, seeing more arrows trained on them, quickly laid down their weapons and backed away.

The first person Charles saw when he entered the hall was Einhard, huddled with a group of servants in the middle of the room. At once they broke into a cheer. It was the first real sound Charles had heard since his arrival. Einhard rushed toward him, grabbing his hands, trembling and sobbing.

"I never doubted you would come back," he said.

"Then you knew more than I did," Charles said with a laugh. "Good to see you, old man."

Einhard beamed up at him. "You look much better than the last time I saw you."

"You look worse."

"It was a hard year."

Charles nodded, his smile fading. "I'm sorry I couldn't get here sooner."

"No matter. You are here now. And you won a great victory. We have been talking of nothing else."

"I can see that," Charles said. It was why he had been able to walk in unopposed. The news of Ambléve had spread through the city like wildfire. The Austrasians had found their courage at last.

"Where is she?" Charles asked. "Is she here?"

Einhard sighed. "In her private chapel, praying for deliverance, I suppose. The boy is at the monastery. She should have gone as well, but she was determined to stay and fight."

Charles turned to Lothar. "I will see her alone," he said. "See to the men. I will be back soon."

# 15

THE DOOR TO the chapel was open. The room had no window, was lit only by dozens of smoking candles. He could make out her slender frame hunched over the kneeler before the statue of Mary, the candles flickering about her, lighting her red hair so it seemed to burn. He watched her a moment, noted the careful set of her shoulders as she steeled herself. He had to admire her; after all that had happened she would not back down, even now.

Plectruda seemed to become aware of his presence. She turned slightly, her profile in the light, then rose with an aged slowness; she was close to sixty now, though he noted that her hair was freshly dyed and her cheeks recently powdered. She pulled her long cape around her and turned to face him.

"Did you come to kill me?" she asked, her voice somehow echoing in the small room, stronger than he had expected.

He looked at her a moment, smiled. "Perhaps. Do you want to beg for your life? I'll listen."

Her slitted eyes widened, revealing the flecks of gold around the green edges. Her lips pursed together. "So it is true … you have defeated the Count of Angers."

"Yes."

"I am not sorry to hear it, I confess. He was an … obnoxious man."

"Yet you turned the city over to him."

"What choice did I have? It was either that or be slaughtered. You would have chosen the latter, naturally. But you are a warrior, Charles. And your commanders did not betray you—"

"Betray you?" Charles said, his voice tinged with scorn.

"As soon as news of your escape was known—"

"What sort of arrangement did you have with the count?" he asked, cutting off her excuses.

Plectruda clasped her hands together, as if in prayer. "I gave him Pipin's treasure to ransom … my grandson's life. Should he learn of my failure …" Her voice trailed off. She looked away. "You killed him, I hope."

"He got away."

Plectruda visibly paled. "Got away?"

"Your grandson is safe, I assure you," Charles said somewhat more kindly. "As is Pipin's treasure."

She breathed a little, conceding to him a small nod. "I suppose I should be grateful for that."

"Do not imagine I did it for your sake."

She sighed and turned back to the kneeler, sinking down as if she no longer had the strength to stand. "So, my lord, what are you going to with me?"

"I have not yet decided," Charles said. He moved to the altar, glancing at the statue, Mary hunched at the foot of the cross, weeping. Plectruda shuddered a little at his nearness.

"I am prepared for whatever you plan to do with me," she whispered. "But I beg you: do not take your vengeance out on Theodoald. You owe that, at least, to the memory of your father—"

"Don't ever speak to me of what I owe my father," Charles said sharply, so sharply she shrank away from him. Then he said in a different voice: "You and your grandson will go to live at the Abbey of Notre Dame. You have a cottage there, I believe? You will not be allowed inside this city again. Or any other, for that matter."

Her eyes widened in surprise. House arrest at Notre Dame, while no luxury, was certainly a more generous offer than she had expected.

"I am content with my fate," she said, "but Theodoald is so young … to condemn him to life imprisonment for a crime he did not commit—"

"He can join the order when he is of age."

"No!" The word came like a slap. "I beg you to take him into your service. He is so young … he is innocent. He should not be consigned to a life as a cleric—"

"It was good enough for me," Charles said drily.

She sighed. "Whatever you think my crimes against you, Charles, have you not had your revenge? You have the city back, and the treasure. You have everything you lost and then some. I, on the other hand, have nothing left. Except Theodoald. I ask you again to be merciful to your nephew. He deserves the chance to prove himself. If he fails, then so be it, send him to the monastery."

Charles appeared to think about this. "Agreed," he said finally. He turned away, preparing to leave, as if she no longer interested him.

"I only did what I had to do, you know," she called after him. He stopped. "I did it to fulfill my husband's final wish. I had to play my part, like Judas in the Garden … for that I will be forever condemned." She closed her eyes, her voice breaking a little. "All I ever wanted, was a son of mine to be king. But my sons were taken from me … " She sighed.

Charles looked at her. She seemed so much smaller than he remembered, so much older, frail even. The thought almost made him laugh.

"Did you have my son killed?" Her green gaze was suddenly taut, focused. "We can be honest with each other now, can't we? It doesn't matter anymore, after all."

Charles smiled coldly. "You never give up, do you?"

Her shoulders heaved. "You will never understand. My life ended the day Grimoald died."

"I notice you live on."

"Answer my question, my lord. Did you have my son killed?"

Charles' smile disappeared. "I would not waste my time killing Grimoald. Grimoald was nothing to me. And don't pretend you cared for him, Plectruda. You used him, that was all, he was a tool, as all men are to you—"

"Shut up!" she commanded. "Don't you dare say another word! You think you have won, Charles, but there is always the final judgment. You cannot escape that, no matter how hard you try. You will pay for the murder of my son … and of my husband! If not for you they would both be alive—"

He looked at her with freezing eyes, and she drew back instinctively, as if the look itself were a physical blow. For the first time she seemed afraid.

"Be careful, woman," he said with chilling softness. "I can still change my mind about killing you. Don't think I haven't thought about it." He left her there and called for his guards.

# 16

## Vincy, near Cambrai
## March 717

FIRES DOTTED THE valley, spread out along the grassy plain to the north of the Somme. It was the first rain-free night the army had experienced since making camp three days before. After an unusually wet winter the Schelde was close to flood stage, making the footing along the banks treacherous. Neither the horses nor the men liked the ground on which they stood. It was not, Charles thought, the ideal place for a battle. But it would have to do.

He had waited out the winter in Kolonia, gathering his forces and consolidating his alliances. The Austrasians had rallied to him at once, eager to reform the shattered army and take back the kingdom. But Charles was in no hurry. He would wait for Raginfrid to make the first move.

In early spring Charles learned that Raginfrid was on the march. Charles moved faster, entering Neustrian territory before Raginfrid had even reached Vincy. They sat now not half a league away from each other on the Roman road north of Cambrai, one of the great cities of the Merovingians, a place where power had shifted time and again since Roman times.

Along with his own army, Raginfrid had brought King Radbod of the Frisians and a large contingent of Burgundians. The Neustrian mayor was taking no chances this time. There would be no surprise attack, no uphill assault to contend with. Raginfrid had united his allies and would throw everything he had into this fight.

Bishop Sigebald listened to Leutgar's report in Charles' tent, slumped on a camp chair, a huge cup of mead in his fist.

"So how many? Two thousand? Including Burgundians? But who counts them? They are useless in a battle. Pure ballast, nothing more."

"Raginfrid will put them in front," Charles said, "to slow us down and make us use our throwing weapons. Once we have exhausted our arrows and javelins, he can go in for the kill."

"Yes, even an idiot like Raginfrid would realize that." The bishop fixed his bleary gaze on Charles. "So … you are ready for this?"

Charles, half lying on his pallet, eyes closed, did not look ready for anything but a nap. "Yes."

"Well, you have my men here, and Peppo's, and Carnivius and Agatheus, that increases your own numbers by half at least. And I understand Rogan of Lyon is with you too?"

"Yes."

"And your Neustrian prisoners? Are you sure they will fight for you? It wouldn't be the first time an army changed sides in the middle of a fight."

"Rogan will lead them. They will do their part."

"You'd better hope so. Should you lose this one, Charles, it will be over for you. You understand that? You let the king get away the last time."

"I know it."

Sigebald did not seem satisfied with his answer. He finished his mead and rose with a belch, readjusting his armor. "All right then. When is supper?"

"The pigs have been butchered."

"Good. You have more mead, I assume?"

"I never forget the mead."

"That is what I like about you, Charles. You remember the important things." Which was true. Charles had built in less than a year an astonishing network of spies and scouts, couriers and messengers, as well as supply lines, training camps, recruiting and foraging parties and every other faction necessary to support an army in the field. His men were better trained and fed than any army since the Romans, and he never, *ever*, forgot the mead. Charles understood what it took to win battles, and it was more than good swordsmanship. Sigebald beamed at him like a proud father. "We'll have some fun tomorrow, yes? I've been looking forward to this all year."

"I told you before, Bishop, you should spend more time forgiving sins and less time committing them."

Rogan of Lyon sat by himself on a rock, holding the reins of his horse while it chewed on soggy grass. He watched the activity of the camp, men building fires, setting up tents, sharpening weapons. The mood was calm, relaxed even, despite the long, forced march at double speed. So different from Raginfrid's haphazard dawdling.

"Rogan of Lyon?"

Rogan looked up then sprang to his feet, startling the horse. Charles was standing before him.

"My lord—"

"Are you going to do this, Rogan of Lyon?"

"You mean fight? Yes, I will fight." Rogan looked away, settling his horse. He did not want to betray his true feelings to this man, whom he had come to admire despite his visceral hatred of all Austrasians. Charles was not like any Austrasian he had ever known. Perhaps it was due to his bastard lineage, or his turbulent history, being rejected by his own father, that made him different. But of all things that mattered to Rogan of Lyon, fighting was foremost. Charles was a fighter, a natural warrior, and the best leader Rogan had seen on any field. "I gave you my oath, my lord. I will fight."

"Good," Charles said. "I won't need you in the initial attack, but you need to be on the right, ready for whatever happens. Do you understand?"

Rogan nodded. His remembered this man's first command to him. *You will do what I tell you. And you will not fail.* He swallowed. For Charles, success or failure was merely a matter of will, not a testing of fate.

"I will not fail you, my lord," Rogan said in a hoarse voice. Charles smiled.

"Come into my tent, and have a cup of mead. You look like you could use it."

Raginfrid was ready for a real fight, itching to face the bastard upstart again and put him in his place. The loss of Kolonia was a disaster, but not an irrecoverable one. There was still time to stop Charles in his tracks.

He was taken off-guard, therefore, when Charles sent a messenger under white flag, requesting a parley. Raginfrid was pleased; Charles already wanted to make a deal. Perhaps he had realized he was severely outnumbered and would not be able to withstand a proper Neustrian attack.

The Neustrian mayor wanted to refuse, but the king insisted on the meeting. Chilperic had decided he would ride into battle, like a proper king. Raginfrid hated it when Chilperic decided to act like a king, which he had been doing more and more, of late. The king had also invited Radbod to join them, another annoyance. The King of Frisia trotted up, ridiculously huge and clearly uncomfortable on a small fat pony. He was an aging warrior, his unkempt blond beard gone completely gray, his weathered skin lying like a wrinkled sheet over his big bones. But he had not given up his quest for vengeance against the Franks, and Charles in particular, who had humiliated him so intolerably on the Crooked Rhine all those years ago.

Charles and his Bodyguard had already assembled at the meeting place, the new *Caroling* banner, the triple flame symbol set on a red cross in a black field, waving above their heads. Horses snorted and tossed their heads impatiently. Raginfrid stared, momentarily unnerved by the size of the man. The eyes were strange too, he thought, pale blue, almost colorless. Raginfrid had the uncomfortable feeling that those eyes saw far too much.

"Well, do you want to surrender already?" he asked as amicably as he could, looking away from the assessing eyes toward the other men, the black horses, all very large and menacing. The Neustrian count felt suddenly very small. *This is his plan*, he thought, *to intimidate us before the battle begins*. He lifted his chin defiantly, fighting the quivering of his stomach.

Charles ignored him, focusing on Chilperic. "Lord King," he said, inclining his head. "I offer you peace."

Raginfrid laughed. The king said nothing, gazing at Charles in astonishment.

"If you give up now, you will save a lot of lives," Charles said. "You can keep your throne and the count can keep his lands and his county. Let us not waste the lives of men today."

Raginfrid snorted derisively. "What sort of trick is this? You think you have even a chance of winning today? We are ready for you this time."

Charles glanced at him. Then he said, "I address the king, not you, my lord." There were mild chuckles behind him. He returned his gaze to the king.

"Why do you make such an offer?" Chilperic asked. He kept his wide, watery eyes on Charles.

"To spare the lives of men on both sides."

"To spare the lives of men?" Chilperic repeated the words as if he could not understand them. The very idea was idiotic to Raginfrid. Had any warlord, any ruler, ever uttered such words before? Had it ever occurred to any general in the field that the loss of men was a price too high to pay? Raginfrid saw uncertainty, wonder, in the king's face. He hurried to intervene.

"Your Majesty, please—" he whispered, "you cannot give the field away today. We must fight!"

After awhile, Chilperic bobbed his head, sighing. "I suppose we must."

Raginfrid breathed with relief and turned to Charles, jutting his jaw. "The king has spoken," he said. "But I will not forget this little meeting,

Charles. You have made your first mistake, and I doubt it will be your last!"

So the battle began, and Charles made no mistakes.

Raginfrid wasted no time in ordering an attack. He had the advantage of numbers, and he would use them quickly and decisively. He noticed, somewhat abstractedly, that the Frankish horsemen were not arrayed at the front, as he had expected. They had stayed in the rear, a last line of defense, a rear guard. Charles was clearly worried that his army would run, especially with so many turncoat Neustrians in his ranks. *Perfect*, Raginfrid thought.

His warriors charged forward, spears held high, shrieking war cries. But the Austrasians did not appear to move at all. Instead they bound themselves together, their shields forming a barricade, waiting for the enemy to fall upon them. There were no flying arrows or javelins. Raginfrid was even more pleased. This would be easier than he expected.

The two lines clashed finally, though to Raginfrid there seemed little violence in it, the Austrasians keeping up their shields, staying on the defensive as the Neustrians tried desperately to break through their lines. The Austrasian shield wall was solid, nearly impenetrable. Raginfrid, increasingly annoyed, ordered all his reserve forces into the fray.

"Break through! Break through!" It wouldn't be long, he thought.

And it wasn't.

Gradually the center of the Austrasian line began to give way, bowing inward. Raginfrid, excited, pushed his men harder, deeper. "They're giving way! Break the line! Break the line!" He kept shouting, madness in his voice now, his captains echoing the command.

And then Raginfrid realized his mistake. But it was too late.

His army was now pressed deeply into the cavity created by the bowing of the Austrasian shield wall. And suddenly the horsemen were in motion, charging around the flanks and coming at the Neustrians with their flying arrows and javelins, not at the front, where they were protected by shields, but from the sides, where they were exposed and vulnerable. Trapped, the Burgundians in front went into a panic, pushing backward against the more hardened Neustrian warriors, who were now hemmed in by the rabid horsemen and Austrasian foot warriors who had suddenly started attacking with spear and sword. Raginfrid's army was now fighting against itself.

It was over then, Raginfrid knew it. He spun his horse and faced the king.

# 17

ROGAN OF LYON was uneasy. The battle was nearly over; it had been easy, too easy. Something seemed wrong. He had stayed on the right, as ordered, but the Neustrians never broke through. They were in disarray, pinned down and unable to escape. Most were surrendering. Still, Rogan felt a tug of something in his gut.

He looked to the rear guard, where Charles sat astride with a few of his captains, watching. He felt Charles' gaze light upon him, the clear eyes piercing even from a distance.

*You will not fail me.*

Charles' gaze shifted to the woods at the far right of the field. Rogan followed it, saw movement. He shouted to his men.

"Come to me!"

Hundreds of half-naked Frisians burst from the woods, brandishing their long spears, as Rogan's men gathered around him. Radbod has been lying in wait until the battle disintegrated, until the Austrasians were preoccupied with plunder.

*You will not fail.*

"Shields!" Rogan shouted.

The men formed a shield wall, crouching low. The Frisian spears were very long, far longer than their own spears and swords. That would not be good. The Frisians would get first strike.

*You will not …*

The men edged closer together, fear stalking them now. Rogan had a new thought.

The spears were long. *Too* long.

"Stay low!" he shouted. "If you let them spear your shields you can get inside their reach!"

The men understood, crouching even lower, their shields raised, waiting. The tattooed warriors were upon them with earsplitting bellows, leaping into the air, driving their spears home.

Rogan screamed and shoved his shield into the nearest spear. He felt the impact, the spear piercing the wood, inches from his head. He gasped, rose up, throwing aside the shield with the embedded spear and thrusting his sword one-handed into the exposed belly of a Frisian warrior, who was still trying to loose his spear. The warrior grunted, eyes widened, blood filling his mouth. Rogan pulled out his sword. The body fell.

He held the sword with both hands, shouting orders to his men, ducking under more spears, thrusting through human muscle and bone, hardly registering what he was doing. He felt the roar of the blood in his temple, in his throat, the sudden burst of energy, like a bolt of lightning through his body. He remembered then Lothar's face, his words: *keep your head, or you will lose it for sure.* He breathed, letting the air rush into the corners of his body. He looked around, saw his men pressing forward, into the spears. He surged ahead, thrusting, dodging. Soon they had all fallen away, except for the king himself, brandishing his long spear and bellowing in his guttural tongue. Rogan's men surrounded him, their swords dripping with blood, forcing the king finally to his knees.

Charles watched the battle from the rear, his scouts and guards clustered around him, awaiting orders. He had not used his sword even once that day. He had known it would not be necessary.

He saw Rogan approach, his soldiers dragging the unrepentant king of the Frisians. He saw the young man's face, bloody, fierce and triumphant, and smiled.

"You bring me a king, Rogan of Lyon."

"Aye, my lord. Shall we kill him?"

"No, he is a great warrior, he deserves to die with his spear in his hand, as every great warrior should. Take him to my tent. Keep a guard on him." Rogan nodded. Charles added: "Well done, Rogan of Lyon."

"Yes, my lord." Rogan did not hide his smile before turning away.

Leutgar rode up next, flushed and panting.

"The king is gone!" he said. "Raginfrid escaped."

Charles sighed. "Lothar will not be pleased."

"Shall we pursue?"

Charles shook his head. "They are long gone I am sure. Go and tell the captains to round up the prisoners and get a count of the dead."

Charles dismounted as Leutgar rode off, glanced around, frowning. "Where's Rodolf?"

The guards shrugged. Charles started to walk toward the main field of fighting, the others following more slowly. He saw Gunther approach, leading his horse.

"Good work," Charles said, smiling at him.

Gunther only nodded and grunted. Charles sensed something wrong.

"What is it?"

The Horse Master turned without speaking and pulled a bundle from his saddle. It took a moment for Charles to realize that the bundle was a body. Gunther held the boy carefully, placing him in Charles' arms. He looked down at the young face, untouched, though the rest was a mass of blood.

"He was supposed to be watching the horses," he said.

"He wanted to fight," Gunther said. "I saw him … but I couldn't get to him in time."

"He was a child."

"We were children when we started," Gunther said. "You fought your first battle when you were his age."

Charles gazed down at the frozen face a long time. He said: "How many have we lost?"

"Not many. They lost many more."

"All these men are Franks," Charles said. "This should not have happened—" He stopped himself. The sheer stupidity of it made the bile rise in his throat. "Gather the prisoners. I want to talk to them." Charles walked away, carrying the dead boy in his arms.

He gave the Neustrian prisoners the same offer he had made in Ambléve. Fight for your freedom, or swear oath to him. This time, no one came forward to fight. They all bent their knees and swore their oaths to him. The few nobles among them swore oaths as well.

Radbod was another matter. It took three men to hold him down. He spat when Charles tried to talk to him.

"Damn your terms of surrender! I will never surrender!" he shouted. "I did that once but ever again!"

"So you want to die today?" Charles asked him in the Frisian tongue.

"You cannot kill me! I am a son of Odin! No mortal can kill me!"

"Really?" Charles drew his dagger and slid the tip across Radbod's arm. Blood poured from the wound. Radbod gasped at the pain, the sight of his own blood. "You bleed," Charles said, "like a mortal."

The king seemed to sag, the fight gone out of him. Charles continued.

"Here's what I want. I want you to go home. Make love to your wife. Raise your crops. You will send me one hundred deniers a year, which can be paid in kind. You will keep your hands and your spears off my missionaries. And you will not show your face in any Frankish territory ever again. Do you understand?"

Radbod swore some more but finally agreed. Charles ordered his bonds cut. The old king rose, still clutching his bleeding arm, and hobbled out of the tent. His remaining warriors were assembled there, their bonds also cut. A groom appeared leading the king's pony, which Radbod mounted. He did not even look at his men, nor they at him. He pointed the animal north and gave a kick to the flanks; it jerked into motion. The Frisian warriors trailed after him. The entire camp stood still, watching the forlorn procession as it disappeared into the woods.

"You let him walk away?" Lothar raved. "Just like that?"

"There is no point in holding him," Charles said. "This was not his fight. He will behave himself. For awhile, anyway." He thought of Rodolf again, felt his heart twist. He would have to find a priest to say a prayer for him, to bury him properly. Rodolf had been a good Catholic. At least he would go to heaven. Where could he find a priest in this place? He thought of Winfrith of Wessex.

He heard a noise behind him and turned to see a boy standing there, freckled and red-haired, a boy he did not know. The boy looked at him with clear blue eyes, standing straight despite his obvious fear.

"My name is Alfric, my lord," he said in a strange, fluting accent. "You need a groom."

"Where did you come from?"

"From Ireland, my lord. I crossed the sea with the missionaries. But I heard of you and I came … to serve you. I do not want to be a missionary."

"Do you know anything about horses?"

"Aye." The boy nodded, his tall frame straightening with pride.

Charles looked at the boy a long moment, then took a breath. "Go introduce yourself to Epone, and if he does not kill you, then you can be my groom."

The boy smiled, a huge, gap-toothed thing, and dashed off.

Charles was about to go back into the tent when he heard a sound, a low rumble that became a chant. He turned, saw his warriors moving toward him in a clump, their spears pumping the air.

"Ham-MER, Ham-MER, Ham-MER … "

The chant grew louder, more joining in. Charles stood motionless, not knowing what to make of it.

"It seems they have finally found a name for you," Milo said, coming up beside him, smiling. "It's better than Bastard, isn't it?"

# 18

## Kolonia

ROTRUDA SAT BEFORE the hearth in her husband's study, watching her children play a boisterous game of Knucklebones with Lothar on the fur rugs. Charles watched also, but his mind seemed elsewhere, as usual. She could hardly believe that they were there at all, together, as they used to be before the death of Pipin Herstal, before the terrible war that had torn them apart. That Charles was finally free. It was a miracle she had prayed for without ceasing. God had answered her prayers. She was His beloved.

It had been a strange homecoming. Little Pipin, who had never set eyes on his father before, had cried in terror when brought to him. Carloman had just stared at him with his flat gray eyes, not speaking a word. How like him the boy is, she thought. Guarded and silent.

But Pipin had gotten over his fright and thrown himself into the game. He loved stealing the bones once they were thrown and not giving them back until he was tackled and tickled into surrender. The children's high-pitched squealing laughter was to Rotruda the sound of angels. Her children were well, her husband was alive, and the kingdom, for the moment, was at peace.

Yet Charles was different. He had cut his beard finally, though he left his hair long, as did all of his bodyguards and horsemen. It was some sort of tribal pact, she supposed, a way of distinguishing themselves from the rest of the world. He looked much older than she had remembered, his face drawn and hard, his eyes still so clear and still, like frozen pools. Lothar had told her something of what her husband had been through: prison, the battles, the long months in exile. The time, and the experience, had placed a wall between them.

She was dismayed that he had chosen Kolonia as his capital, rather than Metz. Kolonia was a depressing city, built of ruins, fronted by a bleak and sinister castrum that had been his prison. It was a grim reminder of what they had suffered; it seemed to overshadow her heart as it overshadowed the city. The river here was wide and bleak with none of the Moselle's curvaceous charms; the land was equally empty, a barren plain fringed by forbidding forest. The palace was a stone fortress built by Romans and inhabited by a world of warriors, so different from the more comfortable, feminine palace of Metz. Yet this was Charles' world, and looking at the stark gray walls adorned with sleek Frankish swords was like looking at his naked body, created for war and immune to love.

Her father Duke Odo had brought her and the children to Metz, but his meeting with Charles had not gone well. The duke refused to swear oath to him until the king was in his possession, though he vowed to remain neutral. For some reason, that made Charles angrier than Rotruda had ever seen him. He told her father that his half-hearted vows were useless to him. Without Neustrian support, Charles could not hope to take possession of the king without another pointless fight. He walked out of the meeting and did not even attend the feast given in the duke's honor.

His rudeness would not be quickly forgotten. Rotruda supposed she would never see her father again. She was cut off, now, from her homeland, her own people, living in exile with a man she barely knew who seemed to take little interest in her. She longed for the company of Plectruda, despite the older woman's treachery; they had been happy, for a time, sitting together in Metz' comfortable solar, sewing baby clothes, talking of children and husbands and womanly things. Plectruda had even served as Carloman's godmother, much to Charles' chagrin. Rotruda had no one to confide in now.

The nurse came in to take the children off to bed.

"Perhaps tomorrow you can take Carloman out riding," Rotruda said when the boys had said their goodnights and were gone. "Lothar brought him a pony just his size."

Charles glanced at Lothar, who did not meet his gaze. "He's a bit young yet."

"He's six! And he's dying to learn." She looked at Charles, sighing a little. "But of course you are busy. Perhaps Lothar could teach him … "

"I'd be pleased to," Lothar said, gathering the game pieces into a small bag. "I have nothing to do these days. You know how agitated I get when there is no fighting going on."

"What about the training?" Charles said. "You have dozens of new recruits to abuse. Don't tell me you have grown bored with that."

"I can make time for Carloman."

"Fine then," Charles said, closing his eyes.

"That boy, Pipin," Lothar said to Rotruda, "could charm the skin off a snake, I think."

"He is rather adorable," Rotruda agreed. She went on to recount all the funny things little Pipin had done in the past year. She hoped Charles was listening, but his eyes were still closed, as if he had fallen asleep. *He is not an easy man*, Plectruda had said. She had known him better than anyone. Rotruda had hoped giving him children would soften his heart toward her, make him see her as somehow more useful to him, more worthy of his love. But still his love eluded her.

At length Lothar rose, kissed her hand with mock gallantry and retreated, nodding to Charles, who nodded back. Rotruda turned to her husband, slumped in his chair, gazing into the fire. She went to him, took the cup from his hand. He looked at her, as if surprised she was still there.

"What are you thinking about?" she asked.

"Saxons."

"Have they attacked?"

"They are always attacking."

"So you are leaving again?" She refilled his cup and handed it back to him.

He took the cup, not looking at her. "Most likely. They've taken the Hellweg. That is the most valuable strip of plowland in the kingdom. I have to get them out before the winter wheat is planted." He drank deeply.

He's tired, she thought, amazed by this. He had always seemed so—invincible. It made him hard to approach. But he was human, after all. And running a kingdom would not necessarily come easily to him. He needed rest. But the summer was only beginning, and the wars never ceased.

She knelt down beside him and put a hand against his cheek. "Charles," she whispered, "let me help you." He looked at her as if he did not know what she was talking about. She reached up and kissed him. She felt the ghost of a response in his body. She slid her tongue around his lips and into his mouth. She felt a soft moan escape her own lips as she slipped onto his lap, gathering up her skirts and wrapping her legs around him.

"Rotruda—"

"Don't think. For once … just feel."

She felt him relax, give in to her; she felt exultant at his surrender. She covered him with her body, taking control of him as she had never done before. Her sunlight hair fell over his face, her hands pushed his clothes aside. She traced the hard edges of his body with her fingers, pulling him into her world of pure sensation, sure that he would never want to go back again.

She awoke alone, in her own bed, though she had no memory of going there. The mead. She had drunk more than usual the night before. It made her bolder. She blushed at the memory of what had happened. Perhaps now she would be pregnant. She wanted that more than anything.

But she had another thought as well, one that had been nagging at her ever since his return. She dressed alone and went to the hall, which was filled with warriors and palace folk eating their breakfast. She saw Lothar, sitting at one of the trestle tables, stabbing at his food absently. She passed by her own seat and went to him. He saw her and rose suddenly, dropping the knife.

"My lady," he said. He was different with her in public, nervous and self-conscious, so unlike the Lothar who played with her children on the hearthrug.

"May I?" she asked, indicating the seat on the bench.

Lothar glanced at the dirty bench and then up at the dais where her chair was held for her, her ladies waiting for her, wide-eyed and curious. She laughed a little and sat, as if unaware of the rough men around her, watching her with knowing expressions. Lothar sat beside her.

"This is not your place," he said in a low voice.

"I can sit wherever I want. And I want to talk to you. Better in a room filled with people than in some private chamber, don't you think?"

Lothar swallowed. "What can I do for you, my lady?"

"Where is Charles?"

Lothar sighed, picking up his knife and stabbing at his meat once more. "He did not tell me where he was going. He does that, on occasion."

Rotruda watched the knife. "It must make you angry. You are supposed to protect him."

"Sometimes—he needs to be alone. And for him, that is difficult."

"I see." She took a shallow breath. "If I ask you something, will you tell me that truth?"

"Of course."

"Does he have … a woman?"

The knife stopped moving. "Charles does not have time for—other women," Lothar said without looking at her.

"That does not seem to be a real answer."

"No. He doesn't have a woman. If he did, I would know about it."

The knife resumed its abuse of the meat. She saw Lothar's knuckles, whitening with his grip on the handle. *He is hiding something*, she thought. "Promise me: if ever you think—if ever you suspect something, you will tell me, won't you?"

"Why would you want to know such a thing?"

"Promise me."

Lothar was silent a moment. Then he said: "I promise."

"Thank you, Lothar." She rose, making everyone around her jump again. She bestowed upon them a winning smile then headed to the dais. She knew he was watching her, as were all the men in the room, watching the seductive sway of her hips, the graceful tilt of her bare shoulders as she walked. She heard a voice behind her.

"I think the lady has taken a shine to Lothar."

Coarse laughter. Then a shriek as Lothar shot out an arm and stabbed the man in the hand with his knife. Rotruda had seen it from the corner of her eye, but still she could not believe it. Lothar pulled the knife from the man's hand and wiped the blood on his pant leg. The wounded man howled in pain, while his comrades roared with laughter. Rotruda turned away, putting a hand to her face, so no one could see her smile.

# 19

## Tolosa
## The Aquitaine
## March, 718

RAGINFRID OF ANGERS stood straight before the tall man seated behind the desk, sweating under his withering perusal. Never before had the count suffered under such a contemptuous gaze, at least not since the last time he had met Charles the Bastard face to face.

When after several minutes Duke Eudo still did not speak, Raginfrid cleared his throat and said in a loud voice: "My Lord Duke, have you heard anything I have said?"

"I heard it all." Eudo's voice was a low hum.

"Well?"

Silence. Raginfrid glanced around the large room, one of nearly a dozen such rooms he had passed through in this giant and garish palace in Tolosa, a palace far grander than the king's palace in Rheims. Eudo himself was even more intimidating: tall, thin, with dark hair cut very short in the Roman fashion and a long, bony, clean-shaven face. There was something else about him, something imperious and relaxed; he possessed the deliberate informality of a man born to rule. The people called him "The Hawk," mostly because of his penchant for falconry, but also because, with his aquiline nose and bright, black, unblinking eyes, he rather looked like one.

When he spoke again, the sound nearly made Raginfrid jump out of his skin.

"So you think you can still win this war with Charles? What is it they call his army? *The Plague?* What a lovely name. I wish I had thought of it." Eudo smiled, not a pleasant sight. "He's beaten you twice now."

"He was lucky," Raginfrid said, throwing back his shoulders.

"Twice? That is not luck, Count."

"If you help us, we can beat him."

"And what do I get?"

"You get your province, Lord Duke. The Aquitaine. All of it. Released from Frankish suzerainty. You have the king's word on it."

Raginfrid handed over the scroll. Eudo opened it, read it, threw it aside carelessly.

"The word of a Meroving is worth spit," he said.

"He is the consecrated king," Raginfrid said, indignant. "The true king. He has the blessing of the Pope. And he is of sound mind, I can assure you." He paused, but Eudo said nothing. "We must do something soon, my lord. Did you know that Charles had already deposed the Bishop of Rheims and replaced him with one of his own leudes? The one they call Milo — a bastard like him! It's scandalous!"

Eudo smiled slyly. "There is one more thing I want," he said slowly, his gaze honing in on his quarry.

"What?" said the count, drawing back slightly.

"Orléans."

Raginfrid balked. "I cannot promise that."

"Then I cannot help you."

"The king must make that decision!"

"The king? Don't make me laugh. The only decision your king has to make is which of his golden pots to piss in each morning. If you do not have the power to make this promise, then get out of my sight. You Franks stole Orléans from my father. I will not help you, unless you give it back."

He waited. Raginfrid chewed his lip a moment.

"Very well," he said. "I will see that it is done."

"In writing," Eudo said. "Send me the necessary declaration signatures from the king *and* the Bishop of Orléans, and I will move my troops. But not before."

"You will have it in a month—or two," Raginfrid said.

"Then I will march in a month—or two," Eudo parroted. "I will require a great quantity of gold as well. I trust you brought your purse?"

"Yes—"

"Good. Now, you'd better go home and put together your army, what's left of it. Gather in Paris. We will march en masse into Austrasia and squash that bird while he's still in the nest."

Raginfrid, pleased with that word picture, bowed and left.

For a long time after he was gone, Eudo sat at his desk and drank his wine and thought about the bastard Charles.

The Aquitaine had suffered for too many years under Frankish rule. Eudo's father had been weak, ceding more and more land to Pipin Herstal, paying ever more tribute. When Eudo first took power he had only one goal in mind: to take his kingdom back. His province was nearly as wealthy and prosperous as the Empire itself; it galled him that he was still forced to pay tribute to those intractable barbarians to the north. Yet the Franks had one advantage over him: they were savage fighters, more ruthless even than the Goths. Eudo had worked for years to build an army that could beat them.

But another crisis had arisen—the invasion of the Arabs, who had taken Septimania from the Goths, denying Eudo access to the best ports, notably Narbonne. The Arabs were nothing more than a nuisance to him, yet Eudo knew he had to deal with them before he had any hope of gaining true independence from the Franks.

Then God had smiled upon him: Pipin Herstal died, and Francia was embroiled in a bloody civil war. He knew his time had come.

Only one man stood in his way now. Charles the Bastard, leaping from his prison cell like Prometheus, had assembled an impressive resistance against the Neustrians and had retaken almost all of Austrasia. But Charles was still relatively weak, and Francia was still divided. Charles, moreover, seemed to have a penchant for horses, which were known to be quite unreliable in pitched battle. Eudo simply could not resist the temptation. Charles, for all his brilliant maneuvering against small barbarian forces, would be helpless against an elite army of Roman-style organization. All he had to do was beat Charles, and the Aquitaine would be his alone.

He finished his wine and called his steward to fetch his mistress. He was feeling happy, for once, energized, and he wanted to celebrate a little before the work began.

# 20

## Metz
## May, 718

THE RIDERS LINED up, knee to knee, holding tight to the reins of the trembling line of horses, waiting. It was raining; it had been raining for several days, and the field was a sea of mud. The horses were already covered up to their chests with it, the riders so mud-splattered no one could tell what colors they wore. Not that it made much difference.

There was a shout, and the line broke, the horses surging forward in a swollen fury, kicking up clumps of mud and earth, the riders leaning into their mounts, shaking their javelins over their heads and screaming a garble of battle cries. The enemy soldiers crumbled, the lifeless bodies tossed violently with the storm of the passing horsemen. There were a few screams of triumph as some of the javelins hit their targets, the circling riders pumping the air with fists.

"You call that an attack?" Lothar shouted, charging onto the field on his big horse. "You struck barely half of them! Good for nothing rams!" He pointed furiously at the stuffed effigies still swinging on their wooden hooks. "Do it again!"

The riders, deflated by the scourging, circled around and returned to the starting place, while hordes of boys rushed around collecting the javelins and rehanging fallen targets. Lothar rode back to Charles, disgusted.

"This will never work," he said, twisting his horse in a circle.

Charles was standing under a large canopy on the sidelines, watching the maneuver. They had been practicing this for over a month, though the results were varied. To kill a foot soldier from the back of a galloping horse was not something that was learned in a fortnight.

The Spring Assembly, the annual gathering of the troops, had become something of a country carnival in Metz. Charles trained his horse warriors with games and tests of skill and strength, drawing spectators from all over the countryside, as well as vendors selling food and trinkets. The warriors themselves came to compete against Charles' own fighters, hoping for a coveted place in his army, perhaps even his *Truste*, his personal bodyguard. Yet Lothar was, as always, unimpressed.

"Rams, all of them," he said sourly.

"Let them rest a bit," Charles said. "Get some food. Perhaps—you can give them a demonstration?" He grinned. Lothar nodded, barely hiding his own grin, and went to get his horse.

"What the devil is going on here?" said a gruff voice. Charles turned to see a large, disheveled man with a heavy red beard dismounting from a shaggy, mud-colored horse. "Those poor bastards couldn't penetrate the ass of a boar let alone a Saxon with those little sticks of theirs. What are those things supposed to be, anyway? Better for pronging meat at the supper table than for killing Saxons." He laughed, hocked up a wad and spit on the ground.

"Nithard, I've missed your biting wit," Charles said in greeting to his Bavarian spy, one he'd hired only recently, much to the consternation of some of his captains, who did not care much for Bavarians.

"Well, it's not as though I've been lollygagging around, sitting on cushioned couches and eating grapes like the lot of you. Peace makes you Franks soft."

Charles ordered the man to sit at the small table under the canopy, and waited until he had drunk and ate his fill before asking him, "What news do you have?"

"Ah!" said Nithard. "I'll tell you. Once I've been paid."

Charles threw a small sack of coins in the table. Nithard took it, stuffing it in his shirt, while still managing to fill his mouth.

"That's better. What do you want to hear about first?"

"Bavaria."

"Ah! Well, you'll be glad to know that Duke Theodo and his son are on their way home from Constantinople. Not sure how they managed that, as the Arab siege is not yet over. Word is the old duke exchanged his granddaughter for safe passage out of the city."

"He gave his granddaughter to the Emperor?"

Nithard nodded. "Not surprising really. He was having a hard time finding a husband for her anyway."

"Is she so ugly?'

"Ugly? No. Beautiful beyond words, Svanahilda. But mad as a stuck pig. Too bad. I'd have tried for her myself if I didn't like my prick so much."

He chuckled. "Theodo will be back none too soon, for Grimwold is starting to get big ideas."

"For taking over Bavaria?" Charles asked. Grimwold, Theodo's younger son, was ruling Bavaria in the duke's absence, and he had proved himself no friend of the Franks.

"Don't think he hasn't thought about it. I believe Grimwold was half hoping his old dad wouldn't make it home at all. Nor his brother neither. No love lost there. Seems to be the way with brothers." Nithard eyed Charles and laughed.

Charles ignored the remark. "What do you hear from Raginfrid?"

"Ah! Your friend the Count of Angers has a new ally." Nithard belched. "Can you guess? It's the Duke of Aquitaine."

Charles sighed, sitting down opposite him. "I was hoping the duke wouldn't be lured."

"Well, you were wrong."

"What did the Raginfrid promise him for his help?"

"I can only imagine the promises that pustule made. But we all know what Eudo wants. A kingdom for himself. If Raginfrid gets all of Francia, then losing the Aquitaine will be a fair exchange for him." He paused, then said: "Rumor has it the count is giving him Orléans as well."

"A big prize."

"Raginfrid is desperate. What do you know of him? This Eudo?"

"Not much." Charles knew Eudo had performed well when the Arabs invaded Septimania, keeping them from taking his capital Tolosa. He knew Eudo possessed a fierce tribe of warriors from the Gascony region that struck fear in men's hearts. He suspected Eudo was well schooled in Roman-style warfare and certainly highly organized if he were able to lead a campaign so far from his capital. He also knew that Eudo of Aquitaine hated the Franks more than anything in the world.

"I wonder," Charles said idly, "why he hasn't tried to get the Arabs out of Narbonne."

Nithard shrugged. "Who cares? The Arabs are not important. What is important is that Eudo has a real army, and if he joins with Raginfrid you will be in serious trouble. You will be outnumbered, for one thing. You will have difficulty in taking this battle to them."

"I have been outnumbered before."

"Eudo is not the dolt Raginfrid is. It will be different."

Charles smiled. "True."

A cheer rose up from the crowd, where Lothar was circling the field on his magnificent horse, sword whipping over his head like a banner, daring someone to come and challenge him. The horse pranced theatrically, its thick neck arched, its knees high. Lothar, wearing only braccos and an abbreviated breastplate, his blond head uncovered, looked the pure pagan warrior in all his glory, and the crowd swooned at the sight of him.

"Look at that peacock, will you?" Nithard said, spitting out some meat that was stuck in his teeth. "No wonder they write songs about him. Does he never get tired of showing off?"

"Never," Charles said with a smile.

"Does anyone ever take him up on the challenge?"

"Not often."

"Then why bother?"

"Because they need it." Charles indicated the crowd, the warriors. They needed a swaggering hero, someone to sing songs about, to lift them from their own miseries. They thrived on this, the drama, the pageantry, the hint of glory. And Lothar himself needed it as much as the rest of them did.

Suddenly another horseman burst onto the field, carrying a spear, point up, a clear challenge. He circled the field at a hard gallop. A wave of murmurs spread through the crowd. On his spear hung a banner with the crest of Lyon.

Rogan came to a stop before Lothar and lowered his spear so it was pointing directly at him. The crowd roared with excitement as Lothar inclined his head, accepting the challenge.

"Are we going to get to see Lothar kill someone today?" Nithard said, rising to stand by Charles, who was watching intently.

"Let's hope not."

The two riders galloped to opposite sides of the field. Lothar demanded a spear from one of the grooms. Murmurs rushed through the assembled onlookers. Hasty bets were made, people digging into their purses for coins.

"You are going to allow this?" Nithard asked.

"I doubt if I could stop either of them."

Lothar turned to look at Charles, who nodded slowly, a look of warning in his eyes. Lothar grinned, shouldering the weapon, spinning his horse in a circle. The spears were blunted, though the force of the impact could still be rib breaking. The two men watched each other, horses bobbing and snorting, sending up sprays of mud and rainwater. The crowd began shouting encouragements. Somewhere a woman screamed Lothar's name.

The trumpeter blew a shrill note, and the horses exploded into motion, the two men hunkering down to their animals' necks, spears swinging over their heads. They closed in fast. Rogan threw first, hurling the weapon with lethal accuracy. Lothar threw a half second later, catching Rogan's weapon in the shaft and sending it spinning away harmlessly. The crowd went mad with delight.

"How many men do you know who can do that?" Charles asked Nithard. "He's worth the trouble of keeping him."

The riders rounded for another try, Rogan shouting for a new spear. Lothar did more prancing circles, milking the audience, who responded with thumps and whistles and wild cheers. Rogan waited, clearly annoyed.

Finally, Lothar was ready for another round. The two men charged each other, shaking their spears, and this time Lothar threw first, surprising Rogan who bobbled in the saddle, his own spear going wide.

Lothar once more dallied for the crowd, but Rogan did not wait for him. He tore another spear from his groom's grip and charged at Lothar at a dead run.

The crowd gasped. Lothar spun, seeing the rider coming at him. A groom offered him a spear, but he didn't take it. Instead, he drew his sword and kicked his horse into a gallop.

The two men charged each other, the crowd now frantic, horrified. Rogan threw the spear. It sailed straight and fast at Lothar, who slapped it away easily with his sword. Someone screamed. Lothar closed on Rogan, striking him with a backhanded blow. Rogan toppled from the saddle. The crowd hushed. Rogan lay face down in the mud.

Lothar circled to a now silent crowd, then drew up before Charles. He lifted his sword in the air. It was unbloodied.

The crowd let out a gasp of relief and began to cheer Lothar, chanting his name. Charles took a long breath. Lothar had used the flat of his sword to knock Rogan from the saddle. Then he saw Rogan pull himself to his feet. He would have an ugly bruise on his ribs, as well as his ego, but nothing more. Attendants came to help him, but he waved them away, walking off the field alone.

Lothar spun his horse and galloped around the field again, his sword still high, the crowd cheering him wildly.

"Seems your crazy man has learned to control himself," Nithard said. "Wonders never cease."

"Seems so," Charles said.

"Well, all of this silly warrior stuff has made me hungry. When's supper? I haven't had a decent meal in two weeks."

"You will need to go to the border as soon as possible. I need to know when Eudo is going to move."

"As you wish. But supper first."

Rotruda had been sitting under her own canopy, watching Lothar parade around the field as the girls screamed and threw articles of clothing at him. He was thrilling to watch. This was his element, he owned this field of battle; no one could really challenge him. She was thankful that he had shown restraint in dealing with the young nobleman who had tried; she knew it was Charles' presence that had stayed his hand. Charles was the only thing standing between Lothar and himself. She had watched them together for years now, had begun to think of them as two halves of the same person, so completely opposite yet so compatible, one completely dependent on the other.

She saw Lothar trot off the field to a waiting groom and shimmy from the horse's back. She turned to one of her younger women, holding out her handkerchief.

"Give him this," she said, "and ask him to come here for a cup of wine."

The girl's eyes widened in surprise. She grabbed the handkerchief and dashed for Lothar, who was already surrounded by a crowd of worshippers. She waved the scarf high in the air, calling to him.

"The Lady Rotruda bids you to come!" she shouted. Lothar pushed several people aside when he heard the name. He looked at the girl and then down the field, to Rotruda's canopy. Rotruda saw him glance Charles' way. Then he took the handkerchief and made his way toward her.

"My lady," he said when he had ducked under the low canopy. He was covered in mud, still wearing nothing but the breastplate and braccos, and he looked embarrassed to be so nearly naked in close proximity to Rotruda and her women. "I am not quite presentable—"

Rotruda did not get up from her seat. "Sit down and have a drink. I thought you might need a respite from the crowd."

Lothar accepted the cup from one of the women and took the proffered seat, a wooden stool with a halfback.

"That was quite a performance," Rotruda said, smiling at his sudden unease. "I enjoyed it very much. We all did, didn't we?" she added. Her women giggled again. Lothar averted his gaze. "That boy—that was Rogan of Lyon, yes?"

"Yes."

"It seems as though he has some sort of—history with you?"

Lothar drank from his cup. "Yes."

"Yet you did not kill him."

"Your husband did not wish it. He thinks the young man is more useful alive."

"I see. Still, I am sure that was—difficult." Lothar did not respond. Rotruda searched for something else to say. "The peasants do love to come to watch the games, don't they?"

"Yes."

"The nobles as well. It has become quite an event."

"I suppose so."

There was another awkward pause.

"Lothar," Rotruda said, her eyes lighting with a new thought. "I've been thinking. I hope you don't mind my saying this, but I think it is high time you got married."

"Married?" Lothar's expression went swiftly from confusion to something like terror. He straightened, his body tense, as if poised to escape.

"You have heard of it, haven't you? Obviously you could have any woman you wanted. There must be some girl in your life—?"

"I don't think I have time for—a wife."

"Never mind that. You *need* a wife, Lothar. I know many eligible girls. I would be happy to help. Perhaps one of my own ladies—"

The girls all seemed to sigh at once. Lothar stood up, setting down the cup. "Thank you, my lady. For the wine. I have to go now." He reached out to hand her back her handkerchief.

"Keep it, will you?" she said, looking into his eyes. "I would be most honored to know that you were carrying it—for me."

Lothar hesitated, taking in the hungry stares of the women in the tent. He clutched the handkerchief in his fist.

"I will carry it for Charles' lady," he said, "because I am her protector, as I am his."

Rotruda's smile waned; she averted her eyes. He tucked the fabric into his belt and exited the canopy. The women watched him walk back toward Charles.

"So handsome," said Ani breathlessly. "Perhaps he will change his mind about your offer, my lady? In which case—"

"Never mind," Rotruda said, the smile gone from her lips. "Clean up this mess. I am going back to the palace."

# 21

## Soissons
## Neustria
## September, 718

EUDO COULD NOT believe it.

He had barely begun his march from Paris, when his scouts informed him that Charles was already on the road north of Soissons. How had he gotten there so fast? It did not seem possible.

It was a dream come true.

Eudo called to a messenger and gave him a verbal message to take to Raginfrid, who was with the king less than two leagues north of his own position. *We have him. Let him walk into our trap. In two days, he will be within reach.*

It was a classic pincer maneuver, one used so famously by Hannibal at the Battle of Cannae to annihilate the Romans. Eudo was an avid student of history. Raginfrid's blundering Neustrians would be the anvil, engaging and locking the Austrasians in position, and Eudo's army, led by his ferocious Gascons, would be the bludgeon to deal the death blow.

"As long as that idiot does what he is supposed to, it will work," he said to his captains. "I want the scouts watching him. I don't quite trust him."

He rode through the camp, checking that his men were ready and understood the plan. It felt good to be on the field again, to be in command of troops. He had spent too much time in his palaces of late, juggling ledgers, listening to people complain about their lots, thinking about what to do about the Arabs and doing nothing. He had been almost solicitous to Raginfrid since his arrival in Paris, which had taken the Neustrian mayor by surprise. Though Raginfrid was less pleased when he learned of Eudo's battle plan.

"You want us to—split up?"

"You will take your army and go north. I will lag behind, staying south of you, so he will think I am still on the march. He will see you and come for you, thinking he can dispatch you easily. Once you are engaged, I will go in for the kill."

Raginfrid objected. "But I thought with our combined forces, we would outnumber him … we would use a direct assault—"

"Throw him everything at once?" Eudo said. "In some grand barbarian shield wall? Don't you think he would see that coming? Don't you think he is ready for that? How did he use his horses the last time?"

"He … flanked us—"

"Exactly. You cannot get around those horses. They will flank you every time, no matter the numbers. If we were to attack him head on, it would be a blood bath, pure and simple. I don't want to lose my army in this fight, and I don't have to."

"But we outnumber him—"

"How crucial have your numbers been in your last two battles with him?" Eudo said with dripping sarcasm. "We need more than numbers this time. We need *strategy*. Something foreign to you Franks, I know. His horsemen are dangerous, to be sure, but they are not going to win this fight for him. He needs his foot army, and a foot army cannot fight on two fronts at once. How many times do I have to explain this?"

"No, no, I understand," said Raginfrid, though his face betrayed his consternation. "But when he attacks, you will be there, won't you? You will be … ready?"

"Just do your job," said Eudo, "and I will do mine."

Nithard say heavily in a camp chair and took the beer offered him by Alfric, downing most of it in a single gulp.

"Piss water," he said, wiping his mouth with the back of his hand. "Did anyone ever teach you how to put up a camp Charles? Where are the rugs? Where is the furniture? You all sit around on wormy camp stools with your feet in the mud."

"Like Bavarians," Charles said, sitting down opposite him.

"Why do you think I quit the army?"

"Did you find Eudo?"

"Of course I did, though it wasn't easy. You'll pay me double this time." He took a scroll out of his pouch and tossed it to Charles, who unrolled it, smoothing out the damp and wrinkled parchment. "Sorry about that. My wineskin was leaking. Anyway, here are their positions, as of a day ago. Eudo has made it as far as the river, here, in these woods just north of the city. Found him almost by accident."

"Where is Raginfrid?"

"Up here … " Nithard pointed, "along those hills there—he's camped out north of the road, waiting for Eudo to catch up. That will happen in less than a day, by my calculation."

"Hmmm." Charles stared at the map. "So—Eudo is not dug in? What's he doing there, do you think?"

"How should I know? I told you, he's clearly on the march. What's the matter with you? You aren't usually so dense as this," Nithard said, annoyed.

"Seems like an odd place to camp," Charles said. "Why didn't they move together?"

"God, but you ask a lot of questions! And for your information, it's an excellent place, with good cover and fine hunting. Maybe he was hungry! He's come a long way, he would need to replenish his supplies."

"Yes, possibly." Charles continued to stare. Nithard watched him, nervous. Then suddenly Charles straightened, shouting for Alfric. Nithard jumped at the sound.

"What the—"

"Get Lothar," Charles snapped at the boy, then spun back around and brought the map to his camp table, where he could study it more closely. Nithard lumbered up from his stool to see what he was looking at.

"What do you see?"

"I see a split army," Charles said.

"So?"

"It may be—an opportunity."

Lothar burst in and crossed to the map. He stared at it a moment, just as Charles had. Then he looked up, a grin spreading across his face.

"It's unbelievable," he said.

"Would you rams mind telling me—" Nithard began, but he never got to finish.

Charles pointed to a spot on the map. "How long will it take to get there?"

Nithard shrugged. "Two days, I would think."

"Then we will do it in one. Get the men up and break camp. We are leaving immediately."

"But," Nithard sputtered, following Charles out of the tent, "we haven't even had dinner yet!"

Charles called a war council of all his captains, explaining what they were to do.

"We'll never make it," muttered Gerold.

"Yes we will," Charles answered. "There are no rivers to cross. We can do it."

"We will drive the horses to exhaustion," said Gunther.

"And how do you expect the men to fight when they have been marching all night and day?" put in Peppo.

"They will fight because they have to. Enough talking now. Let's move."

# 22

EUDO WAS DRINKING wine. His head throbbed, as it usually did in humid weather. He was on edge. Raginfrid had not reported all day. The Neustrian mayor was hopelessly tardy in everything. It was no wonder he had lost two battles against an outnumbered enemy.

His own scouts had told him Charles was moving and moving fast. There would be battle in the morning, he could feel it. Eudo had given the men a few hours of rest. They would move before dawn. He still felt uneasy about Raginfrid; though the Neustrian count's only obligation was to sit still and allow himself to be attacked, even that might prove beyond his capabilities.

His steward came in with a tray, demanding he eat. He pushed the food away, his stomach turning. He could not remember the last time he had eaten. He lay down on his pallet, closing his eyes, hoping to assuage the pain in his skull.

He was awakened by a shout from outside, a cry of alarm. He jumped up, tearing through the tent flaps. A crowd had gathered around a scout, who looked winded and frightened. He slid from the horse and came toward Eudo, who felt his stomach turn inside out.

"My lord," he said, "I saw them!"

"Where?"

"Less than a league from here, my lord!"

*From here?*

"What do you mean?" Eudo demanded. He got hold of the boy and shook him. "What do you mean? Speak some sense!"

"It's the black army … they are coming now! They are horsed—they will be here in minutes! I only just managed to get ahead of them—"

Eudo threw the boy aside, forcing this information to penetrate his brain. It was not possible. "It's a trick," he said, almost to himself. "You must be seeing things. Probably a scouting party." But Eudo felt something cold in the pit of his belly. He turned to the scout. "Quick, take a fresh horse and ride to the Neustrian camp. Tell the mayor to come to us at once! At once! Do not wait for the morning!"

He was shaking. He knew everyone could see it.

He called for Noma, his Gascon commander. The man came to him, a mountain of a man with swarthy skin and a thick, black beard, reflecting the Basque heritage of his people.

Eudo spoke without greeting him. "Form up. It is nearly dark. This must only be a skirmish party, to rattle us. He cannot have his whole army here—" He shut his eyes against the thought, the pain wracking his brain. "Get your men ready! Now!"

He called for his horse, dressed hastily in his armor and mounted. He would have to lead this army himself.

He knew that Charles had seen through his plan and turned it on its head. He cursed himself. He had planned on using his army to deal a hammer blow, not as a defensive force. He had no fortifications, he was completely exposed. And now the Hammer was coming for him.

He moved them out of the trees into the open meadow where they would have more room to maneuver. Almost at once the black riders appeared, straight out of the descending twilight like some childhood nightmare. The Gascons charged to meet them, bellowing and swinging maces and axes and long, metal-studded spears. They were tough and fearless fighters, but they were helpless against the speed and force of this attack, the brutal hooves of the massive horses, the flying arrows and whip-fast javelins that brought them down before they could even get close enough to wield their demonic weapons.

Once the attack began, Eudo saw plainly that this was no small maneuver. Charles had somehow managed to move his entire army to meet him. Rather than waiting for first light, as anyone else would have done, he had attacked immediately. How had he done it? Eudo would spend the rest of his life wondering.

He called to his captains. "Shields!" he shouted. "Move back to the trees! Get your men behind shields! We will wait for help to come." The captains relayed the message. The Gascons, already overrun, were helpless now. He could only hope to get the rest of the army in a firm defensive position, under shields, and wait until help came.

Raginfrid did not know what to do. The reports seemed unbelievable.

"Move now? But the sun has nearly set! How can we go in the dark?"

He conferred with the king, who insisted upon leaving at once to help Eudo.

"If we hurry we will be there in an hour," Chilperic told him.

"No no, we cannot go now. It is far too dark. By the time we get there it will be over anyway. We must wait for the dawn," Raginfrid said, though truthfully he hated getting up so early. "Eudo will last the night."

"But what if he can't? He would not have demanded our help if he thought he could handle this alone."

Raginfrid would not budge, so Chilperic called for his own entourage. He managed to round up only twenty volunteers. He set out, moving slowly in the dark, leaving Raginfrid behind with the rest of the army. He followed the noises, which grew in ferocity the closer he got to Eudo's position. When he finally found the field of battle he could hardly make out who was fighting whom. It all seemed to be chaos. The scouts led him to Eudo's command post, his men surrounding him to keep him safe.

Eudo had formed a shield line behind a thick copse of trees. His men had piled everything they had in a defensive perimeter, to keep the Franks out. The trees helped. But it would not last long, even the king could see that.

"Did you come alone?" Eudo asked, though he knew the answer. Chilperic nodded.

"Raginfrid is not coming until the morning … can you hold out until then?"

"No."

"Then what are you going to do?"

"Retreat."

The king stared at him, wanting to argue. Then he changed his mind and nodded sadly. "But where?"

"South," Eudo said. "To Orléans."

"But … "

"It is my city now. And it is fortified. I can hold him off there. And if all else fails perhaps I can … negotiate. I cannot lose my army to this—*plague*—" He looked away, setting his jaw. And he called for a retreat.

"We should go after him," Lothar said, still breathless from the battle, his body trembling as if with orgasmic heat.

Charles shook his head. His lungs heaved, every muscle in his body rippled with exhaustion; it was difficult even to hold his sword. It had happened so fast, a mad scramble in the night, men like demons, hard to even know whom they were killing. But they killed many.

"No. We have pushed these men hard enough. They need to rest."

"Raginfrid?"

"He is not important." Charles did not even care where Raginfrid was anymore. He was only thinking of Eudo now. "He retreated too soon," he said idly, almost to himself. "He might have held out longer."

The Austrasians had already fallen upon the Aquitainian camp, looting and drinking wine, grabbing food left on cooking fires. The retreating army had left almost everything behind.

"The king is gone, again," Milo said, riding up to him. "For such a slow-witted sort he has proved remarkably slippery. The prisoners say he is in Eudo's possession."

Charles sighed. "Then he will go to Orléans. Make a stand there."

"So we are in for a siege?"

"Perhaps." Charles could hardly think straight. They had marched for nearly twenty hours straight. He needed sleep, they all did. He could not push them any more tonight. "Sleep now. We will move in the morning."

Once the men and horses were fed and settled and the pickets posted, Charles lay down with his guards and tried to sleep. Yet the battle, so fresh his body still quivered from it, played in his mind. Eudo had been taken completely by surprise. He was overrun almost immediately, and yet he had managed to keep his men together, establish a rudimentary defense and execute an organized retreat. That in itself was wholly remarkable.

The duke's plan had been a good one. This was a man who understood what it took to win battles. He had simply miscalculated this war. He had brought too small a force and relied too much on clever tactics, underestimating his enemy. Still, in a proper fight, Charles sensed Eudo of Aquitaine would be a force to be reckoned with.

Charles tried to imagine what the duke would do now. He would go to Orléans, certainly. But would he treat with him there? Or would he make a stand, force Charles into a fight? Eudo was a proud man, a Roman. He would be difficult to break.

"You need to kill him." Lothar's voice broke into his thoughts. He was not sleeping either. "Kill him and the Aquitaine is yours. Then we can go to Paris and take care of Raginfrid. No more second chances."

Charles looked over at his friend, who lay on his back, staring at the sky. *Kill Eudo of Aquitaine. Destroy his army*. It is what everyone expected him to do. It was the smart move. Eudo would forever be a thorn in his side.

He lay back, looking at the stars. *So many*, he thought. *So many stars.*

# 23

## Orléans

CHARLES MOVED HIS army in an impressive array before the main gate of the city of Orléans. He had expected to see men on the walls, trebuchets and other war machines ready for attack, but there was nothing. The city looked deserted, the only movement the snapping of Eudo's banners from the towers. The walls were largely intact; there had not been a major battle here in three hundred years, yet like all cities of Francia it held an air of neglect—stones crumbling from the towers, making a jagged silhouette against the white sky.

Charles waited, expecting some sign from within that Eudo wanted to talk or to fight. But there was nothing.

"Perhaps he's already gone. He has no intention of facing you again," Milo remarked.

"He is here," Charles said. "His banners are flying. He might be waiting for me to make him an offer. So he can refuse honorably."

"Refuse?"

"He needs a reason to fight."

"And you will give him one?"

Charles sighed. "I will give him—an offer."

He sent Nithard into the city under white flag with his terms of surrender.

There was no response the rest of the day. Charles paced about his tent anxiously, certain that his spy was dead, half-expecting the Aquitainian army to throw down an attack from the walls. But still nothing happened.

"Why aren't we breaking down that gate?" Lothar asked him, storming his tent uninvited.

"I am waiting for his answer."

"You know what that will be," Lothar retorted.

*But I don't.*

This was what troubled him. Eudo was a duke, a general of high order, but also a man who did not spend his troops frivolously. He had a fortress that might hold out for weeks, for months. But to what purpose? Eudo, he thought, would know how to pick his battles.

"You could destroy him," Lothar said. "Draw him out. Make him fight."

"I don't want to destroy him."

"Why not?"

"Arabs," Charles said. "Eudo is the only thing standing between us and them. We need him. He's the best duke we've got."

"He is your enemy."

"That doesn't change anything."

Lothar swore aloud. "God in heaven, Charles, you are making a mistake. He will never ally himself with you. Show him this clemency now, and he will only think you are weak."

"He knows I am not weak, any more than I think he is a fool," Charles said. "He is a defeated man. Leave him some of his dignity, or he will rise up again."

"All the more reason to kill him." Lothar stalked out of the tent.

Nithard returned the next morning, much to Charles' relief.

"Sorry I'm late," the spy said, sitting down to a mug of beer. "The man likes to keep people waiting."

"So what happened?" Charles said, standing over him. "Did he hurt you?"

"Hurt me? No … not unless you count making me sit in a room with no beer for a day and a night torture."

"What did he say?"

"Nothing at first. I could tell he was angry. He didn't like your terms at all." Nithard paused to take a swig. "But in the end he accepted."

Charles let out a long breath. "When will he meet?"

"He will not meet." Nithard handed Charles a scroll. Charles opened it, glanced at the contents, then handed it to Milo. "He's already gone. Left in the night, while I was shut up in a closet with a howling drunkard who might have been the king. Hard to tell." He paused, looking at Charles, who had not moved. "You didn't give him much choice did you? Your terms. What were you thinking? You let him keep his duchy and his army intact. All you asked for was the king. He wanted to fight, but you didn't give him a reason. That was cruel, Charles. Clemency is a bitter pill. Don't think he will thank you for it."

Charles nodded, sighing. He went to the tent flaps and looked out, onto the walls of Orléans. No banners flew. *Already gone.* This, the only man he had ever found himself wanting to meet, face to face.

"This could all be a trap, you know," Sigebald said. "A clever ruse. He might still be there, and as soon as the gates open he overruns us. It happened before right here in this city. When the Huns were attacking. It didn't work that time. But who knows? Eudo seems to be a man who knows his histories."

"I guess we will see, won't we?" Charles said. He called in a messenger and gave a command.

The city gates opened within the hour, and Charles entered peacefully with his army. There was no sign of an Aquitainian force. He found the king in the palace, exhausted and disheveled but unhurt. He looked much older than the last time the two of them had met, on the field of Vincy. Charles could tell from his pallor and his perpetual cough that he was not well.

Chilperic was seated on a wooden bench, a pillow under his bottom. The room appeared to be a bedroom, with a wide window overlooking the courtyard. The Count of the Palace hovered nearby but backed away when Charles approached.

"Charles," the king said with a deep sigh. "Thank God this is over. I'm tired of all this fighting. Did you catch the count?"

"Not yet," said Charles.

"Ah well, you will. There is nowhere for him to run now." Chilperic coughed, wiped his chin. "It was a mistake, all of it. I see that now. Raginfrid was a fool, but so was I. To think I could be king again. A real king. Not this sham, this "do-nothing" charade. I had a hope, once … do you understand?"

Charles nodded. "Are you well enough to travel, Your Majesty?"

"I suppose. Where are we going then?"

"I will take you to Paris, and then Rheims."

"And then what? The monastery, I suppose."

"No."

"No?"

"You are the king," Charles said.

"But—aren't you going to choose your own king?"

Charles shrugged. "It does not matter to me who is king."

Chilperic laughed, the laugh turning to another prolonged cough. "That is the truth of it," he said when he could speak again, though his voice was guttered by sickness and sorrow. "Do not worry, Lord Charles. I will not last long, I promise you."

"I am sorry," Charles said. Chilperic looked at him, blinking.

"You are now the ruler of all Francia. How does it feel?"

Charles shrugged. "I don't know."

It was the truth. He had been fighting for so long, he had never imagined there would be an end. Though he knew this was really only the beginning. Again.

"When do we leave?"

"A few days. You need rest, and so does my army."

"Ah. Good."

"And you need a doctor."

Chilperic shook his head. "A doctor will do me no good. I know my fate. It is the fate of all my fathers before me." He coughed some more, as if to prove his point. "But you, Charles, what will you do now?"

"Do?" Charles seemed taken aback by the question. He had not thought past this moment.

"After you have secured the oaths of the Neustrians ... what then? The burden of ruling is far more onerous than the taking of a kingdom. I should know. I come from a long line of failure on that score."

Outside a noise arose; it took Charles a moment to realize it was cheering. They were calling the king's name.

"Your people call you," Charles said.

"It is you they should be calling," said the king. "You are their ruler now."

Charles helped the king out onto the balcony to greet the cheering crowd. The people of Orléans did not seem to care who had won the war, so long as their king was safe.

Charles left the room and went back to the main hall, where his men were waiting. They looked at him expectantly.

"The king is well," he said to them. "We'll leave in a few days for Paris, to secure the oaths of the Neustrian nobles. And deal with the Count of Angers."

There was a long silence, the men glancing at each other in near disbelief.

"So—it is really over?" Gerold said aloud.

"I think so."

"And we won?" said Milo, wonder in his voice.

Charles sighed. "Yes. I think we did."

# 24

## Paris

RAGINFRID SHOOK OFF the guards holding him and walked, with as much dignity as he could muster, into the courtroom. It was lined with people, nobles and bishops, Austrasian and Neustrian. They watched him silently, their expressions a mix of triumph and pity.

He was a shambles, his normally well-fitted clothes in rags about him. His beard had not been trimmed in a month. Yet he held his head high as he crossed the long room, his gaze focused on the king who sat on his throne, hunched and listless, at the far end. *He doesn't look well*, Raginfrid thought. He supposed he was partly to blame for that.

He tried not to look at Charles, who stood on the floor off to the side of the throne, flanked by his massive warriors. The other warriors, the ones who had come to fetch him from his home in Angers, pulling him bodily from his bed while his wife screamed and children cried, stayed behind him, spears at the ready.

He thought he was ready for this, but he realized, standing before this man and his retinue, that he was not. *This is what it will feel like*, he thought, *on the Last Day. The Day of Judgment. Only this will probably not go so well for me.*

"Nice of you to join us, Count," Charles said, breaking the awful silence.

"I had little choice in the matter," said the count, his voice still haughty, despite his ordeal. "Have they all sworn oaths to you then?" He indicated the room.

"Most of them," Charles said. "The Bishop of Rouen and the Bishop of Paris refused. So I deposed them and put my nephew Hugo in their place."

"You deposed two sitting bishops?" Raginfrid said, his mouth dropping open.

"I'm sure more will follow. But most in Neustria are seeing the light. Time for you to as well."

"You expect me to swear oath to you? Before or after you have me killed?"

The crowd murmured. Charles cocked his head slightly. "What makes you think I am going to kill you?"

Raginfrid glanced around, feeling a sweat tickle down his temple. "You dragged me here, before the king, to pronounce the sentence, surely."

"No. I dragged you here to get your oath. To the King of the Franks. And to me."

"But—"

"Swear oath to me, and you can keep your county. And your life, such as it is. You'll pay your tribute, and you will vow never to raise arms against Austrasia again. Those are my terms."

Raginfrid was aghast. "But—?"

"I want peace, Count. I'm not interested in retribution. But this offer is made only once. Make your choice."

Raginfrid felt all the eyes of the court bearing down on him. Then he remembered how Charles had offered him peace once before, on the field of Vincy. He had thought that offer a sign of weakness. Now he saw his mistake; that had been the offer made by a man who had nothing whatever to lose, who had offered peace for its own sake. How very strange; Raginfrid still could not grasp it. He wondered, fleetingly, if Charles had decided not to kill him because he was afraid of reprisals from the nobles. But, peering into those glittering eyes, he saw the truth: Charles did not consider him important enough to kill.

So he knelt, before the king and the Leader of the Franks, and recited the oath of fealty and subjugation. The king rose from his seat, stepped down on frail legs to accept the oath. Charles, almost at once, turned and left the court, his bodyguard trailing after him.

After that the king was put into his resplendent litter and paraded through the streets of Paris, waving wanly as the people showered him with cheering and flowers. Then he was given a great feast, and packed off quickly to Rheims, where he would die only a few years later.

And Charles, at the age of thirty-one, became the Mayor of the Palaces of Austrasia, Neustria, and Burgundy, Leader of the Franks, king in all but name. His people took to calling him *prince*, despite the fact that he had been born a bastard of no royal line. But to his soldiers, he was, and forever would be, *The Hammer*.

# 25

## Kolonia
## December, 718

WINTER HAD COME again. The countryside around Kolonia was barren, abandoned. Animals and people were shut inside their longhouses, the smoke from their fires seeping from thatched roofs, the only sign of life in the valley. Charles rode through the forest alone, the horse's hooves snapping on brittle twigs. It was the kind of day he liked best: a breathless, cold, unbending day, filled with silence.

He had left his family in Paris and returned to this city, where he would make his home, his capital, the center of his power. *Power.* It was a strange word to him, a word full of portent, ominous. And yet he owned it now. He had done this, conquered a kingdom. And he still was not quite sure why.

He thought of his wife, his sons. They had spent Christmas together, at least, perhaps the last Christmas for a very long time. He did not know what was coming, but he knew his life would be different now, that there might no longer be room for a wife and children, if, indeed, there ever was.

He would miss them. They brought a light, a warmth to his world, something he'd never had before. Little Pipin, in particular. No one could be in his presence without smiling. He was the soul of his mother, dazzling in his sweetness. Carloman was all of him: cool, detached, serious. Unyielding. He will make a great soldier, Charles thought. But he will never be happy.

He walked Epone across a little stream, still running despite the cold, and loped up a small hill through the trees. He saw a roe deer, foraging at the saplings, lift her head and look at him, ears flapping. She stared at him a long time, motionless, then twisted and leapt back into the trees. She should not be alone, he thought. But the roe preferred to be alone, convening with others of its kind only during breeding season.

What would come now? He thought again. Saxons, of course. They would always come. Frisians, eventually. As long as Radbod was alive they would never stop. The Germans—there would be trouble there as well.

And Arabs. A giant, amorphous mass that loomed in his mind like a tumor, pressing on his every nerve. For this, he felt certain, he had been born, to defeat this enemy, or die in the trying. He would do either or both, it would not matter. Had God put him here for this, to stand in the gap against this one enemy that seemed unstoppable yet had to be stopped? He thought of this often, especially in these moments, when he wandered alone, searching for he knew not what. An answer. Or perhaps, the right question.

He rode on, to the top of the hill, where the trees thinned and he could see the entire valley. Snow swirled around him in mad patterns, clinging to his eyelashes. Epone nickered, eager to go home to his warm stall and hay. Charles sat still, staring out over the uneven splotches of villages, the deadened fields, the pockets of forest. In this world, he thought, he could forget about the Arabs, about the Saxons and Frisians and Germans, about bishops and counts and everything, he could be free of it all. He could disappear into the fabric of ordinary life, he could forget, for a time, the burden of his journey, the weight of destiny. It called to him, this world of infinite peace and forgetfulness. He longed for it.

He heard a sound, like a piercing bark. Something crashed in the underbrush and the roe reappeared, darting toward him into the glade, then veering away, its eyes wide with fright. More noises followed, and Charles saw dark shapes emerging from the wood. Wolves, snarling riotously, deranged by hunger. It was too early for wolves—they were night hunters. But they were starving, as the herds were in for the winter and the pigs had been rounded up. He saw the whitened rump of the deer as it disappeared again into the trees, the wolves at its heels. It would not be long, he thought. The deer did not have a chance.

He waited for the sound of the wolves to die away. Then he breathed in the last of the frozen air and turned his horse toward home.

# DECEMBER, 731

## Invasion

## Saint-Emilion
## The Aquitaine

SVANA AWOKE TO the sound of the monastery bell, tolling in the distance, calling the monks to Mass. She lay still, listening. The sound was sad, mournful—wasn't Christmas supposed to be a happy time? She understood the sound.

She heard a scuffling noise and sat up, thinking Gryffin might have awakened from another bad dream. He had them most often in the mornings. But he lay on his pallet on the floor, lost in sleep. She sighed, pulled a cloak over her shoulders and went into the main room.

She stopped, her breath catching in her throat. Eudo was there, seated at the kitchen table, a cup of wine in his hands. He often appeared like this, unannounced, usually bearing gifts.

"Merry Christmas," he said, yawning. "You look beautiful this morning. As usual."

"What are you doing here?"

"I ran out of wine."

"There was no wine in all of Bordeaux?"

"None like yours, my lady."

He smiled at her, the smile transforming his stark, ascetic face. She saw the suppressed longing in his dark eyes. She pulled her cloak more firmly over her shoulders. "Are you hungry?"

"Famished."

"I'll give you breakfast, as long as you go out and get me some partridges for Christmas dinner. You brought your bird with you?"

"I rarely travel without her anymore."

"Good. Get me some wood for the fire."

"As you wish, my lady."

He went out for the wood while she pulled bacon and bread from the larder and began preparing a breakfast.

"Come to Bordeaux tomorrow, to the palace, just this once. For a real Christmas feast," he said as he ate the food she prepared.

"No."

"Why not?"

"I have my people to think about … "

"Your people," he said irritably. "Orphans and widows."

"They deserve a feast as much as your lords and ladies. More, I think. They work harder." She smiled, knowing he didn't like her life among peasants, especially around so many young boys who worshipped her like a goddess. He didn't understand her attachment to the vineyards, to the peasants, she who could command a palace if she wanted. In truth, she did not understand it either. It would never have been the sort of life she would have imagined, had she thought she would live this long.

"You prefer this … all this … to my palaces?" he said scornfully.

"Because it is mine."

"Because it is yours," he repeated, as if he had known she would say it. "You want to live out your days picking grapes? Until you die of a broken back?"

"If God will allow," she said, smiling.

"Have you found God, Svana?"

"Perhaps … He found me."

"In the vineyards?"

She shrugged. "Didn't Christ have a certain affinity for grapevines?"

He pushed the plate away suddenly. She sensed he was angry.

"Have you heard from him?"

Svana took a breath. Eudo had never before mentioned *him* in her presence. Not since that day, three years ago. Was it three years already? Yet he was always there, between them. Unacknowledged and yet acutely present.

"No." She picked up his empty plate, refilling his cup of wine.

She had not heard from him. She had sent no message. Yet still she could not shake that day from her memory, the Roman house in Vichy, the infinite weariness in his spectral eyes, the way he had held himself away from her. *I can wait. I have forever to wait.*

"I asked him if he thought the Arabs were God's punishment," Eudo said, jarring her thoughts.

Svana looked at him. "Is that what you think? The Arabs are a punishment?"

"Yes. What else can it be?"

"What did he say?"

"He said if we fought them we would know the answer." He laughed bitterly. "Typical of him."

"Perhaps … he's right."

"I'd like to believe it," Eudo said, his gaze drifting to empty space, to dust motes playing in the sunlight from the window. "If only we lived in a world where such things were true."

"He lives in it," Svana said. "He does not accept any other sort of world. He makes his own rules."

Eudo laughed again. "I have done the same thing," he said caustically. "All my life, I thought I could make the rules and everyone would bend to my will. Then the Arabs came, and I found I was at the mercy of rule makers over whom I had no power whatsoever. He hasn't learned that lesson yet but … he will. I promise you."

Svana said nothing. It was the one thing she feared more than anything in the world. She picked up a bucket from the floor.

"Where are you going?"

"To get more water."

"Can't you get one of your boys to do that?"

She glared at him.

"Never mind, I'll do it," he said, grabbing the bucket from her hands. He went outside into the freezing morning. He was not cold; he loved the cold as he loved extremes in everything. He went to relieve himself around the side of the house before taking the bucket to the cistern. He filled it, feeling as though he would like to crack through the thin layer of ice and immerse himself totally. He needed some way to numb himself from the constant frustration of being near her. Svana, with her black hair and dark, fathomless eyes, her beauty almost beyond bearing. Even after all this time his longing never lessened.

He wondered why he continued to come here, to see her, knowing he would never be able to touch her again. He wondered why he did not hate her for what she had done, how she had used him, luring him to that house in Vichy with the promise of her body, only to trap him there with his greatest enemy. Charles the Bastard. Her lover. The father of her child. Anyone else he would have killed long ago.

He heard a soft fluttery noise and turned to see Alarria, his peregrine falcon, fussing where she was tethered and hooded on the fence post. He went to her and held out his arm and the bird, sensing his presence, stepped onto it. He stroked her chest soothingly, trying to work out his own anger.

He felt a movement behind him and turned to see a small figure standing in the doorway. Gryffin. His black hair was tousled from sleep, but his clear gray eyes peered intently at him, or rather, at the bird.

The falcon squawked and flapped her wings, aware of a disturbance.

"Can I … pet him?" the boy asked softly. It was the first time he had ever spoken to Eudo directly.

"Her," Eudo said. He nodded to the boy to come forward. *Gryffin*. The image of Charles Martel—and Svana too. A deadly combination. He was five years old. He seemed to be an intelligent boy, Eudo thought, though it was hard to tell, for he rarely spoke. But there was something in those pale, gray eyes that didn't exist in his father's, something molten, unstable.

Gryffin stroked the bird carefully, staring at it in rapt amazement. Eudo, warming to his interest, said: "I was going to take her out this morning—your mother wants partridge for dinner. Do you want to come? I could use a flusher."

Gryffin's eyes grew wide, he nodded eagerly. He ran into the house, where his mother was stoking the fire in the hearth. "I'm going hunting," he announced. Then he went into the bedroom to find his boots. Eudo came in with the bucket of water, setting it down beside her.

"Do you mind?" he asked.

"Of course not. But how—"

"It was the bird. Not me."

Gryffin emerged wearing a heavy coat and boots and followed Eudo out to the courtyard. They set out in silence through the vineyards, where the vines lay in deathlike poses about the hills, covered in a thin layer of frost. They walked for over an hour, not speaking, the only sound the wind and the crunch of their boots on the hard ground.

They made it to the river, where the vines dissolved into wild heath, the perfect hiding place for partridge, which preferred being near the water. Eudo took the hood from Alarria's head, talking to her softly. She was his favorite raptor, though he had more than a dozen in his mews in Tolosa. He had trained her himself and she would fly only for him. Many called her his "other" mistress.

Eudo explained to Gryffin what he would do, them sent him ahead to flush out any quarry that was lurking in the tall grass. Gryffin ran forward, shouting, making as much noise as he could until a covey of partridges flew up clumsily from the earth, wild wings flapping. Eudo immediately let go of the jess, and Alarria took off, shooting into the sky as straight as an arrow. Gryffin gasped. Then she banked and dived into the flustered birds, stretched forward her long talons and snatched one of them out of the air. Gryffin screamed with pleasure. Eudo sounded a whistle through his teeth, three short calls; the falcon banked again and shot toward him, dropping the partridge on the ground at his feet and returning to her perch on his arm. Gryffin clapped excitedly, panting.

"I never saw anything like her!" he said.

Eudo gave the falcon a piece of meat. "You hold the birds," he said to the boy, who seemed only too glad to help.

Alarria took four more partridges that morning, a good day's work for her. Eudo found himself enjoying his role as teacher, explaining to Gryffin how to tell a partridge hen from a cock, how the falcon was trained to kill only the male birds, as the females were needed on the nests. When they were done, Eudo allowed the boy to carry the falcon home on his arm wearing the leather sleeve. It was something he had never allowed anyone to do before.

Gryffin couldn't wait to tell his mother what had happened. Eudo had never heard him use so many words at once. Svana smiled with genuine pleasure; she ruffled his hair and congratulated him.

"Can I have one? Please Mama?" Gryffin pleaded. Svana glanced at Eudo.

"We'll have to see," she said. "A falcon is not an easy animal to keep."

"Birds have a habit of flying away, when they get the chance," Eudo said, glancing back at her. "But I will be happy to teach you, if your mother approves."

"Please mama!"

Svana was uncharacteristically disarmed. Gryffin rushed off to tell everyone about his first adventure with a falcon. She turned to Eudo.

"Thank you," she said. "It is the first time I have seen him … truly happy about anything."

"Next time I come I will bring another one … for him."

"You would give him one?"

"Why not? My own son doesn't care for them. And the boy has talent, I can tell already."

"Yes," Svana said, distantly. A gift passed down from his father, or from her? She had her own talent for hunting. She had been a warrior once. A long time ago.

"I should go," Eudo said.

"Will you be back?"

"Not for awhile. I must go to Tolosa after the new year. For another pointless council with Othman." A servant brought his horse and he mounted, gathering the reins, the falcon perched on his shoulder.

He paused, glancing at the door of the house where Gryffin, amidst a group of friends, was showing off the partridges. "That's a fine boy you have there, Svana. You ought to tell him so, once in a while."

"So he can get a swelled head like you?" she asked lightly, touching his leg.

"Men need swelled heads," Eudo said. "Why is the male peacock the one with the plumes? It is the way nature intended it."

"And the male peacock is the first to get shot," Svana said. "I should know—I've shot one or two, in my time."

Eudo looked at her, laughed, shook his head. "There's no point in arguing with you. I'm going to see my mistress. She, at least, does not contradict me."

"Somehow I find that hard to believe."

"What?"

"That you would want any woman who didn't despise you a little."

He glanced down at her, his dark eyes flattening shrewdly. Then he laughed, a robust sound, full of pleasure. "Enjoy your partridges," he said. "They were male. That should make you happy." He laughed again, kicked his horse and rode away.

# Part Two

## The Swan

# 26

## Ratisbon, Bavaria
## September, 725

THE DAWN CAME without sun. Morning brought only mist, coiling around the trees, drowning the grass, skimming over the silent river. The towers of the fortress of Ratisbon looked as though they were perched on clouds, suspended. The mist consumed everything, even sound. It was late summer in Bavaria, though it could have been any time of year, for nearly every day began the same as this.

Then a banner rose, making the mist shiver and flee. A red cross on a field of black, overlain with three tongues of yellow flame, the middle standing straight, the other two curling outward. Some said the symbol looked like a flower. Others said it looked like the hilt of a sword, the sword that belonged to the one who had, for the second time in history, united the provinces of Austrasia, Neustria and Burgundy into the Kingdom of the Franks.

A warrior, tall and slim, dressed in a flowing white robe and wearing a bronze-winged helmet and breastplate, stood in the shelter of a crumbling temple at the river's edge, gazing at the banner. Over one shoulder was slung a short bow and a sheaf of arrows. Nearby stood a horse, pure white, with a pretty dished face and dark eyes. The warrior's eyes, barely visible over the mail face veil, were nearly black as night.

Suddenly another banner tore at the mist: the Golden Lions of Lombardy. The warrior smiled. *So.* The Lombard king Liutprand had made a treaty with the Franks. He also had a treaty with the Bavarians. Apparently, this day, he would not be on Bavaria's side.

The great gates of Ratisbon creaked open and Grimwold, Duke of Bavaria, marched out with his army, spreading across the meadow before the walls. The Bavarian warriors looked proudly terrifying in their wolf and boar headdresses, the sound of their spears thumping the ground like thunder blooming from the earth. Their faces were streaked with the blood of animal sacrifices made in the night, unbeknownst to the priests who blessed them for battle.

Grimwold rode a stout Bavarian Rotteiler, a horse so comically short that his feet seemed to brush the ground. He was a typical Bavarian, tough, square and durable, with a long reddish beard and a bald head under his boar tusk helmet. His son Odilo walked at his side, slight yet regal, his chin still smooth, his dark curly head uncovered.

Grimwold had brought this moment on himself, refusing to pay the tribute, defying the new Leader of the Franks in a manner no one else dared. Bavaria, like all the Germanic provinces, had been under Frankish rule for decades. The old Duke Theodo had been more than accommodating to the Franks. But he was dead now, as was his son and legal heir Theudebert. Grimwold had taken power from Theudebert's hapless son Hucpert, determined to rule Bavaria as a sovereign kingdom under his own control.

If the new duke was daunted by the sight of two enemy banners rising against him, he gave no sign. He should have turned around and marched back behind his walls. Instead, he formed his shield wall and pressed his attack, his rabid warriors charging into the still unseen enemy, their screeching battle cries scattering the mist. They were met by a hail of crossbow bolts, halting their momentum, forcing them to cower under shields. Yet Grimwold was undeterred; he growled and bellowed, his voice rising above the sounds of pain and blood and death, pushing his men onward. Miraculously, their assault had its intended effect; the Franks and Lombards began to fall back in retreat. The Bavarians, screaming victory, pushed deeper into the field, farther and farther from the fortress. *A mistake*, the warrior in white knew. *A fatal mistake.*

They burst from the low-lying mist, materializing from thin air. Black-clad riders on huge black horses thundered onto the field, shredding Grimwold's unprotected rear lines, their long swords and javelins cutting men down like stalks of wheat.

Grimwold should have seen them coming, should have had scouts watching the forest, a rear guard protecting his back. He had been foolishly brazen, and now it was too late; his army, caught between two fronts, collapsed into chaos. Bavarian warriors trying to retreat to the fortress where cut off by the horsemen, who had already taken the gate. And then the Lombards, with their Frankish cohorts, came upon them, arrows and crossbow bolts flying, spears impaled in bellies, francas and hammers and other more gruesome weapons smashing heads, severing arms. It was no longer a battle. It was a massacre.

The mare nickered softly. The white warrior put a hand to its neck, stroking, whispering words of calm. *Almost time.*

Then the sun burned through the blanket of mist, sweeping it to nothing, and the field lay in ruins.

The Duke of Bavaria swung his long-handled axe in a desperate circle to keep the Frankish warriors at bay. Blood gushed from under his tusked helmet, so that he resembled a crazed, cornered boar.

"Come on then! Fight me! See if your puny swords can withstand my axe!" He goaded them; they stared at him curiously. Bellowing, he raised the weapon intending to split open a nearby soldier, who stepped lithely out of the way. The axe buried itself in the mud.

Before Grimwold could free his axe to raise it again, there was a sound like a devil's shriek. He looked up to see a massive black horse parting the crowd of soldiers surrounding him. It pranced and fretted as it advanced, tossing its long mane, its immense hooves like feathered cudgels ready to flail him. Grimwold swallowed, took an involuntary step backward. Such a beast, he thought, remembering the horror of those horses bearing down on him. He reached for the axe, but it was held firm by the mud.

"Do you swear oath to me, Grimwold?" Charles asked in a voice that could cut through ice. Grimwold looked up into his eyes, eyes as pale as winter. He steeled himself, though his mouth was too dry to spit.

"Never," said the duke. "Kill me, if you must."

"I don't kill unarmed men." The men around him laughed.

"Is that what your brother would say, were he here to speak?"

Swords rent the air, spears upraised. Charles spurred his horse forward, nearly trampling the Bavarian duke.

"I came because you have not paid your tribute," he said.

"You have no right to demand tribute from me!" Grimwold growled.

"I think I just proved to you that I do." Charles turned to his guards. "Take him to the tower."

"Wait!" Grimwold shouted as the guards came to grab him, his voice stippled with fear. "Where is my son? Where is Odilo?"

"Your son is dead." Lothar rode up, his sword dripping blood.

"Liar!"

"Come. I will show you his body, though I'm not sure where his head has got to."

Grimwold wailed in anguish. The guards seized him roughly and dragged him off, though he gave no more resistance.

Charles sighed and turned to Leutgar. "Is the fortress secured?"

"Yes, Master, Lord Arnulf is taking care of it. The count of the palace is waiting for you to discuss the ransom."

"Prisoners?"

"A few. Bishop Milo is taking charge of them."

"That will be a problem. He will read them bible verses until they decide to slit their own throats. Where is Goon?"

"Off somewhere, rounding up horses."

"I need him. We must send out foragers."

Lothar interrupted. "The town's stores are full. There is no need—"

"We'll take only what we are owed, no more. Make sure Arnulf knows that." Leutgar nodded and rode off. "Now, we need to talk to Liutprand." Charles took a breath, swinging his horse south, toward the Lombard position. He stopped suddenly and turned, remembering something.

"Where is my nephew?"

Lothar snorted. "The Prince of Turds? Probably halfway to Kolonia by now."

The men chuckled. Charles looked at Herne.

"Where is Theodoald? You were supposed to be watching him."

Herne shrugged. "I saw him fall off his horse," he said. "After that I got a little busy, lost track."

"Find him." Charles turned toward the Lombards. Lothar followed.

"Forget him, Charles. Leave him to the crows. The boy's a coward and a spy for that bitch your stepmother."

"He survived your training, didn't he?"

"You wouldn't let me kill him," Lothar retorted.

The Lombard guards watched them warily as they entered the compound. The king himself was standing before a group of surly prisoners, giving orders. Charles slipped from his horse and approached on foot. The bodyguards stepped in, but the king waved them aside.

Liutprand was a tall and regal man with a narrow face and a long, blond beard, exquisitely combed. He looked none the worse for wear; there was no dirt or blood on his blue velvet tunic, emblazoned with his seal. He smiled when he saw Charles approach, though there was little warmth in his flat blue eyes.

"My lord," said the king, looking Charles over.

"Lord King," said Charles, inclining his head.

Liutprand glanced uneasily at Lothar. "I suppose I have chosen well in making my alliances."

"You had a treaty with Bavaria, which you broke today," Charles said evenly. "Cross me like you crossed Grimwold, and you will regret it."

Liutprand's smile faded, his expression hardened. "I think we understand each other," he said. "I will take my share of the treasure, in that case."

"The treasure belongs to the new duke, Hucpert. He will need it to establish his rule. You can take the border towns I offered you, as well as whatever you find on the field here today."

"That is not enough," said the king, his voice still friendly and yet betraying a hint of warning at the edges. "I came a long way Charles, and it is a long way home. I have given you my oath that I will not attack Rome. I think I deserve something more than your measly spoils and a few nothing towns in Bavaria."

Charles smiled. "You will have me for an ally."

Liutprand gazed at him a long moment, as if he didn't know whether to be affronted or amused. He cleared his throat. "Those horses of yours, the blacks, where do they come from?"

Charles and Lothar exchanged glances. "We found them in Frisia," Charles said. "They roam there in large herds. The Frisian people themselves are terrified of them and worship them as gods."

"Interesting. Well, I will be satisfied with our arrangement, if you give me some of those horses."

"How many?"

"A hundred should do it."

Charles shook his head. "I could not spare that many. The Frisians are slow to breed and difficult to catch. But I will send you some colts, as soon as we have them ready in the spring. Do you have a good Horse Master?"

"Bridian is the best in Italy, I can assure you."

"He will need to be," said Charles. "You will also guarantee my priests safe passage to Rome without having to pay your tolls."

"What? You're mad!" The king's guards moved in, on alert, hands on hilts.

Charles did not move. "Am I?"

Liutprand pursed his lips, then sighed. "I shall expect a sum of one hundred deniers from your treasury to make up for my losses."

"I will give you fifty."

The king looked about to refuse this offer, then changed his mind. He signaled his guards to stand down. "I suppose that is acceptable. But remember, Charles, you have made promises to me as well. I expect you to keep them. Should I ever need your help—"

"I will not forget, Lord King." Charles inclined his head once more. "Can I offer you lodging in the palace?"

"No, no, I can make my own camp, thank you all the same."

Charles nodded. He had seen Liutprand's supply wagons and imagined the king's camp would be far more comfortable and elaborate than anything the Bavarians had to offer.

"Give Grimwold my greetings, won't you?" said the Lombard king. "And tell him my wife—his sister—sends her regards."

"I don't think it will improve his feelings toward you at this moment."

# 27

CHARLES AND LOTHAR headed back to the fortress, which lay along the river like a lounging sow, clusters of huts and longhouses dotting her walls like suckling piglets. The work went on, the requisite looting, the piling of the dead for burial on the field or for burning on the pyre. Herne rode up to them.

"Look what I found!" he shouted, holding in one hand a sack of something Charles recognized as his missing nephew, Theodoald. Herne dumped him unceremoniously on the ground. "Hiding under a stack of bodies. Doesn't know where his horse is."

Charles looked down at the boy. He was covered in blood and slime and excrement, the last no doubt his own. His round face, still soft-looking despite the years of wear, gazed back at him forlornly.

"Are you hurt?" Charles asked. Lothar made a noise of disgust. The others snorted and held their noses. Theodoald shook his head, trying desperately to hide his soiled pants.

Charles sighed. "Go find your horse."

Theodoald nodded without looking at him.

Charles turned abruptly and continued his trek to the fortress, speaking to men as he passed, giving orders, often stopping to check on the wounded. Theodoald limped across the field in search of his lost horse. He called out the stallion's name ... *Here Grasshopper* ...

The horror of it. The battle. All the brutal years of training had been nothing compared to this. When the charge began Theodoald had stayed close to the man on his side, as he had been trained, but something snapped when the truth of the enemy came upon him. He thought perhaps he had fainted, tumbled from the horse, and would be trampled to death. But then someone else had fallen on top of him, a heavy body, very dead, clearly Bavarian. He'd started to shove it off him but then changed his mind. He lay still and waited for it all to be over.

It would all come out. The others would tease him, taunt him, humiliate him as they had been doing for the past four years, calling him "Plectruda's Lapdog" and "Prince of Turds," starting almost every morning by throwing him in a dung heap. He was a coward. A failure. Charles tolerated no failure in his army, let alone the *Truste.*

He breathed, almost with relief. Perhaps now it would be over. He could go back to the monastery, become a cleric, live out his life in peace and quiet. He could give up this insane quest to be a warrior. But his grandmother—what would she say? She had hoped, all these years, that he would regain his rightful place as Pipin's heir. "But you cannot get the support of the nobles until you prove yourself as a warrior," she told him. She was actually pleased when he was chosen for the *Truste.* He was appalled; to him it was a death sentence.

She would understand, wouldn't she? After all, he was all she had left. She didn't want him to die.

Did she?

Theodoald thought about this question as he walked far to the east of the fortress, toward a shambling stone structure that appeared to be the remnant of some ancient Roman temple. The goddess temples were often built near the town, a talisman of protection. He did not know which goddess this temple belonged to, for the statues that had once marked the entrance had fallen over long ago. Stone steps led up to three stone arches, the largest in the middle. Behind the arches were crumbled walls and piles of broken stones, the statues and altars inside shattered. He thought about just hiding out there for awhile, hoping Charles would simply forget about him.

Then he saw his horse grazing in front of one of the side arches of the temple's façade where the grass grew tall and thick. *Grasshopper!* he called out and broke into a run. The horse raised its head and looked at him, ears pricked. Theodoald grabbed hold of the horse's bridle, scolding him for running off. Grasshopper nodded his big head as if in agreement then bent it again to tear at the grass.

Theodoald pulled at the reins, swearing at the horse. Just then he caught a spray of light, a blur of white motion, the sound of hooves clattering on stones. He turned, saw a figure emerge from the center arch, a figure so incongruous he had to blink several times to make sure of what he was seeing. A white horse, its rider also in flowing white, with an exotic bronze breastplate and a conical winged helmet. It leapt over the crumbling steps, flying, suspended a moment before crashing down on the hard ground. It took off across the meadow, toward the fortress.

Theodoald was too stunned to move. Then, as if propelled by an instinct he did not know he possessed, he jumped on Grasshopper's back and kicked hard into his flank. He grabbed the mane and held on as the horse exploded under him, charging after the rider.

Charles reached the city gates and dismounted before his nephew Arnulf, tossing the reins to Alfric. "Give him a good rubdown and some hay," he said to the boy, who nodded and led the horse away.

"The count of the palace is waiting for you to negotiate the ransom of the city," said Arnulf. "I've recovered the treasure, though the duke did his best to hide it. What do you want—?"

He was interrupted by a shout.

Charles turned, frowning. The shout had been a word, a strange word, yet distantly familiar.

*Valkyrie!*

He squinted into the sun. The shout came again.

"What in hell … ?" Arnulf began. Lothar unsheathed his sword.

A figure suddenly appeared, out of the sun, taking on the shape of an armored rider on a white horse, white robes billowing like the wings of a swan.

*Valkyrie.*

Charles stared as the horse bore down on him, his soldier's instincts deserting him. He had time only to admire the peculiar beauty of the pose, the body perched in weightless balance on the galloping horse, the golden armor shimmering like the sun itself. He had seen such images before, depicted on the walls of pagan temples, sung about in the age-old songs of the jongleurs. Yet such things did not exist.

Time slowed, noises died away. The arrow left its string.

Something hard slammed into him and he felt himself fall, his breath knocked out of him. He lay still, a great weight on his chest, but no pain, no pain. He opened his eyes, saw Lothar looming over him, a scowl on his face.

"What sort of idiot stands around gaping when people are shooting at him?"

He rolled to his feet, dazed. Lothar was screaming at the other guards, leaping to his horse. Herne and Frido scrambled to their mounts. The assassin had not stopped. It was headed west now, straight for the forest.

"Take him alive," Charles said, grabbing Lothar's bridle. Lothar grunted, hauling his horse's head out of Charles' grasp and taking off after the assassin with more guards in tow. He shouted for Ragnor, who soon joined the chase, notching an arrow as he rode at a flat out gallop.

Charles mounted his horse and followed, watching the white rider, fast and fluid, evade the guards and archers, headed for the forest. There was no way any of them could catch that horse. But Ragnor didn't need to. He raised his bow and let fly an arrow, just as the assassin was about to reach the safety of the trees.

He saw the rider tumble from the horse, who kept on running without direction. His guards were upon them both instantly, catching the horse and pulling the limp body upright.

"You're welcome!" Ragnor said gleefully as he rode past Charles, bow held high in triumph.

Charles ignored him and trotted to where the guards held the assassin captive. The arrow was lodged in the rider's shoulder; Ragnor had aimed his shot perfectly, to wound rather than kill.

"He's alive," Lothar said, "though probably not for long." He jumped from his horse and pulled off the assassin's helmet, releasing a great mass of black hair. His mouth dropped open, then shut into a tense line. Charles took a breath.

She raised her head slowly, painfully, her hair falling away from her face. Her eyes were lightless black, long and slanted, like shards of obsidian. Her dark brows slashed toward a thin nose, a full mouth. It was a face drawn with the savage strokes of a child's charcoal pencil, an uncommon, feral beauty. Her eyes moved to Charles'. There was no fear in them. He was used to seeing fear in people's eyes. But her eyes held something else, a quality of accusation, a consuming hatred that ate through fear itself. He felt the pulse of something he knew to be desire; the feeling astonished him.

"What the hell is this?" Lothar slurred in shock. "Who is she?"

"I suspect … she is Grimwold's niece," Charles said softly, not taking his eyes from her. "The old duke's granddaughter, Svanahilda."

Svanahilda. *Battle swan.*

"An assassin? For Grimwold? A *woman*?"

Her eyes closed, revealing no more secrets. He turned to the guards that held her.

"Take her to the convent. Tell the nuns to keep her alive until I can question her. Hurry."

He watched as the girl was borne on a shield. There was not yet much blood; the arrow checked the bleeding for the moment. She would last a few hours at least.

He remembered then the stories of the Valkyries: they were the goddesses sent by Odin to secure from the battlefield those warriors who had died bravely. But they could also kill the warriors they hated.

The white horse was brought to him, winded but agitated. Charles did not recognize the breed.

"Arab," said Alfric, who had magically appeared, as usual. "Or Persian. Gunther told me about them."

"Take it to him," Charles said. "He will be interested."

Alfric nodded, grabbed hold of the mare's bridle. She jerked her head up nervously, side-stepping, eyes rolling. He spoke to her quietly; she pricked her ears, listening, then relaxed and followed the boy obediently toward the fortress.

Charles' gaze fell upon Theodoald, who had ridden up behind them. The boy caught his look and turned quickly as if to hurry away.

"Theo."

He froze and waited. Charles rode toward him.

"What did you see?" he asked.

Theodoald swallowed hard, nodding slightly. "I was looking for my horse. I saw a rider … coming out of the ruin. He—she—must have been hiding there. I tried to catch up, to warn you—I didn't know what else to do." He hung his head in shame.

Charles smiled at him, and his smile was open and friendly for the first time. "That was quick thinking. You might just make a *Trustee* yet."

Charles kicked Epone into a canter and headed back to the walls. Lothar threw a disdainful glare at the boy before following. The other guards looked at him with begrudging approval; one even gave him a knock on his shoulder. He stared after them, too stunned to move or speak. *Perhaps*, he thought, *I will not be so bad at this, after all.*

# 28

SVANA AWOKE TO pain. She felt wrapped in it, like a shroud, pulled ever tighter the more she tried to get away.

"I must loosen the shaft a bit before I can pull it out. Then you must be ready with the iron so she does not bleed to death. Pray God it is not a barbed arrow. Do you have her held firm?"

The voice came as if through water, liquid and trembling. Svana felt pressure on her shoulders, hands holding her neck still on a hard wooden surface. She heard that voice again, stronger now, barking, "Hold her still!" then a brace of agony as the arrow was pulled from her shoulder, sucking out her breath. A second later another, more terrible torture, a hot iron sizzling on her damp skin, the smell of burnt flesh sending her into a dead faint. For a few moments there was blissful nothing, then the pain burned through her consciousness once more, and she jerked violently, gasping.

The old nun spoke again, calm and observant, oblivious to the pain she inflicted. "Ha, look, the bone is out of joint, I think. Hold her still whilst I reset it." Again, an explosion ripped through her shoulder, coursing down her arms and back. Her vision blackened, yet she could still hear the voice of her tormenter through the liquid pulse of pain.

"Keep her still. Change the dressing twice a day and keep the poultice on it. It may stem the fever." The voice seemed to hold little hope.

"She will not die," said another voice, young and high, quietly certain.

Svana opened her eyes, the space around her coming into focus. She saw stone pillars and sarcophagi; she was in the crypt beneath the cloister church. For a moment she wondered why they were all clustered around her, gawking at her with stark, worried faces. Then she remembered.

"I always knew she would be trouble," said the first voice again. "But this."

"Poor thing is mad," said a whispery voice.

"It's a miracle she survived this long."

"May I pray for her?"

Svana strained to see the owner of this new voice, soft and lilting but decidedly male. She saw a tall, gaunt monk in the black cassock of the Benedictines, his golden eyes vaguely familiar. He bent down to speak. "Can you hear me, child? It's Boniface—Winfrith—we met many years ago, although I don't suppose you remember."

The monk put a hand on her brow and began to say the prayer for healing in rapid Latin: "Heavenly Father, Creator of the universe, and Author of its laws, You can bring the dead back to life, and heal those who are sick. We pray for our sister, that she may feel Your Hand upon her, renewing her body and refreshing her soul. Show to her the affection in which you hold all Your creatures, and grant her an early recovery. Amen."

The words seeped into Svana's brain, somehow cutting through the pain. She felt an odd sense of peace, knew she was losing consciousness again. She was grateful.

When she awoke again it was dark. A bandage was wrapped tightly around her shoulder. She tried to move, but no limb obeyed her. She felt the walls closer than before, the darkness. She tried to lift her head; a stabbing pain shot through her shoulder, her head dropped. She shut her eyes against its violence.

"Don't try to move," said the young female voice. "I've coated the wound with pitch. You mustn't move until it has sealed and the bone has properly set."

"Who is that?" she whispered.

"Freddy— Fredegund. From the convent. Hush now." The round, doe-eyed face of a young novice smiled down at her. "Here. Drink this." She raised Svana's head carefully, enough to touch a cup to her lips. "For the pain. It will make you sleepy."

She wanted to spit it out, push it away, but she could not. She took small, slurping sips. The liquid was bitter, burning in her throat. It tasted like poison. How long had she been sleeping? She did not want to sleep anymore. Yet being awake meant pain, every breath a torture.

"You'll feel better soon," the girl said softly. "Just lie still—"

"Is she awake?"

Svana flinched; the voice was low yet commanding, impatient. She saw the flit of a torch in the doorway, a looming shadow. Freddy jumped, straightened, dropped something, clattering on the floor.

"Yes, Master," the girl whispered. "But I've given her a draught ..."

"Leave us then."

Freddy glanced at Svana once more, her eyes still soft, apologetic. Svana closed her eyes, as if willing them both away. She heard the soft steps retreating and the heavy tread of boots on the floor. Then they stopped. She forced her eyes open, though they felt heavy as lead, saw him standing there, looking down at her, his mail shirt blood-stained, the eyes so shockingly light, empty, still.

"Svanahilda," he said softly, saying the name not as a form of address but as a declaration of some new discovery. "You are lucky to be alive."

"So are you," she murmured, her own voice like molasses, slow and thick. It hurt to speak.

He smiled at that. The smile had an odd effect on his face, like an intrusion, something unwanted, unnatural.

"Did your mother teach you how to shoot? I have heard tales of the Slavic women, riding with their husbands into battle. I never believed them, before today." He held up a bow, *her* bow. He turned it over, looking at it from all angles, as if trying to unravel some secret mystery. But it was an ordinary composite bow made of yew reinforced with strips of horn. It was flexible and small, built for a horseman, or a woman. The Slavs were famous archers. They were also a conquered race; their very name had given birth to the word "slave."

She felt him move around her, circling. She could not follow him with her eyes. She fought to stay awake, Freddy's potion pulling on her eyelids. But the pain was indeed lessening, did not fill her whole consciousness anymore. *Think, think.*

"Did Grimwold enlist you?" His voice was sudden, sharp.

"Why don't you ask him?"

"I did."

"What did he tell you?"

"He said he had you put in the convent to get rid of you."

"Then you have your answer." She closed her eyes. Just for a moment. *Save your strength. You are going to need it.*

The footfalls stopped. He was no longer moving. "You expect me to believe you acted—on your own?"

"I don't care what you believe."

"Why?"

She heard something new in his voice: pure, raw wonder.

"You are the enemy," she whispered.

"Am I? Not your uncle? After he killed your father and usurped your brother's place as duke?"

"That is the way of things in Bavaria."

"But your brother—"

"My brother is an idiot."

There was a long silence. Then the footfalls resumed, coming closer. She opened her eyes, found him peering down at her, the eyes once again reading her, discerning whatever it was she would not admit. She understood the fear of this man's enemies, suddenly. Those eyes saw everything.

"Your brother will be here soon to take his rightful place as duke. I will ask him for a ransom for you."

"And if he does not pay?"

"Then you will remain my prisoner for the time being."

"You will have to kill me," she said with a new edge in her weary voice. "For I will not be your slave."

He bent toward her, and she felt his nearness like a weight upon her.

"But I don't want you for a slave."

She fought to keep focused, to not look away, for she sensed he would take that as a sign of her weakness. She may be wounded, she thought, but she would not be weak.

He straightened abruptly, went to the door and called for the girl. Svana heard him say something she could not understand. Then he was gone. She breathed, her heart hammering against her ribs, the blood pulsing in her throat.

"How are you feeling, my lady?" Freddy loomed over her once more, her face etched in worry.

"What did he say to you?"

"He wanted to know—if you would live."

"What did you tell him?"

"I told him would." Freddy smiled. "Whether you wanted to or not." She laughed a little. "Perhaps you misjudged him, my lady. I mean, he has proved himself honorable, he has not even looted the treasure! He has treated the prisoners and the people fairly, and is restoring your brother to his rightful place! He is a great man, but I think he is also a good man—"

"Great men are never good men." Svana turned her head, closing her eyes.

# 29

WINFRITH OF WESSEX, christened "Boniface" by a Pope who could never manage to pronounce his Anglo-Saxon name, trudged through the dingy courtyard of the fortress toward the central keep. It was late, past vespers. The guards stationed around the walls watched him, unmoving. He kept his hands folded together, his fingers making a sign of blessing as he walked.

Two guards stood at the entrance of the main hall, watching him warily.

"I wish to speak to your master. I am Bishop Boniface."

At the name the guards straightened and parted, nodding for him to pass. He brushed by them, blessing them as he did.

The hall was quiet but for heaps of snoring warriors lining the long trestle tables and dogs nosing for scraps on the littered floor. He crossed to the round hearth in the center of the room, where he found Charles alone.

"Winfrith." Charles rose to greet him, smiling. "I was surprised to learn you were here. Why aren't you in Frisia?"

"Ah, the Pope has called me to a new mission." There was regret in his voice. "In Hesse."

"Hesse?" Charles frowned.

"Yes, it appears the Irish missionaries there have become a bit too fond of pagan ways. He wants me to go in there and—straighten them out."

"I take it you are not pleased."

Winfrith gave a small smile. "It is God's will. My mission is to save as many souls as I can before I cast my own into eternity."

Charles nodded and indicated the bench. "Sit down."

Winfrith sat, accepting a cup of wine. Charles sat as well.

"How can I help?"

Winfrith blinked, gazing at this tall, fierce-eyed man in wonder. How was it that this great warrior was so solicitous to him—Charles, with his notoriously bitter taste of priests? If only the bishops could see Winfrith here, sharing a cup of wine with their avowed enemy. He blushed at the thought.

"You know I can do nothing without your aid and protection, my prince. The pagans are far more afraid of you than they are of their own gods." He drank his wine. "I must ask you, though, because I have long wondered ... why have you taken such an interest in my work? You do not seem the sort of man who spends much time in church."

Charles regarded him, the play of light making his eyes glow like a cat's. "I remember well what you said to me."

"What was that?"

"The people will never bend their knees to the Franks until they bend their knees to Christ.'"

Winfrith's brow lifted in surprise. "I had no idea you would take my words so to heart."

"It was good advice."

Winfrith smiled a little nervously. "I am pleased you think so. But I must ask you something, my prince, about your treaty—with the Lombard king."

"Yes?"

"You realize that the Pope will not be happy when he learns of it. Liutprand is his most vehement enemy."

"He has promised, as part of our treaty, to keep his armies out of Rome."

Winfrith let out a breath. "Well, that will help. So long as you are alive, of course. I will pray for your continued good health." Winfrith raised his cup and smiled awkwardly. "You've had quite a summer, I hear. Now all of Germania is yours once again."

"So it would seem. Will the nobles support Hucpert, do you think?"

"Well, to be honest, my prince, Hucpert is not much of an improvement over Grimwold." Winfrith chuckled. "What have you done with Grimwold, by the way?"

"I'm allowing him to keep one of his estates, where he will be confined."

"Generous." Winfrith paused. "Odilo?"

"Dead."

"Ah." Winfrith crossed himself. "I do pity him. To lose one's only son. Though I suppose Grimwold himself is the cause of it. This whole business, the suspicious death of his brother, his usurping the rightful duke's place—I would have thought Svanahilda would have set her bow on Grimwold rather than you."

"So would I. Bishop Erhard says she is mad."

"Mad?" Winfrith arched an eyebrow at the notion. "It's possible, though I doubt it. But I do think she likes people to *believe* she is mad."

"Why would she do that?"

"Well, there are no rules for a madwoman. Perhaps it is the only way she has of … being free." He paused, thoughtful. "She's had a hard life, you know. With her mother killing herself when she was so young. And there were rumors …"

"What rumors?"

Winfrith shook his head slightly. "From her time in Constantinople. But I do not like to spread gossip."

"Was there a man involved?"

Winfrith made a noise in his throat. "I cannot honestly say. Perhaps the girl herself will tell you—in time."

"Perhaps." Charles did not sound particularly hopeful.

Winfrith cleared his throat. "I understand your nephew was instrumental in your—salvation?"

"Yes."

"Wonders never cease! Plectruda, you know, has still not given up her quest to restore Theodoald to your place. She has been writing letters, petitioning the bishops—"

"Let her plot," Charles said, pouring more wine for himself. "It gives her something to do."

"Charles, you should not take this so lightly—"

"I'm not afraid of women, Bishop."

"No, but perhaps you should be."

"Spoken like a true celibate."

They smiled at each other. Then Charles grew serious once again.

"There is something else I wanted to talk to you about—"

"Bishops," Winfrith said grimly. He shifted uncomfortably on the bench.

"Is that not really why you are here?" Charles said gently.

Winfrith looked rueful. "I have had a letter from Bishop Eucher of Orléans. The Council is not happy with your latest practice of seizing church lands to finance your army."

"So he sent you to intervene on his behalf?"

"He seems to believe I have some small influence on you."

Charles nodded. "All right then. Influence me."

Winfrith took a breath. "This is difficult for me. Truth be told, they have a strong case against you. But you also have a case. I see what you have done for the missions, for the spreading of the gospel in pagan lands, which to my mind is far more important than fattening the coffers of the bishopric Sees. I understand why you had to take them on. They operate as independent rulers with no regard for the authority of the princes, they had to be brought in line. However, I must tell you what I truly believe: you are a great warrior, Charles, but you cannot win a battle with the Church. At least, not *your* way. You don't possess the right weapon."

"So … what weapon do I need?"

Winfrith thought about this. "Perhaps—you need someone who knows how to deal with them, and who will advocate for you."

"You?" Charles asked.

Winfrith shook his head. "That is not my gift. Nor is it my calling. I am a missionary, not a politician. But perhaps there is someone … "

"Yes?"

Winfrith thought a moment. "Recently I was in Liège, and I met a young cleric there, on sabbatical at the Abbey of Saint-Trond. He struck me as very resourceful and clever, and he was a great admirer of yours as well, though he was careful not to let anyone know it. His name is Chrodegang. He is currently serving as chief cleric to the Abbot Sigebert of Saint-Denis."

"Are you sure he can be trusted?"

Winfrith laughed. "This fellow seems to be the type who can draw any man into his confidence. A rare gift. He will be in Liège for the rest of the year. You should go and talk to him, Charles. He may be able to help you."

"I will," Charles said.

"Well, I should leave you now," Winfrith said, rising stiffly. "It's been a long day, I'm sure. I pray that, for a time at least, there will be peace."

*Peace.* The word sang in Charles' memory like a long-forgotten hymn. He had been fighting almost constantly for seven years. He did not know what peace felt like.

He watched the tall monk shuffle from the hall, his thoughts returning to the Valkyrie.

*Svanahilda.* She had come closer to killing him than anyone else, and many had tried. How was that possible? And why? It didn't make much sense to him, though he was often mystified by the motives of women. Still, by his own laws, her crime was punishable by death. He would have to kill her.

And yet.

He had never wanted any woman as much as he wanted this one.

# 30

HUCPERT, THE RIGHTFUL Duke of Bavaria, was received in the city like a conquering hero, paraded through the streets on one of Charles' blacks and planted at the parish church where he received the blessings of both Bishop Erhard and Bishop Boniface. The nobles in attendance took turns kneeling to him, giving their oaths. Hucpert, still reeling from the news of his rapid ascension and more than a little drunk, nodded and smiled and trembled inside.

He was pale and scrawny and slow-witted, dulled by drink and idleness, as different from his half-sister Svanahilda as it was possible to be. He had been scared out of his few remaining wits by Charles, who had told him bluntly that if he did not pay his tribute and bow to Frankish suzerainty, he would suffer a fate ten times worse than his uncle Grimwold.

"But what if my uncle tries to come back?" he asked.

"Your barons will have to keep him in line. I can't be here babysitting the lot of you every minute. They won't go against me if they know what is good for them."

"I wonder if they *do* know what is good for them," Hucpert replied.

Now he sat beside the Frankish leader at the high table, presiding over a feast in his honor, though he felt more like the lamb offered for the sacrifice. Once the formalities were over, Charles seemed to take no more interest in him, except to ask if he would pay the ransom for his sister. Hucpert had only laughed.

"You think I want her back? You can have her. Make her your concubine. Only make sure your confessions are up to date first. They say she is like a black widow spider. Her kiss is lethal. Men have died trying to bed her."

Since then Charles had ignored him.

Hucpert looked forlornly at his mother, Belectrudis. He knew he had been a great disappointment to her. She had consented to marry

Grimwold only to escape the convent, the fate of most noble widows. But now she had a smile on her face, a rare thing, and he wondered at it.

"What is it, Mother?" he asked, leaning toward her, his balance wavering. "Are you pleased with my—return?"

"I am going to Kolonia," she said, sipping her wine.

He stared at her, shocked. "Why?"

"As a hostage, apparently. Charles wants to make sure that you—and my dear husband—behave yourselves."

"How can he do this? He cannot take you from me!"

"He can, and he will. And I don't mind. I shall be with my sister again. I have not seen Plectruda in many a year."

"She is a prisoner," Hucpert said. "Charles hates her."

"My dear, you are so naïve. Charles does not hate anyone. He has no feelings whatsoever. I must say I admire that about him."

There was only one time in her life that Belectrudis had taken a stand. She had seen a midwife accused of witchcraft and savagely beaten by a priest, just for curing a woman of bleeding. The midwife had died of her wounds. Belectrudis had that priest thrown in prison where he was whipped daily. But the bishop appealed to her husband Theudebert, who allowed the priest to go free and sent his wife to a convent for forty days as punishment. She never tried to intervene again.

"Mother, you can't leave me. I will be all alone here!"

"My son, you were always alone."

"But I can't do this—" Hucpert was sweating now, his breath in short bursts. "I can't … I don't know how … "

"You will succeed or fail on your own," she told him. "You will either become a man or … you will die a boy."

Not very comforting words from his mother.

Charles left the feast early. He wanted to see her. He had not spoken to her since that first day, when he was certain she would die. He almost wished it. That would have made everything so much easier. But she had not died, thanks to the constant ministrations of the young novice. And perhaps also to the woman's own stubbornness.

He'd moved her out of the convent, away from the prying eyes of the nuns, and into a small upper room of one of the fortress towers so he could keep her close and heavily guarded. He had many questions still, though he knew she would never give him a satisfactory answer. Now he climbed the steps and pushed open the door.

The room was cramped and dark and rather cold despite the smoking brazier. The woman was sitting in front of the fire, wrapped in a blanket.

Her back was to him. The novice jumped up at the sound of the scraping door and stood trembling, a hairbrush in her hand.

"Master," she said, bowing low. She was very young, probably no more than fifteen, her brown eyes very large and wide in the round face. She still wore her novice's veil, covering her hair.

"Leave us," he said.

She nodded and rushed toward the door. He stopped her before she could go.

"What do they call you?"

"Freddy, Master. Fredegund."

"You are a novice?"

"Yes, Master."

"You wish to remain in the convent?"

Freddy's large eyes widened even farther. "I wish to—be of service, Master."

"Then go tell the abbess I will need you here awhile longer. You may want to move your things here. You can sleep in the room below."

"Oh—" The girl's mouth opened wide. She fled from the room. Charles closed the door.

"You scare everyone."

He turned to look at the woman by the brazier. "Not you."

He moved around the room so he could see her face in the dim light. She glanced at him, though it was clear she could not move much without pain. Her eyes again took him by surprise.

"You are better," he said.

"Better than what?"

"Better than dead. It would seem you've made a miraculous recovery."

"That must be very inconvenient for you."

He thought he saw a smile, but it was hard to tell. Her fingers gripped the worn wood of the chair arm. She turned her gaze to the fire, avoiding his.

"You've met my brother," she said.

"Yes."

"I told you he was an idiot."

"He's young. He has a lot to learn."

"You've made a mistake in making him duke. But it won't last long. I give him six months at most."

"Does that please you?"

"I could not care less."

He wondered if that were true.

"Your brother will not pay your ransom."

He thought she seemed actually surprised at this. "He never liked me," she murmured.

"You make it hard for people to like you," Charles said. "I have the same—tendency."

She looked at him then, the first look she gave him that was not filled with loathing.

"So, what am I to do with you, Princess Svanahilda?" he asked softly.

"I believe you already know the answer."

"There is another way. If you swear oath to me—"

"No," she said, looking away, her voice flat, resilient once more. "You will have to kill me."

He gazed at her a while, wondering if she meant this. She was difficult to read, her eyes and her voice so contradictory. "Do you really want to die?"

"I am ready for it." But she did not look at him again.

He sighed, turning to the door. "Have it your way then. You will return to Kolonia with my army, to meet your fate."

She didn't answer. He stopped in the doorway, glancing back at her. He remembered a story he had heard long ago, perhaps from his own mother, about a swan who was captured by a hunter. The hunter took away her feathered robe and forced her to live with him, marry him, have his children. For many years she lived as a wife and mother, seemingly content in her new life. Then one day, years later, one of her children found the feathered robe that the hunter had hidden. The child showed it to her mother, and she put it on and flew away, back to her own world. The hunter searched for her, but never found her again. He realized she had never been his at all.

Charles left the room, shutting the story out of his mind.

# 31

GUARDS BROUGHT SVANA and Freddy to the courtyard where the caravan of horses and wagons was preparing to leave. Freddy huddled close to Svana's side, fearful of the activity in the courtyard, the huge horses, the shouting of men.

Svana carried no baggage. Freddy had found her a gown to wear from her own mother's coffer, as well as a hooded mantel, lined with rabbit fur. "You'll need it," Freddy had said. "It will be cold in the nights."

A man approached them, tall and exquisitely handsome with a mane of white blond hair that hung loosely around his powerful shoulders. He wore nothing but braccos and a mail tunic; the black band of the *Truste* encircled one arm. He looked at Svana with cold blue eyes. She remembered him suddenly, from that day of the battle, the one who had saved Charles' life, who had chased her down and wanted to kill her. She wondered now if this was how she would meet her death; Charles might not want to kill her, but this man surely did. All she had to do was give him a reason.

"Put her in the litter," the man said to the guards. He was about to walk away when Svana stopped him.

"I wish to ride," she said. "I have my own horse. Tether her to your guards. There is no point in wasting manpower on a litter, is there?"

The man appeared to think about this. He turned to the guards. "Get the horse." Then he approached her, so close she could feel his breath on her face. "If you try to escape, I will kill you. But first I will give you to the men. There is no point in wasting a body such as yours."

Svana nodded, though she met his gaze levelly. There was clouded violence in his eyes. Yet something held him in check. Perhaps this was what he wanted—to give her a chance to escape. So he could kill her and be done with it.

He stalked away. A few minutes later her white horse was brought. She stroked the mare's neck, whispering her name softly. "Aura." One of the guards lifted her to the saddle. Two other horsemen tethered her horse to theirs. Freddy chose to ride in the wagon with the other women.

"Who was that?" she asked one of her guards, pointing to the blond warrior in charge.

"Lothar," said the guard. "Captain of the Truste."

*Lothar.* She knew she had come face to face with her most dangerous enemy.

Lothar was never out of her sight on the journey. She watched him move, saw the constant, quivering tension of his body, so different from Charles' cat-like languor. He was always in motion, every nerve poised for battle. It was his job, after all, to be ready. But she thought it was also his nature, something he could not escape. Though he never spoke to her again there were moments, especially during times of resting and camping for the night, that she would catch him watching her and would feel the iron blue warning of his eyes.

They traveled hard, relentlessly, Lothar unmindful of the delicacy of the women in his charge. The constant jolt of the horse's motion made Svana's barely knitted bones ache until tears came to her eyes, but she rode straight-backed and silent, the pain itself keeping her upright.

In five days they reached the crumbling Celtic fortress at Wirtenburch, which sat like a great stone idol amid the grape-laden hills of northern Franconia. There she and Freddy were given a separate room, away from the men; Svana was surprised at this inexplicable show of mercy from her reluctant guardian.

"You can see for leagues," Freddy said as she stared out the small window.

"You have never left Ratisbon, have you?" Svana watched the girl glory in the new world she was witnessing.

"I've never been anywhere. I thought my whole life I would be staring at the four walls of the convent, except for the times I was allowed to tend the garden."

"What about your family?"

"My father is a blacksmith. I have four brothers; they all work at the forge. I was the only girl … a girl is not much use in a family unless she can be married off. And he had—no takers for me."

"How did you learn your skill?"

"My mother was a midwife. She taught me all about healing plants and herbs. Women came to her when they were having—difficulties. She saved many mothers and babies, though many died too. But the priests hated her; they accused her of witchcraft and had her beaten. I tried to heal her, but nothing I did helped. She died." Freddy paused. "That is when Father sent me to Niedermunster to be a nun. He thought it would be for the best. I went to tell him I was leaving. But he was very busy that day. The Franks—all those horses! I'm not sure that he heard me." She was silent a moment. "Well, anyway, I don't think he will miss me. I reminded him of my mother, he always said. He didn't like to be—reminded."

Freddy bowed her head. Svana could see she was fighting tears. How sweet and sad, she thought, to want the love of a father. To miss the presence of a mother. She herself did not know these things. Her own mother was a faint shadow upon her life, her father a wilted memory; he had been a ghost long before his actual death. She could remember no yearning for their love, no sense of loss when they abandoned her. She had never realized, until she saw Freddy weep for her family, that there might be something wrong with her, that she was somehow incomplete.

They left early the next morning. Svana's shoulder throbbed, her legs and back were stiff and sore from riding, but she again refused the litter. Freddy joined the rest of the women in the wagon, the sound of their giggling conversation joined with the snorting of horses, the rattle of wagon wheels and the brisk, rustling wind.

As the days dragged on, the cheerful chatter died away. Svana began to feel as though it would never end. The rolling hills of Franconia gave way to rugged uplands, so densely forested that it was often difficult to tell day from night. Four days later the forest thinned to open heath and the town of Ascaffa, a Roman garrison whose castrum had been turned into a monastery, thanks to Bishop Boniface.

From there the land flattened out and the going was much faster, until they came upon the Main River. They crossed at the Franconoford. It took half a day to get the entire party over the ford, including wagons and horses. Once across, Lothar gave them the rest of the day to dry out and rest. They slept in yet another Roman castrum, this one more of an abandoned ruin, though it did provide some shelter from the worsening weather. From there they skirted the foothills of the Westerwald, the densely wooded low hills of the Rhineland massif, passing many Celtic ruins, temples and standing stones, a few isolated hermitages, but few villages. By then no one was much interested in the scenery. It rained steadily, the wind grew colder; everyone just wanted the journey to be over.

At last one afternoon Svana heard a cheer from the marching men, and she saw the outline of Kolonia, rising from the banks of the Rhine like an artfully designed pile of rubble.

Kolonia had been a great Roman colony, the birthplace of the Emperor Claudius' wife, though barbarian rampages had destroyed most of the city's fine Roman buildings. The people of Kolonia, ever resourceful, had used the stones from the ruins to reinforce the walls and build new homes. The materials of Kolonia had stayed the same, only the shapes had changed.

They passed through the old Roman castrum of Deutz, once Charles' prison and now the garrison of his standing army, and then crossed the bridge into the main city. People came out of their homes to stand in the street and gawk at the new arrivals. Svana, wrapped in the hooded mantel, went unnoticed. She watched young women throw themselves at Lothar, tossing him flowers and baring their breasts, hoping to get his attention. She watched his horse toss its dark head and skitter nervously and wondered how a horse trained for the chaos of battle should be so flustered by the screams of worshipful young girls.

The city was laid out in a rough square, with the main road leading from the river gate directly to the palace, which had once been the Roman Praetorium. The palace was a massive oblong edifice fringed with battlements, more of a fortress than a house. Across the plaza stood the basilica, a once imposing Roman courthouse awkwardly repaired. The plaza teemed with people, for a market was in progress, and the soldiers had to push aside vendors with their carts to make room for the caravans from Bavaria. A guard helped Svana down from her horse and led her up the steep steps to the palace entrance, where she joined Freddy and the other women.

She stood in the great hall as soldiers and servants rushed about busily, though many stopped what they were doing to gawk at her, plainly curious. She was pushed into the hands of an army of women, accompanied by palace guards.

"Follow them," Lothar said to Freddy. "They will take you to your quarters."

Svana did not move at once. Freddy gave her a gentle nudge.

"My lady?"

Svana allowed Freddy to lead the way, following the women up the stairs. Guards trailed behind.

When they entered the room, Svana nearly gasped. Silken draperies lined the walls, and fur rugs adorned the plain rush-covered floor. The wooden bed was low, but the mattress had been recently stuffed and covered with fur pelts and quilted blankets. A small table with food and wine stood by the glowing hearth.

This was not a jail cell.

Freddy darted about the room delightedly, running her hands over the draperies and furs. Svana stood still, her stomach roiling. She knew the game he was playing. The people of Kolonia knew nothing of the events in Ratisbon. They did not know she was a prisoner of war, guilty of a capital crime punishable by death. He had no intention of executing her. Instead, he would present her as a token of his victory, his hostage or his concubine, or both. He knew that, for her, this was a fate worse than death.

Svana felt pain stab through her shoulder; she moved to the bed, where a gown lay across the covers, an old but serviceable gown of white damask. Freddy followed her.

"I'll bet it belonged to a Merovingian queen!" Freddy said happily, lifting up the rich garment to inspect it more closely. Svana doubted that any Merovingian queen had ever set foot in Kolonia.

"They say the Lord Charles has gone to fetch the king," Freddy continued, oblivious to her agony.

"The king? Here?"

"For the victory feast. It is a tradition. Can you imagine? We will see the king himself!"

So Charles was bringing the king to Kolonia. He was going to make a big fuss over this Bavarian victory. She closed her eyes, fighting the rising bile in the back of her throat. He would make this as difficult for her as possible. He would leave her no way out.

# 32

CHARLES ARRIVED TWO days later, accompanying the king, Theuderic IV, who rode in an elaborate litter with a considerable entourage. The palace burst into frenzied activity, servants swarming like insects along with the townsfolk curious to get a look at their king, who required several men to move him from the litter to his sedan chair. Apparently he was not in the habit of walking.

One of the servant girls burst into Svana's room, her face flushed.

"The king is here! The king is here!" she shrieked. She and Freddy began chattering excitedly. Svana, sitting by the window, felt her shoulder throb.

"My lady." Freddy approached her. "The count of the palace says you must be present tonight, for the feast."

Svana shook her head. "I cannot—"

"Yes, you can. You must bathe. And wear a proper dress." Freddy held up the white gown.

"No," she said, shutting her eyes, trying to breathe against the heaviness in her chest.

"My lady—" Freddy drew close to her, her smooth face compressed in worry. "It's going to be all right. You'll see. You must look your best. Show them … who you are."

*I am a trophy of war.*

She did not protest as Freddy put her in a bath and washed her hair, setting it in a severe plait, and dressed her in the white gown. When she was ready they sat together before the fire, waiting. Svana stared at the flames, her hands folded tightly in her lap.

A steward arrived, flanked by guards, to take her to the hall. She rose, disengaging from Freddy's grip and offering her a brave smile. Freddy stood as well and followed her mistress out the door to the stairs.

Svana was stunned once again by the sheer size of the great hall. Charles' banners with their peculiar triple-flame symbol lined the upper walls, along with a mammoth display of weaponry: brightly painted iron and wooden shields, francas, spears and swords, the sum of the Frankish aesthetic achievement. Frankish swords were renowned throughout Gaul for their unsurpassed suppleness and strength; it was said that one could bend a Frankish sword from hilt to tip and it would not break.

The hall was packed: warriors and their women, local nobility, a smattering of clergy and an army of servants. They stopped talking and stared at her as she descended the stairs, their gazes a mix of curiosity and malice. She heard the low murmurs of gossip and felt her skin under the heavy dress grow hot and prickly. She clung to the railing, forcing her body to straightness and severity, as if the eyes upon her had no effect at all.

Charles stood at the bottom of the stairs. He was dressed very simply in braccos and a plain black tunic with wide leather belt from which hung a short sword, the only mark of his office. If not for his height and his startling eyes he might have passed for a common peasant.

Beside him stood Belectrudis, her uncle's wife. She smiled coldly at Svana, raising her chin slightly. She must have traveled with Charles, Svana thought, for she had not been in Lothar's wagon train. Belectrudis looked very pleased with herself, and with her new host, whom she gazed upon admiringly.

Charles took her hand when she reached the bottom. He led her to the high dais, where she was seated at his side. The place of a wife—or favored mistress. Belectrudis was beside her. She could see the long-haired king seated at the opposite end of the room in his gold-filigreed sedan chair. His thin body seemed to have a permanent bend—he listed like a wounded ship. A river of reddish drool slid down his chin. A servant wiped it with a cloth.

"What is drooling from the king's mouth?" Svana murmured as she watched him, fascinated and horrified. "Is it blood?"

"Honey balls," Charles said. "His cook makes them for him."

"I think it has caused him to lose his teeth."

"We prefer our kings without teeth."

Servants brought trencher after trencher of meats, fish, winter vegetables and pitchers of wine and beer. Bowls of garum, a foul-smelling condiment made from fish intestines, were passed down the tables. Musicians played their harps and tambours, jugglers and clowns performed before the inebriated crowd.

Svana picked at her food, her stomach lurching. Men gawked at her, women glowered. Belectrudis laughed merrily and drank cup after cup of the sweet wine, occasionally leaning over to Svana to make some disparaging comment about Franks.

Charles never looked at her, did not acknowledge her, as if she were a piece of furniture. She felt a growing anger at being put on display, the same phrase running through her brain: *I am a trophy of war.* She wanted to scream, to throw the trenchers of food on the floor, to run from this room. But she suspected this was what he wanted. So she sat still, staring dully into space, willing her mind to silence, all the time aware of him beside her as if she were held in her seat by the sheer physical force of his presence. All her life she had been able to dismiss and ignore people as she wished, but this man would not be ignored. It was this that made her afraid.

A troupe of comedy players took the stage and performed a parody of the great civil war between Austrasia and Neustria. The actor playing Plectruda wore a gorgon mask and carried a small straw doll—her grandson Theodoald—that she used to shield herself from pelting rocks. Raginfrid wore an idiot's mask and kept bumping into everyone and falling down comically. Radbod, the Frisian king, dressed in fur pelts like some marauding Northman, went around whacking the other players with a huge club. The actor playing Charles walked on stilts so he towered over everyone and swung a giant, stuffed hammer this way and that, the smallest tap sending his enemies flying. The people laughed and hooted, demanding the scene over and over until the actors were too tired to go on.

Once the pageant was finally over, a jongleur began to sing. Svana lifted her head, listening. It was a song she knew, a song from Germania: *The Rubezahl*, "The Radish Counter." In the story a wizard steals a girl and imprisons her in a tower, where he turns radishes into animal companions for her, to keep her company. First he makes a bee, then a bird, but none of them seem to please her. Finally, the girl asks for a horse. When the Rubezahl complies, the girl steals the horse and rides away to freedom, leaving the wizard so bereft he takes out his own eyes.

This jongleur had changed the song to *The Rappenzelle*, "Prison of the Black Horse." In his version a prince comes upon a radish garden and feeds a radish to his black horse. The horse changes into a beautiful woman with black hair. The prince, not wanting her to change back, keeps her locked in the garden and visits her daily. But then the garden's owner, a wizard, returns and drives the prince away, claiming the girl for himself. The prince is so despondent he tears out his eyes and wanders forever in the countryside, alone.

*So she comes, the Dark Horse Lady*
*To her master's secret tower*
*Where the wild rampion grows*
*Where the river meets the wall*

*And her mane she lets him ride*
*And his heart she holds*

Svana felt Charles' eyes on her as the song progressed, growing increasingly melancholy as it described the prince, lost in the wilderness, blind and grieving. She prayed for it to be over.

When finally she was taken back to her room, she fell onto the bed, burying her face in pillows to muffle her screams.

"What were you trying to accomplish?"

Milo, lounging on a pile of furs by the big stone hearth in Charles' sitting room, gazed at him with wine-glazed eyes. "I know she tried to kill you and all, but still—it seemed rather cruel."

"He's right," said Lothar, perched on the ledge of the room's only window. "She should be dead."

"You really should just be done with it. Why torture the girl?" Milo raised his cup to be refilled by a serving girl. He touched the girl's bottom appreciatively; she kicked him in the groin and scurried away. He made an injured noise. Gerold, sitting next to him, laughed loudly.

"Careful now, Bishop," said the big Rhinelander, sputtering. "Must not strain your Saint Peter, seeing as how it's yet unused." The others joined in the laughter.

"You are an imbecile," Milo shot back at him.

"I don't know what that is, but it sounds fierce enough," Gerold said.

Milo shook his head in disgust, returning his gaze to Charles. "So why *are* you keeping her alive? Other than the obvious, I mean."

They all looked at Charles, awaiting an answer. He said. "I am still … curious about a few things."

"Like what?"

"The horse, for instance. Arabian. From the Empire, most likely. Or Iberia. Where would a Bavarian woman get such a horse?"

"A gift, no doubt," Milo mused. "Wasn't she in Constantinople with her grandfather the duke for a time? During the Arab siege?"

"Yes," Charles said. "If it was a gift, it came from someone with means. And position."

"Ah," Milo said knowingly. "I'm sure a girl with her looks had many admirers in the Empire."

"Or from Duke Eudo. He has access to such horses, being so near the Arab stronghold. Perhaps *he* sent her to kill you," Gerold added. "It would be like him, to send a woman to do a man's job."

"I thought of that. But the breast plate and helmet are Imperial," Charles said. "Of the Varangian guard, the Emperor's bodyguard. Curious, don't you think?"

"You don't mean to imply," said Milo carefully, "that she is part of some *Imperial* plot ...?"

Charles shrugged. "I have made an alliance with Lombardy, which may not have pleased the Emperor."

"Ah yes. The Emperor would no doubt believe that such an alliance would hamper his own plans to conquer Rome." Milo's dark eyes lit with intrigue. "Your sudden death would eliminate a large headache for Leo. But still—a woman assassin? Was she the Emperor's whore, perhaps?"

"It's possible," Charles mused. "Winfrith hinted at some—rumors about her."

"Well, you need to get it out of her then," Milo said with finality.

"Get it into her first," Gerold bellowed loudly.

"Shut up, Imbecile."

"The bow was not Roman," Ragnor interrupted. "It was of the Steppe people of old. A Slavic bow."

"*Her* bow," Charles said. "Or her mother's. Her mother was a Slavic queen, captured by Duke Theodo in battle. Given to his son as a gift."

"And a fair shot she is too," said Gerold matter-of-factly. "At any rate, I hope you have bedded her by now. You have, haven't you? It's the least you should do for all the trouble she has caused." He chuckled and added: "Because if you haven't I would gladly do it for you—"

"Ach, God help us," Milo said, slapping the side of Gerold's head. "You have four wives, did you forget? And none of them are very satisfied. Besides, Charles does not share his spoils."

"I say bed her and then kill her," Gerold said, downing his beer.

"Just kill her," Lothar said.

"This is getting us nowhere," Milo said impatiently. "Charles, you have other things to think about now. More important things. The Assembly, for one. The bishops are gathering, like vultures. There has been an awful lot of plotting going on around this place. The halls are humming with intellectual activity, and little of it is distinctly religious."

"We eat bishops for breakfast," said Lothar with a savage grin.

"And will you have the pope for lunch?" Milo snapped icily. "Guard your tongue, Lothar. Your soul is more fragile than most."

"I am not the one who recites scripture to his victims while he guts them," Lothar sneered.

"Just because I kill them doesn't mean I don't want their souls to be saved," Milo shot back. Everyone laughed.

Charles rose suddenly, bringing them all to silence. "Go to bed, all of you. You need to be in church and *sober*, by midday. We have many sins to confess."

They groaned and shambled to the door. Gunther was the last to leave.

"Goon," Charles said before he had stepped through the portal. The huge man turned his distorted face to his friend. "Can we get more of them?"

"More of what?"

"Those horses."

Gunther looked surprised at the question. "You want to go to the Empire?"

"I would think they would be traded in the Aquitaine. Since the Arabs occupy almost all of the southern coast."

"Perhaps."

"Then you shall go."

"When?"

"In the spring. We will need them, Goon. A proper cavalry horse. The Frisians are too rare and expensive. We need to start breeding our own."

"Such ancient breeds do make the best stock. But I—"

"You will go."

# 33

THE NEXT NIGHT Svana was again seated beside Charles at the feast, forced to endure the lurid stares of the congregation while Charles himself paid her little attention. Belectrudis had retired to the monastery at Notre Dame to be reunited with her sister. Svana was alone now.

The jongleur sang a different song this night, the *Song of Sigurd*, the great love story of the Valkyrie Brynhilde and her itinerant prince Sigurd. The song had been written, it was said, for Queen Brunhilde, a kind of battle maid herself, and her husband Sigebert who had been King of Austrasia.

In the song, the great warrior Sigurd falls in love with the beautiful Valkyrie Brynhilde, but she refuses to marry him. So Sigurd marries another woman, making Brynhilde insanely jealous. She, in turn, marries Sigurd's wife's brother in revenge. But the brother cannot ride into her castle for it is surrounded by fire. So Sigurd does it for him and sleeps with Brynhilde, keeping a sword between them so as not to betray his brother-in-law. But Brynhilde learns of Sigurd's deception and demands her husband avenge her honor.

*Back shall I go where I used to be,*
*Living together with my father's kin,*
*There will I sit and sleep my life away,*
*Unless you make sure of Sigurd's death …*

Svana felt the heat rise in her throat, cutting off her breath. She turned to Charles, saw him looking at her intently, the force of his gaze transfixing for a long moment. She rose suddenly, upsetting a goblet of wine, begging to be excused. Charles gave a small nod to the guards. Freddy, who had been standing with the other waiting women against the back wall, ran after her mistress, who fled up the stairs. Charles watched her go.

"Did the song disturb you?" Freddy asked as she brushed Svana's hair slowly. It took a long time to brush that long, dark hair to shining smoothness, and Freddy took particular pride in it. Svana felt drowsy and warm, though the song still swam in her brain, refusing her any peace. She closed her eyes but saw only his eyes on her with their perfect knowledge. Those eyes, those unnaturally pale eyes—they haunted her every waking moment.

"It's disturbing that men should write such beautiful songs for such bad people," Svana murmured.

"Who? The Merovings, you mean? I always thought Brunhilde was a good queen. And Sigebert as well, a great king."

"They were the best of the lot, which is not saying much. The fighting between Queen Brunhilde and Queen Fredegund was what tore apart the kingdom and caused the Merovings their downfall."

"Fredegund? The Neustrian Queen? I wonder if I was named after her," Freddy mused. "Do you know the story?"

"I have heard it."

"Tell me please! I have always wanted to know." Svana sighed as Freddy settled herself at her feet.

"You won't like it."

"Please!"

"Very well. There were three kings of Francia then—King Sigebert of Austrasia, the good king, King Chilperic of Neustria, the bad king, and King Guntrum of Burgundy, the stupid king. They were brothers, but they hated each other and were constantly making war on each other. Fredegund was Chilperic's mistress, but she wanted to be queen. Chilperic refused to divorce his wife, however, because that would make the Pope angry, so Fredegund solved the problem by having Chilperic's queen strangled in her sleep."

"Oh! Then, did Chilperic marry her?"

"No," Svana went on. "Unfortunately for Fredegund, Chilperic's brother Sigebert had married the Gothic princess Brunhilde, and Chilperic, not to be outdone, wanted a real princess for himself. So he asked the King of the Goths for the hand of Brunhilde's sister, Galswinthe.

"Chilperic tried to be faithful to Galswinthe, but eventually Fredegund wormed her way back into his bed. Galswinthe found out about his infidelity and demanded a divorce, but Chilperic begged her forgiveness and, being a good Catholic, she forgave him. Soon after she was found strangled in her bed."

"Fredegund?" said Freddy, her eyes wide. Svana nodded grimly.

"So Chilperic finally married Fredegund and she became queen. She thought her worries were over. But there was one thing she had not counted on, and that was the vengeful fury of Galswinthe's sister, Brunhilde.

"Brunhilde urged her husband to start a war with Chilperic, which Sigebert did. And even though Guntrum joined Chilperic, Sigebert was a great warlord and won every battle. He even captured Fredegund and had her imprisoned. But from her prison cell she hired two assassins to kill Sigebert. One day, as Sigebert was being born up on his shield in a victory celebration, those two assassins appeared and killed him."

"Oh no!" Freddy said, gasping.

"Brunhilde did not give up. She refused to relinquish Sigebert's crown to Chilperic; she had her young son crowned King of Austrasia with herself as regent. So she managed to hold on to the Austrasian throne."

"That's it?" Freddy asked hopefully.

"No, there's more, much more. Too gruesome to talk about. Fredegund killed her husband eventually. Even after she died she managed to torment Brunhilde from the grave. In a strange twist of fate Clothair, Fredegund's son, was eventually named King of Austrasia. He had Brunhilde arrested and tortured, then tied hand and foot to a wild horse and dragged until she was nothing but a bloody pulp."

Freddy had both hands over her mouth. She looked as if she might be sick. Svana smiled at her, picked up the brush she had dropped. "So you see," she said softly, "there is a reason why no one mourns the passing of the Merovings."

The next evening Svana refused to go to the hall. When the steward came for her she lay on her bed as if she couldn't hear, couldn't move. The steward finally gave up. Freddy brought her a tray, but she did not eat.

It was the same the next night, and the next. She ignored the pleadings of Freddy and the steward. She stopped eating, could hardly sleep. She paced the room like a caged animal, refusing to speak to Freddy or to anyone.

In desperation, Freddy screwed up the courage to go to Charles and ask that the woman be allowed out of the tower, to get some air. Charles consented, even giving her a guard to accompany them.

So Svana walked the crowded, rain-strewn streets of Kolonia as children pranced and darted around her, as market vendors peddled their wares, as beggars grabbed her skirt and implored her with their toothless despair. She walked past soldiers loitering menacingly in doorways, past women nursing their babies by the side of the road, past carts lumbering from the farms to the marketplace. She walked to the bridge and stared out at the castrum on the other side of the Rhine, and the plains beyond. She walked until she was too exhausted to walk anymore and then returned to her tower room to sprawl on the bed, her wet clothes molded to her body, the *Song of Sigurd* still playing in her head.

She noticed, on occasion, a strange little beggar watching her from the corner of her vision, always ducking and hiding when she turned his way. But there were many beggars on the streets. Her guards normally just kicked them or poked them with their spears when they got too close to her.

"He has forgotten I am here," she said to Freddy one morning as the girl brushed her hair by the window. "He will leave me here to rot. Until I go mad for good."

"No—he is just busy," Freddy said, sounding less than assured. "Nobles keep arriving for the Assembly. The whole palace is in an uproar."

Svana knew better. Charles himself had spent nearly a year in prison; he, more than anyone, would know what torture this would be for her. She tried to imagine him in prison, could not picture that towering body, that enormous presence shut up in a tiny, dark cell. She suspected that he had allowed himself to be imprisoned on purpose, to wait out the dissolution of Plectruda's rule. His intrepid escape had been carefully plotted as well; the humiliation cost Plectruda what was left of her authority. This is what frightened her: Charles never did anything without a careful, thought out plan. He was patient and precise; he waited for the right moment and then destroyed his enemies utterly.

And she was such an enemy.

"Freddy," she said suddenly. "Tell him I want to speak to him."

Freddy hurried to obey.

She was taken to his reception room, a huge, virtually empty room lined with sconces that seemed to give little light. He stood in shadow behind a long table, the only furniture she could see. He watched her enter, curious, but otherwise expressionless.

"What do you want?" he asked her.

"Justice," she said, her own voice like lead in her throat. "Do you mean to keep me here—forever? So that everyone in your kingdom thinks me your pampered slut? I am a prisoner of war, I request a warrior's justice."

He seemed to consider this. "Why are you so anxious to die?"

She shook her head. "Death would be preferable to—this."

He smiled coldly. "I don't believe you. If you had really wanted to die you would have killed yourself by now. There are no bars on your windows, Battle Swan."

"Is that what you want? You want me to kill myself? To do the dirty work for you?"

"No."

"Then what do you want, my lord?" she asked hotly.

He leaned close to her, so she could smell the wine on his breath. "I think you know what I want," he said softly. He straightened, signaling his guards to take her back to her room.

# 34

THE DAYS DRIFTED by endlessly. Svana felt close to despair. The window beckoned, but try as she might she could not bring herself to take that path. He had known she wouldn't. He taunted her with every moment of her confinement. She wondered if this was what madness felt like.

She walked most days, the only thing that calmed her nerves. Freddy always accompanied her, as did two or three of Charles' guards. They let her go where she wanted; they did not interfere, as if they did not care. She wondered why.

One day she came upon a street fare and wandered toward it. A man was performing tricks with exotic animals; she stopped to watch, amused. Freddy laughed delightedly. The guards, too, seemed absorbed in the funny show. None of them noticed the small, shambling creature approach her, crouching, walking crablike across the stones.

"Please, help!" the creature screeched, grabbing her hands. She looked down, startled. Freddy gave a yelp of fear. The guards came to her side immediately to throw the beggar off, but he pulled on her hands, forcing her to bend toward him, mumbling frantically.

"Be off, you lazy drunk!" yelled one of the guards, kicking the vagrant in the ribs. The man cried out but did not let go. Svana felt him press something cold and hard into her hand. A second kick from the guards and the man released her and scrambled away, yelping like an abused dog.

"You all right?" Freddy asked, distressed.

"Yes," Svana said, hiding her hand in the folds of her mantel. "Just a poor beggar, it was nothing. I think I'd like to go back now. I'm tired." Freddy looked at her quizzically; they had been out barely an hour. But she nodded and followed obediently as her mistress turned and headed back to the palace at a fast walk, the guards struggling to keep up.

When they got to her quarters she dismissed Freddy, telling the girl she had a headache and wanted to lie down. After Freddy was gone, Svana pulled her hand out from her mantel and opened her fingers, her breath locked in her throat.

In her palm was a copper medallion engraved with the crest of her father's family, the Agliofings. She stared at it, puzzled, turning it over. On the back she saw something scratched into the dull metal, as if with a knife. The letter O.

*Odilo.*

Her fingers closed over the medallion and she held it to her chest.

Odilo was alive. And he knew where she was.

That night she waited until Freddy went to bed, until the noises died down in the hall below and the palace fell to sleeping. She had decided already; she knew what she had to do. She had but one weapon left to her. She slid the medallion inside a small hole she had made in the mattress. She undid her hair, letting it fall loose down her back. She pulled a long mantel over her shoulders.

She knocked on the door and waited. After a few moments she heard shuffling footsteps, a sleepy voice on the other side.

"What is it?"

"I wish to see your Master." Her voice sounded surprisingly steady to her own ears.

She heard the scraping of the bar being pulled off and then the door opening, the stiff hinges creaking. The guard's face appeared, a young face, twitching in fear. She smiled gently. He pulled the door open wider, so she could see the spear he carried.

"Too late. The Master has retired for the night," he said brusquely.

"This cannot wait," she answered.

The guard looked down the darkened passage and back at her. He seemed to be deciding something. "Wait a moment." He shut the door. She waited. After a long time the door opened again. A new guard stood facing her, this one older, with a weathered, unsmiling face.

"This way." The guard waited for her to step through the door and then followed closely behind her, giving cursory directions. She had no doubt his spear was aimed at her back, only inches away. They walked silently down a maze of hallways and up another long set of stairs, lined with torches. Other guards stared at them as they passed. Svana kept her gaze focused straight ahead, pretending she didn't see anyone at all.

At the top of the stair they came to a wide, oblong landing lined with ancient wooden shields, carefully and intricately decorated. There were weapons as well, equally old but perfectly preserved: francas, the throwing axes that were once the favored weapon of the Franks, javelins, long swords and scramsaxes, the shorter, broader single-edged blades, all in lethal array. She paused, gazing at them, transfixed.

There was only one door, heavy old oak with iron braces. Two guards stood on either side at full attention, their spears held straight at their sides. Svana's guard went to confer with them briefly. They gave her a long look. Then one of them rapped on the door with his spear and opened it without waiting for a response.

The guard stood aside, indicating she should go in. Svana felt her feet move, though she was not aware of any conscious effort to walk. She took a breath and stepped into the room. The door closed behind her.

The room was dark, except for a few candles and a spill of white moonlight from a single, wide window. She stood a moment, gazing about her, watching shapes appear as her eyes adjusted. It was a room big enough for a king, yet looked as though it were inhabited by a monk. An undraped bed with four bare posters stretching purposelessly to the ceiling. A table with wine. A wash basin. A trunk of plain, unvarnished wood. A chair, strewn with clothes. A stone hearth where a fire smoldered, neglected. There were no treasures or bits of plunder soldiers were usually fond of collecting, nothing to indicate anything about the man who occupied it but a vast emptiness, which seemed to suit him somehow.

She thought at first he was not there at all. Then she saw a movement in the window, a dark shape unfolding; she saw his long form stretched out on the deep ledge. He was naked to the waist, the outline of his body etched in the silver light. It was a body of sweeping lines and sharpened edges, a body honed for war; it reminded her of the weapons on the wall outside the door. She stared at him, aware of a tremor in the pit of her belly, a tightening in her throat. He turned to look at her, his eyes reflecting the lambent light, glowing like a cat's. She waited for his slow smile, but it did not come.

She quelled an impulse to bolt. She moved toward him, slowly, as if straining against his will to draw her in. His face held a calm expectancy. She breathed, feeling the blood pulsing in her cheeks, down her throat. The wound in her shoulder, now healed to a puckered scar, seemed to burn through her skin.

With shaking hands she loosened the ties of the mantel and let it fall over her shoulders until it collapsed in a puddle at her feet. She wore nothing underneath.

She stood spear straight, letting his eyes move over her, take in her body, sculpted and curved and taut like a bow. He slid from the ledge in fluid silence and moved toward her, setting down the cup he had been holding. She looked at the cup, trying to concentrate, to avoid looking into his eyes. She felt him draw near so that his breath fell softly on her cheek, his fingers on her breast, the skin calloused and rough; she held her breath, her heart deafening in her own ears. His hand moved up, to her throat, a hand that had killed men, could snap her neck like a twig. She saw a long jagged scar raked across his chest; she wondered at it. His hand moved around the back of her neck and drew her into him, his body folding, his mouth closing around hers. His kiss was like water that filled her entire body, so she felt suddenly liquid, her skin seeping into his. She tried to pull away but found herself unable to move, riveted to the floor, her arms limber and useless. Her body was not hers anymore, she realized. It belonged to him, was controlled by him.

He released her, and she sucked in air as one drowning. He lifted her, carried her to the bed, laid her down gently, and she felt his naked skin pressed into her, his body like hot metal pouring into hers, filling her with heat and smoke. She heard a wordless groan come from somewhere deep within him; his mouth found hers again, drawing out her breath. She arched against him, disappearing into him, her body molded to the shape of his. She could feel the roar of his breathing in her ear as his body shuddered; she heard a cry, thought it might be her own voice, a cry of victory, or surrender, she could not tell.

# 35

SHE AWOKE SHIVERING, wondering how it was that she had fallen asleep. The sky outside the window was black, starless. He lay sprawled on his stomach, one arm thrown over her, in protection or imprisonment. His eyes were closed. She moved slightly, thinking she could slip away; she felt his fingers close over her arm.

"I'm cold," she said, reaching for the furs.

She felt his body like a burn on her skin, a heat that ran down her legs as he pulled her under him. She found her strength then, suddenly, mysteriously. She clawed at him like a wildcat, her nails ripping into his back, her teeth sinking into his shoulder, as if his flesh were not enough for her, she needed to burrow under his skin, to feel his blood and tissue running into her own. He laughed softly, caught her hands and pulled them over her head, his body heaving, convulsing. He collapsed beside her, his breath heavy, sonorous in her ear. They lay there a long time in silence.

"Hammer," she said softly, into the blackness around them. "Why didn't you come for me and take me by force to your feast?"

"Is that what you wanted me to do?" He laughed when she did not answer. "Go to sleep, Battle Swan."

"Aren't you afraid I will kill you in your sleep?"

"You already have."

They slept for a time, entangled in each other, their sweat and blood and fluid fusing them into one being. When she awoke again the sky was soft gray, the hour before dawn. She heard the clear call of a hunting horn somewhere outside the window, in the world beyond, a world that no longer existed for her. She traced the purplish bruise on his shoulder, the long, swollen welts on his back, smiling, knowing she had left her mark on him. She wondered at the pleasure she felt from that knowledge. She leaned up on one elbow, gazing at his face, so young in sleep, the deep ridges smoothed to unworried planes. She reached out a finger and traced the scar on his chest.

He grabbed her hand reflexively, his eyes open. He did not waken slowly, but instantly, as a warrior does. He looked at her, waiting, expectant.

"They are calling you," she said softly. "The pig hunt."

"The pigs can wait." He pulled her on top of him.

"Bastard."

"Witch."

Her hair fell over his face, she could feel his heart beating against hers, consuming her once more, and she thought she might die from this, her heart would burst from her skin, shattering her body into shards, that those shards would pierce him and he would die with her, and she would take him into the darkness beyond.

Then he got up. She pulled the furs over her body, though her skin was so raw that even the touch of them made her wince.

"So what am I supposed to do now?"

"What do you want to do?"

She watched him pull on his braccos and black leather tunic, his back to her. "I want to ride."

He turned to look at her. Dressed, he looked unknowable to her, not the man who had possessed her in the night, but the enemy she had wanted to kill. She saw the dilemma in his eyes; he sat on the chair and pulled on his boots.

"I'll have your horse readied," he said finally.

She blinked. "You are not concerned that I might try to escape?"

"Will you?"

She turned away, on her side, pulling the furs over her. She heard him laughing, she sighed in annoyance. She felt his weight on the bed; he turned her over to look at him.

"There will be guards with you all day, watching your every move." He smiled, his hand sliding down the side of her face, to her throat, to her breast. He lingered there a moment; she went rigid, breathless. He looked into her eyes, his smile fading. "You won't escape, Battle Swan, because you haven't yet gotten your revenge. That's what *you* want, isn't it? I'm not a fool. I know that—this—will not come without a price. But I am willing to pay." He kissed her hard and deeply, then bounced off the bed and was gone.

Svana lay back a moment, as if released from some dark power, shivering and sweating. She scrambled from the bed, ran to the other end of the room, pulled aside the heavy curtain of the garderobe and fell to her knees, retching violently into the brass pot. There was nothing in her stomach, she heaved trickles of bile, reminded of the trails of drool on the king's face. When the heaves subsided she sat on the pot, a burning pain between her legs as she tried to pee. She felt dizzy, too weak to stand, she lay on the floor, her whole body trembling, the blood thudding in her ears.

After a time she got up, found her cloak, pulled it over her shoulders. She walked back to her room, passing the guards at the door, pretending not to see them. She shut the door and leaned against it, struggling to stop the shaking in her knees, the tremulous emptiness of her whole body against the hardness of the wood.

*What have I done?*

She went to the bed and pulled the medallion out from the mattress. She held it tightly, trying to remember why it was so important. *Odilo*. He was alive. He would come for her. This is why she had done it. But something had happened that she had not expected. The wound in her shoulder began to ache anew.

She lay on her bed, the mantel still twisted around her body, which felt sore and bruised as if she'd been through a battle. She lay unmoving until Freddy came in with her breakfast tray.

"My lady?" said the girl, setting down the tray. "Are you well?"

"Yes," Svana said.

"You slept?"

"Yes, I slept." Did she? She could not remember sleeping. Or perhaps it was all a dream.

"I brought you some breakfast … "

"Thank you. Can you leave me alone for awhile?"

"Of course … "

"And do me another favor, will you? Find me some clothes to wear. I'm going riding."

"What?" Freddy looked at her mistress in wonder. Svana did not meet her gaze.

"Just find me something, Freddy."

The hunting horn sounded in the distance, and Svana gasped softly, pulling the mantel tighter around her, the sound like a lance in the pit of her belly.

"The pig hunt," Freddy said. It was the time when the pigs, that had been let loose to roam the forests all summer, growing fat on roots and nuts and truffles, were rounded up for the slaughter. The Slaughterfest followed, a fortnight of celebrations, of drinking and gorging, the last big feast before the winter.

"Yes," Svana said quietly. "Time for the slaughter."

# 36

THE PIG PAWED the earth, grunting, swinging its huge head from side to side. It glared at the men who crouched in the wood, watching it with fear and determination, their long spears poised to strike. They had been chasing this pig all morning to little avail. The beast appeared to be immortal. It already had three spears stuck in its hide, which seemed to be more of an annoyance than anything else. The hunters eyed each other, no one wanting to make the first move. Finally one of them did, stepping forward, his foot cracking a twig. The noise seemed to jolt the animal to life; it charged the hunter who threw his spear in a panic and missed. The others began to yell, and the pig swerved, confused by the noises, the movement. It ran pell-mell into the clearing.

Charles saw the pig coming. He turned to Lothar, who was stuffing a meatstick in his mouth. They had been lounging on a small circle of boulders in the clearing, having a snack and watching the spectacle of men chasing pigs.

"Pig," Charles said, and the two of them sprang to their feet, spears in their hands. The pig skidded to a stop at this new obstacle and grunted, sniffing the air.

"Go left," Charles said. Lothar ignored the command and bolted directly at the pig, howling like a lunatic. The pig was so surprised it seemed to forget to move for a moment, giving Lothar enough time to ram his spear into its hide. The pig bolted, squealing in pain, dragging Lothar, who refused to let go of the spear.

"Damn fool," Charles muttered to himself, crouching in the tall grass. He watched the pig as it tore around the clearing in crazy circles, trying to oust the weight from its back. Lothar had managed to get a leg over the top of the animal and was trying to drive his spear deeper. It rammed Lothar against a rock; he grunted in pain but still did not let go. It swung its head around wildly, trying to gore the human who clung to it, just out of reach of the deadly tusks.

"What are you waiting for?" Lothar screamed as the pig rammed him against the boulder again.

Charles sighed and made a barking noise, rustling the grass. The boar stopped a moment, listening, then bolted toward the sound. Lothar let go and rolled off its back. The boar charged, squealing, blood oozing from the embedded spears. Charles waited until it was nearly upon him then rose up and with all his strength rammed the spear into the boar's head. The other men could hear the crack of the skull splitting open. The beast shuddered and collapsed, twitching its useless legs, then heaved a great sigh and went still.

Lothar ran to look, blood-streaked, his clothes nearly torn off him. But he was smiling hugely. Charles was breathing hard, shaking his head at Lothar's condition.

"You're an idiot."

"What a beauty," Lothar said as if he hadn't heard. "Too bad we had to kill him." It was not the intent of the Pig Hunt to kill all the pigs at once; most were simply rounded up for the winter. But this pig would never have been captured alive.

The hunters gathered around to see the prize, one of the biggest any of them had ever seen. They set about gutting the carcass, preparing to butcher it there in the clearing, for it was too big to move intact.

Another horn sounded distantly from the palace, signaling the call to the Assembly. Charles sighed. He and Lothar left the hunters to finish the work, mounted their horses and headed down the long wooded path to the city.

"Have one of the women see to you," Charles said sternly, glancing at him. "You look as though you've been skinned alive."

"Speaking of wounds, how's the bitch?" Lothar asked caustically. "Healing nicely, I presume?"

"She is not your concern, Lothar."

"She *is* my concern, Charles. She tried to kill you once, she will do it again."

Charles did not answer. They rode awhile in silence. His mind returned to the night before, as it had all morning, to the fevered, black-haired woman writhing snakelike in his arms, her nails raking his skin, her molten eyes sucking him in. It felt like a dream, yet it seemed more real to him than anything that had happened during the day. When he closed his eyes he could still smell her, still feel her teeth in his flesh, the heat of her against him. He thought of her riding her white horse outside the city gates; he wondered if he had made a mistake in letting her go.

"Charles!" Lothar said. "Did you hear me?"

Charles glanced at his friend. "What?"

Lothar grunted. "I was talking about the Assembly," he said. "The bishops are planning something, Milo said so. What are you going to do about them?"

"There is not much I can do. I will try to reason with them."

Lothar scoffed at the idea. "The only thing to do is kill every last one of the bastards," he said. "No point in talking to them. Just get rid of them."

"Easier said than done."

"Dead men don't get in your way."

# 37

BY THE TIME Charles and Lothar got to the Assembly, held in the large courtroom of the palace, the attendees were already stamping and grumbling impatiently. On either side, lined up on benches, sat the bishops, with the nobles standing in packed rows behind them. The Neustrians, as usual, were on one side, the Austrasians on the other. Despite the unity of the kingdom, this old antipathy had not dissipated much, the Neustrians considering the eastern Austrasians uncouth barbarians, and the Austrasians liking the western Neustrians to their Roman ancestors: obsolete, effeminate, and short.

The king sat on his ornate sedan chair at one end, busily picking his nose.

"I trust the hunting was good, my lord?" said Bishop Eucher, seated at the center of the Neustrian side. He was a small man, frail looking, with a surprisingly deep voice that dripped with irony.

"Good enough, Lord Bishop, thank you for asking," Charles said. He glanced to his right, saw Milo seated with his nephew Hugo, whom Charles had named Duke of Neustria as well as Bishop of Paris. Hugo looked nervous, as always. His brother Arnulf, Duke of Burgundy, was standing before the group, obviously in the middle of a heated speech.

"We've been here almost an hour," grumbled Bishop Savarry of Auxerre. He was older than Eucher, and more bellicose, with a florid complexion.

"I thought you needed more time to pray before we started," Charles said, to the snickers of the Austrasians. "What did I miss?"

"I was just telling them," Arnulf said, "that there have been raids all along the Burgundian frontier, *Arab* raids. They've looted two monasteries at Luxeil and Autun. The Arabs are getting bolder, Charles. They have crossed our borders. You need to do something about this."

"I plan to," Charles said.

"Then you will invade the Aquitaine?" Arnulf looked hopeful.

Charles shook his head. "We cannot invade. Eudo has a treaty with us, he pays his tribute."

"He clearly cannot handle these Mussies—"

"We will not invade. We must take care of these raiders ourselves."

"My lord," said Duke Odo tiredly. "You have been dealing with Saxon and Frisian raiders since time immemorial. Surely these Arabs cannot be more of a threat—"

"They are far, far worse, Duke," Charles said.

"But Eudo defeated them not four years ago—"

"The Arabs have already conquered half the world," Charles interrupted. "They destroyed the Goths of Iberia in a matter of weeks, they took Septimania, they stream over the Pyrenees in ever increasing numbers every year. They have plundered all of southern Aquitaine. I can promise you they will not be satisfied until they have taken over the whole of our world as well."

Whispers of assent came from one side, grumblings from the other.

"So I suppose you will want a bigger army now," Savarry said unhappily. "And you will pay for it how? By stealing more church land for your soldiers?"

Murmurs of alarm shot through the crowd. Lothar tensed, his hand on his sword. The other guards did the same.

"I do not steal church lands," Charles said. "The kings of Francia had beneficed large tracts of land to the bishops in the desperate hope of saving their own souls. A benefice, as you well know, must be returned to the giver once the recipient is dead. That land should have been returned long ago—"

"The land was given to the *Church*, and the Church does not die, my lord," said Eucher placidly.

"I have already given much of it back to the Church—"

"For the *missions*," Savarry put in, his voice rising with his rancor. "And that is purely to advance your own agenda in conquering pagan lands! What we see, my lord, is merely your attempt to undermine the established Sees of Francia, against the wishes of your own king, I might add!" There were cheers of agreement. The king, upon the mention of his name, sat up and looked around, interested.

"And when a bishop opposes you, you simply remove him!" Savarry snapped. "It is completely illegal! You have no authority to do such a thing—"

"Yes, I do," Charles said.

"My lord, I beg your pardon, but you do not," said a new voice in the crowd, haughty and slightly derisive.

The crowd parted to reveal a small, smartly dressed young man, bowing a courtly bow.

"Who are you?" Charles said.

"Theodouin, Count of Vienne," said the man.

"Vienne? Your father is dead?"

"Yes, sadly … May I explain?"

"As you will," said Charles with a note of warning in his voice that the count missed entirely.

Theodouin stepped into the center of the room, smiling pleasantly. "If I may, I draw your attention to the Edict of Paris, ratified by your own great grandfather, the Mayor Pipin of Landen, which decreed that, and I quote, '*Upon the death of a bishop, there shall be appointed in his place whosoever shall be elected by the archbishops, the bishops of the province, the clergy and the people of the city, without hindrance, and without gift of money*.' There, you see? Only in the case of the *death* of a bishop may another be called to his place, and in that event, that person must be elected by the clergy and the people without interference from the lay ruler. Therefore, my lord, you cannot remove a bishop from his See without being in direct violation of your own Salic law."

The room was silent, amazed. Bishop Savarry beamed with pleasure. Eucher was conspicuously silent. Hugo clasped his hands together in prayer, murmuring under his breath. Arnulf rolled his eyes. Gerold looked murderous. Charles glanced at Milo, who stepped forward, smiling with cold pleasure.

"I commend you, Count, on that interesting interpretation of the law," Milo said, mocking Theodouin's pompous manner. "But allow me to enlighten you on some rather unpleasant facts. The law you quote states what to do in the *event* of a bishop's death, but it doesn't say anything about removing said person by another means. Then, of course, there is a bit of wording you quite conveniently left out: '*if the elected person is worthy, he will be consecrated by order of the prince.*' Do you know what that means, Count? It means that the lay ruler, in this case Charles, acting in the best interest of the king, *does* have the power to put on any bishopric See anyone he sees fit, and there is not a lot you or"—he glanced pointedly at Bishop Eucher— "anyone else can do about it."

This last part took the room by storm. The Austrasian counts did not know whether to be triumphant or terrified. Everyone began shouting at once. Savarry rose to intervene, but Theodouin beat him to it.

"Well then," the Count of Vienne replied in a shrill tone, forcing everyone to silence, "may I remind you of *another* law, ratified by Sigebert II, the King of Burgundy, which states that no bishop may be removed without the unanimous approval of the Council of Bishops. Or had you actually forgotten, my lord?"

Lothar took a few steps forward. The shriek of steel against scabbards filled the room.

"The law you speak of Vienne," said Milo in an almost bored voice, "it is an *ecclesiastic* law, is it not?"

Theodouin opened his mouth to speak then closed it again. There were low murmurs, snorts of laughter behind him. He drew himself up defiantly.

"It was ratified by the King!"

"Sigebert II," Milo said, nodding. "Who was never crowned, as he died before his grandmother Brunhilde could arrange his coronation. He was also a child of seven at the time, which means that his signature was most likely forged."

"That's a lie!" Theodouin trilled, the Neustrians echoing his outrage. "And so what if it is Canon law? Is not the Church expected to abide by the Salic law as well?"

"The Church manages to ignore those Salic laws it finds—inconvenient," Charles answered dryly, "such as the law of financing wars and of beneficing. I don't see why I can't do the same."

The bishops descended into rants. The nobles did not know what to do. Theodouin continued to stand straight, seemingly serene, yet there was a kind of violence in the way he stood there, not saying anything. Bishop Eucher called for order.

"My lord King, I beg your intervention on this matter," he said, turning everyone's attention back to the child-like king who had started to fall asleep. A steward nudged him and he jerked awake, gazing around him.

"What's going on?" he demanded.

"With your permission, Your Majesty, I think it is time we called a Synod," Eucher said. There was a collective gasp. There had not been a Synod convened in over fifty years. It was the most powerful weapon the bishops had against the lay ruler.

"A Synod?" the king repeated slowly. "Yes, of course, if you think it is needed."

"I do. Most definitely." The bishop turned his steely gaze to Charles. "You do realize, Lord Charles, that the Synod has the power of excommunication?"

The other bishops murmured nervously, the air in the room grew warm with anxiety. To excommunicate the *de facto* ruler was a terrible risk to the security of the government, not to mention a horrible stain on the entire kingdom.

Charles set his jaw. "I would think," he said slowly, "that the threat of an Arab invasion would be far more worrisome to you than the ownership of a few plots of land, Bishop."

"An Arab invasion? Do you really believe in such a thing?" Savarry said incredulously.

"I do," Charles said.

"It is a fantasy!"

"Is it?" Charles answered. "Was it a fantasy when the Goths invaded Rome herself? Certainly the Romans thought so. And yet it happened. Rome thought the unschooled barbarians were no match for the mighty Roman army. But they were wrong. We are in danger of making that same mistake. The Arabs are faster, stronger, and far more numerous than we are. How do I know this? I know because I have been watching them. For ten years. They have conquered half the world while we sit here and squabble over who owns what bit of land. We have a choice, my lords, to defend ourselves or die. We can no longer live blindly under the fatal illusion that we are invincible."

These words, coming from the man who had already conquered most of Gaul, fell like a hammer blow on the assembled company. Charles was not a practiced orator, but his words were taut and sharp-edged, as if he spoke not with his voice but with his sword.

"Amen, amen," said someone softly. Others joined in, a general assent. The bishops were silent. Savarry looked confused, while Eucher's face held no expression at all.

The king spoke up in the confused silence. "I'm starving. When's dinner?"

Most of the company fled the room once the king was gone. Theodouin was the first to find the door. Milo waited until only Charles was left.

"Well," he said, "you've asked for it."

"Better to have it out now," Charles said. "I'm tired of these games."

"Games are what we do, Charles. You know that."

Charles sighed, rose and went to the door, desperate to get out into the air, the light, where he could breathe again. He had been rash, dangerously rash, but there was nothing to be done about it now. He wanted no more of the charade.

He thought of her then, as he had all day. She filled the center of his mind, not so much a memory as a constant presence. She had come to his bed, had given him her body, but she had not given him her oath. He wondered if that were the one thing she could never surrender.

# 38

SHE ENTERED THE room alone. It was late. He was sitting on the window ledge as usual; the air was cold but the room was smoky—there was a fire laid. She knew he had done that for her. He did not turn to look at her, accepting her presence as if she were a part of the room itself. She went to him, took the cup from his hand and drank from it.

"Did you get a pig?" she asked.

"Yes." He took the cup from her. "Take that off."

She shrugged out of her gown. He looked at her and smiled faintly. He reached out, pulling her to him. She shivered in the cold as he kissed her, his hands sliding down her back. She felt her own body relax, fold into his in a way she now felt to be the most natural thing on earth. Yet she did not touch him, could not for some reason.

"I'm cold," she said.

He stood, lifting her, and carried her to the fur rugs laid at the hearth.

She awoke much later, alone on the floor before the hearth, the embers glowing slightly. Was she dreaming again? She sat up, thinking about his hands, his mouth, his body etched into hers. It had seemed very real. She closed her eyes, breathing in the memory.

She heard a noise, the whisper of movement and turned, saw him sitting in the open window, naked, a wine cup in his hand. She felt the cold suddenly, enveloping her, and pulled the furs up to cover her nakedness.

"I hate the cold," she said aloud, into the air. "Once I tried to cure myself of this weakness. So I stayed outside in a storm, all night. I got a terrible fever and was in bed for weeks. I was cured of the fever. But not the cold."

He did not respond at first. He put the cup to his lips and drank, and she saw that this gave him a certain strength, a strength he seemed to need.

"Who was he?" he asked.

"Who?"

"The … other one. The first one."

Svana looked away from him. He must have known from the first time he had taken her that she was not a virgin. "Is that important?"

"It might be."

She took a breath. "A Roman."

"When you were in Constantinople?"

"Yes."

He paused. "Did he rape you?"

"No," she said quickly. Then, after a moment: "I was married to him."

There was a silence.

"You were married?"

"Yes."

"I never heard about that."

"It didn't last long."

Another pause.

"Who was he?"

"One of Leo's court."

"What happened to him?"

She paused briefly before answering, her voice almost forlorn. "He loved his king more than he loved me."

Charles looked at her. "But you—loved him."

"Yes. As much as I could love anyone." She felt the pain of that memory like a knife edge pressed to her chest, a burning sensation. She kept her eyes on the fire, so he would not see her tears.

"Is your wife … very beautiful?" she asked when she could speak again.

"Yes."

"Why is she not with you?"

He was silent awhile. "She doesn't like it here."

"Will you go to her?"

"Yes."

"When?"

"Soon. Perhaps."

"Do you love her?"

He did not speak, but she knew the answer.

"What are you going to do with me, Hammer?" she asked after a moment.

"What would you like me to do?" He sounded weary. "Let you go?"

She didn't answer. He sighed, his head falling back to the hard stone.

"Svana, I cannot let you go."

She got up from her cocoon of furs and went to him, pressed her naked, shivering body against him, as if she could pull the heat out of him into herself. She did touch him then, running her fingers over his face, down his neck, tracing the scar on his chest. She had always thought it odd, that scar. That Charles would expose himself to such a wound seemed ludicrous. She wondered vaguely if a woman had done it. "Where did you get this?"

He hesitated. "It is a reminder of a mistake I made once."

"You make mistakes?"

"I make many. But never the same one twice." He took hold of her hand, pulled it away from his chest gently, holding it still against her.

"Is that why you always win?"

"It's why I am still alive."

She laughed a little. "It's all a game to you, isn't it? The battles, the courts, even me. I heard about your sparring with the bishops. The council is up in arms. You got the best of them too, didn't you? It's a game you play, and you always win."

"Sometimes I don't mind losing," he said. He wrapped his fingers around the back of her head, tightening in her hair, pulled her to him and kissed her hard. She drew away slightly, breathless.

"I almost got away today," she said softly. "Your guards couldn't keep up with my horse. She is a desert horse, born for running. I could have kept going. They would never have caught me."

"Why didn't you?"

She shrugged. "Maybe I will. Tomorrow."

"So it's a game to you too, isn't it?"

"I don't like losing."

She did not ride the next day. There was a market going on, she wanted to go; she had to find the beggar. She walked up and down the stalls, pretending to look at the goods for sale while Freddy chattered about finding cloth for a new dress.

She saw him, finally, heaped against the side of a wooden box, apparently asleep. She sidled up to the stall near where he sat, fingering a piece of linen cloth. When she glanced his way, she saw he was looking at her shrewdly, waiting.

"Oh my lady, this is lovely," Freddy said, coming beside her and taking the cloth from her hands. Svana half-turned, dropping something on the ground at the beggar's feet.

"Oh no, it won't do," she said, "but that over there …" She pointed, hoping to distract Freddy. She glanced at the guards, who watched her intently. She kicked the thing she had dropped with her foot, saw the beggar from the corner of her eye, scurrying over to pick it up. A guard lunged at him, poked him with his spear.

"You again! Get away!"

The beggar obeyed, the object tucked into his fist, crab-crawling away.

She never saw the beggar again, and she was glad of it. Her initial joy at knowing Odilo was alive had given way to a growing uneasiness. When it was not raining she rode her white horse, but the pleasure in it was gone. That sense of freedom she had once known, the taste of escape on the edge of her tongue, she could no longer summon those feelings. She was tied to him now; there was no getting away.

She tried staying away from him as long as she could, a test of will, railing against her own weakness. But after one or two nights, once Freddy was gone and the servants asleep, she would go back to him. They clawed and raked and fed upon each other like starving animals, and in the stillness that followed they lay in a tangle on the bed, listening to each other's scorched breathing until it slowly subsided. Then they would sleep, deeply and profoundly, as neither of them had ever slept before.

One night he came to her. She had decided to take a bath, to clear her head. She sat in the steaming water, so hot it seemed to burn through her skin, erasing any other sensation, emptying her mind. She had longed for this, the complete loss of feeling, the numbness she had once embraced as the way to survival. Freddy sat beside her on a stool, sewing and chatting inanely.

Then the door flew open and he was there, striding into the room. Freddy turned and fled, leaving her sewing on the floor. He pulled her from the tub, the water running down her skin. His hands moved over her, drawing her into him, the length of her body molded to his. She did not try to resist. She felt ashamed, exhilarated, lost.

"So you know now," Svana said bluntly when Freddy returned the next morning with her breakfast.

Freddy set the tray down. She would not look at her. "There were rumors. The guards talk, sometimes," she said in a small voice.

"What do they say?"

"That … you are a witch and you put a spell on him."

"What do you think?"

Freddy shrugged. "I think he is in love with you," she said simply.

Svana sighed. "What he feels for me—is not love, Freddy."

"Are you sure of that?"

Svana shook her head. It was no use explaining such things to the girl. She was far too innocent.

# 39

"DO YOU BELIEVE in God, Hammer?" she asked him one dark night. She lay on her side, turned away from him. His fingers traveled down her arm, across the valley of her waist to the silky hollow below her hip bone. He loved this place the best, the softest part of her. He rested his hand there, breathing into her hair.

"Most of the time. Why?"

"Do you think He will punish us for what we are doing?"

"What we are doing is its own punishment," he said with a laugh. "Don't *you* believe in God?"

"I used to. I did want to be a nun once, you know ... What's so funny? I was in love with God. Well, I was in love with the *idea* of God. The God of perfect justice. Perfect love. Perfect freedom. I went looking for Him. I prayed. I fasted, I lay on the floor of great cathedrals, waiting for some sign ... *something* ... but there was nothing. God never came for me. Then I learned the truth. I had not suffered enough. Suffering, that was the key. Suffering is what makes you holy, beloved of God."

She turned to him, her sunless eyes fixed on his. "It came clear to me then. Jesus Christ's great gift to the world, his ultimate sacrifice, had become just another form of slavery. But a special, sinister kind of slavery, for the Church preaches that to be wretched is our natural state, that suffering and poverty and disease and death bring us closer to Him. The God of the Catholics makes us long for death, and then makes us love Him for it. It's a magnificent swindle, a colossal fraud, all proclaimed in the name of Love—what are you laughing at?"

He shook his head, rolling onto his back. "Nothing."

She shrugged and sat up, pulling her knees to her chest. "The God I fell in love with doesn't exist," she said finally. "Perhaps I was wrong to look for Him in cathedrals in the first place."

"All right then," Charles said finally, "So you are mad at God. But that does not explain why you tried to kill *me*."

She sighed, turning to look at him. She had thought he would have asked her this long before, and she had prepared an answer. Instead, what she heard coming from her mouth was the truth, so far as she knew it:

"You are the real danger to the world, Hammer. Men like Grimwold, they are nothing. They are their own worst enemy. But you—you make people believe in things. Things that don't exist."

"Like what?"

"Like—freedom. You think you fight to keep your people free. But it doesn't work that way. The power you wield—can only enslave them to yourself."

"No one is my slave."

"That's what you think. But this is the nature of your power. You will have to use it, eventually, to control them. To *survive*. It's the only way it works." She paused. "They know it too."

"Who?"

"The bishops. That's why they need you."

He laughed. "Apparently you haven't been reading their missives. They would rather I were dead too."

"Don't believe it. You are their agent, Hammer, you work for them, even if you think you don't. You build missions and spread the gospels everywhere you conquer. And you *will* conquer everywhere. Your friend Boniface knows it. You are their greatest weapon, their tool. It is through you that the Church will rule the earth."

He stared at her, bewildered, then shook his head and sighed. "I think maybe you *are* mad," he said. He got up and started getting dressed.

"Where are you going?" she asked. It was still dark.

"I have some work to do. I'll be back in an hour. Do you want to go back to your room?"

"No."

He pulled her up from the bed and kissed her.

"You are so beautiful," he said.

She felt a silken warmth at those words.

"Marry me."

She stiffened. "You have a wife."

"Does that matter?"

"It might to your wife."

"Many men have two wives."

"Is that what you want? What many men have?"

"What difference does it make?"

She turned away from him, pulling the blankets around her body, as if in defense. "My mother was a slave," she said. "She killed herself when I was twelve. She could not bear to be a slave any longer."

"You are not a slave, Svana," Charles said tiredly. "I would marry you to prove it, if you would let me."

"I am not a slave," she said tonelessly, "except you will not let me go."

"That's the way things are."

"Why does it have to be? I didn't think you were one to play by other people's rules."

"Some rules you cannot change."

She rose up again to meet him. "Why not? You don't have to go on with this. You could leave it all. We could go far away from here, to the sea, perhaps—have you ever seen the sea? It's beautiful, magnificent, endless. We could live under the stars, I would cook your meals, we would have children, lots of children, and you can teach them to hunt and fish and take care of themselves, and we can forget about the world, and nothing else would exist, and we would be free—" She stopped herself, gasping, fearful of what she had said, realizing she had meant every word. He said nothing for a long time. She looked into his eyes, saw what she was afraid to see.

"Svana—you cannot split me apart and take only the pieces you want."

She lay back down, turning away from him. "This will end badly, Hammer."

He didn't answer her. Instead, he said in a different voice: "I'm going to Liège tomorrow."

She looked at him, genuine fear in her eyes. "Why?"

"There is someone I must see. I will be gone just a few days—what's the matter?"

"Nothing."

"Think about my offer."

"You cannot be serious—"

"I am serious. And I have an idea. I have an estate, at Quierzy on the Oise River. The Merovings had a fortress there to guard the northern approach to Paris. It's a ruin now, but the land is beautiful. I was thinking of building a house there. I would build it—for you."

She looked at him, shock and sadness in her eyes. "A Rappenzelle?" she asked, her voice hard as glass.

"No! Not a prison. A home. You need a home. We both do."

"And what would you do? Put me in your house, a caged bird, so you could come and visit me when you had the time? Once a year? How often do you see your present wife, Charles? Don't do that to me. I can be alone. I don't mind being alone. But not in a prison built by you."

He sighed. "Your options are few, Svana. I am offering you my protection, a safe place to live, and the freedom to do whatever you want. Is that not enough for you?"

She didn't answer.

Hours later she roused from sleep, feeling his body move against hers. She lay awake, pressed inside the fold of his embrace, breathing in the safety he offered, the perfect, yet perilous, peace. *Is this not enough for you*, he had said. He was bargaining with her. Giving her an alternative to her own, inevitable choice. She would be a fool to refuse.

# 40

## Liège
## November, 725

THE RIDE TO Liège was dreary and cold, even for November; a harsh, drizzly rain coated Charles and his guards as they made their way along the Roman road. Despite the weather Charles welcomed the change of scene, the peace of the road and the still countryside after the chaos of court, the belligerent nobles, the recalcitrant bishops, the impossible, unfathomable woman. He had decided to take Gunther, leaving Lothar in charge of the palace. Lothar had been furious, but Charles needed time to think, and Lothar just wanted to argue with him. Gunther was like a faithful hound, he didn't speak unless spoken to; he was quiet company. The two bodyguards Frido and Herne rode in front; Alfric, leading spare horses, brought up the rear.

It was late when Charles arrived at the Abbey of Saint-Trond, and since his visit was unannounced there was no one to receive him. He went to what looked like the abbot's house and knocked loudly on the door.

After a long time the door was opened by a tiny, scattered little monk who stared at him in shock and shuffled quickly away. A few minutes later the abbot appeared, looking slightly annoyed at being awakened, and then utterly surprised when he realized who it was standing in his antechamber. He was small and spare, with an ageless face common among monks and unruly eyebrows that curled into his eyes, making him blink continually. He quickly turned to his servant and gave precise orders for stabling the horses and bedding down the men. Then he led Charles down a hallway to a small room, which seemed to be his office.

"My lord Charles, I do apologize, but the hour is late and you were not expected."

"I know that," Charles said. "I'm sorry to get you out of bed. I need to speak to a monk named Chrodegang."

The eyebrows waggled. "Chrodegang? What do you want with him? Has he done something wrong?"

"I just want to talk to him."

"Tonight?"

"I don't have much time."

The abbot sighed. "I will have him sent for immediately."

He called in his servant to do the search, but Chrodegang, it turned out, was not in his bed. The abbot sighed again, very heavily.

"There is only one other place he would be at this hour," he said.

"The chapel?"

"No, the kitchen." The abbot managed a smile. "I'll take you to him."

"No, I'd rather go alone. Go back to bed, Father. Thank you for your help."

The kitchen was dark and smelled of fish. Charles could see a light in the passage that led to the refectory. He told Gunther and the guards to wait for him and went in alone. The light came from a single candle, from which he could make out a pleasantly fat monk with a crown of blond hair sitting at the long table alone, a leg of mutton in his mouth.

"Brother Chrodegang?"

The monk froze, mutton still locked in his teeth. He turned very slowly to see who was addressing him. Then even more slowly he set his leg of mutton back on his plate and crossed himself.

"Lord, I have sinned. I am a miserable glutton. Have mercy on me, for my weakness—" He prayed rapidly, eyes closed. Charles smiled and came into the room, setting his torch in a wall sconce.

"Relax, priest. I've not come for your soul."

The monk stopped praying, opened one eye to look at him, too frightened now to speak. Charles moved closer, into his circle of light.

"Do you know who I am?"

Chrodegang leaned toward him, peering intently. Then all at once he lurched to his feet, knocking the stool out from under him. "Mother of God!" He crossed himself. "Can it be—Lord Charles? Mother of God!"

"I need to talk to you," Charles interrupted, "on a matter of great importance. Can you spare any of that?"

Chrodegang stared at him in incomprehension. Then he looked down at the food. "Oh … yes … help yourself."

Charles sat opposite him and picked up the mutton leg, tearing off some meat. Chrodegang righted his stool and sat down, blinking, as if trying to wake himself from a bad dream.

"My prince, forgive me. I was not expecting the Leader of the Franks to sneak up on me in the middle of the night. I don't recall the abbot mentioning your visit—"

"I don't like to give advance notice of my movements."

"Ah. Very wise, I'm sure." Chrodegang nodded, breathing more easily, recovering his wits. "Well, now that we have that out of the way—what can I do for you?"

"I have a problem," Charles said. "With bishops."

"Ah … regarding your confiscation of church lands?"

Charles stared at him. "You know about this?"

"My prince, *everyone* knows. We talk of nothing else. But how did—"

"Winfrith—Bishop Boniface—recommended you to me."

"Really? Well, now. I'm flattered. I think."

"Perhaps you should tell me your position on the issue first," Charles said. "You can speak freely."

Chrodegang was silent awhile, considering his answer.

"What I think is this," he said finally. "The bishops are right to oppose you. Their job is to protect the Church from any threat to its power. You are the biggest threat to Church power since the Romans were feeding Christians to the lions. The Merovingian kings quaked at the very thought of taking on the ruling clergy. To oppose the Church is to oppose God himself. Not even the boldest king would dare do that." He paused to take a long draught of beer and then handed the mug to Charles. "The monks make the best beer in the world. They drink it on fast days, to stave off hunger. Clever, eh? After all, there is no law against *drinking* during a fast, is there?"

"So you will not help me then," Charles said, putting the mug to his lips.

"I was not quite finished, my prince. As I said, while I see the bishops' point, I also think they have made a fatal miscalculation. They believe that the Church must always override the needs of the State. But in truth, the Church can most help itself by *helping* the State. In order for the Church of Francia to be great, *Francia* must be great. Just as Rome, the center of political power, became the center of Catholic worship. So—what is their game?"

"They plan to convene a Synod."

Chrodegang's smile disappeared. "Ah, I see," he said. "So they will resort to that already? I think perhaps Eucher might be bluffing just a bit. In order to excommunicate you, he will need the backing of the Pope. And I don't believe that Gregory will cooperate. He needs you too badly, you are the only thing standing between Rome and Lombardy—and the Emperor too, for that matter. Leo wants Rome as much as Liutprand, worn out and jaded as she is. And Leo is a man of high ambition, bless his barbarian soul. He has already started a war with the Church with his banning of icons. Rome has no ruler anymore, nor does it have an army. Rome has few protectors. The Pope would not want to make them angry."

Chrodegang paused to take back his mug and down another gulp. He smacked his lips in satisfaction. "Where were we?"

"Bishops."

"Right. Well—as I see it, you might have a legal right to the land that was beneficed to the bishops, though they will argue the point to death that the land was beneficed not to the bishops themselves, but to the Church. Whether or not that is strictly true, they could muster enough sympathy from the populace to force you to back down. The Church will always have the support of the people, my lord, no matter how popular their ruler. That's why you must be very careful how you proceed. What else did they try to throw at you?"

"Brunhilde's edict," Charles said.

Chrodegang threw back his head, snorting with laughter.

"No, really? My goodness, I didn't think anyone remembered that one. Poor Brunhilde, she was getting desperate then, but after all she was running out of grandsons. You can't really blame her for trying to raise the dead."

They were interrupted by footsteps. Gunther peered into the room, sword drawn, along with Frido, Herne and Alfric.

"What, more warriors?" Chrodegang said.

"My men."

"God in heaven, have they not eaten either? My dear Lord Charles, why didn't you say so in the first place? Tell them to come in. I know where Brother Jonah keeps the meat. He has a special hiding place; that is why he is the only man in this abbey who is fatter than I am. Come in! Come in!"

Chrodegang set about bringing in more platters of food and pitchers of beer. Once the men were seated and eating properly, he returned to his place by Charles.

"You should have told me they were waiting for you," he said.

"They are used to waiting for me."

"So that is how it is to work for you, eh?"

"Yes. So will you come and work for me?"

Chrodegang eyed the warriors at the end of the table. "As long as you feed me better than you feed them," he said. "I don't operate well on an empty stomach. It is perhaps the reason I have been such a failure as a monk."

"When can you come to Kolonia?"

"I will ride with you tomorrow."

"What about Bishop Sigebert?"

"He is your servant, as am I. We will send him a letter. He may not be happy, but don't worry, I will make him think that I am a kind of double agent, that he will now have eyes and ears at court. He will like that. He's all about the intrigue, Sigebert."

"Then I will make you my chancellor," Charles said. "Your job is to keep the bishops quiet, and happy, if that is possible."

The fat monk looked pleased. "Happy, I cannot promise, but quiet, I believe I can. It all hinges on Eucher. The council will sway to him. I did find it curious, I must admit, that you did not just—remove him, as you have others who have opposed your rule."

Charles sighed ruefully. "I thought he was an honest man, sincere in his faith."

"Hah! He is most certainly honest and sincere, which does not make him any less dangerous. But I will talk to him. We will have a pleasant chat. We will come to an understanding, don't worry. You'll need to give him something, I will tell you what that is later. Once Eucher sees the light, the rest will follow. Besides, there are always things that people, even bishops, don't want the world to know."

"Secrets?"

"Oh, indeed." Glancing again at the other men, Chrodegang leaned forward and whispered: "You'd be surprised how many of our august clergy have a fondness for young boys—and girls—I believe one of your own followers is the son of a bishop?"

"I didn't think anyone knew about that."

"You are too much the innocent. Such knowledge, however, is very useful."

"Something tells me, Chrodegang, that I should be grateful you choose to be on my side."

Chrodegang raised his cup of beer and grinned. "To Francia," he said.

They left the abbey the next morning. The rain had abated, but the monk's overloaded pack mule made the going slow. They stopped for the night at a small compound called Aquis Villa, once a Roman bathhouse now used mainly as a guard post that housed relief horses for passing scouts. Chrodegang, stuffed with food and beer, told stories late into the night, keeping his audience entertained.

"My favorite is the one about old King Radbod—King of the Frisians—a crusty pagan to the last! After one nasty war with Pipin Herstal, in which he lost, as usual, he finally agreed to be baptized as part of the terms of surrender—that crazy missionary Willibrord had been after him for years! But with one foot in the baptismal font, he asked, 'Where are my ancestors who have gone before me?' to whit Willibrord told him, 'They are in hell with all non-believers!' At that, the old king removed his foot from the font and said, 'I would rather feast in the Hall of Odin that wallow in heaven with those fasting little Christians of yours!'" He laughed until tears streamed down his face, and the rest joined in.

They were awakened at first light by shouting in the courtyard: a messenger from Kolonia on a blown horse. Charles went outside to meet him.

"Badilo," he said, recognizing him. "What are you doing here?"

The boy nearly fell from the saddle. "My lord," he said, dropping to his knees, as if fearing he would be punished for his news. "Kolonia has been attacked."

Charles stared at him. "Who?"

"Bavarians," said the messenger breathlessly. "A small group, but organized. They took the palace, they are holding hostages—"

"They took the *palace*?" Charles stared at the boy in disbelief.

"Lothar believes they had help from inside. From the—" he paused, clearly nervous, "—the woman."

Gunther came out of the house, weaving slightly, the after effects of the previous night's drinking.

"What's going on?"

Charles turned to him, his eyes diamond bright. "Mount up. We are leaving at once." He shouted for Alfric.

"Leaving so soon?" Chrodegang stood in the doorway.

Charles glanced at him. "There is trouble in Kolonia. We must leave now. You can follow later."

"I think I should come with you."

"Can you keep up?"

Chrodegang nodded. Gone was the cheery buffoonery of the night before. "Lend me a horse. I'll leave my baggage behind. Someone can bring it along later."

"Fine. Let's go then."

# 41

THE CITY WAS quiet. Charles, entering through the south gate, could feel something charged, volatile in the unnaturally empty streets, could see people peering from windows, watching him pass, crossing themselves. He kicked Epone to the trot. Gunther and the two guards rode ahead of him, leading the way, forcing anyone who dared to be out back inside their houses.

The palace courtyard spilled over with soldiers gathered around small fires, trying to keep warm. The palace itself looked dark, deserted.

"That bitch of yours. She did this."

Lothar stood before him, his face a portrait of suppressed fury. Charles slid from his exhausted horse. They had ridden hard all day. He faced Lothar, his voice low, taut, his expression carefully neutral.

"Tell me what happened."

"They were disguised as fruit vendors. The rams at the gate never checked their load. There were a hundred carts coming in that day. It was market day—"

"Who are *they*?"

Lothar hesitated a moment. "The leader calls himself Odilo, son of Grimwold."

Charles stared at him. "You told me he was dead."

"He *was* dead! I saw his body—"

"But you did not see his head."

Lothar spat angrily.

"Where were you when this happened?"

"Hunting," Lothar said tightly. "Most of us were hunting. I was gone barely three hours."

"How many of them are there?"

"I don't know! No one saw anything. By the time I got here it was all over."

"They have hostages?"

"Yes.Two dozen at least. Einhard is in there. And the count of the palace. And the parish priest. Servants …"

"Guards?"

Lothar shook his head. "All dead, I think."

Charles sighed. *All dead.* "Has this Odilo said anything?"

"Only that he will kill the hostages if the doors are breached."

*Odilo.* Charles knew almost nothing about him. Grimwold's son, Svana's cousin. But something more than a cousin? Why would he risk his life to rescue her, if it were not so? Had she passed information to this man, about Charles' movements and those of his men? About where the guards of the palace were stationed, and when the watches changed? She would have known these things. She sat by her window day after day, watching the activity in the courtyard. She would have known—everything.

Charles turned from Lothar and walked toward the main doors, the crowd parting before him. He drew his sword and set it point down on the ground.

"I want to speak to Odilo, son of Grimwold," he shouted.

There was no answer. He saw no movement from the windows. He shouted again. Finally, a voice came from within, though no face appeared.

"Give me your word you will not attack if I come out."

He scanned the windows but could see no one.

"I give you my word."

"Clear the courtyard of your soldiers."

Charles told Lothar to clear the courtyard.

"This is madness!" Lothar ranted.

"Do as I say. Stay alert. I will give you a signal if I need your help."

Charles waited until the soldiers had moved to the perimeter. He wondered where Svana was. Was she there, with this man, watching? Gloating, perhaps? Had she played him to get his trust? He had offered to marry her, to give her a house, to protect her. And she had refused him. Had this been the reason? He shook his head. He could not think about that. It would only distract him from what he had to do now.

After awhile the main door of the palace opened a crack, and a young man stepped out waving a piece of white cloth over his head with great enthusiasm. He carried a torch. He wore a plain brown tunic overlain with a leather vest. He stopped a few paces away from Charles and smiled casually.

"Things really do run amuck around here when you leave, my lord."

Charles took in the impish smile, the calculating eyes, the pleasant, handsome face framed in curly dark hair. He said nothing. Odilo grew visibly nervous under the scrutiny.

"I am Odilo, son of Grimwold." He held out his hand to show Charles his ring. "Sorry about that pretending to be dead business. I switched tunics with some poor headless ram. An old trick, but never fails." He grinned, waited. Finally, Charles spoke.

"What do you want?"

"Only one thing. That you free the Lady Svanahilda."

Charles was silent.

"In exchange, I will return your palace to you. Along with the hostages." Odilo smiled winningly.

"You did all this," Charles said slowly, "for—a woman?"

"Well, Svana is no ordinary woman, as I am sure you realize."

Charles let a moment pass, then said: "What are your terms?"

"Give us safe passage, in writing, with your seal, and fifty horses with supplies enough for the journey. And shall we say—two hundred deniers? That shouldn't be too difficult for you to muster in a hurry. I will even take Merovingian coin, though it is nearly useless in most parts of the world these days. What can I say? I am a reasonable man, as you are, my lord. No one else needs to die because of this."

Charles glanced up at the windows, his gaze caught by sudden motion, a flash of light. The flame of a torch, and then a woman's face, *her* face. He saw her hand appear on the window's outer ledge, her fingers splayed. Odilo turned to look up at the window as well.

"What is she to you?" Charles asked, still watching the window. He saw Svana's fingers close then reopen, spread on the dark stone.

Odilo regarded him thoughtfully. "She is my cousin," he said softly. "Why do you ask? Did you think we were lovers?" He laughed. "Well, I did ask her to marry me. Several times, in fact. She always refused. Wants to give herself to the church or some such nonsense. Can you imagine a greater waste of womanhood than that?"

"How many hostages do you have?"

"That would not be quite fair if I told you, would it? But they have been treated gently, even the women, so far."

Charles glanced up again at the window. He could still see her hand resting on the sill, though her face was in shadow. He was glad. He raised his voice. "How many horses do you require?"

Odilo looked annoyed at the question. "I believe I said fifty," he said. "And the writ of safe passage, signed and sealed."

"That will take some time," Charles said. "The writ will have to be drawn up, and the clerics are ten miles away in Gladingen."

"No matter, I will have the priest write it, and I will send it out for your seal."

"I'll need time to assemble the supplies. And the money."

"You have until dawn. Then I start tossing your people off the battlements." Odilo's face momentarily lost its amused expression. "It would not be a pretty sight, would it? Of course, you could storm the palace. But we will kill the hostages if the doors are even breached, not to mention the inevitable loss of your own men, and for what? A woman. One woman. Is she worth such a price?"

Charles glanced up again at the window. The hand was gone.

"Send out your writ and I will sign it," he said with a tired sigh.

Odilo, somewhat surprised and more than a little relieved, inclined his head. "Thank you, my lord. You've made the right decision, I promise you. Your reputation for wisdom is well-deserved." He turned and disappeared into the palace, the doors heaving shut behind him.

Charles glanced up once more at the darkened tower, then turned to face the men who gathered around him.

"Fifty horses!" Lothar spat out. "Can he really have fifty men in there?"

"No," Charles said. "He has twenty."

"Twenty! How do you know that?"

"She told me." He remembered her fingers opening and closing. Four times she had done that. "He wants us to think he has fifty."

"Why would she give him away to you?" Lothar said. "Perhaps it is a trick."

"It could be. But I don't think so."

"How do you know that? You trust her so much? Charles! Don't be a fool—"

Gunther cut him off.

"We cannot give him what he wants."

"I know that."

"Then we storm the doors," Lothar said. "If there are only twenty of them, it will take no time at all."

"No," Charles said. "They will kill the hostages. We need to get inside without them knowing."

"But how?"

"The tunnel."

The men stared at Charles in incomprehension.

"What tunnel?" Lothar demanded.

"This city was a Roman stronghold, built to withstand a siege. There was an aqueduct that brought water into the city and the palace through an underground tunnel. The tunnel is still intact—mostly—and big enough for a man to crawl through."

"How do you get to it?" Gunther asked.

"There's an access well outside the walls, by the south gate."

"Why have you never told us about this before?" Lothar demanded.

"I did not imagine a use for it," Charles answered. "I was planning to have it filled, as it made the palace vulnerable. Now, it might prove useful after all."

"I'll go," Gunther said.

"You are too big. Lothar will go. Take the smallest men you can find. The tunnel may be collapsed in places, so bring picks and a shovel."

"Where does it lead?" said Lothar.

"To the kitchens. From there you will have to gain access into the palace by whatever means necessary and find the hostages. My guess is they are in the armory; that is the only room inside the palace that can be locked and easily defended. Once you have secured the hostages, get the doors open and we will do the rest. And Lothar, I want the woman taken alive. Do you understand?" Charles glared at Lothar, who glared back.

"What if she resists?"

"I want her taken alive."

"And the leader?"

"Do what you need to do."

Lothar turned away and began shouting for men. Charles turned to Gunther. "Start gathering horses and wagons. Make it look good. And bring in every man from the castrum, but keep them hidden for now."

They went to work. There was a lot of shouting, Gunther bellowing orders loudly, guards attempting to clear the courtyard. Chrodegang, the only one left, made a noise in his throat. Charles turned to look at him.

"Well," said the fat monk, rubbing his stomach absent-mindedly, "this is quite a way to begin my service to you, I must say. Anything you want me to do?"

"Do you have any advice for me?"

Chrodegang chuckled under his breath. "Well, I'm not sure there is much I can offer. You handled the—negotiation—quite well, I think. And that young man—he believed you completely."

"Did he?"

"Oh my yes. Men believe what they want to believe. But you know this already, don't you? Truly my lord Charles, I'm not sure you really need me at all."

"I don't have much of a gift for speaking to bishops."

"Ah, well. That is a special talent, I admit. So this woman—she is valuable to you?"

Charles hesitated, off-guard. "What makes you think so?"

Chrodegang shrugged. "Because you are a practical man, Charles, and you would not go through all of this trouble for a woman you cared nothing about. And by the way, I saw what she did."

"Did you?"

"It's my nature, to be curious. I do a lot of penance for my curious nature. I believe God has given us weaknesses on purpose, so that we don't begin to think too much of ourselves. Don't you agree?"

"I've never thought about it."

"Yes, well … perhaps He has not given you quite as many as the rest of us." Chrodegang laughed. "All men have their blind spots, don't they? The key is to know where they are and take advantage—am I right?"

"You are full of sage words. But not very useful ones."

"Ah, I am new to this job still. Just getting my feet wet."

Charles smiled grimly. "Why don't you start by going to the church and praying for us? And get some supper, while you are at it."

"Supper? Who can think of food at a time like this?" The fat monk chuckled. "No rest for the weary, eh? I have known you only two days, and I am already worn out. What does that bode for our future, my prince?"

"You will learn to keep up."

"I rely upon God who gives me strength in all things."

# 42

SVANA WAS STOKING the embers in the brazier when Odilo returned. There had been no wood or coal since the Bavarians had arrived. All the servants, except for the cook, had been locked up. Freddy sat in a corner, wrapped in a blanket, shivering with cold and fear.

"He took my offer, can you believe it?" Odilo went to the wine table and poured the last drop of wine into a cup. He drank it, sucking it dry. "Isn't there any more wine in this palace? You there," he pointed to Freddy, "go and get some wine."

"You do not order her about," Svana said. "Get one of your men to wait on you."

"My men have better things to do," Odilo snapped. "Did you even hear what I said out there?"

"Yes, I heard," she said without looking at him. "I could not help but hear."

"Well, what do you think?"

"I think you are a fool."

Odilo's face fell. "What do you mean?"

"You gave him until dawn."

"So?"

"That is too much time."

"He needed time to gather supplies—"

"You should have given him an hour. He has more than five hours now."

"And what can he accomplish in five hours? Svana, you worry too much."

"And you worry too little."

"Look! You can see from here they are assembling the supplies!"

Odilo was at the window, looking down on the courtyard. Svana felt like screaming. She rose and went to stand by him, whispering harshly so Freddy wouldn't hear.

"Since you have so much time, you need to prepare for battle. Barricade the doors. Stockpile your weapons. Get your men posted. You need to cover the windows—" She saw he was not even listening. She grabbed his arm so he would face her, made him look into her eyes. "Do you really imagine he's going to give in without a fight?"

"Relax, cousin! If he were going to attack he would have done it already. Why wait? He likes to attack when the enemy is unprepared. Svana, he's not going to fight. I saw it in his eyes! He gave me everything I asked for."

She practically screamed. "How can you be so blind? Do you really believe that Charles Martel is going to let us walk out of this place alive—" she stopped, biting her lip, looking away.

"What's the matter with you? What are you trying to tell me?"

"I'm trying to save your damned life," she said through gritted teeth. "Please Odilo, I beg you. Give yourself up. There is still time to surrender. He won't kill you. He'll probably just send you home with your tail between your legs."

Odilo regarded her with new eyes.

"And what about you?" he asked softly, stepping close to her, inches from her face. "Will he let you go with me?"

She did not answer. She turned her head, could not look him in the face.

"So," he said slowly, "I am too late, after all."

Still, she did not speak.

"He has already made you his concubine," he went on with quiet fury. "For that, I shall have to kill him."

"Don't be ridiculous," she said, her eyes snapping to his. "You do not kill a man like that. You beg for his mercy."

"Did you do that then?" Odilo asked coldly, moving on her, forcing her backward. "After you were captured? Did you beg for his mercy? Or was it something else you begged for?"

She raised a hand to slap him; he grabbed it in the air, held it fast, his eyes beating into hers. He spoke in a low growl, like a dog baring his teeth, his face so close to hers she could feel the touch of his lips against her cheek.

"There was a time when you wanted nothing but vengeance on the Franks. Now you are that man's whore. If I did not know otherwise, I would think you actually had—*feelings* for him. You think he cares so much about you, that he would risk his soldiers and those hostages for you? I think not. You are an amusement to him. A conquest. Nothing more." He dropped her arm, pushing her away, and went back to the wine table. He picked up the carafe, seemed to remember it was empty, and threw it across the room. It shattered against the wall, shards of clay flying everywhere. Freddy shrieked.

Svana stood still, breathing against the coiling knot in her chest, amazed at how much his words had hurt. Finally, Odilo turned to her, his face sagging, contrite.

"Svana, I'm sorry. I know you have been through hell. I am sorry for what has happened to you. But it's almost over. Trust me. Tomorrow, we will be free." He went to her, took her hands and kissed them, holding them together. "We will both be free."

She saw that he believed this absolutely. "I hope you are right."

# 43

LOTHAR WAS NOT happy. The tunnel, over three hundred years old, was in worse shape than he expected. Several areas had collapsed and his men had to spend precious minutes digging out debris to get through. They often had to crawl on hands and knees, scraping their skin raw on the crumbling stones. Rancid water made the air fetid and stale, rats skittered around their legs. Lothar could not go ten paces without banging his head on a timber beam overhead and swearing colorfully each time. The tunnel twisted and turned with the pattern of the rock, sometimes so narrow they could barely squeeze through sideways. Their torches went out after the first few minutes, so they had to feel their way in the dark with only a small lantern to guide them.

At last they reached an opening where the tunnel widened into a dry well. Lothar shone the lantern around until he made out a wooden trap door built into the ceiling.

"This better be it," he whispered hoarsely. He ordered the men to stand on top of each other. They balanced precariously while Lothar nimbly climbed up their legs and backs until he was within reach. Carefully, he pushed at the door, which gave way with a creak, sending a shower of dust and dirt down on his head. He swore silently, pushing the door all the way open and hoisting himself onto the dusty floor.

Rats scurried, a dog raised its head and whimpered. He stood up, stretching his aching muscles, and looked around. He sniffed and made a face; the air was redolent of sour wine and onions. This was definitely the kitchen. He heard a sound like a snore and whirled to see the cook collapsed on a table, one hand still clutching a jar of mead. The central fire pit sat cold; the stupid man had fallen asleep and failed to keep it lit. Scraps of food and empty wine flagons littered every surface, more trash was spewed on the floor.

Lothar turned back to the opening in the floor and crouched down. One of the men below threw him a rope, which he used to pull the three others up with him into the kitchen. The cook continued to snore.

Lothar told them to wait and moved stealthily toward the slumbering cook. He drew his scramsax and grabbed the man by the hair, whipping his head back and holding the blade to his neck. The cook flailed, knocking over a jar of mead.

"If you make even one squeal I will cut through your gullet," Lothar said. The frightened man nodded, not breathing. Lothar loosened his hold only slightly. The cook sucked in a breath, his face red as a sausage.

"I don't know anything—"

"Shut up. Where are they keeping the hostages?" Lothar demanded.

The man stammered, sweat pouring down his face. "In the—armory, I think. I don't know for sure. They keep me here to do the cooking. The door is barred and guarded …"

Lothar glared at the door, as if he could will himself to see what lay on the other side. He knew it led to a narrow passageway that went directly into the main hall of the palace.

"How many guarding the door?"

"Only one I've seen."

Lothar nodded to one of his men.

"Thorn," he whispered. He indicated the door. Thorn, a baby-faced young man with a slim build, nodded and, pulling a dagger from his belt, crept toward the door as silently as a cat.

"Call for him," Lothar said to the cook, his blade still nestled in the folds of the man's neck. The other two men moved into the darkness, drawing their scramsaxes. The cook called out something unintelligible. They heard the scrape of a bar being removed. Then the door opened and a sleepy Bavarian appeared.

"What do you want—?"

Thorn stepped in behind him, grabbed him by the neck and swiftly slit his throat. The man fell silently, mouth working with no sound. Thorn peeled off the man's tunic and pulled it over his own head. Lothar dropped his hold on the cook and moved to the door, stepping over the dying man. He signaled to the rest of them to follow him and stepped out into the passage. Patches of dove gray light filtered down through the holes in the thatch above. Lothar swore to himself. It was already past dawn.

They slipped into the hall, hearing voices, a man shouting angrily. Lothar halted his team to listen.

"When did you send out the writ?" said the angry man, no doubt Odilo.

"Three hours ago."

"Damn it! Why hasn't it been returned? The time is up. Get the priest and meet me on the battlements. Once the Franks see one of their priests splattered on the stones in the courtyard they will know I am serious."

Lothar realized he had only seconds to act. He slithered along the wall, keeping in the shadow of the balcony. They reached a corner where a hallway jutted off toward the back of the palace and took the steps down to the underground armory. Lothar stopped at the bottom and took a shallow breath. Then he nodded to Thorn, who signaled down the line. Three of them fanned out over the entrance. They crept toward the armory door.

An oil lamp revealed a single Bavarian standing guard. Stupid, Lothar thought. These men were rams. The guard straightened when he saw Thorn approaching but did not draw a weapon. He yawned.

"Are you here for the priest—?" That was a far as he got, before Thorn's knife met his throat. His mouth gaped open. Thorn guided him gently to the floor. He pulled out the blade and wiped it on his tunic.

"What is this?"

Lothar spun around at the new voice, saw two more Bavarians coming down the steps. He threw a franca, catching one of them in the chest. The other whirled, alarmed, but before he could fumble for a weapon Gordo lodged a scramsax in his belly. Both men slumped on the steps, one on top of the other. Gordo drew out his blade and retrieved the dead men's weapons, returning the bloody franca to Lothar.

"Rams," Lothar whispered disgustedly, stuffing the franca back in his belt. "One of them has the key. Open the damned door."

Thorn found the key wrapped around the second guard's neck. He handed it to Lothar, who fitted it in the lock. A great commotion arose from the other side as the hostages realized the door was opening.

"Shut up!" Lothar hissed at them. The hostages gazed at him in terror, unsure whether he was their rescuer or their destroyer. He grabbed the lantern, slipped past Thorn and went inside.

The room smelled like a slops pot. Women whimpered, shrieked. The servants huddled together. Lothar glanced around, saw that the weapons had all been removed.

A man approached whom Lothar recognized as Dorian, count of the palace.

"Lothar! Thank God—"

"Quiet," said Lothar sharply. "Are there any guards here?"

"No, I'm afraid. They were all killed … "

Lothar swore again. "I need the priest."

"What?" The count looked confused. "But I thought … "

"Shut up and bring me the priest."

The count sighed and called for the priest. A round man with the purple stained fingers of a cleric was brought before Lothar.

"*Gloria Patri, et Filio, et Spiritui Sancto* …" the priest prayed rapidly, quaking with fear.

"Shut up," Lothar barked at him. He glanced over the men in the room. "You and you," he said, pointing to the youngest and strongest looking among them. "You will guard this door. Use the Bavarians' weapons. If anyone tries to come here, kill them."

"But—"

"Just do it. No questions." He dragged the babbling priest out of the armory. "Gordo, put on one of those tunics. You and Thorn will come with me. You, Baudoin, is it? When you hear the signal, get to the doors and get them open."

"What is the signal?"

"Bavarian scum dying." Lothar turned to the priest. "We are taking you to the battlements. You can scream if you wish. Make it look real. If your God is with you, then you won't get thrown off and smashed into pieces."

"Please forgive me, Father," said Gordo nervously.

"*Sancte Michael Archangele, defende nos in proelio; contra nequitiam et insidias diaboli esto praesidium. Imperat illi Deus* …" the priest prayed the prayer of protection to the Archangel in blubbering gasps.

"Take him," Lothar said in a harsh whisper. "I will follow behind. Don't let the others see your faces. Get up the stairs quickly. We will kill the leader, the one called Odilo. You all saw him last night, didn't you? Hopefully that will draw the others to the stairs, and give Baudoin a chance to open the doors. Understood?"

All the men nodded in unison. Gordo and Thorn hauled the priest up the steps and through the hall, keeping their heads down and pretending to struggle with their captive who bellowed very convincingly. In truth, the priest was probably not sure that the intractable heathen Lothar would not throw him off the battlements just for the fun of it.

The men guarding the door glanced at them curiously but did not seem alarmed. They made it to the main stairway and were halfway up when another man barred their way.

"Ren … is that you—" The man stopped in mid-sentence, staring at Thorn. "Ach!" he shouted loudly. He reached for his sword but Thorn beat him to it, hurling a franca into his belly. The man shrieked and fell down the stairs. Below, the sleepy Bavarians who'd been lounging at the trestle tables looked up, alert, a few rising to their feet, grabbing weapons.

"Damn," Lothar said from behind. "Change of plans." He drew his sword, the shorter, broader scramsax in the other hand, and his men did the same, arraying themselves shoulder to shoulder on the steps. Gordo shoved the priest down, begging forgiveness.

"Come and get us, Bavarian rams!" Lothar screamed. He hoped Baudoin was listening. It was three against ten at least, but the Bavarians would have to fight while balancing backwards on the steps.

The Bavarians took the bait, surging up the stairs, brandishing their thick swords and cudgels. Weapons clanged together, the shriek of steel against the duller grinding of iron. Lothar and his men fought seamlessly, stepping back with each turn of the sword, drawing their opponents farther up the stairs. Lothar shouted at them, insulting their mothers and their entire race, keeping an eye on the main doors below. What was taking Baudoin so damned long? Lothar met a Bavarian sword with both his own blades at once, crisscrossed in front of him, then shoved his attacker in the chest with his boot, sending him hurtling down the steps with a mighty roar, taking three more men with him. *He must have heard that.*

Finally, a bright light swept over the hall. The Bavarians stopped fighting and turned, confused, seeing the great doors opening. Frankish warriors poured in, screaming their battle cries. The Bavarians froze in panic.

"Look out!"

Lothar ducked as an axe flew over his head. He turned to see more men coming from the upper landing. "Get them!" he yelled to Gordo and Thorn, who raced up the steps to face this new threat. The men below them had turned to run down the steps, hoping for an escape, perhaps, but there was no way out. The hall was teeming with Frankish warriors. The Bavarians fought back anyway, though they had no chance of survival, let alone retreat. It would be over quickly. Lothar knew he had only a few minutes. He turned from the fighting and raced up the stairs.

# 44

SVANA PULLED HER bow out from under her mattress.

"Where did you get that?" Freddy whispered.

"Never mind. You need to hide now. Quickly."

"Why? What's happening?"

Svana paused, listening to the sound of battle below, the ring of steel, the blood-laced screams. She looked at her maid, who was huddled in a corner of the room, shivering.

"Charles is here."

"He got in?"

"Of course he got in."

Svana strung the arrow, tested the string. Freddy watched in horror.

"What are you going to do? Are you going to help that man?"

"I'm going to try."

"But why?"

"Odilo did a very foolish thing, but he did it for me."

"But Charles—"

"Charles can take care of himself."

The door burst open. Odilo stood there, shaking. Svana whirled and looked at him, her heart racing, the bow, still strung, pointed at the floor.

"How did they get in?" Odilo said in a trembling voice. *"How did they get in?"*

"I don't know."

"You are lying! You knew all along!"

Svana swallowed, watching him, clenching the bow. "I told you he would get in. I told you he would not give in without a fight."

"You told me—nothing!" Odilo swore in despair. "I loved you Svana. I would have died for you. I went to war for you. And you … betrayed me … "

"Odilo—"

*"Stop!"* he shouted. He took a breath, drawing himself up. He spoke again, his voice an abyss. "I am dead now, I know it. But I will not let him have you, Svana. I'm sorry, but I won't."

He drew his sword and advanced on her. Freddy screamed in terror. Svana raised the bow.

"Don't take another step." She drew back the arrow, the weakened muscles in her shoulder shaking with the effort. The bow wavered. "Odilo, please. It's not too late. Just surrender. Lay down your sword and he will spare your life. I promise—"

Odilo laughed harshly. He took another step toward her. And then another. "You aren't going to shoot me, my swan. You can't do it. I love you, remember? You love me too—"

"Yes, I love you, Odilo. But that doesn't mean I won't kill you. I have killed many things I have loved." She struggled to keep the bow level, the pain ripping down her arm.

"You don't know what you're saying—"

"Well, isn't this sweet?"

Both of them turned to see Lothar leaning casually in the doorway, his arms crossed. He was covered in mud and dust and blood, though his blue eyes gleamed with a particular, feral light. His swords were sheathed.

"But you aren't going to kill her. I am." He looked, to Svana, as if he were about to explode, yet he maintained a veneer of utter calm. This was Lothar at his most dangerous. But Odilo did not see it. He turned on this new threat, advancing slowly, his sword at the ready.

"Odilo, no! Stop!"

He ignored her. There was a moment of poised stillness, of two men frozen, of a decision that had to be made by one or the other. Odilo made it, lunging forward, his sword thrusting toward Lothar's unprotected chest. But then Lothar was not where he had been; the sword slipped past him, and he met the forward momentum of Odilo's body, grabbing his head and twisting it with terrifying strength. There was a sickening sound, like a tree limb being ripped from the trunk, and Odilo hung suspended a moment, a look of utter surprise on his face. Lothar let go, and the body fell, the head cocked at a cruel angle. Freddy wailed. Svana closed her eyes and moaned softly.

Lothar stepped over the body and came toward her. She knew he would not give her such a quick death. He would make her suffer, as he had wanted to do from the beginning. She let the bow fall to the floor.

He grabbed hold of her neck with one hand, nearly lifting her off her feet. His strength was unimaginable, born of cold hatred. She closed her eyes, feeling the blood drain from her face, the air run out of her body. Her throat burned, the light dimmed; she could not feel the floor under her feet. From somewhere she heard Freddy screaming.

Then she heard another voice, cutting through the unfurling blackness.

"Let her go."

She collapsed to the floor, struggled to breathe through her crushed windpipe. Black dots burst in her vision, exploding into white stars. She fought to stay conscious, registering the voices above her.

"I told you she was to be taken alive." Charles' voice was a low hiss, as angry as she had ever heard him.

"She's a murderer, Charles! She was going to kill you as soon as you walked in the door—"

"Listen to me now, Lothar. This woman is my concern, mine alone. If any harm comes to her, any at all, I will hold you personally responsible."

"Are you *mad?*"

"You are her keeper now."

There were no more words. Svana opened her eyes, saw the two men staring at each other, nose to nose. Charles' sword was drawn but lowered. Lothar's face was a jumble of shock and outrage. They stood there a long moment. Then Lothar turned in silence and walked out the door.

Svana lowered her head, closing her eyes. She heard the heavy scuffle of boots and Charles giving terse orders for the disposal of the body and the removal of the whimpering maid to the servants' quarters. The noises faded eventually. She waited. But he did not come to her.

She was breathing again, though every breath cost her something; her throat ached as if Lothar's fingers still gripped it. She did not look at him, though she knew he was still in the room, his unleashed fury vibrating through her very bones.

"Was this your plan?" he asked finally, his voice like shattered glass.

"No," she said. Her own voice sounded as though it belonged to someone else, strained and tattered, a voice in ruins. She pulled herself to a sitting position.

"But you knew what he was planning. The beggar told you."

"You knew about that?"

"My guards tell me everything."

She nodded slowly. "I sent him a message—I told him to wait. That I would come to him when it was safe."

"When I was gone, you mean?"

His voice was so cold it made her shiver.

"I was going to escape. I knew I could outrun your guards when I was riding. But I didn't—he did not wait for me."

"So … you loved him?"

She licked her lips, the pain of each breath seeping into the edges of her being. She knew her life was in the balance, but suddenly she did not care anymore. She would tell him the truth, because it was all she had left to give him.

"Yes, I loved him. He was like a brother to me. We grew up together. He would have done anything for me. He came to rescue me."

"And yet you gave him away to me."

She let out a low sob. "I did want to destroy you, Hammer. You were everything I hated in the world. War. Power. The Church. Slavery. I had seen too much of it. I wanted Bavaria to be free of you. I was even willing to let my lying, murdering, scum of an uncle have it—" She stopped, the air run out, waiting for her breath, her voice, to return. "Odilo loved me, stood at my side, had come to save me. And I betrayed him. For you. Because … I love you, Charles. And love is the exception to every rule."

She felt desolate, drained. She wanted to lie down and sleep for a hundred years, sleep until she could not remember anymore. It was a long time before he spoke again.

"You will get your wish then." His voice was full of grief. "You'll have to leave Francia. I'll give you the safe passage your cousin died trying to get for you."

She looked at him, her wide, black eyes startled, fearful. He looked like a man facing his own execution. "Where will you send me?"

"Where do you want to go?"

She turned away, glancing toward the window, streams of light touching down on the floor. Light. How long the night had been. "To the sea," she said finally. She looked at him again, saw the fear in his eyes as well. She had lived once by the sea, in Constantinople. But she could never go back there. She was running out of places to hide.

"The sea," he said. Hadn't she told him this dream of hers, before he left for Liège, before their world came apart? She had wanted him to go with her. But he had refused. He was locked in his destiny, and she could not change that. "I'll arrange your transport. You must leave at first light tomorrow. It won't be safe for you here. Not anymore."

He left her alone.

He returned many hours later. It was well past sunset, the room had grown dark and cold. Svana sat on the small stool by the unlit brazier as if trying to glean any bit of warmth it may have left. She was shivering violently. Her throat still ached. She did not look at him. He picked her up and carried her to the bed. He laid her down, gently, as if she were a wounded child. He hovered over her, uncertain, and she could see the long sleepless day in his eyes, the dead men littering his feasting hall, the immutable ache in the pit of his soul. He moved as if to leave and she stopped him, her hand folding over his. He gave in then, pulling her hand to his mouth, his body collapsing. She pulled him down on top of her, holding him hard against her body. They lay like that a long time before he moved against her, pulling away her clothes, holding her as a drowning man clutches for the safety of the sand.

They clung to each other after, knowing that letting go would be like falling from a great height into the darkest pit. They slept and woke again and it started over, and neither of them knew where their waking ended and their dreams began.

They lay pressed together, his face nestled against her breasts, her arms cradling his head. She could hear him inhale, slowly, breathing her in, as if taking her body into his aching lungs.

"Are they all dead?" she asked in the darkness. "All of them?"

"Yes."

Her body lurched, as if run through with a sword. "Charles—I tried to stop him. You have to believe me—"

"I believe you." He leaned up on his elbows to look at her. "I wanted to hate you." His fingers traced the purple bruise on her neck. She winced, shut her eyes, trying to push it away, the horror of it. But she would never escape it, she knew. Waking or dreaming, it would be there, ever-present.

"How do you do it?" she whispered. "How do you—sleep? Eat? Breathe? How do you go on?"

"You just do. You have no choice."

She looked at his face, his eyes still burning, as if with a fever.

"Don't be too hard on him," she said softly. "He was trying to protect you."

"I shouldn't have trusted him. I know what he is capable of."

"Is it any worse than what you, yourself, are capable of?"

He didn't answer. She gazed up at the ceiling, the swirling patterns in the dark, weathered wood, studying the cracks and whorls as if this alone would help her to forget this night. She could not imagine what would happen now, where she would go, how she would live. She did not think she wanted to live at all. But the mere fact of his existence in the world made it impossible for her to die.

She felt his lips on hers, silencing her anguish.

When she awoke in the morning she was alone, her breastplate and bow lying on the side of the bed where he had been.

# 45

## Paris
## December, 725

THE PALACE AT Paris was decorated for Christmas in pine boughs and holly, with thousands of candles filling the long tables of the feasting hall and hanging on the huge, iron chandeliers. Rotruda greeted Charles happily, pleased he had decided to join his family for the feast. She had dressed herself like a Roman goddess in a shimmering silk gold dalmatica with a belt of small gold plates hinged around her neck and waist. Her golden hair was bound up and covered in an Imperial-style headroll from which strands of tiny pearls dangled like delicate drops of rain. She looked like a statue of herself, a sculpted icon cast in gold, beautiful and expensive, an object of worship. She sat quietly at the high table next to Charles, feeling the eyes of every man—and woman—in the vast hall upon her. All eyes, that is, but her husband's.

After the feast she invited Charles and Lothar to her sitting room. Lothar's presence eased the strain between them; he entertained the boys, playing Kings with a set of wooden playing pieces old Einhard had whittled for Charles when he was a boy. Charles had brought them to his sons as a gift, which pleased Rotruda enormously.

Pipin regaled them with stories of his adventures at school. "The other boys used to tease me because I'm so small," he announced, "then one day I climbed the tallest tree and went out on the smallest limb and I stood there and yelled, "I am Pipin the Short and one day I will be King of the Franks!" He stood tall when he said this, one hand raised as if it held a sword. Rotruda laughed indulgently.

Charles' smile was strained. "How are you doing in school Pipin?"

"I hate school. School is stupid."

"You're stupid," said Carloman without looking up from his game.

"Carl, that's enough," warned Rotruda.

"When can I go to war with you?" Pipin asked his father, his purple eyes wide with hope.

"Not for a while," Charles said. "But I could take you hunting, I suppose—"

Pipin nearly leapt into the air, whooping happily. Rotruda glanced at Carloman, worried he might feel left out. But he did not seem to hear; he was intent on his game. "Death," he said calmly, knocking one of Lothar's pieces over.

"Your son is a devil," Lothar said to Rotruda, laughing. "How do you do it, Carl?"

Pipin begged for a story, one of the wild tales Lothar usually constructed, half truth, half fiction, of his and Charles' boyhood adventures roaming the northern frontier, hiring themselves out as mercenary fighters to local seigniors tired of Saxon and Frisian raiders. It was Pipin's favorite pastime, and Lothar was always eager to oblige. But not this night. Rotruda saw him glance at Charles, saw something strange in the look, a strain between them she had never seen before. Charles did not seem able to meet his friend's gaze. She wondered at it.

"Perhaps—another time, Pip," Lothar said finally. "I'm worn out from Carl's beating."

"One more," Carloman said.

Lothar agreed to another game; Pipin loudly protested. Rotruda turned to Charles, searching his face, his translucent eyes, so unreadable to her. "Is there—something wrong?"

He looked at her as if just realizing she was in the room. "No," he said.

She looked back at Lothar, who though he had resumed the game seemed markedly quieter, his eyes averted. She cleared her throat, eager to bring them all back together again. "We missed you this summer. Things in Germania went well? The mission was a success?"

Lothar did not look up. Charles nodded. "Yes."

"I'm glad to hear it. We've had a lot of rain this year—more than usual, I think."

Neither of them responded. She looked at Charles. "Will you be staying in Paris long?"

"For a few weeks perhaps."

They watched the boys play in silence, until Carloman won again (Rotruda was certain Lothar let him win). Then Lothar made a hasty retreat, and the boys went off to bed. Rotruda retired to her room, calling for her maids to dress her properly for bed. He might come to her, she thought. She had to look her best. But Ani was nowhere in sight.

Annoyed, she went to the maids' room to see what was keeping them. Ani and the other maids were often too busy gossiping amongst themselves to pay attention to their duties. She stood at the door, about to go in and reprimand them, when she heard snatches of their words, feeling her own heart cave in.

"They say he's mad about her … who is she? … a Valkyrie … what is that … he's keeping her hidden …"

She listened a long time. Then she turned and went back to her own room, alone.

Charles did not come.

She descended to the hall the next morning to find it largely empty but for servants and dogs. She saw Lothar, sitting at one of the tables, tossing an apple into the air and catching it absently, occasionally taking a bite. He was staring into space, did not hear her approach.

"You look pensive," she said.

He sat up, suddenly alert. "My lady," he said and started to rise.

"Don't get up." She sat down beside him on the bench. She felt him stiffen, look around furtively, searching for prying eyes. "Why are you here alone?"

He leaned forward, his elbows on his knees, tossing the apple from hand to hand. "Charles is out hunting with Pipin. I took Carloman out for a ride, but he didn't want to hunt today. He said he was going to church."

Rotruda smiled. "Carloman is a different kind of boy. I don't think he cares much for soldiering. But he will be good at it, nonetheless. Carloman is good at everything he does."

"Yes, I can see that. Like his father." He paused. "It's surprising that they don't—get along better."

"Carloman barely knows his father." She felt his eyes skim over her, questioning. She shrugged. "He likes it when you spend time with him."

"He did once. But he's growing up. He's found—other interests."

She met his gaze. "Things seem different between the two of you."

She was not referring to Carloman. Lothar shrugged. "It can be difficult, being his friend."

"Try being his wife," she answered, laughing a little. "He has a woman, hasn't he?"

She felt him stiffen, though he said nothing. She searched his face, knowing his eyes could not mask his soul the way Charles' could.

"So the rumors are true," she said quietly. "About the … *Valkyrie?*"

"It seems that rumors fly faster than a man can ride in this kingdom," Lothar said sourly. "What did you hear?"

"Not very much. The maids were talking … who is she?"

"She was—a hostage. But the duke refused to ransom her."

"I see … is she beautiful?" Rotruda was afraid to speak the words.

Lothar turned away. "Some might think so."

"Charles thinks so."

"I do not know what he thinks. He does not share his thoughts with me," Lothar said quickly. "And anyway it doesn't matter. It's over. She's gone."

"Gone?" Rotruda's heart pounded. "Do you mean—?"

"She's gone, my lady. She won't be back."

Rotruda felt a small seed of hope grow in her breast. The Valkyrie was gone. So God had not abandoned her. She was still His beloved.

"He'll forget her," she told him confidently. She laid a hand on his arm, feeling oddly as though she were comforting him rather than the other way around. "Oh, I almost forgot! I have a present for you. Wait here, will you?" He nodded, smiling, and she fled up the stairs, returning a few minutes later with a bundle of cloth in her arms.

"I've been working on it for awhile," she said. "The one you have is so tattered."

Lothar unfolded the heavy black cloth, lined in rabbit fur and trimmed in red embroidery.

"It's a mantel," she breathed excitedly. "I made it. Do you like it?"

He fingered the fur lining. "You shouldn't have done this," he said softly.

"Charles will approve, don't worry. He knows you need a new one. You need a wife, Lothar, you need someone to tend to your clothes. What happened to that lovely girl I saw you with last time, the one with the red hair … Oh well, they come and go in your life, don't they? I can't wait to meet the one who finally captures your heart—"

Lothar rose suddenly, startling her. Then he turned and looked down at her, and he smiled. "I should see to the men—thank you, for this." He bowed to her awkwardly.

She gazed at him with her large violet eyes. "You're welcome." They looked at each other a moment longer. "Think of me when you wear it."

"I will." He turned reluctantly and walked out of the hall, still cradling the cloak as if it were a living thing. Rotruda watched him go.

# DECEMBER, 731

## Invasion

## Saint-Emilion
## The Aquitaine

IT WAS A steady, rumbling rhythm—far off in the distance. Thunder, Svana thought, and was about to turn over and go back to sleep when something made her sit up and listen. Thunder did not sound quite like that. Thunder was sporadic, fitful. This sound was regular, insistent. She froze.

*Drums.*

She slipped out of bed, pulling her shawl over her shoulders, and went into the kitchen. Freddy was already there, Erik beside her. Freddy looked pale, her large doe eyes wide and frightened. Svana turned from them without speaking and went out to the yard.

It was dawn, the air hung cold and breathless in the small yard like a fine mist. At first all was still, then the guard captain Otto broke through the fog, coming toward them on foot. Mattheus, Erik's brother, was with him. He was a big, hulking young man, the complete opposite of the thin, wiry Erik. They both looked very grim.

"What is going on?" Svana asked him, almost afraid to ask. She already knew what it meant. She had heard the sound before.

Otto gazed into the distance. "Drums," he said, "that is how they come. Beating drums. It sounds like death. It is an effective weapon." He spoke dryly, factually.

Svana felt her head swim. "It can't be."

"There are raiding parties headed this way. They bear a banner with a red flame."

"That is not Othman's banner," she said. Otto nodded grimly.

It could only mean one thing. Someone had seized power from Othman, someone bent on conquest.

Freddy started to cry. Erik pulled her close to him. "What should we do?" he said. "What *can* we do?"

"Leave," said Otto. "Take nothing. Just run. Perhaps you still have time to get away, get to the river. The river will slow them down."

"And if we are caught in the countryside?"

"Then you will be killed."

"It's the dead of winter. The river is half frozen. It will not slow them down."

"Perhaps not."

"And we will not survive for long out there."

"No, but you will survive longer than if you stay here."

"I'll get the horses ready," Erik said. "We will gather what food we can carry. I'll alert the people—"

"No," Svana said. "We aren't leaving."

Freddy gasped.

"My lady—" Erik began. Svana ignored him, turning to Otto.

"How long until they get here?"

"A few hours, perhaps. They will find the town and the monastery first. That may hold them awhile."

"All right." She took a breath, turned to the others. "Go and tell everyone to come to my house at once. Don't tell them what is happening yet."

"You think we can fight them?" said Erik, doubtful.

"No," Svana said. "We cannot fight. But I have an idea. I lived in Constantinople many years ago, during the Arab siege, I know these people. I speak a little of their language. I will try to talk to them. Go now. We don't have much time."

Freddy and Erik nodded reluctantly and went to gather the people. Svana turned her gaze to Otto.

"You are making a mistake," he said.

"We'll see. How many men do you have?"

"Seven."

Seven. It was a pittance. "You should leave," she said.

"I don't take orders from you, only from the duke."

"The duke—may be dead by now," Svana said. "If they are on their way here, then Bordeaux has already fallen. If you stay, you will die."

Otto hesitated. "We will stay," he said finally. He turned away to prepare his men.

Within an hour the entire population of the estate was crammed into Svana's little house. She told them calmly what was about to happen. There was a moment of fragile silence then the room burst into sound, crying and shouting. They wanted to run. Some wanted to fight.

"If we fight, they will kill us," Svana said coldly. "If we run they will track us down. But if we give them what they want without resistance, they may spare us."

"Then we will have nothing!" someone shouted.

"You will have your life," Svana said stoically. *Perhaps.*

"They might kill us anyway," said another.

"Yes," she said. "We have only a slim chance. If you decide to follow me, this is what you need to do: gather all your possessions and bring them here. Anything you have: silver, furs, beads, food, anything, bring them and we will make a collection for the raiders. When you have done that, come back to this house."

"We could hide them—" said someone.

"They will find them," Svana said bluntly. "They will burn your houses, they will look for newly dug holes in the ground. They will torture your children until you give them what they want. Then they will kill them, and they will kill you for trying to hide your treasure."

Their eyes grew wide with fright. But they did as she told them, for they believed her. Many of them were refugees from villages destroyed by Arab raiders; they knew this enemy all too well.

Otto returned to tell her that a scout had arrived who confirmed their fears: Bordeaux had been sacked by a new Arab force. Eudo had tried to stop their advance on the Garonne; there had been a terrible battle. The duke's army was annihilated; the duke himself was dead.

"Eudo is dead?" Svana said, unable to believe it. Hadn't he been at her house only a few days ago? Hadn't he taken Gryffin hunting with his falcon? Hadn't he laughed and joked about peacocks with her? And now he was dead ... Bordeaux sacked ... How could the world change so quickly, in the blink of an eye?

"That is the report," Otto continued. "They put his head on a spear for all the world to see."

Svana shut her eyes, struggling for breath. "Who is their leader?" she asked when she could speak again.

"He calls himself 'Rayman', the Fire of the Desert," Otto replied. "They say he is the new Emir of Cordova."

"So, it has come to this. As he always said it would," Svana murmured. No one listened to him. No one believed him. Eudo, like all the rest, had refused to face the reality that loomed before him. And now—

The monastery bells began to toll, not steady and mournful but clanging, erratic. Svana froze, her heart in her throat. The bells suddenly stopped altogether.

"They are at the monastery," said Otto in a soft voice.

Svana's heart ached at the thought.

The people began scurrying to her house, carrying bundles of food, children clinging to their skirts, wrapped around their legs. Sacks of grain and vegetables were piled in the wagons, along with furs and what few items of gold and silver they possessed. The animals bleated pitifully. Children cried, clinging to their lambs. Chickens ran about squawking madly.

Svana tried to calm them, to reassure them, to appear certain of her decision, even though she was screaming with terror inside.

*Charles ... I need you now.*

How often had he done this? Made decisions when hundreds of lives hung in the balance. He did it every day. It was why he slept so little.

*Please God. Please.*

She felt foolish praying. Why should God listen to her? Why should He care? After she'd insulted him and rejected Him, after she'd turned her back on Him all those years ago.

She went into her room, shutting the door, leaning against it. She felt the fear wash over her, the understanding of what could happen, what might happen. She wanted to weep, to moan, to keen like the widows over the bodies of their loved ones. Gryffin. Freddy. Erik. Mattheus. All of them. They had put their lives in her hands.

She closed her eyes.

*Help me.*

The words filled her mind, her body, her soul. She didn't know who she was asking, or who would answer. She waited, listening. She heard only the cries and bleats and the distant drums, growing ever louder. But there was something else too, a kind of music perhaps; it grew in strength, deadening the noises of fear and sorrow, breaking open inside of her, clear and steady and unbearably true.

She opened her eyes, breathing so that the air filled her lungs, reached to the tips of her fingers. She nodded once, as if in answer. Then she opened the door and went out again.

# Part Three

## The Hawk

# 46

## The Aquitaine
## October, 727

EUDO OF AQUITAINE was angry.

He slid from his gray Andalusian stallion and walked over to the dead body lying in the dirt. There were a dozen of them in this small village, all dead. The longhouses, which held the precious winter stores, were burned. Slaughtered goats and chickens littered the courtyard. A village decimated in a single night. It had happened over and over in the past five years all along his border, and Eudo had been powerless to stop it.

He gazed at the survivors huddled together amidst the destruction, weeping and moaning. Widows and orphans. He would give them money, but it would be a small comfort. And the winter would be long.

He had not come to see the dead villagers, however. He had come because strewn among the wreckage of the town were the bodies of four white-robed warriors. Arabs. He walked over to one of the bodies and examined it. The man's head had been almost completely severed from his neck.

"Theurin!"

One of the captains hurried to his side.

"Do you see what I see?" he asked, in a way that did not favor an answer.

Theurin shrugged. "He's dead, sir. Someone—killed him."

"Who, do you think?"

"One of the villagers must have done it."

"This man was on horseback. Yet his head is nearly cut off. How does a villager on foot, armed with an axe, make such a wound, do you think? These men do not look like giants to me."

Theurin nodded, clearly confused. "Then who?"

Eudo turned away and spoke softly, more to himself. "They come in the night, and no one sees them, not the raiders, not the villagers. No one. They come on horseback, that is how they effect such speed, and how they are able to kill other horsemen. They are completely invisible until it is too late to stop them. Only one man I know fights like this." He stopped, painful memories creasing his brow. A battle in the nighttime, men on horses. "This was the *Bastard's* doing."

The men around him quieted. There was only one man on earth whom Eudo referred to simply as "The Bastard." His name was not to be uttered aloud in his presence.

Eudo turned swiftly to his horse and mounted. "Get rid of them," he said.

"The bodies?" asked the captain uncertainly. But Eudo had already spun his horse and was gone without answering.

He rode along the Garonne River toward Tolosa, trailed by his bodyguards, silent, morose. The Bastard Prince was back, haunting him again. He knew it was Charles' black riders who had killed those Arabs. Charles needed to protect his Burgundian borders, which had become vulnerable to the raiding. His horsemen seemed able to track and intercept the raiders while Eudo's own patrols failed to find even a trace of them until after they had struck. This was not his kind of war, and he knew it. This was Charles' kind of war, a war of stealth and subterfuge, a slippery game of cat and mouse. Eudo, the Roman general, was out of his element.

Pain snaked across his brow, circling his skull. The piercing ache that always came when thoughts of Charles, of Soissons, invaded his memory. He should have been over it. He should have felt vindicated after his victory against El-Samah in Tolosa. He had decimated an army of 20,000 Arab warriors, sent the remnant packing all the way back to Septimania. He had done what most men considered impossible.

Yet it had not been enough to erase the humiliation of Soissons. That failure still hung ripe and heavy in his soul, a mutant fruit that would not fall from the tree and die, too ugly to be eaten. Moreover, he was still, despite his great wealth and power, a vassal of Charles Martel, subject to his will. He knew he would never be free until he had defeated him, once and for all.

He was tired and troubled when he arrived at his opulent palace in the center of Tolosa, so he avoided his wife and children and went to see his falcons. No sooner had he coaxed one of his favorite birds to his arm, when his peace was broken by the shrill, petulant voice of his daughter, Lampegnia.

"Father? Where have you been? I wish to speak to you."

Pain thudded through his skull. "I'm busy."

"You do not look busy. And you've been avoiding me."

Eudo turned to find her beautiful brown eyes fixed mercilessly on him, her chin lifted as if preparing for a parry. He knew this look. This was how she always came to him, ready for battle. He shut his eyes a moment, willing the pain away.

"Well, what is it now? More money again? Your gowns aren't good enough for you anymore?"

"Father, I wish to marry."

Eudo opened his eyes, relieved. He stroked the bird. "Fine. I will find you a husband."

"I have already found one."

"Really?" He put the falcon back on her perch and turned to her fully, his arms crossed over his chest. "And who is this man you think you are going to marry?"

"His name is Richard."

"A detestable name. Is he rich? A capitoul? A senator at least?"

"No—"

"Does he have money to pay your bride price?"

She looked away. "I don't care about that."

"Ha, but I do," Eudo said. He turned and walked down the row of birds, stopping to pet them as he went. Lampegnia followed.

"He's a good man, Father. He will take care of me."

"Does he have any idea of how much money is required to take care of you?"

"We won't need money."

He laughed. "He doesn't know you very well, does he? Let's see, you don't need money, your love will sustain you, love conquers all—"

"Don't mock me!" Lampegnia shouted.

Eudo stopped, whirling on her. But his voice remained soft, almost gentle. "Never mind, you'll understand one day. You will marry a man suitable to your station—a man I will choose for you. Forget this poor church mouse of yours. I forbid you to even think of marrying him."

"No!" Lampegnia screamed. "You cannot do this!"

"Yes, I can," said Eudo, advancing on her, so she had to step back. "My decision is final. Never see him again, for if I find out you have not broken it off with him, I will find him myself and kill him."

"Then I will kill myself!"

Eudo almost smiled. "No, you won't. By the way, if you try running off with him I will find you both, and I will kill him while you watch. But listen, don't fret. Once you are properly married, you can carry on with this goat of yours as much as you like. I don't care about that. But if you present yourself to your husband on your wedding night as anything less than a snow-white virgin, you will not live to see the morning. Do I make myself clear?"

"No!" Lampegnia wailed. "You can beat me, starve me, chain me to the altar, but I will never say those words to a man I don't love! Never!"

Eudo laughed. "We'll see about that. Go away now. Go slam doors in some other part of the house where I can't hear you."

Lampegnia ran from the mews, shrieking and wailing. Eudo left his falcons and returned to the palace, retreated to his office and shut the door. Distantly he could hear doors slamming in the rooms above. He poured himself a large cup of wine and sat behind his desk, eyes closed, every door slam like a dagger in his temple.

A steward knocked and stuck his head furtively around the door. "My lord?"

"What is it?" Eudo snapped.

"The Emir, my lord."

"Who?"

"The Emir. Othman of Septimania. He's been waiting for quite some time …"

Eudo rubbed his face as if trying to draw the pain from his skull. "All right. Let's get this over with. Send him in."

A few minutes later Othman-ben-Abi-Nêssa was ushered into the room. He was a great, handsome warrior with an expansive brown face that narrowed to a sharply pointed beard. He was dressed in flamboyant court regalia, flowing robes belted in gold, with gold bands around his neck and wrists and a huge, gold-trimmed turban on his head. He bowed gravely, his big hoop earrings jangling. Eudo did not stand to greet him, pretending to be absorbed with the scrolls on his desk.

"Can I help you, Othman?" Eudo asked.

"I have been endeavoring to see you for some time," said Othman in passable Latin. "You do not answer my messages."

"That must mean I have nothing to say. What do you want?"

"I want the same thing you want, Duke. Peace."

"Then leave the Aquitaine," Eudo said. "You will have all the peace you want."

Othman ignored the remark. "You have a daughter of age to marry. I wish for her hand."

Eudo looked at him, clearly surprised by this offer. Then he laughed. "The only way you will get her hand is if you chop it off with that great, curved sword of yours."

"That is very arrogant, considering your position."

Eudo was on his feet. "My position? I am Duke of Aquitaine."

"I could take your rule away from you any time I wish."

"Really? Then what are you waiting for?"

"I, like you, wish for peace between us."

"Splendid. Then go back to Iberia."

Othman sighed. "If we cannot come to some—arrangement, I am afraid that the raiding will continue."

"You think you can threaten me? I have faced far worse than your measly raiding parties."

"You cannot hold us off forever, Duke."

"Perhaps not. But I can hold you off for a long time. Long enough to weaken you, to demoralize your troops and make your Caliph in Cordova grow impatient with you. And I will do everything I can to see that happens."

"Do you imagine the Great Caliph will simply give up and send us home?"

"If he is a wise man, that is what he will do."

"Then you are bigger fool than I thought you were," Othman said. "You do not know our people very well. But you will learn, Duke, as the rest of the world has already learned. Allah is with us."

Eudo sat back down, returning to his scrolls. "We are finished here, Othman."

Othman waited a moment, then turned in a great, glowing huff and left the room. Eudo went to the wine table and poured another cup of wine. He drank shakily.

There was another knock at the door.

"What now?" Eudo snapped. He turned to see his wife hovering in the doorway. He blinked; he often forgot what she looked like, mistaking her for a servant.

"What is the matter with Lampegnia? She's quite—agitated."

"She needs a husband, that's what's the matter with her." Eudo drank the wine in a single gulp. "I'm going to have to find her one before she does something stupid."

"Do you have someone in mind?"

"There's a fellow in Bordeaux I've had my eye on, the son of a shipper. A nothing bloodline, but very rich. I will go to Bordeaux and talk to him."

# 47

## Saint-Emilion
## The Aquitaine
## March, 728

THE CHILD CRIED.

Svana paused in her sweeping, gazing at the little pallet where he lay, thrashing and wailing, still half-asleep. This was how he awoke, always, as if in torment. What sort of dreams did a two-year-old child have to distress him so?

She set aside the broom and went to kneel beside the pallet, pulling him into her lap. He looked up at her, sniffling. The eyes, she thought. They were hard to look at. Clear as glass, so utterly familiar. She rocked him softly, cooing.

"Gryffin," she said. "Wake up child."

The crying softened to sobs, the boy not yet fully awake, sticking his thumb in his mouth. She wiped the tears from his sticky cheeks. It always took a few minutes to calm him down, and in an hour it would start all over again.

She had been in Saint-Emilion almost three years. It was a peaceful place: a landscape of rolling, vine-covered hills, dominated by a monastery built within a warren of caves and grottos overlooking the drowsy, wine-soaked town. It was not where she had intended to go. She had headed, initially, to the sea, to find a ship that would take her to Britannia. A new place, a wild land. But the sea when she came upon it was not the deep calm of the sea she'd known in the Empire. It was savage and dark, beset by storms, flanked by steep cliffs and rocky beaches that proved no safe haven. So she headed south. Someplace warm, she thought. Out of the wind and pounding rain. The Aquitaine. Iberia. As far from Charles as she could go. She thought with distance would come oblivion. Forgetting. Freedom.

She knew she was pregnant, had woken every morning of the journey to gut-wrenching nausea. She hid this fact from the guards charged with escorting her, knowing they would report back to Charles. If he had known, he wouldn't have let her leave.

Freddy knew though. She had insisted on accompanying her, much to her surprise. Svana would have thought that the events in Kolonia would be enough to make the girl shun her forever. But Freddy had become a different person that night, had somehow grown from girl to woman, had stared down death and survived.

By the time they arrived in Saint-Emilion, Svana could go no further. They found the abbey almost by accident, and Freddy insisted she should stay there. Her mistress was ill, she told the guards, too sick to continue. She gave the abbot the money Charles had provided them, to insure his cooperation. And his silence.

The small community of nuns welcomed the two women with smiles that made their wrinkled faces crinkle like tiny walnuts. They filled Svana with ginger tea and special herbs to curb the sickness, praying over her every day. She grew to love them as she loved the grotto itself, with its dark airless passageways and its sweet, dusty, long-forgotten smell. It was like being entombed, she thought, but there was comfort there also, like a mother's womb. In the grotto she felt safer than she ever had, except when she had lain in Charles' arms. She tried not to think about that, for to remember brought a well of grief to the pit of her soul that was almost too much for her to bear.

The baby was born in late summer, a boy with black hair and ice-blue eyes. The nuns crossed themselves upon seeing him, making the sign against evil, for there was something rather unsettling about those eyes. She named him Gryffin, and the named proved apt, for he screamed night and day, forever wakeful and unhappy. Svana thought she would go mad for real, was afraid she would hurt the child in her sleepless despair. But Freddy and the nuns again came to her rescue, walking with the baby up and down the narrow passageways so that she could snatch patches of rest.

She had planned to leave once the baby was born but found she could not summon the will. Instead, she offered to help the monks in the vineyards, baby strapped to her back. Freddy followed her, dragging the baskets in a small cart. The monks seemed not to mind; they showed the women how to pick the grapes so as not to damage them, explained the process of crushing and fermenting and aging. Svana was familiar with the pale wines of Franconia, but the wine of Saint-Emilion was deep red in color with a strong, smoky flavor completely unlike the sweet and fruity wines of the north. The Romans had called it *Vinum claratum*, clarified wine, which had been shortened to "claret." The work was hard, the sun relentlessly hot, but the child on her back quieted with the steady rhythm of the work and the many sights and sounds of the vineyard, and Svana began to feel an odd, transcendent peace.

She discovered an old hermitage on the land, a small wood and mud cottage that had not been used in years. She had an idea. She went to the abbot and asked if she could have it. He was hesitant; the monks were not inclined to take on renters, especially unmarried women with small children. But she persisted until he finally relented, giving her a share of the vineyards to tenant. The monks could not maintain all the vineyards themselves, and they did not sell the wine, making only what was needed for Mass and trading what they had leftover for food and supplies from the town.

She hired two brothers, Erik and Mattheus, to help her with the work. The orphaned brothers had made a living by piloting barges up and down the Garonne. Erik built a machine that would press the grapes faster than the ones used by the monks. Mattheus was extremely useful for hauling lumber and digging holes, and he was perfectly happy doing anything she asked of him. He was also a skilled boatswain, and soon was poling the casks up and down the river to Bordeaux for sale in the local marketplace.

Mattheus rebuilt Svana's house of stone, and built a smaller house for himself and Erik, as well as a longhouse for storage and a small barn for Svana's horse, a donkey they used for hauling grapes from the vineyard, and a goat for milk.

More boys came. Erik and Mattheus had spread the word up and down the river that the woman needed laborers. They were orphans or runaways, at the age where no one cared to take them in. Others soon trickled in, women and children whose villages had been burned and their men murdered by Arab raiders.

The small estate grew steadily. Erik was now working on building a crusher, so that their operation would be completely independent from the monks. Svana had never worked so hard in her life; her beautiful horse became a wagon pony, her hands and feet grew calloused, her pale skin darkened in the relentless sun. She went to bed at night with every muscle in her body pulsing and lay exhausted in the smoky dark, aching for Charles, his absence more acute than his presence had been.

She had sent him no message. She had considered it, many times, but could not think of any words to say. What she wanted to say was beyond words, as it always had been with him. She would close her eyes instead and remember his body against hers, his hands on her breast, his mouth. The eyes she did not have to remember, for she saw them every day in her little son, eyes that missed nothing but revealed nothing either.

Sometimes when the pain was bad, when it threatened to consume her, she would stop whatever she was doing and breathe slowly, taking it into her lungs, letting it course through her like blood. She did not try to get rid of it, she tried to own it, to make it a part of her, something she could not live without. When she breathed it breathed with her, like a living being inside her.

The child was quiet, asleep, sucking his thumb. Freddy rushed in through the open front door, a basket of herbs under one arm.

"I heard something—"

"It's nothing. Just a dream, I think."

"He has a lot of those, doesn't he?"

Svana nodded, regarding the fierce little face, still scrunched up with tears. She laid him back down on his pallet and took up her broom again. "Have you finished?"

"Almost. I found some wild dandelion. It will make a nice salad. And Erik's got two rabbits. It will be a feast tonight!" Freddy giggled, running off. Svana watched her scamper across the courtyard toward her garden. The air, for once, felt sweet and warm, the herald of spring. It would be good to be out, in the fields again, watching grapes grow, tending vines. She turned her attention back to sweeping.

# 48

## Bordeaux

EUDO DRANK HIS third glass of wine, half-listening as the tremendously fat man across from him droned on about the perils of shipping from Bordeaux since the arrival of the Arabs.

"It's not only piracy," said the man. "It's embargoes! It's sabotage! There's no getting around Iberia anymore; there's no getting through Narbonne! And these Mussies don't drink, so what's the use of them?"

Eudo nodded sympathetically, glancing from time to time at the younger man at the table, the son. Nothing much to look at, but Eudo sensed a sharp mind. He would need it, to outwit his daughter, though he would probably find himself constantly outmuscled.

"This claret," Eudo said, trying to change the subject. "Where did you get it?"

"It's the latest vintage from Saint-Emilion," the shipper announced.

"Saint-Emilion? The monks sold this to you?"

"No, no, not the monks. They have a tenant, haven't you heard? A woman, of all things."

Eudo leaned forward, suddenly interested. "Who is this woman?"

The fat man shrugged. "Some wayward woman the monks took in. She's decided to set up shop on their land! But the wine is quite good. Who am I to judge?"

"She has not sold to me," Eudo said thoughtfully. "But I haven't been to Bordeaux in quite some time. I shall have to pay her a visit. I must get some of this for the palace stores."

"I would be happy to get it for you, Lord Duke."

"Kind of you. But I think I will go and see for myself."

Eudo had a house in Bordeaux that was smaller and plainer than the one in Tolosa, but only here, without his pestering wife, bratty children, and nosy ministers, could he be truly alone. It sat on the north bank of the Gironde, an unfashionable district of small, clay-roofed houses outside the main walls of the city. Bordeaux had been an auspicious settlement under the Romans, a center for learning and scholarship, but it had suffered badly in the aftermath, as had so many of the fine Roman cities of Gaul.

Yet Eudo liked Bordeaux. It was quiet. It was quaint. It had just enough squalor and decay to feel comforting to him. He had built an empire on his wits and his will, but he had come to discover there was not much joy in it for him anymore.

He did not mind being unhappy. It was the *need* for happiness he found so strange, so unsettling. It was a sign of age, he knew, a sign that he was getting to the time when he would look back on his life and realize that, after all, it had not been enough.

He thought of this as he rode along the road to Saint-Emilion. He did not need to go personally—he had plenty of servants who could buy wine for him—but today he simply wanted to wander, to escape this vague unease that had settled upon him since the dinner with the shipping magnate and his son. Was it merely forming a marriage alliance with this odious family that disturbed him? Facing Lampegnia's wrath when she laid eyes upon his choice for her? Did he actually want her to be happy, after all?

He found his way to the estate, surprised to discover a complex of small beehive huts, pens and longhouses, crawling with laborers busy in the fields. He stopped before the tiny walled-in courtyard where a child and a young man were playing some sort of game, the boy chasing the man with a stick and shouting, the man laughing. The man's clothes were old and purple-stained.

Then a woman came through the front door to watch, holding a small bouquet of flowers. She was tall, black-haired, with the bearing of a queen and the face of a goddess. Eudo stared at her, riveted.

Suddenly the child stopped running and pointed directly at him, yelling something. The young man turned as well. Eudo paid no attention to them. He did not take his eyes from the woman.

She straightened as he walked his horse into the courtyard. She did not speak, looking up at him warily.

"Are you the … owner of this place?" She nodded. "I would like to buy some of your wine." He paused. "I am Eudo, Duke of Aquitaine."

The young man gasped. But the woman did not show any reaction at all.

"My lord," said the young man, bowing. "We are most honored."

"I was in Bordeaux and heard of your wine. I came to see for myself. It is not customary for the monks of Saint-Emilion to rent land to— anyone."

The woman finally spoke. "Come in, and I will give you a sample." She turned abruptly and went into the house.

Eudo dismounted, tossing the reins to the man as if he were a groom and followed her. The man held the reins, not sure what to do with them. Eudo entered the house, taking in the dank stone walls, the rush covered floor, the handmade stone fireplace. Even the monks of Saint-Emilion lived grandly compared to this.

He watched the woman move about the small kitchen, setting her flowers aside and taking up a wine carafe. He thought that she didn't belong there at all, this was not her world. She was a jewel that required a magnificent setting, a setting only he could give her. He decided, then and there, what he would do.

There was a rough wooden table in the center of the room. He sat in a chair while she poured wine into a cup and handed it to him. He glanced out the window, at the child who still stared at him with clear, unblinking eyes. He looked away.

"Your son?" he asked.

"Yes."

"What's his name?"

"Gryffin."

"He doesn't look so fierce to me."

"You didn't give birth to him."

He laughed aloud at that. He thought she might have smiled, but it was difficult to tell. She would not look directly at him, keeping her eyes on her work.

"What is your name?"

She hesitated. "Svanahilda."

He sipped the wine, letting the name flit over his mind. "You are from the north, I think. Bavaria, perhaps?"

He saw a faint flicker in her eyes. "Franconia. My husband was a vintner. He had heard of the grapes of Bordeaux and wanted—to see if there was a way to transport them to our land. But he died of fever … the monks were kind enough to take me in."

Eudo gazed at her awhile, not speaking. He knew this story was a lie. Suddenly she seemed vulnerable, exposed, and that gave him new confidence.

"So your husband is dead?"

"Yes."

"How very tragic." He drank the rest of the wine and set the cup back on the table. "I will take ten barrels. But you must deliver them. To my palace in Tolosa."

"I don't go to Tolosa. The roads are too dangerous. Even the river is unsafe."

"Then I will give you a guard to accompany you." He pulled a small leather pouch from his belt and tossed it on the table. "That should be enough, I think."

Svana picked up the pouch and emptied it onto the table. Ten gold triens poured out. She gasped.

"Is it not enough?" Eudo asked, eyeing her carefully.

"I have never seen—so much gold. We usually deal in silver." She paused. "It is far too much."

"Take it, for your trouble," Eudo said. "But you must come before the end of the month. I will send the soldiers."

She said nothing.

He rose and went to the doorway, where the young man still stood holding the horse's reins. He mounted and rode off at a clipped trot without looking back.

Svana stood in the doorway, watching him leave. She breathed deeply, leaning against the door frame for support. Erik moved to her.

"What did he want?"

"To buy wine, I think."

"That's all? Did you tell them—who you are?"

"I am a woman who has wine to sell. That is the end of it." She turned away quickly and went into the house.

# 49

## Tolosa

TOLOSA HAD SEEN better days. Once it had been a thriving Roman metropolis, due to its strategic location on the Garonne between the two seas, a center of trade and an important military outpost. After the Romans left, the city fell victim to barbarian raiders, as did every other wealthy city in Gaul, culminating in the Frankish kings, the Merovingians, who were so busy making war on each other that the governance of the Aquitaine had fallen to rival warlords. Somehow, despite war and plague and bad government, Tolosa had survived.

The Roman part of the city had been mostly destroyed, but the palace still stood, a long, basilica-like building of white stone ringed by a colonnade. It rivaled the Emperor's palace in Constantinople, a building Svana knew too well.

Eudo was waiting for her when she stepped into the cavernous hall, accompanied by Erik and Freddy, leading a bewildered Gryffin by the hand. Svana wondered, not for the first time, why Eudo would pay so much for wine from a provincial estate in Saint-Emilion, when he lived in a city where goods from every corner of the world were readily available. Clearly Eudo had more on his mind than wine. Did he know who she was? Was this a trap? Or did he want her for—other reasons? She had thought of little else on the journey. Now, standing before this man and his elaborate guard, she tried to quell the tremors in her stomach.

"Welcome, lady."

She inclined her head to him, keeping her eyes on him steadily, so he would not sense her anxiety. Freddy and Erik stayed behind her, huddled together.

"Bring in a cask. I think we should taste it, to make sure it is the same as the wine I tasted in Saint-Emilion." He gave some orders and soon servants appeared carrying a barrel. Eudo's wine steward came forward to tap the barrel and draw out several cups. Eudo talked about the claret of Bordeaux, displaying a keen knowledge of grapes and vintage. He seemed to be enjoying himself immensely, savoring the trepidation he created in his guests.

"I have arranged for a private dinner, just some of my acquaintances and business partners," he told Svana. "You should be able to harness many new clients."

"Dinner?" She saw that he enjoyed taking her off-guard. She struggled to muster some of her former haughtiness. "That is kind of you, but … I am not dressed for such an occasion," she said. "And my son—"

"We can take care of all that."

Before she knew what was happening, she and Freddy and Gryffin were whisked away to the women's quarters, where a nursemaid took charge of Gryffin. A dark-skinned maid curtsied before them and brought them to a room of nauseating extravagance. The walls were covered in sheer draperies, the floors with exquisite Persian rugs, the furniture stuffed with pillows and covered in silky fabrics. Svana was given a hot bath and dressed in a Roman-style gown of deep red, her hair arranged in an intricate pattern of interlocking braids pinned up on top of her head and studded with tiny crystals. Freddy giggled through it all. Svana found herself curiously unable to protest.

"My lady, you look most beautiful," Freddy said, gazing at her mistress when the transformation was complete. Svana could hardly breathe against the tight girdle that encircled her middle. The pointy slippers pinched her toes. The dress was scandalously low cut, but a lorum made of a shimmery gold fabric draped over her shoulders, hiding her breasts from plain view.

"I feel ridiculous," Svana said.

She was taken to the dining hall, a vast room built of white marble, where a dozen of Eudo's friends gaped at her. Their duke, they whispered, had found himself a new mistress and a spectacularly beautiful one at that.

Eudo sat her beside him at the long table while the dinner guests gushed over the wonderful dark earthiness of her wine and inquired how they could buy some. She could barely understand their Latin. She felt the color rise in her cheeks, the humiliation of it all, dressed up and put on display like some exotic animal. They seemed not to notice her discomfort, asking her presumptuous questions about her barbarian homeland, the whereabouts of her husband, how she came to be in Bordeaux. Eudo answered for her, repeating the story she had told him but adding his own embellishments, as if to make her aware of the fact that he knew her own version of events was every bit a lie. Svana sat mutely through it all, smiling at the sympathetic faces that mooned over her sad story, trying hard not to avert her eyes in shame.

"There is news that Bavaria has turned against Charles again," said a fat elderly man at the far end of the table. "The upstart Grimwold has returned."

This Svana understood. She looked up from her plate, alarmed. Eudo was grinning wickedly. "Yes, it's true," he said. "Grimwold has retaken Ratisbon. But I could have guessed as much. Charles was a fool to leave the man alive."

"What has become of the—young duke?" Svana asked carefully, not wanting to betray too much concern about her brother.

Eudo glanced at her. "I haven't heard. But I don't imagine Grimwold would let him live … do you?"

She shrugged, avoiding his gaze, afraid of what she would see there. Was he trying to bait her? To force her to reveal herself? Her heart throbbed against her ribs, her lungs straining against the constricting girdle. "Your hatred of Charles is well known. Perhaps this is your chance to get even with him. But I suppose you are too busy now, fighting Arabs."

There were nervous chuckles around the table. Svana kept her eyes locked on his.

"I have already defeated the Arabs," Eudo said tightly.

"Really?" Svana said. "Then why are your roads and waterways so unsafe? Why does your countryside teem with refugees? If you won the battle, my lord, why are the Arabs still here?"

The room went deadly silent. Eudo did not move. She gazed at him unflinchingly, knowing she had crossed the line, that there was no going back. She waited for his anger, his outrage. But Eudo surprised her.

"You have a gift for frankness," he said gently. "What we expect from our northern neighbors." There was some humor in his tone; everyone in the room breathed in relief and returned to their own conversations.

"You enjoy taunting me," he said, softly so only she could hear.

"I'm sorry. It's been a long journey and I am tired. I beg your leave, my lord." She stood abruptly. Eudo rose with her. He took her hand and led her out of the room.

He walked her to the hallway where the women's quarters began.

"I will send for you," he said.

"I will not come."

He stopped, staring at her. She knew he was not often refused. And after her performance at dinner she was already on delicate ground.

"Then why did you come here?" he demanded.

"Because you bought my wine," she said simply. "And you paid in gold. The gold—it was for the wine, was it not? Because you would not think, merely because I am an unmarried woman with a child, that I am also a whore."

She saw a flash of anger slide across his face then disappear again. Of course that is what he thought. He knew she had lied about her husband. But the truth he suspected was still wrong.

"My apologies." He looked at her, then looked away. "I did not mean to offend. Sleep well, my lady." He bowed to her gravely and walked away.

Svana put her hand against the wall. She realized she was shaking. She had wondered, all evening, what she would say to him when the time came. She had thought she might even go to his bed, for there seemed to be no real reason not to. She felt drawn to him, an attraction that defied the rules she had set for herself.

But there was a reason: *he* was still there, he was always there; she was tied to him as long as he existed in the world. She would never be free.

# 50

THE MINOS PUBLIC Inn was owned by a Greek named Agrius, an ex-warrior from Byzantium who claimed to have been unjustly accused of some crime or other and forced into exile. He loved to tell his sad story over and over to anyone who would sit in his inn long enough to listen. Gunther listened, though he was tired and hungry and understood nothing of the man's Grecian tirade.

He had come to Tolosa to buy horses for Charles, but he was missing the war in Bavaria, which did not make him genial company. Charles had insisted he stick with his mission, that he was not needed in Ratisbon, but still it rankled him that others would get to kill Germans and he would be stuck bartering with two-faced horse traders.

The inn was crowded with men engaged in a game that entailed throwing daggers at a large mural of a bull/man painted on the wall: the Minotaur. The object was to hit the bull directly in its one visible eye, whereupon everyone would yell "Bull's Eye!" and do more drinking. The game got rather dangerous as the drink made the men's aim more precarious.

Gunther noticed one man who never seemed to miss. He was tall and fair, which made him even more conspicuous in that squat, swarthy crowd. He was apparently quite well-known, for the others cheered him on as they threw coins into a pool on one of the tables. Another man challenged him, each of them taking turns until once again the tall man triumphed. Gunther watched.

The innkeeper refilled his tankard.

"Who is he?" Gunther said, startling the man.

"Him? That's Brand."

"What does he do?"

"Nothing, and everything. He's a singer, mostly. But he has many talents, as you can see."

"Tell him I want to speak to him," Gunther demanded. The innkeeper shrugged and called out.

"Brand! Come! This one wants to buy you a drink!"

Brand looked over at the innkeeper, then his eyes fell upon the hulk of the man at the table. He turned and said something in Arabic to his friends, who groaned in disappointment. He collected his winnings and ambled over to Gunther's table.

"Can I help you, Friend?"

"Perhaps," Gunther said. "Sit down."

Brand sat, still smiling but wary. A servant girl inserted herself in his lap, pressed her breasts against him and kissed him hard. The men shouted and laughed. Brand returned the kiss appreciatively and then slapped her away, ordering food and more drink.

"Are you familiar with the Minotaur?" Brand asked genially. "I know a song about it. I'll sing it later. The monster born of the Greek ruler Minos' wife and a white sea bull, a creature formed by Poseidon. Very tragic story." Brand smiled, though he saw no return smile on his new companion's face. "It sounds better when it is sung."

"You speak Arabic," Gunther said.

Brand nodded. "One needs to speak just about everything in my line of work. You are a Frank? I can tell by your lousy Latin."

Gunther grunted.

The food came, a roast chicken and boiled carrots. Brand ate ravenously, washing huge pieces of food down with wine.

"I need a translator," Gunther said, when he had finished. "Are you available for hire?"

"Possibly. Why do you need a translator, may I ask?"

"I need to buy horses."

"Horses? I know nothing about them."

"I do," Gunther said. "But I don't trust these horse traders."

"I don't blame you. They love to take advantage of foreigners."

"You are a foreigner as well," Gunther said, eyeing Brand shrewdly. "Where are you from?"

Brand hesitated. "Nowhere."

"Where were you born?"

"Burgundy. Vienne."

Gunther raised an eyebrow. "You do not look like a Burgundian. Who was your father?"

"I never knew my father. He died before I was born, or so I'm told."

"What about your mother?"

Brand glanced at him, suddenly off-balance. "She is dead too."

"Her family?"

"Why do you want to know about my family?"

"I like to know the sort of man I'm dealing with."

"I've told you everything I know."

"I think you are lying."

"People tell me I am a remarkable liar."

They stared at each other. Gunther saw a hardness come into the man's blue eyes, a defensive sheen. He did not think Brand was lying exactly, but he sensed there was much he was leaving out.

"I will pay you ten deniers for two weeks' work."

"Twenty."

"Fifteen."

Brand shrugged, his grin returning. "Fair enough. Plus food, of course, and wine. And women."

"I will not pay for your women."

"No, I get mine for free. But you will have to pay for yours, I think." He laughed, his teeth showing white against his tanned skin.

"Be ready tomorrow at dawn," Gunther said, rising. He tossed a coin on the table.

"Dawn is not an hour I am familiar with," Brand said. "But I will be ready after breakfast. Right before lunch anyway."

Gunther regarded him, made a noise like a growl and then barked at the innkeeper: "My men and I need beds. Now!" The innkeeper hopped to obey.

The sun was well up, shining weakly through white clouds when Gunther, Brand, the guards and servants ambled past the palace on the way out of the city. Gunther, on horseback, stopped to stare at the huge building. Brand, on foot, glanced at him.

"Admiring the palace? You should see the ones they build in the Empire—they put this one to shame."

"It's big," Gunther grunted.

Suddenly he saw the iron gates pushed open by slaves and a caravan of horses and carts emerge from within the palace walls, accompanied by soldiers. And then he saw a woman who looked far too familiar, a woman with long black hair and dark eyes, riding a white horse. She looked and acted like a queen in a procession. People in the streets stopped to stare at her, whispering amongst themselves.

"Who is that?" Gunther asked, staring in disbelief.

"One of the duke's many mistresses," Brand said. "Every year or so he gets a new one—where are you going?"

Gunther had spun his horse and was moving in the opposite direction.

"That's not the way to the bridge," Brand called after him.

"Is there another way?"

"Of course. There is the long way around if you want to waste time—"

"Then we go the long way," Gunther said.

Brand shrugged, chasing after him. "Very well, it's your time and money to waste," he said.

# 51

## Ratisbon, Bavaria
## September, 728

THE GATES OF Ratisbon opened, and a horse emerged at a dead run, dragging something behind it. Charles' men ran out to catch the horse and its cargo, which turned out to be the erstwhile Duke of Bavaria, a dagger still lodged in his chest.

Charles stared down at the body and heaved a great sigh of relief. After four months, the siege of Ratisbon was finally over.

An hour later he rode through the city with his victorious army. People lined the streets to watch. They looked haggard, half-starved, but relieved, as relieved as he felt. It had been a long summer for both sides.

Grimwold had retaken Ratisbon easily, the nobles abandoning Hucpert like rats from a sinking ship. But this time, when Charles came for him, he shut himself inside his fortress, daring Charles to break down his walls. It would be a siege, and a long one, for Ratisbon was well-fortified and defended.

Charles knew he could never breach the walls of that city without great loss of life. He knew as well, thanks to his Bavarian spy Nithard, that the city was peopled not only with soldiers but citizens who had sought protection from the invading army. So Charles decided not to attack at all. Instead, he barricaded the town in an effort to keep the people inside from getting out. Then he let his soldiers loose to pillage the countryside, stealing and destroying crops and livestock, taking Bavarian women and parading them half-naked before the walls, taunting the men inside. They cooked mutton and boar over fires so that the smell wafted over the meat-starved city. At night they bombarded the walls with flaming arrows to keep the guards awake and on edge.

As the months passed, nerves frayed inside the fortress. People grew hostile to Grimwold and his soldiers, who had brought them to this predicament. The soldiers too, grew agitated, demanding a fight on open ground. Grimwold refused, certain Charles would eventually be forced to attack. But Charles did not attack.

So the people took matters into their own hands; they killed the duke and his captains, sending his body out as a peace offering and opening the gates to him.

Charles rode to the palace and stopped, turning to face the crowd.

"Grimwold is dead. Your rightful duke will be restored to his place. I have no quarrel with you, and I want nothing but your loyalty to your duke and to me. This war is over. And for your service to the Frankish king, we will take nothing from this city and hold no ransom. You may go in peace."

More cheering, and a thrum of a chant, "Ham-MER, Ham-MER," louder and louder. Charles inclined his head to them, drew his sword, grabbed it by the blade and held up the hilt like a banner for them all to see.

"Incredible," said Nithard, lounging at the long dining table, a large mug of beer in his fists, as usual. "I didn't think it would work, to tell you the truth."

"Fortresses are built of people, not walls," Charles said. "And people crumble more easily."

"True, I suppose. At least you won't have to worry about Grimwold again."

"And Hucpert?"

Nithard snorted. "I can't promise you much. Grimwold died without heirs, so there will be no more challenges to the seat, anyway. And there is some good news: the boy hasn't had a drink in months. They kept him in the crypt, and once he had gone through the communion wine there was nothing left." He laughed.

Charles drained his cup and slumped against the hard back of the chair. He felt as though he had been holding his breath for four long months, and for a few days at least he might be able to relax. He longed for sleep, the kind of dark, dismal, dreamless sleep that lasts for a century, the sleep that heals, restores, forgets.

"What will you do now?" Nithard asked. "Go to Quierzy?"

*Quierzy*. The house he was building, his place of refuge. He had wanted to build it for her.

"If there's time. After Christmas, perhaps."

Nithard eyed him. "Well, you should go. You need a rest. You look half-dead, if you want to know the truth."

"I don't."

Bavaria secured, Charles returned to Kolonia to settle his standing army and disperse his levied troops, most of whom were anxious to get back to their farms in time for the harvest. Before long the Autumn Assembly would be upon him, the yearly battle with the bishops he had come to loathe. Chrodegang helped enormously. The chancellor had arrived in Kolonia before him and was eager to share his news of the latest negotiations.

"Eucher has seen the light," he told Charles over a hearty meal in Charles' private dining room. "But he does have some conditions."

"Which are?"

"That you stop removing bishops without the consent of the Council," Chrodegang said. "Which is reasonable, I think. And he wants a tenth of the rents, naturally. In addition, he demands that you turn over a tenth of the land you—acquire—for the building of a church."

"A tenth?"

"It's actually not a bad idea, when you think about it. Churches breed towns, and Francia needs more towns."

"True, I suppose."

"Of course it is! And here's another thing to remember, my lord: if you agree to not remove any more bishops, it doesn't stop you from *adding* them, does it? You can put bishoprics wherever you like   your good friend Boniface has already helped you there, with his addition of Eichstat in Bavaria. And didn't you put your own man in as Bishop in Alemannia?"

"Duke Lantfrid was not too happy about that."

"And what is he likely to do about it?"

"Good question."

Chrodegang picked up his cup. "You needn't worry about a toad like Lantfrid. I can handle him."

"You'd better be careful that the bishops don't come after you."

"They won't. They are still afraid of you. They know you are not one to bluff. The bishops, on the other hand, are excellent bluffers. Truthfully, I think Eucher was relieved to make a deal, given his failure to convene the Synod. Still, I believe you should avoid such confrontations in the future. It wouldn't be good for your image. Give him this small concession, and he will be placated."

"For how long?"

Chrodegang shrugged. "For now. In the meantime, your missions will grow, and the Church will gain tithers, which is what the Church wants most of all."

"I thought it was saved souls."

"Aha! They leave that to the irritants like Boniface and his ilk. Better to have them out in heathenland converting pagans than hanging around the parishes, nagging the bishops about their morals. If there is anything bishops despise, it's priests with morals. I heard your excursion in Bavaria went well, did it?"

"As well as it could."

"Lord, Charles, where did you get such modesty? Certainly not from your father. Your mother must have been a saint!" He paused, realizing what he had said. "I'm sorry Charles. My mouth runs away with me sometimes."

"It's all right, Chancellor."

There was a silence. Then the monk said thoughtfully, "Whatever did happen to your mother?"

Charles hesitated. "She was executed. For adultery."

Chrodegang raised a bushy eyebrow. "Adultery?"

"That is what Pipin claimed. She was pregnant—he said the child was not his. So he had her beheaded."

Chrodegang crossed himself. "Good Lord, Charles. I'm so sorry. I can't imagine—"

"It was a long time ago. I don't remember her." Charles' voice was flat. Chrodegang regarded him critically.

"Well, still. One never gets over the loss of a mother. I understand now your ... well, your *attitude* toward your father. That he would do such a thing—"

"As I said, it was a long time ago," Charles said, more sharply.

"Of course, forgive me. By the way, whatever happened to your poor unfortunate Bavarian princess? Have you heard news of her?"

Only Chrodegang would dare to mention Svana to him directly.

"No."

"Ah, well, I am sorry, my prince."

"Why?"

"Just because I am a priest does not mean I am not a man, you know."

Charles gave him a sideways look. "I could not tell under all that blubber."

Chrodegang laughed. "Well, if a man cannot have women, he might as well have food."

There was a knock at the door.

"Come in." Charles poured more wine into his cup. He saw the door open and grinned broadly when a large man wearing a filthy mantel entered the room.

"Goon! Where the hell have you been?" Charles rose to greet him. "God, you stink. You were supposed to be back weeks ago. I was getting worried. Did you run into trouble?"

"Some." Gunther glanced at the monk at the table. "I can come back later—"

"Nonsense!" Chrodegang said, lurching to his feet. "I was just leaving. Must roll myself into bed and sleep this bounty off. Charles, good night. See you at breakfast!"

When he was gone, Charles turned to Gunther. His smile faded. "What is it?"

The big man shifted uncomfortably "I have news."

Charles nodded. "Sit down. I'll get you some wine."

Gunther sat heavily in Chrodegang's vacated chair. Charles handed him a cup and sat across from him.

"You got some horses?"

"Yes. That part of the journey went well." Gunther drank and set the cup down. He looked into Charles' eyes. "Eudo has given his daughter in marriage to the Arab governor Othman ben abi-Nêssa. They have formed an alliance. And—they are on the move."

Charles straightened. "What do you mean?"

"I mean they are intending to attack us. They were headed to the Dordogne, last we saw. We think they are going to move into Burgundy. Your loyalties are weak there. They also know you have been in the field all summer and your armies have gone home."

Charles leaned his elbows on the table, head in his hands. There would be no winter of rest, after all.

"I don't believe it."

"Well, believe it."

"How do you know all this? You said 'we.' Who is 'we'?"

Gunther paused before answering. "I met a man. Calls himself Brand. A Burgundian, he tells me. I hired him as a translator and a guide. For buying the horses."

"And?"

"He infiltrated Eudo's camp. That's how we learned what was going on."

"Infiltrated? This man is a spy?"

Gunther shrugged. "He is a jongleur, a wastrel, a player of tricks, but he has some ... unusual talents. In fact, I suspect ... " Gunther stopped, took a drink from his cup.

"What do you suspect?"

Gunther looked at Charles. "You will think me mad, but I believe this man … may be your brother." Charles stared at him. Gunther went on. "He looks like you. But it's not just the looks. There was much he could not explain. He was raised in Vienne. His mother never told him who his father was—"

Charles turned his gaze to the fire. "My mother died a long time ago, the child with her."

Gunther shrugged. "What if she didn't? What if your father hid her and kept it a secret?"

"Why would he do that?"

"Perhaps—he loved her. And he wanted her to be safe from Plectruda."

"No—this is impossible—"

"Just talk to him. Decide for yourself."

"He's here?"

"Yes. Waiting outside. He didn't want to come; I insisted."

"Does he know of your suspicions?"

"No. I told him nothing. Just that I wanted him to report to you directly about Eudo."

Charles did not move for a long time. He said, very softly, "Send him in."

# 52

A FEW MINUTES later Brand stood in the doorway. He gave a short, awkward bow.

"My lord."

Charles could say nothing for a long time. In some ways, it was like looking in a mirror, though this man was younger, his eyes bluer, his face open and appealing. Brand seemed to color a bit under the scrutiny, but he remained still, waiting.

Finally, Charles spoke. "Sit down."

Brand moved to the table and sat. Charles sat as well. They looked at each other.

"Goon tells me you have information about the Duke of Aquitaine."

"Yes, Lord."

"How did you get into Eudo's camp?"

"With wine, lots of it. Soldiers like to drink, and when they drink they talk, and I am a good listener. They say he had to drag his daughter to the altar kicking and screaming." There was an awkward silence. Brand eyed the carafe of wine. "Do you mind?"

"Help yourself."

Brand poured himself a cup, trying to avoid Charles' intense perusal.

"Gunther says you are from Vienne."

Brand drank deeply from the cup. "I was … once. But I left a long time ago. I didn't much care for the life of a country farmer." Brand drank some more.

"Where did you go?"

"Nowhere in particular. I traveled. I like traveling. I am a singer, mostly. I ended up in Tolosa because the wine and the money were better—"

"Your mother," Charles said, interrupting. "Tell me about her."

Brand's face closed in, his eyes narrowed. "Why do you want to know?"

"Did she look like you?"

"Well—yes, I suppose—"

"What do you remember?"

Brand closed his eyes, as if trying to picture her. "She used to sing … I think that is where I got my penchant for singing. A song about a sparrow … I can't remember how it goes … " He started to hum a little.

Charles let a moment pass. "And your father?"

"She told me he was dead." He paused. Then he looked directly at Charles, a new expression on his face. "But that was a lie. I know who my father was."

"You do?"

"Yes. I've known it, perhaps, since I was seven or eight. I was playing in the square with some of the village boys, and they were taunting me. About my name. It was then that I learned the truth. My name, you see, is Childebrand."

He paused, looking at Charles, who closed his eyes briefly.

"You see what I mean? It is a Merovingian name. The boys in the village knew it before I did. It was quite common, there were Meroving bastards all over the kingdom. My mother tried to protect me. She didn't want me to know that I was the product of a diseased and degenerate line, doomed to die at an early age. That's when it all came clear to me. I had imagined my mother was a kind of enchanted princess. But it wasn't true. She had been some Meroving's concubine, banished and forgotten. So I ran away. Ended up in Septimania. As if I could escape my fate."

"How did you live?"

"I worked on ships first, traveling around the Middle Sea, port to port. That's where I first started singing. Drinking songs. I had learned other things on the ships as well: magic tricks, storytelling, games. I became a prime amusement for wealthy men—and their wives—" his voice dropped off. "It was better than swabbing decks anyway. I went everywhere, Italy, Greece, Mauritania, Asia Minor, even Constantinople, for a time. I learned Greek and Arabic. Somehow I ended up back in Tolosa, working the alehouses. The money was good enough, and I was free, I could drink as much as I wanted, and I did not have to think about—the future." He stopped, drank more wine, tipping up his cup to get the last dregs. After a long silence Charles spoke again.

"Did you go back to see your mother again?"

"Once. She was dying by then. I waited for her to die. Then the count arrived, with a deed saying her land had been a benefice and he was taking it back. I had a deed stating the land had been a permanent gift from the King of the Franks, but his deed was backed up by quite a few more armed guards than mine, so his deed won." Brand sat back in his chair, winded by the tale, his face emptied.

Charles closed his eyes a moment, breathing slowly. When he opened them again they were soft, almost warm. "Brand," he said, "you are not a Meroving."

Brand stared at him. "How do you know?"

"Because I believe that your mother and mine—are the same."

Brand sat perfectly still, blue eyes wide with shock. "That cannot be."

"I remember the song," Charles said. "The song about the sparrow."

"It is a common enough song."

"Is it?"

Brand shook his head, turning away, his body bent as if in pain. "I beg your leave," he whispered. Then he left, as if escaping with his life.

# 53

THE NEXT DAY Charles and Lothar went out hunting, though the game was scarce and both their moods subdued. The day was unusually warm, the heather was high, the fields not yet mown. They stopped for awhile to let the horses graze and sat on rocks by the river, skipping stones into the water, one of their favorite pastimes from the old days. Charles still felt the tension between them, Lothar's morose silence in the wake of the disaster in Kolonia. Everyone, even Rotruda, sensed there was something wrong. He knew, despite his own lingering anger at what Lothar had done, he needed to mend some fences with his oldest friend.

So he told Lothar about meeting Brand.

"Of course he wouldn't believe it," Lothar said irritably. "Who would? You cannot be sure anyway."

"He does look like me."

"That is not proof."

"Gunther is convinced."

"Gunther believes that pigs have evil spirits too. You can't listen to him all the time." He paused, then sighed. "He's probably right anyway. It's much more plausible that he is a Meroving bastard than your brother."

"He does not act like a Meroving. Or even look like one. I think it is very likely that my mother created that ruse herself, to protect him from Plectruda. It may be why she even gave him a Merovingian name."

"So you believe it too?"

"When I looked at him—I knew. A man should know his own brother."

"Well, fine for you. It's the least of your problems now. What are you going to do about Eudo?"

Charles sighed. "I don't know," he said. "It will take weeks, months even to recall enough men to put together a decent force. And if I do that the harvest will not be brought in and the winter wheat will not get planted. People will starve next year."

"If you don't meet him, he will ravage Burgundy unopposed. Arnulf cannot handle that alone."

"I know. Neither can I stop him with my standing army alone. We can try to delay him, perhaps, until I can recall enough troops. Gerold and Milo will come, and Peppo and Sigebald. I doubt very much that I can count on any of the Burgundian nobles. It is grape-picking season. They may send a few companies, but their obligations are done for the year."

Lothar scoffed. "I told you this would happen."

"Yes, yes, I know you did," Charles said tiredly. "I still can't believe that he did it—gave his own daughter to an Arab—"

"He would do anything to get back at you for Soissons. You should have finished him off when you had the opportunity. You let him go, and this is how he repays you."

They rode back to the city in the early afternoon, as clouds began rolling in from the west, threatening rain. Gunther met him at the stables and took the reins of the horse.

"Rain coming," Gunther said, sniffing the air like a hound.

"Yes. Everything all right?"

Gunther glanced at Lothar, who was engaged in conversation with other men milling about the stable. He drew closer to Charles and spoke softly.

"There's something I didn't tell you last night ... " he began, then faltered.

"What is it?"

"Your woman the Valkyrie I saw her in Tulosa."

Charles stared at him. "That's not possible."

"It was her. They say she is Eudo's mistress now."

Charles gazed at him a long moment, then turned away. "Give him extra hay," he said, giving the horse's neck a long stroke. "I'll see you at dinner."

# 54

## Aquitaine
## October, 728

SVANA SAT ON a small wooden bench in her little garden on the side of her house, watching Gryffin play in a mud puddle. The boy was laughing and slapping the mud, sending up shoots of brown goo on her skirt, but she did not scold him. It was rare that he was simply happy. Her own heart was disquiet. She looked out, over the vineyards, as if she could see the army of the Aquitaine moving east.

"My lady?" Freddy, carrying a laundry basket, stopped in front of her. She followed Svana's gaze to the distant hills and then sat down beside her. "Eudo has ten thousand men," she said idly. "How many can Charles muster this time of year?"

Svana said nothing. This was partly her fault; she had chided Eudo in his palace in front of his guests. Yet she had never imagined it would come to this: that Eudo would form an alliance with the Arabs and attack Charles directly. She wished she could take it back, every word. Perhaps if she had slept with him, told him who she was, it would have been enough for him. He would have considered the conquest of Charles' mistress victory enough. But she had been proud, and stubborn, and foolish, as she had always been.

Yet Eudo continued to buy her wine, and she had picked up several more prominent customers since that time. Her vineyard was a bustling, thriving place, as more and more displaced villagers came to settle and work. Eudo never returned himself, always sending his agents to place orders and pay in gold. He never sent her a personal message. She had wounded him deeply, she knew. He would not face her again. But she thought the crisis was passed. Now she saw that she was wrong.

"Perhaps there is still time to stop him," Freddy said cautiously, gazing at her mistress.

"I don't see how."

"Don't you?" Freddy said softly. "Eudo would do anything for you, I think. And Charles … he would too … " she broke off. Svana looked at her.

"Freddy … are you thinking what I think you are thinking?"

Freddy blushed. "I think so."

"It would never work," Svana said doubtfully.

"Maybe not, but what is there to lose?"

Svana thought of what there was to lose—she could not bear it. If there was even a ghost of a chance she could help avert a war, she would have to try.

"Send Mattheus into the village, tell him to find some men who can ride very swiftly and are not afraid of danger on the road. They will be paid well. Hurry."

Freddy nodded excitedly and dashed off. Svana looked down at her son, *his* son. What would he say when he knew the truth? Would he be angry? Would he force her to return with him to Francia? Perhaps he had wiped her from his mind and would not care at all. She didn't know if she could bear that—his indifference. She'd rather he hated her.

Erik appeared, wiping his purple-stained hands on his shirt. "My lady? What has happened?"

Svana turned to look at him. "We are leaving tomorrow."

"For where?"

"Vichy."

# 55

CHARLES LEARNED FROM his scouts that the Aquitainian-Arab army had already crossed the Cevenna mountains east of Tolosa and were headed toward the Burgundian frontier. Eudo seemed to be hovering near the border, raiding towns and monasteries, waiting for the Franks to come to him.

Yet Charles was hesitant to move right away. He did not like being pushed into a fight, and he could muster barely a quarter of Eudo's strength. So he waited. He stayed in his study, staring at his maps day and night, struggling to figure out what to do.

Then the matter seemed to be decided for him. A letter arrived from the Aquitaine. It was very short.

"Vichy. House on the square with black shutters. Come by the 5th. No later. S."

*S.* He held the scroll a long time. The large letter S seemed burned into it, the force of that single symbol so real he could almost feel her hand upon the paper, gripping the quill. She had been gone for three years, yet every day seemed like the first day; he would lie in bed, breathing deeply, moving through the numbing ache toward the will to rise. He had been amazed at his own weakness. And then, when Gunther had told him what he had seen, the unhealed wound that was his memory had opened to bleed anew.

Why was she summoning him now? After all this time? And why there? Vichy? So close to Eudo's position …

*Eudo.*

He went back to his maps. Vichy was more than a week's ride away. If he left immediately and traveled alone he might make it in time. But it would be difficult; Lothar, in particular, would want an explanation.

Charles always travelled with the army; it was his policy to make sure the men who fought for him knew he was with them.

He sat at the table and poured a cup of wine, thinking.

After awhile he was interrupted by a knock at the door. The sound jarred him from his reveries. "Come in," he said, rolling up the scroll and tossing it on the fire.

"My lord."

He looked up; Brand stood in the doorway.

"Call me Charles," he said.

"Charles." Brand came into the room slowly. "That will take some practice."

"Sit down."

Charles sat and waited for Brand to sit across from him and pour himself a cup of wine. He took a long drink.

"Spiced wine," he said. "Something you northern Franks are fond of. Burgundian wine does not need such—adornment." He smiled painfully, setting down the cup. "I came to apologize … for the way I left last time."

"You don't have to."

"I do though. The thing is … I've had some time to think. I was telling myself that your notion—Gunther's notion—was sheer nonsense. It could not be true. But then I remembered something. About my mother." He paused, turning the cup of wine in his hands idly. "You remember how I told you I had gone back home? I don't know why I did. I had left the Empire, wandered through Asia Minor … then something told me to go home. I just felt as though I had to, maybe it was God … I don't know.

"She was very ill. Some sort of growth in the throat, the doctor said. She could not eat; she had wasted to nothing. A girl from the town attended her, feeding her broth and washing her. She could barely speak.

"I prayed for her to die quickly. I am a coward when it comes to death. I have avoided ugliness all my life. And she had been so beautiful. To see her like that was torture. I thought of ending it for her. But I didn't have the courage even for that.

"I couldn't understand what was keeping her alive. I had the idea she was waiting for something. Maybe someone … I thought it might be my father. She never married, and she had spurned all suitors. It was possible, after all, that she might have loved him.

"Sometimes she would try to ask me questions. I could not understand what she was saying. But there was one word I understood: 'war.' I thought it odd. We Burgundians never paid much attention to the war between Austrasia and Neustria. It all seemed very far away. I thought she was losing her mind.

"I spent a lot of time in the taverns, drinking my problems away. It worked, for awhile. Then one day news arrived about Ambléve—the battle, *your* battle. It was a shock, I can tell you. Most everyone thought you were dead, or still in hiding. People began to panic; I guess they thought we would be next. You know, most people have no idea how close or far away other places are? Anyway, there was general mayhem.

"That night I went home and told her what I had heard. 'Charles defeated the Neustrians at Ambléve.' She looked at me with her mournful eyes, and for an instant, I thought I saw her smile. Six hours later, she was dead."

He paused, taking a long breath. "It occurs to me now, what she was waiting for all that time. It wasn't my father. It was news of you. It was *you*, all the time."

He looked at Charles, who did not speak. He laughed a little. "Life is strange, isn't it? One minute you are the unknown relation of the dreaded Merovings, the next you are the brother to the greatest Frankish ruler since Clovis. How can it be?"

Charles did not answer. He was remembering his mother, Alpaide. He saw only unfinished sketches of her face, the shape of her mouth when she scolded him, the sound of her voice when she sang him to sleep, the Sparrow's Song.

*This leads me to the lonely mourn*
*The song of the sparrow, song of woe*
*That carried me to a faraway place*
*Where I can dream, where rivers flow …*
*Is not the sparrow loved of God?*
*For sold for farthings, a price so low …*
*Fear ye not, for ye are loved*
*Far more than the lowly sparrow*

He had not thought of her much in the past twenty years. He thought of her now with a sudden, inconsolable sadness. And, finally, he mourned.

*Vienne*. She had been there all the time. *So close*. Yet he had never known, his father had never told him. Pipin, it seemed, had won that last battle, after all.

Brand went on. "I'm sorry … this must be very hard for you. You are so much like her. I should have seen that from the first. She was the kind of person you could never live up to … that's why I left home, I think. I knew I would be a disappointment to her. Just as I will surely be a disappointment to you. So I will be leaving soon—"

"No," Charles said, as if awakening from some dream. "Brand, listen to me. I don't care what you've been before. I need you now."

Brand shook his head. "No, you don't. I am nothing like you. I am not brave. I am not a warrior. I am a useless wastrel. Don't get any ideas of fashioning me into something I can never be."

"You have eyes and ears," Charles said. "And you know how to use them. You know languages. You were brave enough to infiltrate an enemy camp with nothing but your wits and a few wineskins. And Gunther says you have pretty good aim."

Brand laughed broadly. "When it comes to killing painted bulls I am your man."

"We shall see." Charles paused, then said, "If you want to go home, I won't stop you. But do this one thing for me. I am riding to Vichy tomorrow. Come with me."

"Vichy? What for?"

"Have you been there?"

"Yes, of course. The town of baths, beloved of the Romans. The springs there are said to promote healing of various lung diseases. But what do you want me for?"

"It's a long ride and I need some company. I can't spare any of my captains. And … this is the sort of mission that needs to be—kept quiet, if you know what I mean."

Brand grinned a little, intrigued. "Ah, a secret mission. My favorite kind. All right, I'll come."

Charles smiled for the first time. "And when that is done, I will see about getting you back your lands."

# 56

## Vichy

SVANA HEARD THE horses in the courtyard and sat down on the marble bench by the fountain, folding her hands in her lap. She breathed deeply, forcing her heart to slow, repeating the words she had recited over and over to herself: *This is for Charles.*

"Svana?" Eudo's voice echoed against the stucco walls of the atrium. He came into the peristyle garden, an open space in the center of this Roman house. The flowers had withered, but the trees still held some green, dappling the stone floor with autumn sunrays. It was a lovely house. The owner had agreed to rent it to her for an exorbitant sum, but she did not care. She told him her child was suffering from a breathing illness and needed the baths for healing; he did not question her story.

She rose to meet him. He came to her, his face clouded with worry. "What is the matter? Are you ill?"

"No."

"Then why did you send for me?"

"I needed to see you … " Her mouth trembled. He waited, watching her. "I have … missed you."

"Missed me?" He looked at her, confused. "The last time I saw you, you turned me away."

"I know. I'm sorry. I was … wrong."

She paused, taking a breath. She did not think she could speak more. But then she didn't have to. He came to her, pulled her to him, his hand on the back of her neck, his mouth on hers. She stood still, allowing him to kiss her. He stood back a moment and looked at her.

"Where?" he said, his voice hoarse with desire.

She pointed to a doorway. He picked her up and carried her into the sleeping room. He pulled off her gown and laid her down, undressed quickly and lay on top of her.

She had prepared herself for this, willing her mind and her body to a state of unconsciousness, building around her a shell as hard and factual as the Valkyrie's armor she once had donned in pursuit of freedom. This was a sacrifice she had to make, was glad to make, for Charles.

Yet there was no shame in it, no remorse. There were only his hands, the hands that knew her in an entirely different way from Charles, the taut and trembling body where she could feel every inch of bone and muscle under his skin. She gripped the coverlet, arching against him as he came into her, his breath hoarse in her ear. He collapsed against her, and she put her arms around him, tenderly, stroking his back. She closed her eyes, so she would not have to see his face.

She awoke sometime later to find him standing in front of the tiny window, naked, his back to her. His gauntness was sharpened in the moonlight, the sinew of his long arms, the individual bones of his narrow back.

"Eudo?" she said softly, as if to be sure it was really him.

After a few minutes, he said: "I am fifty years old." He paused. "How old are you?"

"Twenty-nine."

He made a sound like a sigh. "I used to wonder, when I was twenty-nine, what it would be like to be fifty. What it would be like to look in the mirror and see an old man, with lines in his face and gray in his hair, to realize that life was almost over. I kept waiting for the day when I would wake up and it would have happened. It did happen one day. But then the next day I was all right, and it might be some time before it happened again … These last few years, though, I began to see that it was here to stay. And now … " he turned to her, "now I am simply afraid, because I've forgotten what it felt like to be young, to be twenty-nine. I think perhaps that twenty-nine year old man was not me, it was some other man, that in the intervening years he was slowly replaced, metamorphosed, like a caterpillar turned into a moth. That's why I'm afraid. Not because I was so happy being a caterpillar. It's just that I am not ready to be a moth." He turned back to the window.

She said, "Eudo, if you could have one wish granted, anything at all, what would it be? To be twenty-nine again?"

She saw his shoulders heave a little. "To be twenty-nine forever."

In the morning he told her he had to go back. She begged him to stay. *One more day*, she said. He tried to resist, feebly. *One more day. But no more.* She hoped it would be enough.

# 57

SHE WAS AWAKENED early the next morning by shrill, childish shrieks emanating from the other sleeping room. She sat up, gently pushing Eudo away, and got out of bed. She pulled on her gown and padded into the other room.

Gryffin lay on his pallet in the throes of a nightmare, still mostly asleep. She sighed, picking him up and holding him until he calmed down. She called for Freddy, but there was no answer. *Erik*, she thought, smiling to herself. She knew they were in love, though neither of them had admitted it to her yet. Freddy must have snuck out during the night.

Svana carried Gryffin out to the garden and set him down on the bench by the fountain. The boy soon recovered his good humor and was trying to get to the water in the fountain, splashing it with the flat of his hand. He shrieked with delight as the water sprayed him in the face. Then he splashed some at Svana, who laughed and splashed him back. Soon they were immersed in an all out water war, both completely drenched, rolling around on the floor in a mock tussle, Gryffin giggling while she tickled him. Neither of them heard the horses in the courtyard or the footsteps echoing in the atrium.

She felt him before she saw him, as she always did, his presence in the room like a pressure on her face, a heat. She rolled to a sitting position, Gryffin still in her arms, still giggling. She looked at him.

He was not looking at her. He was looking at the child, and his face was white and still with shock. She sat still, watching him, waiting.

He looked the same. She had remembered the details correctly: the stone-cut face, the sun-colored hair, the crystal eyes. He was dressed in his peasant costume, as usual, in leather tunic and braccos. He looked not like a man but a force of nature, part of the ordained order of the world. She thought it odd that he should be there, in that Roman house with its Corinthian columns and stucco walls, a place made by men in affront to nature. She thought he looked all wrong there—but perhaps it was the house that was wrong.

She didn't think more; he moved to her, pulled her to her feet, his mouth seizing hers in an embrace that contained every month and hour of their separation within its grasp. She gave herself up to this, pulling his mouth more deeply into hers. Gryffin, alone on the floor, began to cry.

It was this sound that made him pull away abruptly. He held her at arm's length, his eyes cooling. He looked down at the child.

"What's his name?"

"Gryffin."

He smiled at that. He touched her face, pushed a shock of wet hair out of her eyes. "He has your face … your hair."

"Your eyes."

He closed his eyes, breathing. Then he crouched to look at the boy. Gryffin stared at him, hiccoughing, suddenly too afraid to cry.

"You ought to have told me."

"I never expected to see you again, Charles. I never thought … you would want to see me again. It was over."

He straightened, looking at her. There was no anger in his eyes. "I would never have abandoned you, Svana."

"I know. We can't talk of this now. There are other things—"

Just then the door of the sleeping cubicle opened.

"Svana? Where are you? What are you doing up so early—"

Eudo came out, pulling a long, Roman-style tunica over his head. He stopped, his gaze honing in on Charles with the predatory focus of the bird for which he was named.

There was shock, then bewilderment, then spellbinding anger in his face. Svana looked to Charles, expecting to see the same in him. But he looked different—tired, perhaps. There was no shock there, only a defused sorrow, the barest hint of a scar. He already knew, she thought, and wondered how that could be.

"So this is him? The father of your child?" Eudo's voice cut sharply into her thoughts. He was looking at her now, his fury clearer, more exposed than she had ever seen it. Perhaps he saw the resemblance—the eyes—in the boy and this man. He was no fool.

"Yes," she said.

"You told me he was dead."

"I lied."

Eudo was silent, struggling. Charles waited, unmoving.

"You have some reason for coming here now, I presume?" Eudo said, addressing Charles for the first time.

"I was sent for," Charles said. His tone was strangely deferential. Svana glanced at him.

"You sent for him?" Eudo said, looking at her.

"Yes."

"Why, in heaven's name?"

"I wanted … I wanted you to meet." It was as near to the truth as she could venture. Suddenly the whole plan seemed ludicrous, paved for disaster.

"What for?" Eudo looked mystified. His eyes flicked from one to the other, roving endlessly. Then they stopped altogether, narrowed on Charles' face. He took a step forward. "Who are you?"

*No!* Svana screamed silently. "Eudo, please … " She moved toward him. Charles put a hand on her arm, stopping her. He drew a silent, shallow breath.

"My name, Eudo, is Charles."

Eudo closed his eyes.

When he had opened them again they were bright as black glass, curiously shining. The anger was gone, but the pain remained. He stood it well, he didn't flinch. She felt oddly proud of him at that moment.

Eudo glanced at her, a queer half-smile playing about his mouth. "So this was your game? To lure me here so I can meet your lover, my enemy … what have I ever done to you that you would desire to punish me in this way?"

"This is not about punishment Eudo. It is about truth. You need to talk to him—"

"Talk? No, I will not talk!" Eudo's eyes flicked to the wall where several Roman swords were mounted in an artistic design. He was there in an instant, ripping one of the swords off the wall and holding it out, the point directed at Charles.

"No!" Svana screamed. She ran toward him; Charles grabbed her, pulling her back.

"Get the boy out of here," he said roughly in her ear. "Now."

She obeyed, sweeping a bewildered Gryffin up from the floor and running to the sleeping room. When she returned to the garden, they were where she had left them, in frozen tableau. She suddenly realized that Charles was not even wearing a sword. She flattened herself against the door, her legs shaking so badly she could barely stand.

"Surely you did not come here without a weapon," Eudo said mockingly.

"I did not come to fight."

"Call your man to bring you a sword."

"No," Charles said sharply. "Not here. Outside. And if you insist on this, I suggest you use your own sword."

Eudo said nothing, but he did not stop Charles from walking out through the atrium into the courtyard.

"Don't think you are doing this for my sake," Svana said when he had gone. Her voice was hard-edged and bitter. "If you do this, you do it to save your own honor, not mine. You want to get back at him for Soissons, now is your chance. But that has nothing to do with me. I love him. Do you hear me, Eudo? *I love him.* He has broken no faith with me. He did only what I asked him to do. He is here because I asked him to come."

"Why for God's sake?" Eudo said, his voice winded with anguish.

"Because I can no longer stand to see the Aquitaine consumed by war and violence because you are too proud to ask for his help. Eudo, please, for your own sake, *wake up*. You must see that what you are doing is … *madness*. You are about to start a war with the only man on earth who can help you defeat this enemy. Your *real* enemy. Charles is not your enemy! He can help you, if you will only let him. Please—"

She stopped, struggling for breath, her chest tightening like a vice. Eudo stood still a moment, not looking at her. Then he turned, stiffly, and went into the sleeping room. He emerged a few minutes later wearing leggings and a mail shirt over his tunic. He carried his sword. He moved past her and headed outside to the courtyard, shouting for his guards.

# 58

SVANA FOLLOWED HIM out. A small crowd had already gathered in a wide circle—guards, servants, and Freddy and Erik, looking disheveled and rather bewildered. Then she noticed another man who looked remarkably like Charles handing him a sword. The two spoke briefly, then the other man looked directly at her and smiled. She gave a small nod of her head, astonished.

Eudo stood in the center of the circle and waited while Charles came to meet him. Charles was not wearing mail, only the leather tunic. Eudo raised his sword, assuming a fighting stance. Svana sighed, leaning against the portal. *Pride*, she thought. He had started it, he had to finish it. *Stupid Roman Pride.*

She saw Charles breathe deeply, raise his sword slowly. Eudo began to circle, gauging, taunting. Charles watched him, hardly moving at all. Then Eudo struck, his sword high, aiming for the shoulder and neck; Charles blocked it but did not make a counter-strike. Eudo pulled back, clearly perplexed. He struck again, this time a slice across the middle, and again Charles deflected the blow and stepped back, disengaging.

Charles let Eudo do all the fighting, countering the blows but refusing to strike back. His failure to attack began to wear on Eudo's nerves. He struck harder and faster, dancing in an ever-tightening circle, slicing sideways then thrusting, a dizzying display. People emerged from nearby houses to watch, curious. The crowd expanded, became more vocal. Money was soon changing hands.

Svana watched helplessly, unable to stop herself from comparing them. Eudo's skill derived from constant schooling—he knew a lot of expensive moves and he used them with great flair; he made the heavy long sword dance and sway like a beam of light. He was not a natural swordsman—each move took a conscious effort, an act of will, each move looked slightly staged. Charles seemed almost dull by comparison. He was not a showman with the sword, he did not make it do tricks as Eudo did, but the weapon seemed to be a natural extension of his arm, a part of his body. He moved effortlessly but with strict economy, as if every movement would exact a price he was unwilling to pay. In Eudo, it was how much he did that was impressive, in Charles, how little.

Gradually, almost imperceptibly, Eudo began to tire. He had ten years on his opponent, and it showed. As his strength waned, Charles' began to expand before their eyes, sucking in his energy as a sponge takes in water.

Finally, Eudo made a mistake. He had gone for a long, sweeping slice to Charles' right side, stopped by the edge of Charles' sword. He hesitated, gathering the strength he needed to pull back and raise the weapon again. It was the briefest of hesitations, but it was enough. Charles made his first offensive move then, sliding his own sword down the length of Eudo's blade and smashing it, striking it from his grip. Eudo sank to his knees as the edge of Charles' blade pressed the side of his neck. He was breathing hard, gulping in air, holding his wounded hand.

"Well, this makes it all nice and neat for you. Kill me and the Aquitaine is yours."

He was not surprised when Charles tossed his own sword to one of the guards. He was not surprised, but he was disappointed.

"You got what you wanted," Charles said to him. "Now, we talk." He turned, talked briefly to his men, and walked into the house, leaving Eudo alone in the circle of now silent spectators.

Charles paused before Svana then continued on, walking through the garden into the dining area. She followed. He sat heavily on one of the carved wooden chairs and poured wine from a clay pitcher into a cup.

She said, "You should have killed him."

He drank the wine. "See my men get something to eat. And a place to sleep. We've been riding all night." He ran a hand over his skull, pushing back the long hair from his face. She saw how tired he was, that hollow, sleepless quality he always had when he was at war. "I'll bring some food," she said. She turned and left the room.

A moment later Eudo came in, a bloodstained bandage wrapped around his hand. He sat on the other side of the table. He poured a cup of wine and drank. They sat quietly awhile, drinking. Svana returned with some bread and fruit and a wedge of cheese. She looked at the both of them, sighed, and left.

Finally, Eudo set down his cup, his gaze focused on the table before him.

"I must have conjured you a thousand times in my head," he said in a winded voice. "The ultimate Frank, big, bearded, muscles rippling every which way, brave and stupid, like your dear ancestor Clovis. You don't look like I pictured you. Except perhaps for the stupid part. At least Clovis knew enough to kill his enemies before they became a threat, while you just let them go on and on, plotting against you, making war on you, doing nothing to stop it."

He paused, then looked at Charles for the first time since coming into the room. "What sort of ruler does that? It's not natural. *You* are not natural. You should not have survived, Martel. You are like a turtle without a shell, a baby born without legs. How have you managed to live so long? If you had killed me out there, the Aquitaine would have been yours. You could have avoided this whole war. Why didn't you kill me?" His tone was curious, not angry.

"I need you, Eudo."

Eudo snorted. "Like a hole in the head you need me."

"The Aquitaine needs you. They would not accept me or any Frank as their ruler. You are the best duke we've got, not to mention the richest, and you command the second largest army in Gaul."

Eudo's eyebrows lifted slightly. "You seem to be forgetting that I made an alliance with the Arabs."

"You can break it. You haven't given Othman anything you can't take back."

"My daughter, you mean?"

"The Pope would annul the marriage."

"I don't think Othman would take kindly to that. He will make war on me if I break my oath."

"You would rather make war on me?"

Eudo leaned in, his voice betraying an almost gleeful derision. "Because I will win this time, Martel. I outnumber you three to one. I have chosen the ground. I cannot lose." He smiled coldly. "I have waited a long time for this. You will not take it from me."

Charles regarded him. "What if you don't?"

Eudo snorted. "Are you so full of yourself that you think you cannot lose?"

"No, but I know the difference between you and me. I go into every battle prepared to die. But you aren't ready for that. You are still afraid of death, while I am only afraid of losing. That's why you lost at Soissons. I studied your battles. I knew you would run when we attacked that night. You would not risk your army in a blind battle. You were not ready for a fight to the death."

"I just fought a duel with you, didn't I?"

"Did you really think I rode all this way just to kill you in a duel?"

"Why not? I would have killed you," Eudo said. He laughed tonelessly. Then his face grew still, he looked into the pale eyes, focusing. "Why *did* you ride all this way?" he asked softly.

"Because she asked me to."

"So you knew what she was planning?"

"I—suspected."

"Ha! Well, more fool me. It never even occurred to me." Eudo paused. "Did you know about her child?"

"No."

Eudo's face changed, softened, as if he suddenly felt this man, this enemy, to be a kindred spirit.

"She's good at secrets. She tried to stay hidden. Thought she could fritter her life away in that vineyard of hers, with the monks her guardians. But you don't know any of that, do you?"

"No." Vineyard? Monks? He had imagined her living at the edge of a cliff, overlooking a boundless sea, free, as she'd wanted to be. There had been comfort in that vision, and impossibility as well. He had thought one day to go and find her. But he had not really wanted to know the truth.

Eudo continued. "I came upon her estate quite by accident. Or maybe it was fate. Do you believe in fate, Hammer?"

"Sometimes."

"Do you believe every man has a destiny?"

"I suppose so."

"I do. And I will tell you what I have always believed: my destiny was to destroy you, or die in the trying. That is what my whole life has been about. Destroy Charles the Bastard. Free the Aquitaine from Frankish rule. That is what I live for."

"And you think you can do that with this absurd alliance?"

"I know I can."

"You would rather be ruled by the Arabs?"

Eudo's face darkened. "You sound like her now." Then he said in a different voice: "I do wonder now—I assume you stole her from one of your Bavarian raids, though I can't imagine how she allowed herself to be stolen. Must have been your rakish charm or was it something else?" When Charles did not answer, he went on. "All right then, tell me this: why did you let her go?"

Charles raised the cup to his lips, shifting uncomfortably in his chair. "I had no choice."

"I don't believe that. You are the Leader of the Franks, you could do anything you wanted. You could have married her. You could have kept her as your concubine. She tells me she loves you. From what I know of her, there is not much she loves. And yet you let her go." He laughed suddenly, joylessly. "She has played us both for fools. And we let her do it, because we are helpless men. Well … despite what you are thinking, she never let me near her before this. And believe me I tried. All of this—was for you."

Charles said nothing, staring into his cup.

Eudo poured more wine. "And what will you do with her now? Will you take her back with you?"

"If she wants to come."

"And if she doesn't? You will let her go … *again*?" Eudo sounded incredulous.

"I do not own her, Eudo," Charles said. "She is free to do what she wants."

"And your child too?" Eudo shook his head. "God, but you are the strangest man I ever met."

Charles slammed down his cup. "Can we get back to the matter at hand? This war. This alliance you've made … what are you going to do about it? You know it cannot last, it's only a stay of execution. Do you think the Emir in Cordova will put up with you forever?"

Eudo leaned back in his chair, gazing up at the ceiling. Charles waited, watching him.

"What about God, Charles Martel?"

Charles sat back, exhausted, as if this were the real duel, this play of words and thoughts and pointless questions, designed to wear him down, to goad him into making a fatal mistake. "What *about* God?"

"Is God on your side?"

"I do not stop to consider whose side God is on."

"Really? That's thoughtless of you. God is either for you or against you, isn't He? He can't be both. What if God sent the Arabs to punish us? He has been known to send infidels against his own people now and then, to teach them a lesson. What if God has had enough of us and wants to finish us off once and for all?"

"There is only one way to know," Charles said. "Fight them. If we lose, then we will know God's answer."

Eudo laughed out loud. "It's so simple to you, isn't it? Everything is simple to you. Fight! The righteous will prevail! How naïve you are. It would be a different world entirely if men prevailed simply because they were right." Eudo drank more wine.

"Whatever side God is on," Charles said tightly, "you must decide whose side *you* are on."

"I have already decided that. Isn't that why we are here? Isn't that why your army is on its way? What little army you could muster this time of year?"

"There is still time—"

"No. Time has run out. You only came here because you know you can't beat me this time."

"I may not have your numbers, but I don't need them. My men are the best-trained fighters in Gaul; every one of them is worth ten of yours. You know this, Eudo. You have seen them in action."

Eudo shifted his gaze away uncomfortably. "You have never faced the Arabs, Martel. I have. And I have beaten them before."

"Then why not do it again?" Charles said, leaning in with a swell of new urgency.

Eudo went still, his voice bereft of energy. "Because I can't do it, anymore. I know I can't. I need an end to this. To all of it. I can't destroy *them*, I know that now. But I *can* destroy you. It is a partial victory, but a victory, nonetheless. I must put Soissons to rest, once and for all."

Charles could say nothing to this. He knew the sort of torment this man lived with day after day, the dreams that kept him from truly finding peace. This was a warrior's hell, a general's nightmare. To have failed, and to have to live with that failure, until it could be undone.

Eudo rose suddenly, picking up the wine carafe. "We are out of wine," he said. He turned and left the room.

# 59

SVANA SAW THE man who looked like Charles sitting by himself on a log stump, a small harp on his lap, strumming softly. A musician. A *jongleur*, perhaps. She sat down next to him, handing him a piece of bread and some grapes.

"It's all we have," she said. She gazed into his eyes, so much warmer and softer than Charles', a deeper blue.

"I could eat a stick right now I'm so hungry." He smiled at her, setting the instrument aside and taking the food. "How's it going in there?"

She shrugged. "I can only hope Eudo will listen to him."

Brand ate a grape. "It doesn't seem to be his habit."

"No."

"But Charles … can be very persuasive."

"Yes." There was a silence. Then she said: "I didn't know he had a brother."

"Nor did I. It was quite a shock, I can tell you. If it is even true."

"You are … not sure?"

"Well, let's just say I'm still adjusting to the idea. It's quite absurd, actually. But perhaps it's not nearly so strange as your story."

"He told you then?"

Brand nodded. "It was a long ride, my lady." He smiled at her embarrassment. "This was a remarkable bit of diplomacy you pulled off."

She looked down at her hands. "Perhaps there is hope—as long as they don't kill each other."

He smiled. "I'm Brand, by the way."

"Brand." She looked at him. "You look like him."

Brand laughed. "That is as far as the resemblance goes, I can assure you." He paused, the smile fading. "He is … the most remarkable man I have ever met."

"Yes."

Brand took a bite of the bread. "What do you think will happen now?"

Svana did not answer at first. She looked at the sky, and then at the house, the doorway beyond which the two men sat together, talking. It was a miracle, she thought, that this was even happening. Why not believe another miracle? Why could not this day be filled with miracles?

She said: "There was a time when I thought God could not be trusted. So I set myself against Him. I became a warrior for Odin. Odin promised freedom. Odin's justice I could understand. But then ... " she paused, blinking against tears. "But then ... there was Charles. When I first saw his eyes, I thought they were the eyes of God. I knew God was with Charles. I cannot explain it. But in all that has happened since then—I have seen God's hand. Charles thinks he doesn't need God. He doesn't realize how much God needs him." She smiled faintly, clasping her hands together. "Whatever happens, Brand, God is in control."

"What will you do after this?" Brand asked softly. "Will you ... stay with him?"

She shook her head. "He has a wife. I have heard she is beautiful. And good. He needs that. A good wife. I have only brought him grief." Her voice drifted off. She was still looking toward the house, her eyes shining. "What about you?"

"Me?"

"Will you stay? With him?"

Brand laughed. "If he will have me. I'm still not sure what use I can be to him, but he's given me a world of material for a song or two. Might prove profitable."

"I'm glad."

Brand cleared his throat, setting down the empty plate. "I hear you are pretty handy with a bow," he said lightly.

She looked at him, startled, then smiled despite herself. "I'm out of practice," she said.

"Well, do you think you might give me a lesson?"

# 60

SHE AWOKE SUDDENLY, seeing his eyes, thinking at first she was dreaming. But he was there, crouched by her sleeping couch, looking at her. It was dark, but the tiny flame from the oil lamp on the table reflected in his clear eyes, making them dance with a warmth they did not possess in the day. She sat up, alarmed.

"Where's Eudo?"

"He's gone."

"He didn't … "

He shook his head.

"Charles … I'm sorry—"

"Don't be." He straightened, moved to the window, putting distance between them. "If not for you this would not have happened. At least, it was a chance."

"So—we failed?"

"We did not have much hope of success. He is—a proud man."

Svana sighed. "Yes." She could barely see him in the dim light. "Charles—"

He turned to look at her. "What is he to you?"

"Nothing."

"Don't lie to me, Svana."

She lowered her gaze. "He is—my penance," she said softly. She could not tell his reaction. His body seemed too stiff, too still. "What will you do now?"

"I have to go. My army is waiting."

"Can't you—stay a little while?"

He hesitated, shook his head. "No."

"Charles." Her eyes reached his, pleading. "What I did … I did for you."

"I know it."

"Does it hurt so much?"

"More than you can know."

"But—"

"Svana, listen to me. You know I want nothing more than to take you now, this moment. To take you back to Kolonia with me, to marry you, to have you with me forever. But you are the one person on earth— besides him, perhaps—who I cannot command. I have no power to make you do anything, and I don't want that power. If you come to me, you have to come freely. Do you understand?"

She pulled her knees to her chest, hot tears pressing the backs of her eyes. "Will I see you again?"

"If I survive this war," he said, and she heard the bitter humor in his tone. "But there is one thing I am going to ask. You have a son of mine, I have a right to protect him. I will send a guard to you—"

"No," Svana said. "Eudo has already given me a guard. We are perfectly safe."

Charles sighed. "Well then, promise me if there is any—trouble—you will go north, north of the river at least, and let me know where you are. Will you do that?"

She nodded, still not looking at him.

"Svana, look at me." She looked up as he crouched beside her. He reached out and brushed the tears from her cheeks. "I will wait. I have forever to wait." He kissed her, so lightly she thought it was only the memory of his kiss she felt. Then he was gone, and she lay down on the couch, curling into a ball, and wept.

Eudo stood on a rock and stared out over the flat, marshy landscape. They were there in plain view. Franks. So few. They would come too late, his armies. Charles had won battles when he was outnumbered, but this time, he had neither surprise nor numbers nor even ground of his choosing. Eudo had every advantage.

He knew he should attack quickly. He knew Charles would wait for him to make the first move. Charles would fight a defensive war, because he had no choice. He already had his men building earthen walls—the Franks were known to throw up fortifications overnight. And there were those menacing horses to contend with—he remembered them all too well. Of course, he had horses of his own now, Arab light cavalry, fast and lethal.

He would win this one. He knew it. There was simply no way he could lose. He had waited for this moment for ten years, ever since that bastard prince had escaped from his prison cell. He didn't care about the price he would have to pay. He knew better than Charles what that price would be, but that was for later. Now he had redemption. Nothing else mattered.

He thought of Svana, felt a bitter laugh in his throat. What perfect justice, that she should belong to him. But then, Svana belonged to no man.

He remembered the things Charles had said to him. He could not get them out of his mind. He tried to identify what he felt about the man, tried to conjure the consuming hatred that had always come so easily, but that passion eluded him now. He had imagined the Hammer of the Franks as some formless monster, a demon of the night as he had first appeared in Soissons, but now the monster had a face, a voice, the monster was a man, and the man was not invincible. The man had shown his weakness. The man did not want to fight at all.

He had not been able to think straight when he was in the room with him. Now he was thinking, thinking hard. And he thought of something that even Charles had not considered. He laughed aloud.

He rode back to the main camp and dismounted, ignoring the questions fired at him by his captains. He strode nonstop to Othman's elaborate tent.

Othman ben-abi Nêssa was seated on a purple cushion on the floor, surrounded by his chieftains, eating some strong smelling stew out of a wooden bowl. He looked up in anger as Eudo barged into the tent. Arab guards surrounded him, swords drawn.

"What is the meaning of this?" Othman demanded.

"I'm pulling out," said Eudo of Aquitaine.

Othman stared at him, aghast. "What did you say?"

"I'm pulling out. I'm going home."

For a moment the Arab governor could not respond. His closest aide jumped to his feet, enraged.

"Are you mad?" he sputtered. "You cannot leave this field! We are about to do battle—"

"You can fight, if you want. But I'm taking my army and leaving."

"You are breaking the alliance?" Othman said, rising, casting the bowl aside.

Eudo did not flinch. "Not at all. I will hold to my part of the bargain. I gave you my daughter, and the promise that I would not fight against you. I didn't say I would necessarily fight *with* you."

"But you agreed—"

"I withdraw my agreement."

Othman's face darkened. He sputtered in rage. "Why?"

Eudo appeared to think about this. "I don't like the odds," he said.

"But … the odds are in our favor! We outman him, outhorse him, we have every advantage!"

"It's not enough," Eudo said. "You've never fought him, you don't know what he can do. He doesn't fight battles he isn't prepared to win. He would find a way to win this one. That is why he is here. We moved too soon. I would wait if I were you, Othman, wait until you are at full strength, wait until you have enough men to beat him."

"How many men will it take? How many will be enough?"

Eudo thought about this, then laughed suddenly. "There may not be enough in the entire world! You can do what you please. I'm going home."

Charles and Brand stood atop a small hill and stared at the army across the plain in disbelief. Stakes were being pulled up, horses saddled, carts filled with provisions. The Arab-Aquitainian army was pulling out.

"It's unbelievable," Brand said. "Is he really retreating?"

"Don't mistake his retreat for surrender." Charles paused, then said more softly, "He will never surrender."

"I think you are wrong. Every man has his limits. Eudo will come to his, eventually."

"As will we all," Charles said.

Brand regarded him. "Well. I suppose we can go home now, right? Came all this way for nothing."

"Not for nothing." He was thinking of Svana, of her hair and her face and her dark, liquid eyes, and despite his relief at seeing the enemy leave the field, his whole body ached with longing. He wanted to ride back to Vichy, take her in his arms, take her back to Kolonia with him. But she wasn't ready for that. He remembered saying as much to Eudo: *You aren't ready*.

So he was letting her go, with his son, back to Bordeaux, back to the protection and possibly the bed of his enemy. He shut his eyes, trying to rid himself of that vision for the hundredth time, knowing that the killing grief would become as much a part of his life as breathing. Sometimes, it seemed, the hardest thing in the world to do was nothing.

After a moment he opened his eyes again and turned away from Eudo's army to face his own men waiting for him.

"Let's go home," he said.

# 61

## Herstal
## December, 728

WET SNOW FELL softly on the house at Herstal, a great gray palace by a gray river under a sullen gray sky. Rotruda rode her mare beside Lothar along the river path outside the palace walls, her first outing since her arrival. This was Charles' birthplace, his father Pipin's family stronghold, his mother's home until her exile. There were too many ghosts here, she thought; too many old, tattered memories. Too much silence.

She had sought out Lothar's company. Since his return from Vichy, Charles' own silence had become unbearable to her. She felt something had changed irrevocably in him since his homecoming, which she had hoped would be a joyous affair after such a narrow escape in Burgundy. Instead, he seemed more withdrawn than ever, staying in his rooms with Chrodegang and his other advisors, rarely even joining the company for dinner. She wished now she had stayed in Paris; coming to Herstal to be with him had been a terrible mistake.

She shivered; it was cold. The gray around her felt imbued in her heart. She could not stand the thought of Christmas in this place.

"Why didn't he want to come to Paris for the holiday?" she asked Lothar. They had been silent too long; she needed to hear his voice.

"He thought it would be better for you here than in Kolonia. He knows you don't like Kolonia." Lothar spoke listlessly, his voice as gray as the sky and the wind.

"I don't like it here, either," she retorted with a short laugh. "It's almost worse here. Perhaps he is brooding … about his mother."

Lothar glanced at her. "He hardly knew her."

Rotruda shrugged. "Then what is it?" She felt a coldness in her belly. "Is it … because of *her*?"

Lothar was silent.

"He saw her, didn't he? You promised you would never lie to me, Lothar. What do you know?"

Lothar hesitated before answering. "Yes, he saw her. She has a child."

Rotruda stopped her horse. "His child?"

"Yes."

Rotruda felt a sob in her throat, pushed it down angrily. "It's happening, just as I thought it would. Perhaps that is why I feel such a connection to Plectruda. We are both spurned wives."

"Charles will not forsake his own sons, Rotruda."

"I know it. But Plectruda's sons died … " she shuddered at the thought of it.

"That will not happen to Carl and Pipin," Lothar said fiercely.

"Don't you ever wonder, at the patterns our lives follow? I thought, when I married him, that I would be different. But instead—"

"He is not like his father. Patterns can be broken."

"Can they?" She smiled wearily. "I pray it is so." She was silent a moment. "Let's go back. I'm tired and cold."

When they arrived in the courtyard of the palace Lothar dismounted and came to her side to help her down from her horse. She stepped away and then slipped on the wet stones. He caught her, held her a moment. She gazed up at him.

"You having always been … my champion," she murmured in his ear. Lothar pulled away and handed the reins to the grooms. They walked together toward the palace doors.

"I will return to Paris," she said. "As soon as the feast is over. But I will let the boys go to Kolonia with their father. They need to be near him for awhile … will you look after them for me?"

"Of course I will. But why don't you come too? There is no use in you being in Paris all alone."

"No, " she said. She stopped and turned to him. "Sometimes I cannot bear it, Lothar, being near to him and yet, so far away. It's easier if I am in Paris. I have much to do anyway. The people in the city are so desperate and winter is so hard … I need to be there to make sure they are taken care of."

"Isn't that the priests' job?"

She shook her head. "The priests of St. Vincent's need a bit of prodding to part with their silver," she said ruefully. "Hugo is a great help, of course, but the people look to me. They need me."

She needed them too, of course. They gave her a purpose beyond herself and made her forget, for a time, that her husband needed her not at all.

She looked at Lothar. "Don't be too hard on him. The heart—wants what it wants. No one can choose whom to love. Can they? If we could, life would be so much easier."

"I will speak to him—"

"No. Don't. It's better this way. Will you ride with me again tomorrow?"

"If you wish."

"I do." She smiled at him.

Lothar straightened, looking away. "Tomorrow, then."

From the window of Pipin's Tower, Charles watched his wife ride with Lothar into the courtyard. Chrodegang, behind him at the desk, cleared his throat.

"Everything all right, my prince?"

"Fine."

"Well then, as I was saying, I do not think it a good idea to let Eudo's treachery go unanswered."

"What do you think I should do?"

Chrodegang sighed. "Some show of strength might be appropriate."

Charles turned to face him. "He had his opportunity and he didn't take it. I don't think he will challenge me again."

"But he won't join you either. So what will he do? Sit on the fence? And what if he falls off? Or is … pushed?" The chancellor's tone turned ominous.

"We have a little time, I think."

"Enough time?"

"God willing."

Chrodegang sighed. "And what will you do now, then?"

Charles gazed out the window, thinking about what to do next. Wait. Wait and train and rest and … prepare. The darkness was coming, he could feel it, but it was a long way off still, barely discernible over the far hills. He needed time. He needed a few years of peace. Then, he thought, he could begin again.

"I was sorry to hear about Einhard, by the way," said Chrodegang after a moment. "I know he was dear to you."

Einhard had died suddenly, in his sleep. Charles had only learned of it on his return from Burgundy. He was surprised at how the news had affected him. It was one of the reasons he had fled Kolonia, had come to Herstal for Christmas.

What else was here? His mother? He wanted to roam the halls she had roamed, as if he could find some piece of her still there. But there was nothing left of her. He felt a strange emptiness in his soul. She had loved him, once. He was certain of that. Yet even her love seemed gone from this world.

He dismissed Chrodegang and sat at the desk, unrolling a scroll he had read a dozen times already, as if searching for some hidden meaning. It said only: "Now we are even." It was not signed, but it carried the seal of the Duke of Aquitaine. He stared at it a long time, then he threw it on the fire and watched it burn.

# DECEMBER, 731

## Invasion

## Saint-Emilion

NOISES FILLED THE courtyard, shouting in a strange language, much commotion. Women wept, pulling children closer. Svana told them to be still, to make no sound. Gryffin looked up at her with eyes full of fear. She could not look at him.

She tried to make out what they were saying. The accent was strange to her, but she knew they were discussing the treasure. They sounded angry. Then hasty footsteps drew nearer to the house. The front door flew open, letting in a sudden wash of light.

A man stood in the portal. He was dressed in a knee-length coat of mail, a blue turban wrapped around his head from which protruded the metal cone of a helmet. Under the mail he wore a long white tunic, his legs were sheathed in baggy blue leggings, the same color as the turban. His face was very dark, his eyes deep and fierce. He carried a sword in one hand. He stared around the silent room at the faces of the people, dumfounded. Others appeared behind him, dressed similarly, looking in curiously.

They talked amongst themselves, arguing heatedly. Finally another man appeared, clearly the leader. He wore a banner over his mail coat and a twisted gold torc around his neck. He yelled at the others and they backed away. He stepped into the room.

"I am Abbas ibn Rahniah," he said in Arabic. "Who is the owner of this house?"

Svana rose slowly. Abbas looked at her, plainly surprised.

"This is your house?"

She nodded.

"You understand what I am saying to you?" said the Arab, amazement and something else in his eyes.

"Yes, I understand … a little."

"How can this be?"

"I lived in Constantinople … during the siege."

The Arab's face darkened at this news. The siege had not gone well for his people. He glanced around the room.

"Where is your husband?"

"I have no husband." She added hastily: "We have brought out all we have for you. We ask that you show mercy, take what we offer and leave us in peace."

He gazed leisurely around the room once more. The warriors behind him pressed in, straining to see inside. The people in the house shrank back, terrified but quiet.

"I see you have left us little to take," he said. He was silent a moment, considering.

"It is all we have," Svana said, trying to keep her voice steady. This was not quite true. She had a stash of silver and gold hidden in the wine casks, which she knew the Arabs, who did not drink wine, would not investigate.

She had a brief moment's hope. Abbas looked uncertain. He was clearly trying to decide what to do. It was one thing to kill people who were fighting or running, but to kill them while they just sat by quietly? It was not something he had encountered before. She had gambled that he would not be able to do it. The Qur'an expressly forbid the murder of innocents in cold blood, even infidels. She'd had a friend, an Arab prisoner in Constantinople, who had told her that.

"I should just kill you all," he said finally, looking her in the eye. "But I may have use for you. So I will make you a deal, woman. I will spare your people, for one thing."

"You can take whatever you want," she said.

"What I want—" he said with a slow leer, " is you."

He pointed at her with his sword.

She swallowed, her mouth dry, the blood pulsing behind her eyes.

"Why is he pointing?" Gryffin asked. She looked down at him a moment, her child. She hoped there was something reassuring in her face.

"It's all right," she whispered.

"What do you say?" the chieftain said, louder. "Do you agree?"

Svana turned to him, her eyes calm now, perfectly still. "Do I have your oath that no harm will come to these people?" she asked. "Your oath … sworn to Allah?"

It was a clever thing to say. An oath to Allah was sacred.

The chieftain looked startled. He shook his head angrily. "I promise nothing," he said. "I can take you anyway, whether you consent or not."

"No," she said. "You can't." She pulled her hand from behind her back. It contained a small, curved knife, the kind used for harvesting grapes. "I will use this first—on myself."

The villagers murmured, alarmed. The chieftain stared at the knife. His face blackened, his eyes narrowed to slits. "You cannot threaten me," he bellowed. He reached down, grabbed one of the children and held her up, holding his sword to her throat. A woman screamed. The child called out piteously. Svana shut her eyes.

"I will kill them, all of them, one by one, until you consent."

"I will be dead." She pressed the knife into her own skin.

He pushed the sword against the child's neck and stared into Svana's eyes. She stared back at him, the knife steady, drawing blood. A long, tense moment passed. Then Abbas cursed something in Arabic, tossing the child back to the floor. She crawled to her mother, still whimpering.

"All right. I swear to Allah the Great and Almighty that none of your people will be killed."

"Not just that," Svana said, "not only killed, but not harmed in any way. That means no wounding, no raping, no torturing, no starving."

"Do you think that little body of yours is worth all this?" the chieftain shouted.

"You will answer to Allah, not to me."

He stood a moment, fuming. "I swear to Allah that no harm will come to these people—*after* I am done with you."

She closed her eyes and dropped the knife. She looked at Erik. "Take care of the boy," she said. He stared at her, questioning, afraid. "It's all right," she said. "Keep them calm, whatever happens."

She felt Gryffin's fingers tighten around her leg. She saw the chieftain smile, displaying sharp white teeth. He turned and gave orders to his men. A few of them moved into the room, taking up positions along the walls, swords drawn and ready.

"Tell them," the chieftain said to her, "not to move. If they move, they will die."

She repeated the order. She saw Mattheus start to rise, defiant; she gave him a look that made him freeze in place.

Abbas came toward her. She indicated the door behind her, at the back of the house. He smiled, grabbed her roughly by the hair and shoved her toward the door.

"You made me swear a terrible oath," he said to her when they were alone in the room. "I will make you pay for that."

She held still as he came toward her, the tip of his sword sliding down her neck. He grabbed the edge of her gown, pressing his sword against her skin and ripped straight down, tearing her dress and cutting into her flesh. The pain of it shocked her, brought her almost to her knees, but he would not let her fall, wanting still to run his sword point over her breasts and belly, sliding it between her legs. She felt a wave of nausea, fought to stay standing, but he shoved her onto the bed, smiling, undoing his clothes. She held her breath against the sour smell of him as he climbed on top of her, forced himself into her. She shut her eyes, willing herself to a place of perfect blackness, a place deep inside herself. It will be over soon, she thought.

But she was wrong.

He rose up, undoing his belt. She watched him, puzzled. The belt was made of linked circles of gold. He smiled down at her, raised it over his head and raked it across her breasts.

She lurched uncontrollably, the sharpened metal links like a fire on her skin. She turned over, struggling to crawl away, but he hit her again and again, the belt tearing the skin of her back, the pain slicing into her very bones. She stopped struggling and lay still, her whole world full of fire and darkness and unending pain.

He grabbed her by the hair and pulled her almost upright. She felt her body ripple away from her, scattered into fragments, separating. She felt the cold edge of his sword against her throat. She sighed, thankful it was almost over. She whispered a silent goodbye to Gryffin, to Charles, and a prayer that the two of them would live to meet one day.

But instead of the sword slicing through her neck, it sliced her hair, cutting it off in a single, savage blow. She fell forward onto the bed. He threw the cut-off hair on her body.

"You do not deserve a quick death," he said with low savagery. "Die slowly, harlot."

Then he turned, adjusting his clothes and his turban, refitting his belt, and left.

Svana drifted into a fog, her eyes closing. She wondered if she were still alive. But the pain was real, her skin burning, the blood pumping out of her onto the linens. Is this what death feels like? But then she could not think, because the pain took over her mind, filling her so completely that no other thought was possible. She prayed again, a prayer without words.

She saw a face, fragile and changing, a face she did not recognize. She tried to reach out toward it, sensing an all-consuming peace in the eyes that looked upon her with pity and care. *It's all right. Everything is all right now. It's over.*

Freddy opened the door cautiously, peering in. Then she put a hand over her mouth, stifling a scream. There was blood everywhere, the bedclothes soaked through. The body on the bed did not look like a human body at all.

Freddy fought the urge to vomit, to faint, to run from the room. She went to the bed, found Svana's face in the tangle of chopped hair, put a hand on the side of her neck.

"Oh my God— she's alive!"

Svana's eyes opened suddenly, she tried to reach to Freddy, to grab her arm.

"Don't let Gryffin—" Her tongue was thick and fuzzy, her throat choked by blood.

"Keep the boy out," Freddy said, turning to the other women that had come into the room. One of them stared down at Svana, blanched, and ran out, holding a hand over her mouth. Erik came in, shutting the door and the prying eyes out. He and Freddy quickly covered her body. Freddy began to shout for water and clean linens.

Freddy had never seen such a horror as this. The belt had torn pieces of skin away—there was so much blood she wondered if the woman had any left at all. "Dear Lord," she whispered, "dear Sweet Jesus—have mercy on us—"

She wondered how a man could wreak such havoc on another human being in the name of his god.

# Part Four

## The Hammer

# 62

## Paris
## December, 731

PIPIN STOOD ON tiptoes, straining to see above the heads of the crowd. He was short for sixteen, and though he didn't normally mind, now his father was coming home—for the first time in over a year—and he could not see a thing.

This was his moment. He would finally have a place in the army, perhaps even in the *Truste*. He had been ready for ages, yet his father had always insisted he go back to Saint-Denis for school in the winter months until he was old enough. Pipin had waited for his sixteenth birthday the way some boys wait for their first time with a woman—with a longing that was almost sexual in its intensity. It was here, now, and this time he would not be left behind.

"Pipin, be still," his mother said sharply, putting a hand on his shoulder. He shook her off, ignoring her stern expression. Yet she looked so beautiful today, in her blue silk gown with silver lorum, her blond hair flowing free under her white veil. She rarely wore her hair unbound. She'd done it for him, no doubt. Her husband.

The palace courtyard was packed with people, the crowd disappearing down the tree-lined cobbled street all the way to the bridge. Pipin needed a higher vantage point. He looked up to the guard tower at the corner of the courtyard wall. He bolted for it, charging through the crowds. The guard at the bottom of the tower stopped him.

"You can't go up there—"

Pipin ignored him, slipping by him before he could raise an alarm and charging up the winding wooden staircase to the top.

"Pipin!" said the surprised guard standing watch on the parapet, nearly turning his spear on the boy. "What are you doing here?"

"I need to see!"

He pushed the guard aside and grabbed hold of the rail, looking out over the city, the wide bridge that connected the island of Paris with the city of the Right Bank. The land here was flat, unlike the Left Bank, the site of the original Roman city. There were no Roman buildings on the Right Bank, only the shapeless dwellings of the poor Parisii. It was a sad place, and Pipin hated traveling that way. But today even the Right Bank rippled with energy, with excitement, with hope.

No sooner had he cast his eyes over the scene then a rumble rose up from the crowd, swelling like a tidal surge, the familiar chant he had learned as his first words: *Ham-MER, Ham-MER, Ham-MER*. Then he saw them, the black horses moving as one body, like a ship floating on a sea of people, the banners with the triple flame symbol snapping in the quick breeze, like black fire against the white sky.

"It's him!" Pipin shouted, to the air, to the wind. He raced back down the steps, nearly knocking over the already befuddled guard, and launched himself into the packed crowd, pushing his way through, desperate to get to the bridge. He made it to the entrance but was waylaid by three guards who stood in his path, their spears crossed to prevent his further progress.

"Let me through!" he shouted.

"Pipin!"

It was the deformed giant Gunther, leading the procession, who saw him first. The guards lowered their spears, surprised. Pipin stood breathless, gazing up at the man on the monstrous horse, smiling hugely.

"Good Christ, boy, you'll be trampled to death."

And then his father was there, riding up beside his Horse Master, the two of them gaping in wonder at the temerity of this boy. The Bodyguard pulled up behind them, the procession all but stopped. Around them the crowd quieted, observing this reunion with keen interest.

"Welcome home, Father." Pipin straightened and bowed, formally. Gunther grunted.

Charles smiled, looking him up and down. "Hello, Pip. I have something for you." He signaled to Alfric, who drew up next to them leading a big bay horse by the reins. Pipin thrilled at the sight.

"For me?"

"If you think you can handle him. This is a stallion, not one of those docile mares you are used to."

"He's beautiful! What's his name?"

"Samson."

Pipin laughed.

"Hop on," said Charles.

Pipin jumped easily onto the horse's bare back and rode to the palace at his father's side, his heart near to bursting. He saw his mother as they approached, her white face even whiter, her mouth locked in a smile. He saw his brother Carloman, his face as ferociously empty as always. How like their father he looked when he was in this mood.

They dismounted together and moved toward the company arrayed to meet them. Hugo came forward to greet Charles, a bright smile carving his narrow, perpetually worried face.

"Uncle! We are so happy you are here at last."

"Really? I don't think you'll feel that way after putting up with this crowd for a week. Is your brother here?"

Hugo shook his head. "Late, as usual. But he will be here in time for the hunt, no doubt."

"Hello, Brother."

Charles turned to greet Brand, clasping arms. "Good to see you, Brother."

"As I am to see you."

"Married life seems to agree with you." He gave Brand's belly a playful slap.

"A little too much, perhaps," Brand said, laughing.

"Where is your wife?"

"Home. Pregnant. Didn't feel up to the journey this time around. She sends her greetings ..."

"Charles! About time you showed up. We've been bored to death for days." Chrodegang came forward, inclining his head, his cheeks dimpled with suppressed mirth, as usual.

"I see you too are staying well fed," Charles remarked.

"Of course. Which is more than I can say for you. You seem to be wasting away before our very eyes! I'm sure your lovely wife will remedy that in due time." He turned his gaze toward Rotruda, who smiled tremulously, embarrassed.

Charles went to her, took her hand and kissed it. The color burned into her cheeks instantly.

"Welcome back," she said, and her voice seemed to shiver. "We were expecting you sooner."

"I stopped in Quierzy for a few days. Gunther had some new horses he wanted me to see."

"I see." Her smile faded. She turned to Pipin. "Is that yours?"

"A gift from Father," Pipin said, straining with pride.

"Long overdue," Charles said.

"Isn't he beautiful?" Pipin said.

"Yes," Rotruda whispered. "He looks … rather big."

Charles turned to Carloman, who had remained were he was, by the door, standing straight and stiff, unsmiling. "Hello, Carl."

"Hello Father."

"Can we go riding now, Father?" Pipin begged.

"Not now," Rotruda said. She looked pleadingly at Charles. "I've arranged for a private dinner, just us. I hope you don't mind. It's been awhile since we've had you all to ourselves. Do you think your friends can fend for themselves for one night?"

"They'll be all right." He looked at Pipin. "Tomorrow. We'll go hunting." Pipin whooped with joy.

"Hugo, tell the Count of the Palace to get this horde fed and bedded down."

"I will see to it myself," said Hugo with a deferential nod.

Rotruda sighed, took Charles' arm and walked with him into the palace, the boys trailing behind, the sounds of the crowd fading as the doors closed.

"Where's Lothar?" she asked, glancing around.

"He said he was going to stay in town tonight."

"A girl?"

Charles did not answer. Rotruda glanced at him, smiling. "Well, I'm glad. He needs a wife. He's been too long alone. You should make him get married, Charles."

"I've tried. He won't even discuss it."

"There is no end of available girls who would have him. My own maids never tire of offering themselves."

She brought him to a private room lit by candles and wall sconces. The table was only big enough for the four of them. She had planned the dinner herself, seeing to every detail. There was roast partridge, onion soup and platters of roasted winter vegetables, chestnuts and fruit. She was pleased that Charles had agreed so readily to this small company on the first night of his return.

Pipin talked nonstop, which seemed to relieve everyone at the table from having to maintain a conversation. He talked about the horrible monks, the escapades of his classmates, his hunting adventures, his victories on the training field. He never waited for a response. Rotruda relaxed, sensing everything was going to be all right.

Then Pipin said something that changed everything.

"We have a plan, you know, me and Carl," Pipin said. "We are going to make a great team … "

"Plan?" Charles raised his eyes from his food and looked at his son with interest.

"Yes, for when we depose the Merovings. Chrodegang says that must happen soon, so that Carloman and I will be named the new kings. We will rule jointly, you see, not dividing the kingdom like the Merovings did, more like partners, you see? It's going to be a whole new thing … "

He stopped, aware that his father's face had changed, his eyes lightless and still, and he wondered what he had said to make him so angry.

"Listen to me, both of you," Charles said quietly, "there will be no more talk of being king. Neither of you will ever be king—do you understand? Not ever."

Pipin fell silent, staring down at his plate.

Rotruda looked at her husband, her face pale with shock. Only Carloman remained unmoved, continuing to eat his dinner as if nothing had happened.

The meal ended in subdued silence. With the boys gone off to their apartments, Charles walked Rotruda to her rooms. They talked idly, mostly about their children; like all parents they had seized upon this topic of mutual concern to carry them through their aloneness. When they reached her doorway, however, she took his arm, her eyes reaching into his with dark purple intensity.

"Come inside a moment … I have something to show you."

# 63

SHE LED HIM into the room, closing the door after him. He took a few steps and stopped, as if uncertain of what to do next. She came to stand before him.

"What was it you wanted to show me?" he asked.

"This." She unbuckled the belt around her waist and let it fall; she undid the ties at her neck and pulled the top of her gown down, revealing herself to him, her chin tilted up, her violet eyes raised to his, daring him to move, to flee. She waited, her breath like a knife in her chest. He didn't run. He stood still, his gaze traveling to her perfect breasts, which prickled with the cold of the room. She moved to him, slid her hands up his chest, around his neck, his skin slick with sweat against the coldness of her palm. She pulled his head down and kissed him, slipping her tongue into his mouth, her fingers entwined in his hair, pressing her body against him.

She felt him respond, the hardening of his body, the shortness of his breath. She felt wicked, witch-like, casting a spell on him, using all her skill to lure him into her. And it worked, miraculously; she drew him to the bed, pulling him down on top of her, feeling the weight of him, the heat of him surging into her, releasing twenty years of liquid silence, of self-enforced exile.

Rotruda could not remember the last time her husband had fallen asleep beside her. She awoke after a few hours, astonished that he was still there. She said aloud, "I think I will have a child now."

"What?" He stirred; he was such a light sleeper, she sometimes wondered if he slept at all. She laughed softly, took his hand and placed it on her belly.

"I can feel it. Can you? I have wanted another child for so long." She was thirty-six, a time when many women were grandmothers, but she still seemed like a child herself, so small and pretty, as if she had not aged at all.

"But why? After all this time? Why go through it again?"

"I cannot explain … you'd have to be a woman to understand, I suppose." She laughed breathlessly. "I think this time I will give you a daughter," she said. "Every man should have a daughter."

"A daughter—would be nice," Charles murmured.

"All right then, a daughter for you," Rotruda said. "If you think you can manage it, at your age." She giggled, poking him in the ribs.

She was teasing him. A lifetime spent almost constantly in the field had kept Charles, at forty-three, as lean and hard as he'd been at thirty— there were no telltale rolls around the middle that usually hit men his age no matter what their lifestyle. It was remarkable, she thought, but he looked younger now than he did when she'd married him; the lines in his face seemed appropriate to him, a sign of achievement, not struggle. And now, for the first time in forever, there was no strain between them.

"I *am* getting old," Charles said, sighing. "I never thought I would live this long. I don't feel it, somehow. Perhaps it's only a numbness."

"No," Rotruda said, "it's that the struggle is over."

"The struggle is never over. In fact, I think the real one is only beginning."

"What struggle do you mean?" She turned onto her side, gazing into his eyes in rapt attention. He was on his side as well, facing her, she could feel his breath on her face, could not remember the last time he was so near to her. She thought of his world, his people, the crowds outside the palace, lining the streets to the end of the city, to the far reaches of his kingdom. How many would give anything to be this close. She had always been in competition with them, all of them, vying for his attention, his favor. Now, finally, she had it. If only for a moment.

"I—I don't really know. I don't have a name for it."

"I can't imagine what it could be. The world is yours Charles, Prince of Franks; you've done everything you set out to do. You've united the kingdom; you've kept the invaders at bay. You've worked all your life for peace, and now you have it. You ought to learn to enjoy it more, to relax."

"It has always seemed to me," he said slowly, "that the minute you begin to relax, that's when things start going to pieces again."

She laughed. "If only the world knew how much you worry." She put her hand on the side of his face and held it there. "Go to sleep, my prince," she said softly. "Sleep."

And he did.

Morning came too soon for Rotruda, announced vociferously by Pipin, who invaded their room at first light with bow and arrow, proclaiming that it was time to go hunting.

"Got to get out early before the deer wake up," he said to Charles, who sat up suddenly. Rotruda protested at the removal of his warm body from her side; in the next moment she realized that he was profoundly embarrassed to be seen by his son in bed with her. The knowledge made her laugh suddenly. Charles looked at her, annoyed.

"Go on," she said lazily, "if you must."

"Get the horses ready," Charles said to Pipin. "I'll be there in a minute."

"Okay!" Pipin sailed across the room and out the door. Rotruda continued to laugh softly.

"You shouldn't allow him to barge in like that," Charles said. "He's not a child anymore." He rose, pushing off the covers, and went to find his clothes on the floor.

"Ah, I think Pipin will always be a child—that is what is so wonderful about him. Still, I don't see what you are upset about—it's perfectly natural to him that his father and mother should be in the same bed together. What could be *more* natural?"

He didn't answer. This talk, as well, embarrassed him. She went on coyly, "I'm sorry if I displease you, my lord."

"Rotruda don't be foolish," he said sharply, tiredly. "I am quite obviously not displeased."

She rose and strode naked to him, slipping her arms around his neck. But it was different suddenly, he was distracted, remote—her body no longer affected him as it had the night before. She looked into his eyes, hurt, questioning. He gently pushed her away.

"I'll see you for dinner," he said, heading for the door.

"Not before?"

"I can't. I have court most of the day and then Chrodegang has me for the rest of it."

"But I was hoping that we could … " She didn't finish.

He turned to look at her, smiled awkwardly, then turned away again and left the room.

# 64

IT TOOK MOST of the morning, but Pipin finally got his prize, a small doe. It was hardly the mighty stag he had been tracking for months, but to have his father all to himself for an entire morning was more than he could have wished for. Pipin preferred the bow to the spear for hunting, a weapon that required much more skill and patience than most men had. Charles himself was no archer, but he watched his son with admiration; Pipin, usually so silly and self-effacing, was totally different on the hunt, sly and stealthy, completely focused on his prize, ruthless in the attainment. Charles got a sense of what he would be like in battle. This charming, fun-loving boy had another side to him that he suspected few people had ever seen.

After the kill was secured they sat on a fallen log and took meatsticks and cider skins from their packs for breakfast. Pipin talked continuously, asking questions about what was happening in the kingdom, why it was happening, and what Charles was going to do about it. Charles was impressed with the boy's grasp of the political climate in Francia; he decided to test him a little.

"What do you think about the Aquitaine?"

Pipin looked very thoughtful. After a long moment he said, "It's a cauldron of boiling hot wax." He took a big bite of his meatstick.

Charles laughed. "You'd better explain that."

"Well, wax doesn't really boil when it heats. It looks very calm, very peaceful. And then, without warning, it explodes."

Charles related the conversation to Chrodegang when the two sat together in his study later that afternoon. The fat monk threw back his head and laughed.

"The boy will crush the lot of us, I guarantee it!" he said, his blue eyes twinkling.

"But he's right," Charles said. "My own nobles refuse to believe it, but this boy understands completely. How can that be?"

"Well, he is your son, after all," Chrodegang said more soberly. "He's got Rotruda's looks but your mind—what a combination!" He paused, thoughtful. "Carloman, on the other hand—an interesting fellow. More like you than you'd care to admit, I think."

"He doesn't approve of me."

"Ha! I doubt he would approve of Christ Himself should he make an appearance!"

"Perhaps so. What news do you have? Any word from Winfrith?"

"Yes, as a matter of fact. Bishop Boniface is headed to Rome."

"Rome?"

"Indeed. A Papal summons. You know what that means. He's getting the mitre."

"Winfrith? An archbishop?"

"And why not? He is the most famous monk in the world now, thanks to you. And to his own work, which is remarkable. He's done in ten years in Germania what the Irish missionaries couldn't do in a generation. And peacefully—that's the real genius of it all. Now—to business."

Chrodegang kept Charles busy into the late afternoon with land distributions, tribute collections, the estates, papal edicts, the latest machinations of bishops, and all the business of running a kingdom that Charles detested but the chancellor seemed to thrive on. When they were finished and had settled back to share a cup of wine before dinner, Chrodegang said something that shattered the peace between them.

"Charles, I think it is time we talked seriously about making you king."

Charles looked up from his cup, startled. "What?"

"I know your ambivalence on this matter, but the time, as they say, has come. This 'mayor' or 'leader' of whatever you call yourself simply won't do. You are not young any longer. You have your sons to think about now; you must insure the future of your line. Just because the people are willing to accept you as the *de facto* ruler of the realm does not mean they will bestow such favor on Carloman and Pipin. Do you want Francia to fall back into the hands of the Merovings? It could happen you know, as long as they are the consecrated kings. I don't understand your reticence on this matter, why you've done nothing up to this point, but you cannot afford to put it off any longer. Charles, you must have the crown, and I for one intend to see that you get it."

"No." Charles rose abruptly, went to stand before the window. Chrodegang waited for him to speak again, but he didn't.

"Charles," he said slowly, "I simply do not understand this. Are you afraid of opposition? The nobles would welcome it, and the bishops would not dare—"

"It isn't that."

"The Pope, then? You need have no fear there. I firmly believe Gregory will support you, even if the bishops don't—"

Charles turned his piercing gaze to the monk, cutting him off. "Listen to me, Chrodegang. I will not be king. I will never be king. And neither will my sons, if there is anything I can do to prevent it. *Never*. That is final."

Chrodegang sighed, leaning onto the arm of his chair, as if he were suddenly very tired. "You could at least tell me why."

Charles did not speak for awhile. He had turned again to look out the window. Chrodegang waited, sensing he was gathering his thoughts, as if he had never had to speak them aloud before. Charles had refused utterly to talk of taking the crown in the past. But it was understandable. The last mayor who had tried was beheaded for his hubris. But Charles' rule was secure; he had the full support of the kingdom. His nephews and his brother were dukes, utterly loyal to him. There was nothing standing in his way. Nothing, except Charles himself.

"Do you know what the name *Frank* means, Chrodegang?" Charles said finally. "It means *free*. I learned this from an old Greek monk I once knew. Roman citizens living in Gaul were being crushed by Roman taxes, so they gave up their Roman citizenship and became free men, *Franks*. That is really why Rome fell, you know. It was not barbarian wars or civil strife—those things didn't help, of course, but ultimately Rome taxed itself to death. Once the taxes dried up, Rome did too.

"Then there was chaos, disorder: Saxons, Huns, Slavs invading everywhere, murdering and stealing. People needed protection; they turned to Clovis, who beat back the invaders and restored order to the kingdom, uniting the tribes into the Kingdom of the Franks. He was a great hero. So they made him a king.

"But what was his legacy? You've seen it yourself: another line of degenerate, power-mad kings, lazy and incompetent, growing more ridiculous with each generation. The people had enough; my grandfathers took power from the kings, and order was restored, for awhile. Things seemed to improve.

"But if I make myself a king, the cycle begins again. Something happens to a man when he becomes king, something strange and stupid. A man becomes a king and suddenly he is not a man anymore—he is a leech, a blood-sucking parasite. Look at that thing we call a king now, and tell me I am wrong. I will not be a king, and neither will my sons."

Charles fell silent. Chrodegang stared at him, amazed. "But Charles," he said after a long moment, "don't you see that you commit the sin whether you call yourself king or not? And don't you see that you will commit a *worse* sin if you allow Francia to fall back into the hands of the Merovings?"

Charles shook his head. "I will not let that happen. When Theuderic dies—which he will, he's not a well man—I will not replace him. And Francia will go on without a king. It is the only way to truly change things, Chrodegang, the only way to break the cycle."

"But how can you ensure that your wishes will be carried out?" asked the chancellor incredulously. "How can you ensure that no man in Francia will ever call himself king again?"

"I can make a law—"

"Laws can be rescinded, laws can be changed, a law is not written in stone," said Chrodegang, gathering momentum. "The truth is, Charles, that unless you intend to live forever—which I do not necessarily put past you, you understand—you will not be able to guarantee *anything*. Not even the actions of your own sons, I'm afraid. You may not want to be king, though—God be praised—you are probably the only man on earth who *doesn't* want to be king—but you, Charles, are an aberration, a freak of nature, a phenomenon not to be repeated. It would be better for you to take the crown now, while your power is secure. Nothing will have to change, only the name. First you were a Mayor, then you are a King. But it is *nomenclature*, pure and simple, it doesn't have to mean anything—"

"But it *does* mean something," said Charles, turning from the window and moving back to the table where the chancellor sat. "Words have meanings. There is a difference between being a mayor and being a king, a huge, unbridgeable difference, one that no man is immune to, including me." He sat suddenly, as if enormously tired. "Trust me, Chancellor, I have been in power long enough to know its terrible charm. It's a sickness, a disease; it makes rational, intelligent, moral men utterly mad. The difference between being a mayor and a king is the difference between being a *leader* and a *ruler*—men often need to be led, but they never need to be ruled, even if they think they do. I cannot allow myself to step over that line. And I cannot allow my sons to do it either."

He picked up his cup and drank it to the dregs. Chrodegang watched him, unable to think of anything to say.

"You understand," Charles went on, "that I am counting on you to help me."

"Help you?" Chrodegang said, aghast. "But how … "

"You will be here when I am gone and they are ready to take over. I'm counting on you to see this through for me, to see my will done. You are the only one who knows how these things work. You have the Pope's ear. If either of them wants to be king, they will need your help. You must promise me that you will never help them. Promise me."

Chrodegang sat in shocked silence, looking up into the implacable gray eyes that bore down upon him. He knew he could not make such a promise. It was against his very nature. And yet he was this man's obedient servant, this man whom he admired above all men, this man for whom he would rather die than disappoint.

He understood perfectly Charles' reasoning. But he understood as well the basic flaw in his theory: the assumption that men actually *wanted* to be free. He himself knew this was not true. For freedom meant responsibility, it meant bearing the burden of one's own life, it meant suffering even. And people did not want that. They wanted to be taken care of, to be provided for. Moreover, they wanted someone to blame for their problems, be it a god or a count or a bishop or a king. Something beyond themselves, something greater than themselves, something remote and abstract enough to absorb the guilt. It was why the people of Francia still preferred a useless and decrepit king on the throne to no king at all.

But he could not say these things to this man whom he admired, because this man would not believe him. For this man, this prince, actually believed in mankind, he believed in the dignity and nobility of men. And Chrodegang could not bring himself to disillusion him. There was a chance, after all, that he might be right. He had proven the world wrong time and again; perhaps he would do so in this as well. It might be impossible, but if anyone could effect the impossible, it was Charles Martel.

Chrodegang took a deep breath. "I promise," he said.

Charles smiled, openly and warmly. Chrodegang looked into his master's relieved, unburdened face, and shriveled inwardly. But he smiled and inclined his head and said nothing more.

# 65

ROTRUDA SAT WRAPPED in furs under a wide canopy, watching her son and Lothar work the new horses on the barren island across the narrow channel from the palace, which served as a troop encampment when Charles was in residence. Her ladies shivered about her, huddled against the brittle wind. Rotruda seemed not to mind.

The two of them raced across the frozen ground at full speed. She could hear Pipin's laughter, carried on the wind, as Lothar shouted at him, prodding him to go faster, faster. Pipin looked far too small for the big horse, yet he rode fearlessly, flawlessly, keeping pace with Lothar easily. They looked almost like father and son, blond hair whipping in the wind like the manes of their horses. Pipin had chosen to grow his hair long, like all of his father's companions, though Carloman kept his hair deliberately short.

Pipin won the race, though Rotruda was pretty sure Lothar let him win, as usual. The ladies cheered. Rotruda noticed some servants had crossed the bridge from the palace to steal a look, girls pointing and giggling. They were there not just for Lothar, who always drew a crowd, but for Pipin as well, her handsome son, who was turning heads with alarming regularity.

Pipin slowed, beaming proudly, raising his arm in the air. The girls responded with claps and cheers. Rotruda shook her head, smiling despite herself.

Pipin raced past her on the galloping horse.

"Mama! Watch this!"

She called to his retreating back: "Be careful, please!"

But he wouldn't be. He was never careful, traipsing through the world oblivious to its dangers, its heartaches. It was something to be admired, and feared as well. She turned to see Lothar looking at her. She felt a blush rise in her cheeks, lowered her gaze.

He kicked his horse into a trot and rode over to her. She rose, stepping away from the canopy, away from the prying eyes and ears of her waiting women.

"My lady," he said softly, looking down at her. He inclined his head slightly. She smiled up at him, hoping the pink in her cheeks appeared as the result of the winter wind, not of his presence. She was startled once more by his breathless beauty, unchanged by time.

"You look well, Lothar," she said, straining to keep her voice poised, polite. "I see Pipin is keeping you busy."

"Yes. He's an excellent rider. Like his father."

"Like you. You taught him, after all."

He smiled, though his smile seemed sad to her, weighed down.

"How are you?" he asked, lifting her from her own thoughts.

"Oh … " She tried to think of something to say, something light and easy. "Well, fairly well, anyway." That was true, she thought. She was well, her sons were well. Did it matter so much, the emptiness of her life?

"And how is Carloman? I haven't seen much of him."

Rotruda shrugged. "Carloman is … himself, as always." She laughed a little. When he said nothing, she asked another question, one that was always on her mind. "Lothar, tell me … has he seen her? The Valkyrie?"

He shook his head. "Not these past three years."

She sighed, closing her eyes. "I'm pleased to hear it. Though, I don't think it matters to him, how much time has passed." She was remembering the night before, the heat of his passion, her fragile hope, his coldness in the morning. Was it because of her? The Valkyrie who possessed his heart, even as she lived in exile, a thousand leagues away.

Pipin came rushing back, that inexpressible joy still on his face. "Come on, Lothar! Race me again!"

"You'd better go," Rotruda said. "I will see you at the feast tonight, of course."

Lothar nodded, gathering his reins. "Of course," he said. He gave one more lingering smile, stilling her heart. Then he kicked the horse and sped away, chasing her son across the field once more.

# 66

PIPIN FINALLY SHOT his stag, much to the delight of the hunters who gathered to gaze at the prize in admiration. Then the servants slit open the belly to spill the innards and the carcass was trussed for carrying to the butchery. Pipin declared a feast in his own honor and led the procession back to the city, shouting at the top of his lungs, "Three cheers for Pipin the Short!"

The rest followed behind, dutifully cheering. Charles found himself walking beside Carloman near the back of the group. Carloman was almost as tall as his father but thinner, his gauntness part of a general aura of relentless moral asceticism about him, an unfailing discipline. They walked in silence. Charles tried to think of something to say.

"You have been very quiet these days, Carl."

"Mother always tells me to keep silent, if there is nothing good to say," Carloman said.

"You are not impressed with your brother's prize?"

The younger man shrugged. "The stag was old. It was his time to die. It happens to all the living." He glanced slyly at his father.

Charles stopped walking.

Carloman turned after a moment, waiting.

"We are alone here. Why don't you tell me what is on your mind?"

Carloman shifted uneasily. "Does it matter what I think, Father? You don't answer to me. But you will answer to God, one day."

"Yes, I suppose we all will." He paused. "I never meant to hurt your mother. Our marriage was a—political arrangement—"

"It is not just against my mother you have sinned, Father. You have sinned against God himself. You've stolen church lands. You've removed bishops without authority. You've been attacking the Holy Church ever since you came to power. You will pay for that, I can promise." He spoke flatly, cruelly. Charles could only listen, amazed.

"And you will make me pay?"

Carloman shrugged, insolent. "I will have no power to do that, will I? You said you would see to it that neither Pipin nor I will ever be king."

Charles stared at his son, the truth dawning on him finally.

"So, you want to be king? Is that it?"

Carloman did not answer at once. Then he said, very softly, "You won't be able to stop me, you know, when you are dead."

He turned and walked away. Charles watched him go, unable to move for a long time. He remembered suddenly his own father staring at him across a fire-flecked room, shaking with anger, with all the frustration and anguish of a man who had fought his last battle against an implacable enemy, an enemy that refused to fight back, refused to surrender. He understood now, that impotent rage, and he felt for a moment a sliver of regret.

On the ride back to Paris, Charles told Brand about his conversation with Carloman. Brand shrugged it off.

"Don't make too much of it. He's idealistic, inflexible, and he is very devoted to his mother. He sees that she is unhappy—"

"How is it that everyone knows everything about my family except me?" said Charles, suddenly agitated.

Brand glanced at him. "Perhaps you aren't paying attention."

Charles fell silent. He thought of Svana, the simpleness of his feeling for her amid the messiness of his family life. He was tired of this game. He would go and get her, he decided, he would bring her back with him, to Quierzy, he would marry her and be done with it.

But when he arrived back in Paris, the world had changed utterly.

Hugo met him in the hall, his pale face even whiter than usual.

"Thank God you are back."

Hugo led him into his reception chamber. Chrodegang was there, with Sigebald and Arnulf. They were all unnaturally silent, their faces grim. Charles stopped in the middle of the room, his eyes locking on a boy sitting on a stool by the fire, filthy and shaking.

"Badilo," Charles said, moving toward him. Badilo had been scouting in Saint-Emilion for the past few years. "What happened?"

The boy rose but wavered and fell to his knees. "My lord," he said softly, "I'm sorry—" He seemed unable to speak anymore.

Chrodegang cleared his throat. "There's been an invasion," he said. Charles turned to him. "Bordeaux has been sacked."

"Bordeaux?" Lothar said, incredulous.

Charles grabbed the scout by his collar and hauled him up. "Tell me!"

Badilo swallowed, his voice trembling as he spoke. "They came on Christmas. Christmas! My brother Baudoin and I, we had heard a rumor of troops marching up the Garonne. We couldn't believe it, but we went to see for ourselves. We came upon a scouting party—we didn't know they were hostile until it was too late. My brother went to speak to them and they cut him down where he stood—"

Badilo stopped, gasping from the memory. Charles had let go of him, had moved away, his arms folded tightly over his chest.

"I escaped … ran into the woods until they gave up looking for me. Then I followed them … I saw the army, a huge force! They had come up the river from Tolosa. They moved fast, so fast … Eudo had no time. He tried. He marched down the Garonne … there was a terrible battle. He had no chance. His army was destroyed. Then they advanced on Bordeaux … " Badilo paused again, shutting his eyes. "I never saw such a thing. They killed—they killed—"

"Who did this?" Charles asked. "Who are 'they'?"

"A new leader, named 'Abd ar Rayman. The new Emir of Cordova. He killed Othman! That is what they are saying, anyway."

"Where is Eudo?"

"He is dead. They put his head on a spear and paraded it through the streets—"

Lothar, the first to react, broke into a cheer. "Finally! God in heaven, I didn't think we would live to see it!"

Charles whirled on him, eyes white with rage. Brand cut in, saying gently, "She's not actually in Bordeaux after all, Charles. Perhaps she escaped … "

Lothar stopped raving, understanding dawning on his face. Charles turned to the boy.

"Where are they now?"

"They are raiding. All over the countryside. Burning villages—killing—" The young scout dissolved into sobs.

There was a long, heavy silence in the room. Then Charles turned to Hugo. "Give him some food and a bed. I'll talk to him again tomorrow."

Hugo nodded and led the distraught boy out of the room.

"How do you imagine he got all the way to Bordeaux with no advance warning?" Sigebald mused. "Quite remarkable."

Arnulf gave a harsh laugh. "It was Christmas. Half the army was probably drunk or in church. And it had been peaceful for so long—"

"Who is this Rayman? I never heard of him before," Chrodegang said. "Is it really possible that he killed Othman? And Eudo? We need more information."

"I will go," Brand said. "I will find out what happened."

Charles nodded. "Take Leutgar with you. And Badilo, if he is recovered enough. He knows the land there better than anyone." He turned to Chrodegang. "We must send word to the bishop. Make sure not to alarm the people. They don't need to know about this … yet."

Chrodegang nodded.

Charles went to the window, staring out.

Lothar threw up his hands in annoyance. "God in heaven, Charles," he said, moving toward him. "This is no time to be mooning over that goddamned bitch. You are better off if she is dead—"

He got no further. Charles' arm shot out, grabbing him by the throat with crushing strength, pulling him close.

"Don't ever speak of her again," Charles said, his voice deadly calm. Then he released his friend, who stumbled back, gasping. "Get out of here."

Lothar stood gaping for a full minute, then turned and fled the room. No one spoke for a long time.

"Arnulf, send out the couriers," Charles said finally. "We will need to muster at Tours in the spring."

"Where?"

"Chinon. There is a villa where we can make our headquarters. Send word to the owner. We will need his house and his lands. All of you. Get out now."

They left silently.

Charles stood still, feeling his heart tearing, sundering. He knew that to get through the next few minutes he had only to stand there, to continue to breathe, to let one moment slip to the next, to just, for the moment, survive.

*Svana.*

He thought of her as he had last seen her, in a sleeping room in Vichy, soft and pale in the early dawn. She had seemed fragile to him then, tears spilling down her cheeks unchecked, her black hair swirling like a storm cloud. He wished now he had gone to her, taken her in his arms and held her as he had wanted to, for now it seemed likely that he would never see her again. Little had he imagined that this enemy who had come for him would come for her as well. That this battle would be hers as much as it was his.

He had been, from the beginning, impervious to death. The terror that came upon most men in the heat of battle had instead delivered him to an almost prodigious sense of freedom. But now, in this room, alone with his tortured imaginings, he felt death's hold upon him at last.

He was amazed that men, when they became aware of the naked fact of death, could continue to go on living, to find things worth living for. What was the point of fighting, when the outcome would be the same, in the end?

He felt suddenly very old. *Old*, he thought. His time was short. Men—rulers, warriors—rarely lived to see fifty. There was much to do, and yet he didn't want to do anything. He wanted only to lie down and sleep. But there would be no sleep until this was over.

# 67

## Saint-Emilion

GRYFFIN ENTERED THE dark cellar, aware of a strange smell, musty and medicinal, spiced with onions. He could see his mother lying on a wooden pallet, piled with blankets, the space around her illuminated only by an oil lamp on a shelf. Sprigs of onions and root vegetables hung above her, like hovering spirits.

Freddy smiled at him, beckoning.

"She's awake. She wants to talk to you."

Gryffin swallowed. He had not seen his mother since the attack, nearly two weeks before. He was certain she was dead, or would die soon. Abbas had insisted she be moved to the root cellar to die; he had taken over the house and the homes of the workers for his warriors. No one but Freddy and Erik had seen her since then. They had forbidden anyone else to enter the cellar.

That terrible day still haunted him, the women rushing about, crying, Freddy barking frantic orders, the Arab warriors waving their mighty curved swords, shouting at them in their bizarre and frightening language. Surprisingly, though, Abbas had not interfered when Freddy insisted upon tending her mistress. He did not want her death on his head, Erik told him. Allah forbade the killing of innocents. Murder was allowed only in self-defense. And Svana had not fought back.

Gryffin had snuck out of the longhouse a few hours later and listened at the cellar door. He had heard nothing but muffled, urgent voices and smelled the putrid scent of burnt flesh. They were cauterizing her wounds. The smell made him nauseous, and he retched violently. Freddy emerged only to give orders to the boys to get supplies, clean linens and spider webs with which to pack the wounds. She had told him only that his mother was sleeping. He thought that meant she was dying. He had heard the noises coming from the room that day; they had all heard the awful sounds of the beating. But he had not heard his mother's voice. He thought he never would again.

He moved toward her makeshift bed, relieved to see that her face looked almost normal, though pale and thin. Her head was wrapped in a scarf. Her eyes looked familiar to him, yet darker and deeply hollowed.

"Gryffin," she said in a voice he barely knew, as if her voice had been burned along with her wounds. "Are you well?"

"Yes," he said. "I thought you were going to die."

"So did I," she said softly. She smiled. Her hand reached out from under the blanket to touch his face.

"I will kill him, Mama," he said savagely, grabbing her hand. She winced.

"No," she said. "If you try, they will kill you … and that I could not bear."

"But after what they did—"

"You must never be ruled by hatred, Gryffin. That is something I had to learn … the hard way. Promise me you won't do anything. Perhaps in a few weeks they will be gone from here. Promise me."

Gryffin was silent a moment. "Mama … does it hurt?"

She looked at him with glassy eyes, heavy with tears. "Not much." This was true. She was barely conscious most of the time, awash in Freddy's potions. She felt nothing but a deep, limitless fog about her. Her son stood staring down at her with fear-filled eyes; she struggled to focus on his face, to reassure him that she would live.

Memories had come only in flashes, disjointed. The last thing she remembered was the sword slicing through her hair. After that there was nothing but glimpses, hushed voices, and great slabs of pain. She felt as though she had slept for a hundred years. She dreamed of Charles, his hands on her body, healing her, his rain-colored eyes smiling at her, his mouth covering her wounds. She was happy there, content in the shadows, unwilling to surface.

Then there was the fire, the shadows turned to rivers of white hot flame that licked at her wounds, making them burn through the linen wraps. She fought to keep Charles' face before her, the coolness of his eyes, but soon even these things dissolved in fork-tongued flames. The fire was brutal and unending, so that she felt in some remnant of awareness that only death could end it.

Gradually the fire subsided, taking with it the hot sheets of pain. She felt her body spinning away; she was flying, suspended over the earth, dipping and wheeling like a bird, soaring, feeling nothing but wind and light and peace, a peace beyond her own enduring.

*You must go back.*

She had seen a face, a face like someone she had known once but could not remember anymore. It was not Charles' face. It was kind, serious, beautiful in a way she did not think could be beautiful. The voice was the same, familiar yet unremembered.

*You must go back.*

She turned away from the face, from the voice. *No.* She did not want to go back. She wanted to fly, to keep flying, the world dissolving. She felt herself being drawn downward, and she struggled to stay in the air, to soar higher. But the earth began to pull on her, like a weight wrapped around her feet, dragging her down, in a wild spiral, into darkness.

Now her son was here, standing before her, shaking with fear. *He's afraid of me*, she thought. *He may never come near me again.*

"Gryffin," she said, "Can you get to the town?"

"Yes."

"Good. Charles will send scouts to see what happened here. You must get word to them. Tell everyone, but do it quietly. Do you understand?"

"Yes."

She smiled. She was not worried about him. He had Charles' gift for stealth. There was much of Charles in him, she thought with a certain pride.

"Watch them, too, the … Arabs … and tell me what you see. But do *nothing*, do you hear?"

"Yes, Mama."

"Good. You'd better go now."

"Okay." Gryffin turned to the stairs, but stopped before taking a step. "Mama … do you think he will come for us?"

"Who?"

"My father."

Svana felt her heart stop. He had never spoken of his father before. "No," she said softly. "He won't come for us."

The boy's small face puckered in consternation. "Why not?"

She licked her dry lips, struggling to think of an answer. "He has all of Francia—an entire kingdom—to worry about. We must take care of ourselves. But we'll be fine, Gryf. The worst is over. We will be fine."

Later she roused from sleep to see Freddy at her side, running a cool cloth over her face.

"What are you giving me, Freddy? I have the strangest dreams."

"Absinthe," she said. "For the fever. And a little henbane, for the pain."

"Henbane? Isn't that a poison?"

"Not in very small doses. Rest now. You need to save your strength—"

"I want to know what they are doing."

Another face came into view. Erik.

"They have taken over the house and most of the others as well," he said grimly. "They have given us the longhouses. They eat all our food, but they have not touched the wine ... " he smiled slyly. "They have kept to their oath. They have not harmed anyone. Abbas is afraid, I think."

"Afraid of what?"

"Of you. He thinks you are a witch. That is how you survived. He's heard stories of witches in our land ... well, perhaps we have told one or two. Some of them seem able to understand us."

Svana smiled faintly. "How many are there?"

"Twenty, thirty. They come and go."

"Saint-Emilion?"

"More there, I think."

"And the abbey?"

"They took everything of value. They took everything of value, and what they couldn't take they destroyed. It was much worse there, as if they hated the very idea of our God." Erik paused. "The abbot is dead."

Svana winced in pain. "Poor Alcien. God rest his soul. What are their plans?"

Erik shook his head. "From what I can make out, they wait for orders from their leader—Rayman. Othman is dead. Abbas says Rayman is going to conquer all of Francia."

"He will have to get past Charles to do that," Svana said softly. "And he will *never* get past Charles."

Erik looked dubious. "We have heard they are still coming, more and more of them. I don't think Charles can stop them."

"He will. He's been preparing for this all his life. He will stop them."

# 68

## Paris
## January, 732

SNOW CAME TO Paris, briefly, a shimmering whiteness that seemed to lift the downcast city from its gray winter hues for a time. Paris had not seen snow in many a year; to some it felt like a harbinger of bad tidings, an ominous sign of things to come. Pipin, however, was delighted; upon waking up to the newly whitened world he led the entire palace in a snowball war, galvanizing servants and soldiers alike into the fresh cold air. For a short while everyone laughed and played and did not think about the darkness on the horizon, the enemy army lurking somewhere in the south.

A trickle of scouts and messengers arrived from the Aquitaine, but none with any new information. The fact that there had been so few told Charles all he really needed to know: there were few survivors. He could do nothing now but wait for news from Brand and begin preparations for war. The couriers had been dispatched, calling in the troops from every corner of the kingdom. They would move as soon as the ground thawed.

One day he returned from Saint-Denis with Chrodegang to find a great commotion in the courtyard. Guards were everywhere, trying to push back a jumble of people crowded around something, jostling and shouting excitedly.

"What is it?" Chrodegang asked nervously. "More news … another messenger?"

Charles ordered his guards to draw their swords and carve a path for him into the center of the courtyard. He spurred Epone into a trot as the people fell away. When they parted he finally saw the object of their attention.

It was not a messenger. It was Eudo of Aquitaine.

He stood motionless, a few of his leudes surrounding him protectively. He was unshaven, his usually impeccable clothes torn and filthy, his thinness turned to emaciation, making his dark eyes appear cavernous. He looked like his own corpse. What was worse, though, far worse than his condition, was the expression on his face. Charles hoped he would never have to see such an expression on a human face ever again.

A stillness fell around them, a charged silence born of the explosive energy that seemed to flow between these two men. Charles did not dismount. He waited. Three years ago he would have gotten down from his horse, met this man face to face. But not now.

Eudo understood. He inclined his head slowly, so slowly it seemed he hadn't moved at all. And then, very clumsily, in the manner of a man who had never had to perform this particular feat, not even before his God, he knelt.

His retainers, somewhat surprised, knelt as well. And the now silent, puzzled crowd heard Eudo, Duke of Aquitaine, recite in a disembodied voice the oath of loyalty and subjugation to Theuderic IV, King of Francia and Charles Martel, Leader of the Franks.

Charles stared at the man, saying nothing a long time. He did not trust himself to speak. Finally, he turned and spoke to the guards. "Take him to the palace. Have him tended. Keep a close watch on him."

They took hold of the duke and his men, leading them away. Other guards moved in to clear the courtyard, turning people back to their business.

"Was that him?" Chrodegang asked softly.

"That was him," said Charles.

"So … he is not dead after all."

"Apparently not."

Chrodegang chuckled. "He comes to you at last. I only pray it is not too late."

Eudo was seated on a low stool before the brazier, a bandage across his brow, several more on his arms and legs. He did not look up when Charles approached, standing behind him.

"They came … so fast," he said, staring into the flames. "There was no warning. I could not believe it. It was worse than … worse than Soissons." He paused, glancing at Charles, his smile a painful thing. "I know what you are thinking. You knew this would happen."

"I only knew that your alliance wouldn't work," Charles said.

"Yes, I know. You told me. Many times. But I had to try, don't you see? I had to try."

Charles sighed. "They said you were dead. We got reports of your head on a spear."

"Not my head. I have many doubles. I was able to escape. But my army ... is gone." Eudo closed his eyes, his head dropping to his chest. "I should have stayed. I should have died with them. God forgive me ..."

He broke off, his face crumbling, his eyes closing. Charles looked away, unable to bear the sight of this man coming face to face with his own, terrible truth.

"What about Svana?"

Eudo's head jerked up, then his shoulders sank lower. "They have taken her estate."

"Who?"

"Arab patrols," Eudo said. "My men who were guarding her were dead. They are using her house as an outpost. I could not get close enough ..." He stopped, overcome once more. Charles wanted to ask more questions but decided against it.

"Rest now. We will talk more in the morning."

He directed the steward to take the duke to a room to sleep and keep him under guard. He did not want to return to the hall. He needed to be alone. He moved along the passage until he came upon an empty room. He went in, shutting the door. He sank down to the floor, drew his knees to his chin, buried his face in his arms, and began to think.

Lothar paced incessantly. Hugo, Arnulf, Gunther, Chrodegang and Sigebald sat at the long table, drinking, watching Lothar pace. They had been there for hours. A smoky haze hung over the room, though the fire had burned low.

"Lothar sit down!" Sigebald snapped finally. "You're wearing out the floor, man!"

"Where is he?" Lothar said fiercely.

"Hiding," Arnulf said with a laugh. "As usual. He does this all the time, you know it."

"He'll come out when he's ready," Gunther said. "He needs time to think."

"What does he have to think about?" said Lothar. "He knows what we have to do."

"Lothar, even your barbarian soul can see the man has a lot on his mind," said Sigebald tiredly.

Lothar stopped pacing and gazed at them. He was beyond fury. He thought if he spent the night sitting in that stifling room, staring at these blank, stupid faces, he would go mad. He headed for the door. Gunther went after him, grabbed his arm.

"Where are you going?"

"For a walk," Lothar said, pulling away. "I'll be back long before him, don't worry about that."

"Lothar … "

"Oh be still. Your precious duke is safe from me tonight."

He went to see Rotruda.

Whenever he was angry with Charles, he went to see Rotruda. She had a way of calming him, and he needed to be calm now. His anger always made him afraid—he knew himself well enough to know that there was a part of him over which he had no control whatever.

He found her still awake, sitting by the brazier in her sitting room, a small tattered prayer book in her hands. She looked up at him, her lovely face flushed by the fire, opening to a smile, her eyes wide and deeply purple. Her women moved into the shadows as he approached.

"He is nowhere to be found, I suppose," she said.

He shook his head, sat on the fur rugs at her feet.

"What has he done now?"

"You know about the duke?"

"Yes. What's the matter, Lothar? You should be pleased he has finally come and given his oath. It is what you wanted."

"No, I wanted him dead." He smiled wanly. "But I suppose you are right."

"So what happens now?"

"We go to Tours, gather the armies."

"Why Tours?"

"It's on the Roman road on the border of the Aquitaine."

"Then what?"

"We march south into the Aquitaine and meet them wherever they are."

"I see." She was silent, staring down at her book. "Lothar … what about her? Was there news?"

He shrugged uncomfortably. "The Arabs took her estate. Most likely she is dead. Her child as well. The Arabs are killing everything in their path."

Rotruda gasped a little and crossed herself. "Lord have mercy," she whispered.

"Mercy? There will be none of that." Lothar lay on his back, staring up at the ceiling beams. He seemed to relax, imagining the events yet to come. "I wish I knew what he was thinking. I can never figure it out. But he's done it, he's done what everyone said he couldn't do. He's got the Aquitaine, Frisia, Germania, Neustria, Burgundy … all of Gaul under a single banner. Think of it, Rotruda. This war will decide the fate of men for ages to come. Can you imagine? And we will have lived it, *we* will have made it happen. Charles will be called the greatest warrior who ever lived, the greatest ruler, the greatest king … "

"No," said Rotruda, her voice racked with bitterness. "He will never be king, Lothar, you know that."

"He will have to be, after this," Lothar said. "He will have no choice. The people will make him king, they will demand it—"

"And when have you ever known him to bend to the will of the people?" Rotruda asked bleakly. "No, he won't do it. He doesn't want to be king. It's about time you accepted that fact. I have. To him, the future does not even exist. He cannot fathom the responsibility he has to his sons. He told them—did you know? He told them that he would see to it that they would never be named kings. He *told* them that, Lothar. I was there, I heard him say it. He had that look in his eyes—you know the look. And that is when I finally realized the truth: Charles is a man without dreams. When he dies, the world ends. He doesn't care what happens after." She was crying now, huge, fat tears streaming down her face, her skin milky white and brittle. "He doesn't care about his sons. He doesn't care about me—"

"Stop it." Lothar sat up straight, his voice very hard. "Don't talk like that. Don't ever talk like that. You know it isn't true."

"Do I? I wonder." She moved to rise, but he grabbed her arm and forced her back into the chair. He stood, facing the two women who lurked in the darkness at the far end of the room.

"Get out," he said in a low growl. They looked at each other, then bolted from the room. He turned back to Rotruda, kneeling before her; he took her face in his hands and kissed her cheek, her throat, her mouth, drinking in her salty tears. He felt her shudder, heard a sound emerge from deep within her. He knew he ought to stop, but he knew as well that he wouldn't. This had been ordained, it was meant to be. He gave himself up to his fate, drawing her to himself, to the furs, where they finished what had begun long ago.

# 69

LOTHAR RETURNED TO the room at dawn—Charles still had not appeared. The rest of them lay about in desultory heaps, snoring. The fire had gone out, the room was very cold, a fresh breeze blowing in from the open window. He was reminded of Gethsemane, the disciples promising to stay awake but failing, the traitor returning with a kiss ...

He went to the window and stared out, over the plaza, the river, the city. The sun had broken the horizon, splattering the cloud-laden sky in washed-out hues of blue and pink, the promise of a storm. He had seen more dawns than he cared to remember, it was the prime time of wakefulness for a warrior. But this one was different. *He* was different.

He tried to contemplate the thing he had done, but he could not—the enormity of it, the depth of his betrayal. And yet all he could really think about was *her*—her violet eyes, her body trembling beneath him, soft and yielding. Her fingers gliding over his scars, as if she could fix them, heal them. The shape her mouth made when he pressed deep within her, the sound in her throat, like the far-off rumble of thunder, rolling over him, into him. Then lightning, swift and brilliant, taking them both by surprise. Twenty years he had waited, suffered. He had whispered love words to her, though she had not whispered back. Her tears, streaking her cheeks: that was how she had answered him.

He knew he should feel remorse for what he had done. Instead he was aware of a vast sense of destiny, a fulfillment. He saw his path mapped out before him, there, in the silent city below him, growing with the light. He felt utterly, breathlessly calm.

The door creaked, swung open, making him jump from the window. The others aroused as well, shaking themselves. Charles stood in the doorway, glanced about as if wondering what they were all doing there. He turned and went to the wine table. Another figure appeared behind him, a man whose straightness of line seemed toppled by an extraordinary weight, and yet whose eyes pierced them in the thin light with the precision of a hunting bird looking for prey. Eudo of Aquitaine.

Lothar looked to Charles, saw he was pouring wine into two cups, oblivious. He saw the Aquitainian duke make his way across the room, toward an empty chair at the table, each step an eternity. This was the great, indomitable Eudo of Aquitaine. Lothar felt a swift stab of pity. Only Charles could do this to a man, he thought.

Eudo reached the chair and stood, awkwardly, his eyes on Charles, who was still turned away. Lothar thought he might scream if this went on any longer.

"Sit down," said Charles, and Eudo sat. Charles turned finally and went to him, set the cup before him. Eudo stared at it as if he had not the strength to pick it up. Charles stood over him, frighteningly huge, silent once more.

The men watched this little ballet in fascination. The presence of Eudo was an odd thing, repressed and volatile, or perhaps it was the combination of the two of them, like opposing storm fronts clashing overhead, in just that moment of stillness before the thunder cracks and the rain starts to fall.

Charles drank his cup to the dregs and set it down on a table. "Tell us about them," he said.

Eudo began to talk.

"There are many untruths about them," he said, his voice groggy, sluggish. "First, that they are a single people. They are a mixture of many tribes, many cultures. Most numerous are the Berbers, from Mauritania, across the strait. The Arabs conquered the Berbers long ago. What they have in common is that they are all, now, followers of the prophet Mohamet, and all believe in Mohamet's ultimate conquest of the entire world."

He paused to lift the cup to his lips, unsteadily. He set it down again. His voice grew clearer, stronger.

"They are not barbaric raiders. They are highly skilled and organized. They fight with sword and bow. They have only light cavalry, no heavy spears, no lances, but very fast. You cannot outrun them.

"You will hear the drums before you see them. The sound will shake an army to its core, if you aren't prepared. It is the sound of death."

He stopped talking, as if lost in memory.

"What about their weaknesses?" Charles asked.

Eudo licked his lips slowly, drawing breath. "They have few. The land, perhaps. They don't know the land north of the Garonne very well and Francia not at all. And they have an aversion to rivers; I don't suppose there are many waterways in the desert. I think that is why they didn't take

Arles nine years ago when they had taken Nîmes already— the river has no bridge and they were loathe to cross it. They don't like forests either. The weather also might have an effect. They prefer the dry air of the desert ... " He stopped talking as if he had run out of breath.

"What about Rayman?" said Charles.

Eudo looked at him tiredly. "I know very little about him," he said. "Othman had mentioned only the elder Rayman, the Governor of Cordova. You must understand something about these people. They are not mere marauders looking for plunder. They want ... to destroy us completely, our way of life, our God. To wipe us off the face of the earth. This is the mission given them by the prophet. Othman meant to do it slowly, to bleed us to death. But Rayman, he is in a hurry, a great hurry. This is the hundredth year of the death of Mohamet. This is his *jihad*, his holy war. He will do to you what he did to us in Bordeaux ... " He paused, catching his breath, closing his eyes, as if imagining a hundred horrors he could not describe.

There was silence. Lothar turned his gaze to Charles. The gray eyes were still and pale, unfocused. He had never seen real pain in those eyes before, but he was seeing it now. Pain, massive and terrible, a burden too heavy even for this man whom he thought could bear anything.

Charles moved to the window. He stood there, looking out, as if he had forgotten about them. They waited, their eyes flicking from him to the duke, wondering what was next. All at once he turned around to face them.

"We cannot attack them in Bordeaux," he said. "They are too strong there, and they are fortified. We must make them move north. We will gather at Chinon and wait for them to come to us."

There was a sound like a collective gasp. No one moved but Lothar, who was on his feet. Before he could speak, Eudo cut him off.

"But that means I could lose every city between the Garonne and the Loire!" The duke had risen from his seat, his voice taking on new dimension.

"You have already lost them," Charles said.

"No! You cannot sacrifice the Aquitaine to save Francia, I won't have it!"

The men jumped in alarm, hands flew to daggers. Eudo stood like a volcano, spitting. Charles looked at him steadily, his voice flat.

"I am not the one who made that sacrifice, Eudo. Sit down."

Eudo stood a moment, blindly, his fists unfolding. Then he sat, slowly. He stared hard at the table in front him. Lothar watched, fascinated. Eudo of Aquitaine was meeting, for the first time, the Hammer in truth.

"Now listen," Charles said slowly. "Listen and understand. It is too late to imagine we can defeat this enemy by simple assault. We cannot. They are too strong. We must let them come north, into our territory. We must let them have victories—sacking cities will make them confident and careless. They will think they are invincible. That is what we want them to think. They will be carrying a lot of treasure, which will make them slow and cautious as well.

"They have many advantages over us, but we have one very important one: we know the land. We will have to use that knowledge." He turned to Eudo, his face losing its crystal hardness, suddenly full of motion. "What shape is your army in now?"

Eudo looked up at him. "I have no army," he said dully.

"Your army is scattered, you need to gather it back again."

"Most are dead. My captains—"

"Then you will get more men. More captains. You will raise a new army."

"Raise a new army?" Eudo blinked in disbelief.

"Rayman thinks you are dead and your army is destroyed," Charles said. "That's good. You can go around him, get behind him, muster a new force. You must make sure he doesn't know you are alive. Rayman is a man who believes in his destiny—it will be up to you to ensure that nothing stands in his way." He paused, gazing at Eudo's stricken face. "You can do it, Eudo," he said quietly. "I know you can. You must. Remember what I told you about fear? You are not afraid of anything, anymore."

Lothar watched the face of Eudo of Aquitaine transform then, understanding. This was what made Charles Martel the great general he was, the greatest since Caesar himself. It was his unique ability to look into the soul of a man, to see the truth of him, and to know what that truth meant. Charles Martel understood the living essence of a man; he knew how to nurture it, to make it grow. He knew, as well, how to crush it. Lothar almost felt sorry for Eudo of Aquitaine.

Eudo's head dropped, his eyes seeming to close. Charles ordered the guards to take him back to his quarters. Eudo stopped in the doorway, twisting around.

"What will you do—about her?"

Charles was silent a moment. "There is nothing I can do."

"Nothing?" Eudo was incredulous. "You are not going to try to save her? Have you thought about what could have happened to her in the hands of those men?"

"I thought about it all night long," said Charles tiredly. "Now go. I'll send for you when I need you again."

Once Eudo was gone, the others left one by one. Lothar lingered in the window, watching his friend, who sat at the table, drinking. He longed to go to him, to sit beside him, to share a cup of wine and laugh about this turn of events. What did it feel like, to laugh? He hardly remembered.

"You ought to be more pleased," Charles said, not looking at him. Lothar tensed. Did he know already? "Eudo of Aquitaine has sworn oath to me."

Lothar let out a breath. "I would be pleased. If it were not—too late."

"Too late?"

"The Aquitaine is already lost. Thanks to him."

"As long as he's alive, the Aquitaine is not lost."

"You really think he can raise a new army? In a matter of months?"

"He has to. We all must do … impossible things now." Charles sighed, rising slowly. He turned to look at his friend, as if seeing him for he first time. "Get some rest. You look as though you've been up all night."

"I could say the same," Lothar said, averting his gaze. "Charles … "

"Yes?"

"You know that … no matter what happens … I am always with you."

He felt Charles' eyes bearing down on him. "I know it."

# 70

ROTRUDA STAYED IN her bedchamber all day, telling her women she was ill, refusing to see anyone. She lay on her bed, the sweat like a fever on her brow, chills in her limbs. She would not be able to see him, to look him in the face. Because he would know, he always knew everything. And he would not be angry. He might be resigned, or accepting, or merely indifferent. But not angry. That hurt her most of all.

Finally, in late evening, she began to doze, fitfully. There was a knock at the door. She sat up, her heart pounding. She waited, not answering. In time the door opened.

But it was not Lothar or Charles. It was Carloman, who had never entered her room unbidden.

"Mother, are you all right?" he asked softly, blinking into the darkness. He carried a lantern, the only light in the room.

"Carl?" she said, and she burst into tears, not knowing if they were tears of relief or disappointment.

In an instant he was beside her. "Don't cry," he said. "I know all of it."

"What do you know?" she said, afraid.

"That you love Lothar."

She drew away, gasping. "No … "

"I know what happened. And I'm glad. Because he loves you, and you love him."

"Carl … don't ever say such a thing!"

"You've always loved him. Everyone knows it. Why not just be honest about it? Father doesn't hide his mistress, does he? He has no shame at all … "

"It's not the same thing," Rotruda said miserably.

"Then there is something wrong with the world," Carloman said, his voice hard-bitten. "The way Father has dishonored you—it's despicable. He should have been excommunicated."

Rotruda managed a smile. "Carl, you are so innocent of the ways of the world. Even bishops have mistresses."

"It should not be," he said. She laid a hand on his cheek.

"You must leave this alone. For my sake. What happened ... it will not happen again."

He looked at her, wounded. He stood up, moving away from her. "I don't understand you. Why would you forsake your only chance for love in this world? For a man who doesn't care whether you live or die, who doesn't care about any of us?"

"He does care, he just doesn't know how to show it."

Carloman laughed bitterly. "You are still apologizing for him. It's disgusting. Why can't you see the truth of him? Why are you so blind? Is this what love is?"

"Carl, please—"

"Never mind. I don't understand it and I never will."

He left her alone to sob into her pillows.

When she did not appear for days, Hugo went to Charles. "You need to go see your wife," he said. "Something is wrong. Her maids say she won't come out of the room. She won't get out of bed. They fear she is very ill."

"Send the doctor to her."

"She refuses to see the doctor. Please, Uncle. Go and see her."

Charles, embroiled in maps, calculations, troop movements, sighed heavily. Late in the evening he went.

The room was dark, hazed in smoke from a languishing fire. Charles threw open a window, let the cold air lash his face, breathing. He turned and peered into the room. A candle guttered on the bedside table. Rotruda was motionless on the bed. She appeared to be asleep.

"Rotruda?"

He saw a movement, a flicker in her body, a reflex.

"Please go away," she said, turning over, hiding her face in the pillow. "I'm fine."

"Hugo says you are not well. What's the matter? Are you pregnant?"

She almost laughed. "I don't know."

"Then what's wrong?"

He sat beside her on the bed, turning her over to look at him. He was surprised at her face, so terribly pale he could see the fine lines of age she managed to mask with powders and potions.

"Charles … what has happened to us?" she said, the words tumbling from her lips in a rush. "That first night, I was so … so happy … I thought you were too … but now you are cold again. The more I try to reach you, the more you turn away. You hate me … I don't know what I have done to make you hate me … "

"I don't hate you," he said.

"No, you don't hate me," she said bitterly. "You don't feel anything for me. That is so much worse."

"Rotruda … " he bent to her, brushing a tear from her face, not knowing what to say. She had been a perfect wife, had given him sons, had cared for his people. She was beautiful and uncomplaining and everyone in the kingdom adored her. He had wanted to love her. How much easier it would have been to love her than the raven-haired Valkyrie who had caused him no end of grief. Yet against this one thing he was powerless.

She clutched the hand that touched her face. "Please, love me … can't you?" She lay back on the bed, holding his hand against her cheek. "Just once more … I won't ask for more than that, I promise. Please … "

She wrapped her arms around his neck and pulled him down. She kissed him hard, forcing his mouth open. She tugged at his clothes, pushing herself against him with a kind of madness, a fevered desperation that made him feel cold and dead to his core. He pulled away from her, straightening.

She shrieked, bolting upright, furious. "How dare you!" she screamed. "I am your wife, damn you! I deserve better than this!"

"You do, you're right," he said gravely. "I'm sorry, Rotruda." He turned as if to leave.

"No!" She scrambled from the bed, beating on him with her small fists. Her eyes were wild, pulsing, her whole body shook. "No, it doesn't work that way! You can't leave me with nothing! I've given up my life for you—everything I have done I did for you! You owe me, Charles, you owe me!"

He let her flail at him until her strength failed, dissolved in sobs. He held her until she quieted, laying her back down on the bed gently. He let go of her, but she grabbed hold of his shirt, pulling him down and hissing in his ear.

"Do you want to know what I have done to you, Husband? I have made a cuckold of you, that's what! I have been with your best friend! I slept with Lothar!"

She let go, turning her face to the pillows to muffle her sobs. He felt the room close around him, the darkness like a shroud, comforting. He took a breath, letting the air fill his body, seeping into the empty spaces. He left her on the bed, alone, shutting the door behind him.

# 71

## Luxeuil, Burgundy
## April, 732

THEODOUIN, COUNT OF Vienne, was ushered into a small room lit by candles set on huge, elaborate candelabra. He blinked, his vision adjusting. The room was spare but expensively furnished with two stuffed chairs and a carved oak dining table, fine oriental rugs warming the bare stone floor. The ceiling was vaulted, rare for a private residence. Bishop Eucher was said to be a man of Spartan habits, but Theodouin saw that he managed to surround himself in luxury nonetheless. He liked this about him. This was a man with whom he could do business.

The bishop was bent over a kneeler before a little shrine of artifacts: the bones of saints, a statue of the Blessed Virgin, a glass case that was said to contain a splinter from the actual Cross. He was worrying a large set of wooden beads, a new invention called a rosary, which aided in daily prayers. Theodouin waited patiently until he was finished.

When the prayers were done the small man rose, wincing with pain as he straightened his knees, and said without turning around, "Well, Count, what can I do for you today?"

Theodouin was startled to hear himself addressed. He bowed to the bishop's back. "My compliments, Your Grace, and thank you for consenting to see me." Eucher turned and shuffled to one of the stuffed chairs. He was not very old, but he was cursed with inflamed joints that kept his body bent and his expression in a permanent scowl.

"Yes, yes, but hurry up. I am busy today." Eucher did not offer Theodouin a seat, so the count continued to stand.

"You have heard by now that Charles is headed to Tours?"

"I have heard," Eucher said in a low voice. A servant bent to give him a cup of wine, which he took eagerly without offering any to his guest.

"I have also heard," said the count, "that he has demanded quite a lot of money from you and the other Sees for his war."

"Yes."

"He says the Arabs have invaded the Aquitaine, but do you believe it?"

Eucher looked at the count for the first time. "Does it matter if I believe it?"

"My dear Bishop," said Theodouin, warming to his subject, "you seem to have lost your enthusiasm for a good fight. It is not like you. Think about it: does any of this make sense? Eudo and Othman have been allies for years now! The Arabs have a treaty with the Aquitaine, so why on earth would they suddenly attack?"

"You believe that Charles is lying?"

"Of course he is lying! What else could it be? It's quite simple, Your Grace: Charles is tired of waiting for an actual reason to deploy his great army in the Aquitaine. Moreover, he wants to strip the Church of any riches he had not yet stolen. He wants not only your land, but your gold as well. Are you going to continue to let him get away with such blasphemy?"

"If God wishes to stop him, God will stop him," Eucher said tiredly. "Charles is a dragon I am tired of fighting."

"You don't need to fight him alone," Theodouin said, moving closer. "I have a proposal for you."

"Yes?"

"Call a Synod."

Eucher stared at him. "A Synod? No … we tried that once, we failed."

"You need to try again."

"Why?"

"Now is the time, don't you see? If you don't stop him now, his power will be limitless. He will wipe out the Church! God put you here to be the Church's protector, didn't He? So how can you sit idly by while Charles destroys the Church completely?"

Eucher looked dubious. "The people will not go along with it," he said. "Charles is too popular. The nobles support his war. I could not oppose him."

Theodouin smiled furtively. "That, Your Grace, is where you are wrong."

Eucher arched an eyebrow. "You know something I do not?"

"You have God on your side! Can Charles fight God? Of course not! It is your moral duty to oppose Charles' war. Charles would not retaliate against you! The people would revolt! They will not stand to see their Holy Sees attacked. Charles knows he can do nothing against you."

"Charles has had no qualms about removing bishops in the past—"

"But he will not do that now! It would look like blatant vengeance! The people know you have only the interests of God at heart; you care nothing for wars and politics. They will soon see that this war is a sham, a lie, and that you are the only one brave enough to stand against him. Your Grace, if the people have to choose between Charles and the Church, whom do you think they will choose? When their eternal salvation is at stake?"

Eucher gave Theodouin a half smile. "You are still angry at him for humiliating you in front of the Assembly, aren't you? Is that why you come to me now? You've been waiting all this time for vengeance?"

Theodouin's lips tightened, he straightened, stiffening. "Charles has stolen from me too," he said.

"Ah, yes, I heard something of that. Your father was his mother's overlord, correct? When she lived in hiding in Burgundy—"

"He had no idea she was Pipin's second wife," Theodouin said sharply. "She was an unmarried woman with a child, a fallen woman—"

"Yes, and your father was unable to get her to sleep with him?"

Theodouin blushed deeply. "Where did you hear that?"

"I have my sources, my young friend. Don't worry. I'm just curious, seeing as you seem to have such a determination to get even with Charles. The woman spurned your father, so he tried to steal her lands after she was dead—"

"He had a deed!"

"Of course he had a deed. Everyone has deeds. They are easy to come by, aren't they?"

"He did not steal that land! The land had been beneficed. He had every right to take it back."

"Well, Charles did not see it that way, did he?"

Theodouin bristled, his composure cracking. "He took twice the amount of land that once belonged to his mother and made his so-called brother—that vagrant!—Duke of Northern Burgundy—my overlord! But that is how Charles operates, as you well know. He takes what he wants, when he wants it, from anyone he considers an enemy. He has taken much more from you, has he not?"

Eucher did not respond.

"You see? You know I am right! My question is this, Your Grace: how long will you tolerate it? How long will you continue to allow this heathen to run roughshod over the Holy Mother Church? How long will you allow God to be mocked?"

Eucher set down his cup. "A Synod … is a very dangerous thing, Count. If we were to call one, Charles would know we were declaring war on him. That we mean to have him excommunicated."

"Yes, of course! That is the point! He would no longer be able to rule. You yourself, as chief of the Council of Bishops, would take his place. That is the law."

Eucher was smiling now, though his smile was still twisted with pain. He turned to the servant standing in the shadows. "Call in my secretary," he said. "I have some letters to write."

# 72

## Chinon, On The Loire
## June, 732

THE WIDE PLAIN of the Loire Basin was said to be the most beautiful land in Gaul. It had been a favorite vacation spot of the Romans, who found in its flower-laden fields and bright, blue streams a glimpse of their homeland. The river, the longest in Gaul, was shallow and wide at this stretch and almost constantly flooded as the land was low and the climate wet, especially in the spring. Yet in the spring the Loire Basin had a lushness unparalleled in the land; tall, stately poplars bowed magisterially to gentle breezes along still, clear pools, and wildflowers of infinite variety lifted their faces to a soft and civilized sun.

There were few real villages here; farming was difficult in the lowlands. But the Romans had built sprawling villas atop the ragged hills that jutted unexpectedly along the southern edge of the Loire, villas that continued to provide shelter for a chosen few. The Loire Basin was the playground of the rich, a lush and peaceful garden of earthly delights, where Latin was still purely spoken, where nature was worshipped like a god, where warfare and bloodshed and all the horrors of the barbarian world did not and could not exist.

It was here that Charles Martel chose to fight the battle of his life.

The city of Tours was most famous for the conversion of Saint Martin, a Roman legionnaire stationed there some three hundred years before. Martin once dreamed of a poor man dying of cold, so he had cut apart his cloak and gave the man half. The poor man turned out to be Jesus Christ, who appeared to him in another dream wearing his cloak. It was proof enough to Martin to give up his soldier's vocation, convert to Christianity, and build a monastery at Tours, the first in the land. Upon his death, his body had been borne along the river to the city, and though it was the dead of winter, flowers sprung up and trees burst into bloom as he passed. A basilica had been built over his tomb, where Christian pilgrims flocked in large numbers to pray before the stone effigy of the saint and perhaps, like Martin himself, witness a miracle of their own.

Many people had experienced miracles, including Clovis the first Frankish king who, after a miraculous victory over the Visigoths, rode through the streets showering the populace with gold and silver. Shortly thereafter, he was baptized a Christian, along with three thousand of his warriors.

That legend neatly overlooked the fact that Clovis' wife Clothilda, a staunch, Burgundian Catholic, had virtually insisted he convert. For no one liked to admit that the greatest of all Frankish rulers could have been under the thumb of his wife.

Tours had also produced Francia's most famous bishop, Gregory of Tours, friend and patron of the beloved Queen Brunhilde, author of the celebrated (and somewhat embellished) *Historia Francorium*, and builder of the abbey that surrounded and engulfed the basilica. If Charles had intended irony in choosing his battleground, he could not have done better: there was no place more suited to defending Christianity in Gaul than the city where it had been effectively born.

Charles arrived in early June and took up residence at Chinon, a Roman villa on the Vienne River, one of the Loire's larger tributaries. The villa sat on a rocky hill, its many stuccoed wings and terraces built right into the multi-leveled terrain, as if it were an extension of the rock itself. The villa commanded the best views of the southern plains and provided plenty of space for bivouacking an army, setting up smithy shops, food storehouses, weapons-making facilities, and latrine pits.

The villa owners, an elderly Gallo-Roman named Arnald and wife Gera, along with their two young grandsons, obediently made room for Charles and his men, moving their personal belongings to a wing on a lower level. They accepted with good humor the presence of Frankish warriors lounging in their dining hall, consuming their wine and eating their food, for Charles had promised to pay them handsomely when their ordeal was over.

The spring rains had ended, and the plain was awash with color — wildflowers, mushrooms, berries and wild rampion sprang up in blanket clusters. Men began the work of building pontoon bridges to carry warriors and equipment over the river, which had reached its high water mark the month before and had been steadily receding. The fishing was glorious, the plains pocked with small game warrens. Hunting parties brought in fresh meat, and herds from Charles' own estates were let loose to graze the grassy meadows. Gradually, the peaceful fields of Chinon became cluttered with tents and fires and bedrolls, as an army took up residence.

Brand met Charles in Chinon after nearly five months spent scouting the land south of the Loire and learning more about Rayman's army. Charles immediately called a war council with all of his captains and his sons, Carloman and young Pipin, who had insisted on accompanying Charles against his mother's wishes.

Brand unrolled maps he had drawn on the journey. "It is not difficult to know Rayman's plan," he said. "He announces it in the plaza square every day. He thinks he is the Chosen One, the Holy Warrior sent by Mohamet to liberate Gaul from the Christians."

"Just how many men does he have?" Charles asked.

"It is difficult to say. Rumors are there are three hundred thousand altogether, but they are scattered now, raiding, gathering supplies for the march."

"Three hundred thousand?" said Milo. He crossed himself. "God in heaven."

"We can muster not even half that many," Gerold said.

"We cannot fight here on open ground," Milo said. "We must go to the walls of Tours—"

Charles interrupted. "They have not started the march yet?"

Brand shook his head. "Rayman was still in Bordeaux last I saw. His army is dispersed. But we set up a courier network, so we will know as soon as he starts moving, I can promise that."

Charles nodded, looking at the map. "What have you learned of the ground?"

"Ah," Brand said. "You said that the duke believed they would stay on the Roman Road, since they don't know their way around Gaul and their army is too big to move without a road. I believe this to be true as well. Rayman doesn't care if we see him, because he thinks his army is too big and too powerful to be bothered. He's already defeated Eudo easily, so he has a very poor opinion of our western armies."

"Good," Charles said.

"Here," Brand said, pointing to an area halfway between Poitiers and Tours along the Roman road, "the Vienne forks to form two rivers. The Roman road crosses the Vienne at the settlement of Châtellerault and then traverses this narrow strip of land between them, getting narrower as the rivers converge. If the Arabs keep to the Roman road, they will be squeezed right here between these two rivers, forced to close ranks. This will concentrate them in one tight place, but it will also make it difficult for them to circumvent our army—to do that they would have to cross one of the rivers."

"Is that hard to do?" asked Gerold.

"It depends on when they come. If they come in summer the rivers may not hold them for long. But if they come in fall, when the weather is rainy and the water level is high, they could very well be trapped."

"So the question is, when will they come?" said Milo, looking at Charles.

"Good question," Charles said slowly, staring at the map. "I'm a bit surprised they haven't started moving already. But if the army is really that big, they will need to carry a lot of supplies, and that will take time to gather. And when they do come, they will stop to sack every town on the way. It could take all summer."

"You mean we could be here all summer?" said Arnulf, tension in his voice. "We cannot keep an army in the field that long, Uncle."

"We should march south," Lothar said. "While Rayman's army is dispersed. What on earth are you waiting for anyway? We should go down there and crush him!"

"Perhaps Rayman will not come this year at all. Perhaps he will wait until next year," said Milo thoughtfully.

"No," Charles said. "Rayman will have to be in Rheims by the end of the year."

Silence. The captains exchanged nervous glances.

"Why Rheims? Why this year?" Gerold finally asked.

"Because," Charles said with a grim smile, "Rayman is a man who believes in Destiny." He paused. They all stared at him, waiting. "When did he invade the Aquitaine? When did he take Bordeaux? *Christmas*. He defeated the Christians at the time we celebrate the birth of our God. And at that time as well, he will march into Rheims."

"Not Paris?" Brand asked.

"Paris is not important. Rheims is the seat of the Merovingian kings, the *real* kings of Francia. He must take Tours and Rheims to make his conquest complete. This is the hundredth year of the death of Mohamet; it has to be this year. And to destroy Francia utterly, he must adhere to all the symbols; he must drive home the significance of his conquest."

The theory was compelling but subject to a thousand variables. The men immediately began to ask questions. What if the Arabs veered from the road, seeing the narrowing of the rivers and sensing a trap? They could move west, leaving the Franks trapped between two rivers and forced to give chase. Then Rayman would get to Tours first, and Tours would be destroyed. The destruction of Saint-Martin's, the symbol of their faith, would be a fatal blow to the Franks. Charles could not let Rayman get to Tours, but to risk throwing all of his forces into the narrow strip on the Vienne/Creuse fork could leave the Arabs with a wide berth to get around him.

The matter was discussed heatedly for a time. "Obviously," Charles said at length, "we cannot let them know where we are until it is too late. We will do what we have done a thousand times before—we will create a screen. We will maneuver in several different areas, to keep their scouts on alert. But we keep the army here until we are certain the Arabs have crossed the river at Châtellerault. Then we move, and we move very fast. We'll have a longer distance to travel than they will—"

"Father," Pipin said suddenly, his voice small and tremulous. Everyone looked at him, surprised that he had spoken aloud at this gathering. "One thing."

"What is it?"

Pipin took a breath. "Well, two things actually. The land there between the rivers is probably very low, isn't it? If the rivers flood, isn't it likely that *we* will be washed out as well as the enemy?"

He paused, waiting for a comment. Charles said nothing. Pipin took this as tacit permission to continue.

"The other problem is, what if the rains don't come in strength? What if the rivers don't flood enough to trap them inside? We cannot put all our hopes on the weather—the weather has been known to fail us."

Silence. Then Charles said softly, "You have a suggestion to make?"

"Yes, as a matter of fact," said Pipin, grinning shyly. "But it will take some time, and some work."

"Go on."

"I think we should build a dam."

Silence again. Then there was laughter, short and suppressed. The men were shaking their heads.

Pipin went on, undaunted. "Consider it. The Vienne flows north. If we dam it at a strategic point, say, here—" he pointed to the map, "—we not only dry out our ground, we force a flood of the southern plain. I realize we've never done something like this before, but it's not a new idea. The ancient Ripuarians used to change the course of entire rivers in order to affect the outcome of a battle. If they could do it, why can't we?"

There was silence again, everyone staring at Charles doubtfully. But Charles was smiling. He turned to Malwolfe, his engineer. "Can it be done?"

"It's a beastly lot of work," Malwolfe said, shaking his head, making his long beard tremble. "And what would we build with? There are not enough trees—"

"We could dig," Pipin said. "Dirt. And rocks. The land is full of both."

Malwolfe growled a little. The men chuckled.

"The men will have to work day and night—"

"Put them on shifts," Charles said. "It will keep them busy and fit. Tell the smiths—we are going to need a lot of shovels."

Malwolfe grunted a reply. Charles looked at Pipin, who beamed up at him, thrilled beyond words. "Good work, son. We have some work to do. Let's get busy."

# 73

BRAND WENT TO Charles' room hours later. The room was small, as were all the sleeping rooms of the villa, the stucco walls webbed with cracks, but it had a large window that overlooked the river. Charles stood there now, gazing out. Brand leaned against the wall beside him and sighed, as if he had come to the end of a long journey.

"She's alive," he said.

Charles did not move, did not trust himself to speak. Brand understood.

"Apparently the people of her estate had been sneaking in and out of the village for months; the Arabs are not paying very close attention anymore." Brand paused, noticing Charles' clenched jaw. "They are still using her house as an outpost, and it was heavily guarded. I could not risk trying to get in there."

"How do you know she is alive?"

"Everyone knows it, apparently. She made some sort of deal with them—"

"Deal?" Charles looked at him in wonder.

"Yes. She bargained for their lives. The entire estate was spared. Which is more than I can say for the monastery, unfortunately."

Charles turned back to the window, staring out in disbelief. "What did she bargain with?"

Brand shook his head. "You know her better than I do, Charles. But from what I know of that lady, I believe she is capable of facing down an army."

Charles smiled a little, nodding, closing his eyes. "Yes." He was silent a moment, thinking. "Can we get in there?"

"You want to try and rescue her?" Brand shook his head. "I don't think that would be wise. Any maneuvering so far south would tip your hand. I would wait until they have left the area. The Arabs suspect nothing now; you want to keep it that way."

Charles nodded again, sighing a little. "I suppose you are right."

"She'll be all right, Charles. She's made it this far." He paused, then said: "You seem more worried than usual."

"Yes. I am worried."

"Because of Rayman's delay?"

"Arnulf is right. Three months is a long time to keep an army in the field, too long. We could run out of local provisions in a matter of weeks. I'm bringing in all I can from my estates, and so are the nobles, but it may not be enough."

"I see."

"And there's another problem."

"What's that?"

"The bishops have called a Synod. They've declared this war illegal and refuse to support it."

Brand nearly laughed. "They can't be serious."

"Apparently they can. God has spoken to Eucher, and told him that by opposing this war he can reassert the authority of the Church."

"And if the Arabs overrun the kingdom?"

"He doesn't believe any such threat exists. He says that this whole war is some sort of ruse of mine."

"Christ in Heaven! What are you going to do?"

"Chrodegang went to appeal to the Council, but it refused to give him an audience. Most of the Burgundian nobles have joined the bishops. Now the Neustrians are starting to get nervous as well."

Brand was silent, stunned. "You think they will refuse your call?"

"If it is a choice between this war and their immortal souls, which one do you think they will choose?"

Brand stared at his brother in shock. "What will you do? Remove the bishop from his See?"

Charles shook his head. "I cannot do that without bringing even more trouble on my head. He knows this. I suspect our friend Theodouin has been talking to him."

"Theodouin? That imbecile! He can't have—"

"He's never quite gotten over having to give your lands back to you. He's been burning for vengeance for a long time."

"Good God."

"Chrodegang may be able to persuade Eucher to relent. He's worked miracles before. We have to hope he can do it again."

"God, Charles, I'm so sorry. This is all my fault—"

"Of course it isn't. It was only a matter of time before the bishops tried to oppose me again. I just never thought … how is it that men can be so blind?"

"Men believe what they want to believe," Brand said. "I suppose we should not be surprised at all."

The grass grew long on the sunken meadows of the Loire, so the livestock, at least, had plenty to eat. The armies of the Franks began to arrive. A few of the Neustrian dukes reported, including Rotruda's father, who brought six thousand men at arms and a flock of sheep. Bavaria sent five thousand men, and six hundred archers came from Alemannia. The army around Chinon spread like a cancer over the landscape. And none too soon, for word came that Rayman, finally, was on the move.

Eudo brought this news personally, riding a white Andalusian stallion into the courtyard of Chinon. He looked much healthier than the last time Charles had seen him—the sunken quality was gone, and his eyes had regained their hard, hawkish gleam. He was putting together an army; the task had given him an almost manic energy.

Charles took him to his rooms for a private meeting. He knew the men still did not trust him.

"You are going to have to empty every town between Saintes and Châtellerault, tell everyone to clear out. There can be no resistance when the Arabs arrive."

"Is that really necessary?" Eudo still did not like this part of the plan at all.

Charles nodded. "Let them spend the summer gorging themselves on Aquitainian bread and gold. I want them fat and happy when they come to me."

It was Eudo who finally put a name to Charles' strategy.

"It's a pig slaughter," he said. "Is that what you have in mind?"

Charles only smiled.

Lothar, below in the dining hall, swallowed a cup of beer and gloomed. Eudo—again. They were up there, together, sharing confidences, sharing wine. As if they were friends—*friends*! Lothar bristled at the thought. He drank, trying to drown the rage in his marrow.

He had said nothing to Charles about Rotruda. She was pregnant again, due in late summer. The news had caused a sensation in Paris, everyone gossiping about the miracle of Charles and Rotruda's reconciliation, the miracle of another pregnancy. Lothar had stayed away from her, avoiding her even in public, and she him. He was sure that Charles would notice this, but Charles did not.

It was this more than anything that convinced him that Charles knew.

*Rotruda*. When he thought of her he could hardly breathe. He still did not regret it. It would be worth the cost, and the cost would be great, he had no doubt.

But for her it was different. She was consumed with guilt. He had gone to see her before he left, to say goodbye. She had been praying, her face streaked with tears. He could not stand to see her torment, her shame.

But Charles did not care. Perhaps he was even relieved. That would be like him. He would not even give his wife the satisfaction of being jealous or vengeful. Was there no way on earth to move him?

There was a way. Lothar had thought of little else since leaving Paris. He had waited only for the right time. And now, sitting there, once again shut out, once again left to imagine what he himself could never have, he knew the time had come.

# 74

HE WAITED FOR the moon to appear, a waxing crescent. Traveling at night meant traveling by moonlight, and for the next week he would need moonlight. He wore a plain leather tunic, no mail. He had a full complement of weapons hidden under his saddle pack. He had some food, enough for a few days, but he was used to living off the land. No one saw him leave.

He rode away from the camps, avoiding the sentries. He crossed the bridge over the Vienne and continued east, staying close to the river until he came upon the proposed battlefield. He could see the silvered outlines of the piles of dirt and rocks that had already been dug, to be used for the dam. Being so near this place pierced his heart, but he put it out of his mind.

The weather was blessedly calm, and after three days he reached a plateau, where the river veered suddenly east. He had a vague idea that he should not travel that way and forded the river, continuing a southwesterly trek toward what he knew to be the Garonne. He had a rudimentary map with him, which he had hastily copied from Charles' desk when no one was around. But much of the land here was unknown, especially to the east of the Roman Road. He stayed off the road and saw no one.

He made it to the Dordogne River in seven days. He rode up the river until he found a ford shallow enough to cross on horseback. He dismounted after crossing, pulled a piece of white cloth from his saddlebag and tied it to the branch of a dead tree at the water's edge. Then he remounted and continued on. The terrain changed sharply from flat heath to gentle hills, many of them covered in vines. Wine country, Saint-Emilion, with Bordeaux just twenty-five miles to the east.

Surprisingly, he saw no patrols on the other side of the river. He was disappointed. He was itching to kill Arabs.

He continued on, meandering between the hills to stay out of sight, until he came to the strange monastery in the grotto. He had overheard Brand telling Charles of this place. He dismounted in the courtyard, hobbled his horse and went inside.

The place seemed deserted. He felt his way through the darkened passages until he came to a wider opening where candles stood on tall wooden holders, heard a smattering of plainsong from within. He saw a small group of nuns and monks kneeling together on the bare floor in front of a crumbled pile of stones he supposed had once been an altar.

He watched for awhile, until one of the praying monks looked up and saw him. He crossed himself, unleashing a stream of incomprehensible Latin. The others turned, startled, staring wide-eyed in utter fear.

Lothar showed his hands. "I will not hurt you. I am Lothar, captain to Charles Martel. I just want information—"

It made no difference. In the next moment all was mayhem, the monks falling over each other in an effort to flee, helping the women as they went. Only one remained, an old nun who appeared to have trouble rising. She looked painfully at Lothar.

"You must excuse them," she said. "Many of our brothers and sisters have been killed. You come in peace?"

"Yes."

"Then you are welcome, my son. I am Mother Beatrice."

"Where is the abbot?"

"Dead. Killed defending this altar. It was a foolish thing. What is there to save but a few gold chalices? God would have forgiven him. But he would not forgive himself." She crossed herself. "They took everything, as you can see. What they couldn't carry they destroyed. A few of us are left. We stay and carry on as best we can. How can we be of service to you, my lord?"

"I am not a lord," Lothar said nervously. "I just need information."

"About—what?"

"A woman. A woman who came here three years ago. She has an estate near here—"

"Ah yes. Svanahilda. I'm afraid you won't get in there. The Arabs have taken it over."

Lothar nodded impatiently. "I know that, just tell me how to find it."

The old nun's face clouded. Lothar could tell that the woman did not quite trust him. Her watery eyes met his; he was surprised to see iron in them. Finally, she nodded.

"Wait here."

The nun disappeared through a doorway. Lothar waited, pacing anxiously. Was she going to get help from those hapless monks?

Finally she returned, carrying a small parcel and a black cassock draped over one arm.

"Use this," she said, handing Lothar the cassock. "I borrowed it from one of the monks who won't be needing it anymore. It will help you be less—conspicuous. And some food, for your journey."

Lothar took the proffered items. "Thank you."

"Take the path—it winds around a bit—up the hill to the south. It is well marked."

Lothar nodded and turned to leave. The old woman reached for him, grabbed his arm.

"My son, the lady is—very dear to us. I pray for her safety, as I do yours."

Lothar nodded again, catching the meaning in her eyes. He turned quickly and left.

He found the villa without much trouble, the stone house surrounded by several tents and hastily built mud shelters. He understood why the Arabs wanted the hill—they had a near perfect view of the countryside in all directions. He was surprised to see people out in the vineyards, working, tending the vines as if it were a normal day. Occasionally he saw an Arab soldier wandering around, looking menacing and rather lazy. They did not interfere with the work. The people of the villa ignored them. How was it possible?

He waited all day, but he saw no evidence of the black-haired woman herself. He went back to the woods where his horse was tethered and waited for full dark. He slept for a time, covered in the cassock. When it was dark he woke up, ate some of the cheese the nun had given him, then ventured back to the villa, following his tracks by memory. He got close enough to the main house to watch the activity in the yard. He saw three guards, one on horseback, the other two sitting by the door. They were talking, laughing. Then another man came into the doorway, shouted an order at the horsed man, who nodded laconically and turned his horse away. He was the one on patrol.

Lothar tracked him, following his route. A few hours later the other man took the horse and did the same route. Careless, Lothar thought, but they had fallen into a fatal routine.

At dawn he went back to his hideout in the woods, ate some more of the food and slept. That night he watched again, saw that the patrols varied their route little, and only did two rounds a night. He noted where the guard posts were, saw who was sleeping and who stayed awake, which ones seemed more alert than others. *Know thy enemy*, Charles always said. *Know them better than they know themselves.*

On the third night, Lothar awoke at moon set. He donned all his weapons and pulled the black cassock over his head. He felt grateful for the nun's gift, it made him virtually invisible at night. He moved into the path of the patrol and waited.

It seemed to take a long time. He let the first patrol go by. That guard would be more alert than the second one, who would be waking from sleep to make the rounds. He waited. He thought about what he was about to do. He thought of Charles' face when he found out. He felt no regret, only that same sense of destiny he had felt the morning after his night with Rotruda. This was his reckoning. This is how they would both pay for that sin. But he did not care anymore. He had loved her from the moment he first saw her. He had loved her on her wedding day, when she gave herself to his best friend. He thought of how cruel God was to give him such a love, knowing it would destroy them both.

He heard the dusky thrum of hooves and went rigid, ducking lower among the grape vines. The second rider ambled along. Lothar waited until he was nearly past him, then leapt from his hiding place, pulled him swiftly off the horse, and swept his scramsax across his throat. The Arab stared at him, surprised, his mouth working, no sound coming out. Then he closed his eyes as if falling asleep. Lothar wiped the blade on the black robe and sheathed it.

Lothar scrambled to catch the horse, which had continued walking as if nothing had happened. He stripped off the cassock and put on the Arab's white robe and turban. He was about to drop the cassock then changed his mind and tossed it over the horse's neck. He mounted and finished the patrol route the same way the guard would have done.

When he rode into the yard the guard at the entrance turned to acknowledge him with a wave. He waved back, then swung the curved sword across the man's neck as he passed. The man dropped without a sound. Lothar tossed the sword on the body. He rode toward the main door of the house. Two guards sat in front of the door, dozing. One of them was supposed to be awake. Lothar shook his head disgustedly. He pulled out his franca and threw it. It hit one of the sleeping men in the forehead, splitting open his skull. The guard's stifled grunt woke up the other guard. He sat up and looked at his companion, but Lothar was already off the horse and had the man by the throat before he knew what had happened.

"Where is she?" Lothar hissed in the Arab's ear. The man's mouth was open, his eyes bulged. He could not breathe. "The woman! Where is the woman? Don't talk, just point!"

The guard, still gasping, pointed. Lothar glanced over his shoulder but saw nothing, so he stood the man up, drew his scramsax and pressed it against his neck.

"Do not make a sound or you will die," he said. He was sure the man understood him. "Now—show me."

He released the Arab, keeping the short sword pointed at his back. The man stumbled across the yard until he came to a gate that led into a smaller yard. Lothar pulled him back by his collar and looked through the gate. He saw a ditch dug in the ground with stairs leading to a small wooden door. A root cellar. He slid the blade through the Arab's back. The Arab dropped silently, his body sliding off the cold steel.

Lothar drew his long sword and descended down the stairs.

# 75

SVANA SAT UP, listening.

For the past six months she had slept in the root cellar, under the wary surveillance of Mattheus and the other boys. Erik had told her that Rayman had already begun his invasion north, and soon Abbas would join them. She did not believe he would leave her alive.

She had spoken to him only once. Surrounded by Mattheus and her other boys, she had told him that if he let the people starve, he would be breaking his oath to Allah. Moreover, if the people were not allowed to work, the Arabs would starve right along with them. Abbas, perhaps amazed that she had faced him directly, without rancor or fear, acquiesced. He allowed the people to go back to their vineyards, to plant their gardens and rebuild their homes, and life returned almost to normal. Spring came, the vines burst with green, the goats had their spring litters. The healing began.

Svana's own wounds had taken a long time to heal. Now they were long, jagged scars lacing her body. She no longer minded the scars; her scourging had been her release. She had survived the worst of it; there was little left for her to fear.

Mattheus snored at the bottom of the stairs. He slept there every night, as his way of protecting her. She got up from her pallet. Gryffin stirred sleepily.

"What is it, Mama?"

"Nothing," she said. "I have to pee. Go back to sleep."

Using a small oil lamp she crept to the sacks of onions and drew her bow from the bottom of the pile. She kept arrows there as well, arrows she had made herself from innocent supplies the boys and Freddy had brought her: birch and oak saplings from the woodlands, arrowheads cut from slate stones at the stream bed, feathers from the gray geese in the yard. She worked on them in the night when the guards slept, and now had almost a dozen, though she had no idea if the arrowheads, attached with strips of her own ragged garments and what sinew the boys had been able to smuggle in, would hold. She set the lamp on the ground.

"My lady?" Mattheus awakened at her movement. For such a big man with a loud snore, he was a light sleeper.

She put a finger to her lips and pointed to the door. Mattheus reached to the ground and grabbed his club. He did not carry a knife, for a knife was a subtle weapon, and Mattheus was anything but subtle.

Svana heard the door start to creak. She straightened, drawing the bow up, nocking the arrow. She drew the string back to her ear and waited, not breathing at all.

The door burst open, knocking Mattheus down. She saw a spray of white and red and the flash of a blade, but she did not loose the arrow. She could make out the figure of a man in Arab clothes, but something about the way he moved seemed familiar. She hesitated, straining against the pressure of the string, until the man came into her circle of light. Then she saw the brilliant blue of his eyes.

"Lothar?"

He stopped. They both stood frozen, their weapons trained on each other. She watched his face, his eyes locked on hers, his body so rigid she thought he might burst into pieces. She lowered her bow.

"What are you doing here?"

He did not answer. He did not lower his sword. He came closer. She held her breath, remembering the night he had come for her, his hands closing around her throat. Her heart thudded dully in her chest; she could feel the blood pulsing in her cheeks, her throat, hot and slow. She gripped the smooth wood of the bow.

She felt a rustle at her skirt, a shadow beside her.

"Mama?"

Gryffin clutched at her, staring at the half-crazed warrior in the Arab robes with a sword pointed at his mother. Lothar froze. Then the energy seemed to go out of him, his body slumped. He lowered the sword. Mattheus was on his feet, coming at him from behind—

"No!" Svana shrieked. Lothar did not look behind him. He ducked to avoid the wild swing of the club, at the same time reaching behind to grab the big man around his neck. He pulled him downward in a choke hold; in another moment Mattheus would be dead.

"Let him go!" Svana raised her bow again. "He's one of mine!"

Lothar hesitated a moment, but seeing the man was not Arab, let go of him. Mattheus fell heavily, clutching his throat and rolling on the ground. Gryffin crawled over to him, calling his name.

"Is that what was protecting you? How lucky you are to be alive," Lothar said caustically. "Come up to the yard. Now." He turned and went out the door. She let out a ragged breath. *This could not be happening.*

Mattheus moaned. Svana went to him, saw he was not badly hurt. "I'm so sorry, Mattheus," she whispered. She took Gryffin by the hand and pulled him up the steps, still clutching her bow.

She almost tripped over the dead body at the top of the steps. Lothar was headed toward the yard where the Arab's horse stood. In the gray, predawn light she could make out more dead bodies by the doorway of the house. She moved toward Lothar, who had taken the reins of the horse.

"Where are the others?"

"What others?"

Just then three men emerged from the house with swords drawn, shouting. Abbas and his bodyguards, who had been lying in wait. Lothar pushed her aside and whirled to meet them, drawing both his swords. Svana raised her bow, straining to see what was going on, watching Lothar dance and weave around the three attackers with the sleek flurry of a leopard at play. He killed two of them, but Abbas, mailed and helmeted, managed to strike him hard in his side. Lothar stumbled and almost fell, blood on the white robe. Abbas swung again for the kill, but Svana's arrow caught him in the neck. He fell slowly, grabbing at the arrow, his eyes finding hers, his mouth twisted in a soundless growl. She watched him die, feeling no pity or victory, feeling nothing.

Lothar jumped to his feet, tore off the white robe and threw it on the body. His wound was bleeding, but he seemed not to notice.

Erik and Freddy ran into the courtyard, followed by a limping Mattheus. Freddy was wrapped in a blanket. Erik carried a torch. From the other dwellings more people emerged, frightened by the noises of battle. Lothar was agitated. Too many people. They were all talking.

"Quiet!" Lothar hissed at them. He pointed his sword at Svana. "Get on the horse! Now, damn you! We haven't got all day!"

"My lady!" Freddy shouted. Erik held her back.

Svana glanced at her, then moved to the horse. Lothar pushed her up into the saddle He grabbed Gryffin by the back of his shirt and tossed him up to her like a rag doll. She groped at him, pulling him over the saddle in front of her. Lothar mounted behind them.

"Where are you taking her?" Erik demanded, coming forward. Lothar turned his sword on him, making him jump backward in fear.

"It's all right," Svana said to them. "They will come up from the village—now is the time to fight—do you understand? Take the Arab weapons and fight them! Do you hear me? Fight!"

She could say no more. Lothar had grabbed the reins and kicked the horse hard. Freddy cried out as the horse spun and galloped out of the yard. Out of the corner of her eye, Svana could see her collapse in Erik's arms. She shut her eyes against the sight.

The sky lightened steadily as Lothar rode hard through the vineyards toward the edge of the woods where his horse was tethered. He jumped down and untied the reins.

"Get on," he ordered.

"Your horse?"

"Yes. Now!"

Svana obeyed. Lothar handed her the boy. Then he remounted the Arab's horse.

"We need to get to the river," he said. "They won't be able to track us after that."

"You're bleeding," she said.

"It's nothing. Follow me."

He began picking his way out of the woods toward the river. Svana followed, numb with fear. Gryffin pointed.

"Mama, I hear them."

In a moment Lothar heard them as well. Horses. He swore under his breath.

He looked to the east along the riverbank. He turned to her and pointed. "Follow the river. Find the ford. It is that way, as the ground rises. It's marked with a white flag. Take the flag with you. When you cross the river stay near the trees. Give the horse his head—he knows the way. You will go east until you get to the next river; follow it north to Chinon. Stay off the road. There's food in that bundle tied to the saddle. It will last a few days. Go!"

"What are you going to do?' Svana said, a cold chill creeping down her spine. "You cannot kill them all."

"I don't have to kill them all," he said, his voice deadly calm. "I just have to delay them."

"No!" she screamed, but the look on his face was so clear and serene she did not, for a moment, recognize him anymore. "Don't do this. We can make it if we keep going."

"No," he said. "I've come too far to fail now. Go. Go!"

The sound of horses grew louder. A white shape appeared on the western ridge, it spread out, becoming several, separate vibrating shapes.

Lothar kicked the horse into a pivot. She screamed at him.

"No!"

But he was already moving, spurring the horse to a flat run, away from her.

The black horse whinnied, pawing the ground, wanting to follow. Svana grabbed the reins, spun around and kicked it into a canter, holding onto Gryffin with one arm.

"Who is he, Mama?" Gryffin asked against the surging movement of the black horse. His voice sounded dreamy, far away.

"An old friend," Svana said. "Hush now. Look for a white marker."

He could see their bright outlines, riding hard toward him. Ten riders, waving swords. He threw a franca, hitting one in the face. He threw his javelins and more fell from their horses. By then they were upon him. He dropped the reins, drew his swords and charged into their midst.

To the Arabs he seemed like a phantom, an unholy spirit. He slipped around them, between them, through them, so quickly that his body lost its definitive shape, became a loose, flowing mass, forever transforming. But his swords were real and deadly, they were everywhere at once, piercing mail, slashing limbs.

Lothar felt supremely powerful, wielding his double-fisted swords like Thor's hammer, the weapons imbued with his energy, as if they had a will of their own. He put on the performance of his life, as he did on the fields of the Moselle to make the girls swoon. It was his last show, but it would be his best. He only wished that Charles had been there for this, his finest moment, the moment for which his entire life had been merely a prelude.

He killed four more before he felt the sword penetrate his leather tunic and sink into his back. And even that he did not mind—there was no pain, no regret, only an enormous sense of liberation the likes of which he had never imagined. At last, it would be over, and there would be peace. With one last great effort he swiveled, swinging his sword in a violent circle, slicing straight through the neck of his attacker. Then he fell with the severed head, reaching for the earth, allowing it to swallow him, comfort him, give him rest.

# 76

SVANA CONTINUED ALONG the river until she saw the flag, glowing in the breaking dawn. She pulled it off the branch and crossed the river carefully; the water was up to the horse's chest, but the ford held and they made it across. She kept moving, following Lothar's instructions, afraid to stop, afraid of the sound she would hear, the drumming of horse's hooves, the shouts of warriors. Gryffin, cradled in her body, seemed to fall asleep, becalmed by the movement of the horse. She was grateful for that.

By full light she could go no further; she rode into a copse of trees and nearly fell from the horse, exhausted, bewildered, unbelieving. The horse lowered its head and nibbled on the fern covered ground. Svana curled into a ball with her son, wrapping them both in the black cassock Lothar had left tied to the saddle. She did not know where she was. She did not know where she was going. Gryffin asked her sleepy questions, which she did not answer. She fell asleep.

The birds woke her at noon, chattering in the trees above her. Clouds had thickened, a breeze kicked up along the tall grasses. She sat up, stiff and sore. She tried to remember what had happened, but it all seemed like a crazy dream, and if she hadn't been sitting with her son in the middle of nowhere she would have thought it was.

They ate some of the bread and cheese and dug at the roots of trees for truffles as they had seen the pigs do. They found a few and ate some, stuffing the rest back into the bundle.

She hoisted Gryffin into the saddle and walked beside the horse, holding the reins, hugging the tree line as Lothar had told her to do. When she was tired, she led the horse into the trees and found a soft place to lie down, holding her son in her arms, covered by the cassock. They slept for awhile, than ate a little and moved again.

After four days they came to the wide river that flowed north. The horse drank greedily and tore at the soft grasses at the water's edge. They ate berries, sat under the willows and tried to sleep. Svana wondered where she was. She prayed that Lothar was right, that the horse knew the way home. She looked back often, expecting to see him following. But she did not see him, and she felt herself slipping with each passing hour, her strength and energy and courage fading. She would die in these woods, and she would never see Charles again.

*Lord, if you are there*, she whispered aloud, looking up into the trees, *please … lead me back to him*. What a paltry prayer, she thought bleakly. She had sought God in great cathedrals and had heard nothing but echoes in darkness. Yet since coming to Saint-Emilion she felt God moving through her life, sometimes in gentle breezes and sometimes in great, sucking gusts, and she had wondered at it. She had been brought back from death more than once. Was it only to die here in the wild, undiscovered? She could not believe it. So she prayed, because she could think of nothing else to do.

*Lead me back.*

Leutgar stopped his horse along the river's edge and stared at the black horse standing alone under a lumbering willow. He held up his hand to halt the rest of the party that trailed behind him. They had been searching for Lothar for days, and Leutgar had felt certain that the warrior had followed the river south. He did not know how he knew this, but his instincts had proven him right time and again. He was the best tracker in Charles' army. He had followed the flattened grass for miles, had found small firepits and rabbit bones, as well as hoof tracks sunken into the dried mud of the riverbanks. Now he was looking at the missing warrior's horse.

"Do you see him?" said one of his men.

The horse appeared to be alone.

Leutgar dismounted, drew his scramsax and approached the horse cautiously. The others stayed behind him, following in his footsteps. Leutgar stopped, noticing a dark shape under the tree. Lothar? Asleep? It did not seem to be the sort of place Lothar would choose for a nap. Perhaps the horse had been stolen. By robbers? Highwaymen? Arab raiders? Did that mean Lothar was dead? He could not imagine Lothar being ambushed by anyone.

He inched closer, grabbed a corner of the black cloth and pulled it away. The body under it came to life; *two* bodies, a woman and a child. They sat up, startled, the child cried out. Leutgar had never been more surprised in his life. He jumped back and nearly fell over, tripping on a root. The others leapt into full alert, unsheathing their short swords.

"God in heaven!" one of them said. Leutgar, recovering his footing, peered curiously at his discovery.

"God in heaven."

She told them her story; they listened in shock. Leutgar decided the only thing to do was to take her back to Chinon and let Charles deal with her.

They traveled up the river for three days until they reached the little village where the river joined the Roman road. Once across the bridge they were met by a patrol, and Svana, with chagrin, recognized their captain. It was Charles' son Carloman.

"Lord," Leutgar said, bowing his head. He, too, looked nervous.

Carloman listened in silence as Leutgar explained the situation, staring at the black horse. Then he turned his gaze to Svana. She was transfixed by the look in his eyes, the cold, impenetrable hatred, a hatred without emotion, without energy, a hatred that seemed divorced from the man, that had a life and a purpose of its own. She had never been so frightened of a human face in her life, not even the face of Abbas, her rapist.

Then Carloman looked away, his eyes passing over the other men and focusing on something beyond them, beyond his own vision. She watched, fascinated, as the man waged war with himself.

"Take her to the villa," he said finally, spinning his horse. He rode away hard, his guards following him. Svana let out a long breath and closed her eyes.

Brand was there when she arrived in the courtyard of Chinon. He helped her down from the saddle, shocked at her condition. She was weak and thin with deep hollows around her eyes; her once luxurious mass of black hair had been crudely chopped off. He swept her up in his arms, shouting for servants to come and help.

"Where's Charles?" she asked faintly as he carried her into the house.

"He went to the battleground to check on things. We will send someone for him," Brand said. "You need rest."

Charles did not return until the next evening. She had bathed and corralled her hair into a short braid. Gera had given her a dress, one belonging to her daughter, who had died two years before. It was too big and hung on her like a sack. She had eaten a little and slept most of the day, not leaving the room. Gryffin was preoccupied with the villa owners' grandsons and their vast collection of wooden swords and shields. She was glad of it. She began to feel an unexpected peace.

But when she heard the commotion in the courtyard, the fear returned. She rose from the bed and went to the window. She recognized him instantly, even in the dim torchlight, his body sloped unnaturally, as if he were being slowly crushed. She saw Brand talking to him. He was still a long time. Then he turned and disappeared into the villa.

She withdrew from the window and stood, wondering what to do next. She leaned back against the ledge, struggling for breath against the tightness in her chest, the heaviness in her legs. She waited.

The door opened finally. He was there, standing in the threshold. He looked like a man who had traveled far too long for a treasure he had been seeking all his life, yet now was too tired to claim it. She opened her mouth to say something, but nothing came out. He moved toward her; she went to meet him. He fell into her arms with a force that astonished her, took her breath away. He held her against him, his arms around her as if he needed the support of her body in order to stand. She slipped her arms around his waist and led him to a chair. He sat heavily; she knelt between his legs, looking up into his rain-spattered eyes.

"Tell me," he said softly.

She told him.

"Why?" he said when she was done. "He has lived his whole life for this battle. Why did he do it?"

She sighed, pressed against his thigh. She was remembering a night long ago, a tower room, Lothar with his hands around her throat. Charles and his terrible pronouncement. The moment that tore the two of them apart.

"You made him my keeper, do you remember?" she said.

His eyes widened, remembering. "So this was his vengeance?"

"Not vengeance," she said firmly, her hand on his cheek. "He was holding to his word. I saw it in his eyes. He did it … because he loved you, Charles. And love is the exception to every rule."

She rested her head on his knee, felt his hand stroke her hair.

"Your hair—"

"It will grow back."

Neither of them moved for a long time.

Much later she lifted her head to look at him. He was asleep. A miracle, she thought. How exhausted he must be. She rose, tugging his arm gently, saying his name.

He opened his eyes and stared at her blankly. She pulled him to his feet, coaxing him to the bed. He allowed her to lead him. She sat him down, pushed his shoulders back to the mattress. He lay still, obedient. She sighed in relief.

She was about to lay down beside him when he came suddenly to life, grabbing her arm and pulling her on top of him. He kissed her, his hands pressing against the side of her head, nearly crushing it. She tried to get away. *Not tonight, not tonight …* her mind shut out the possibility. *Not yet … he's not ready yet …*

But it was not to be. He seized the collar of her gown and pulled it down, over her shoulders. His hands roamed down her back, over her naked skin—he stopped.

He sat up suddenly, holding her at arm's length. His eyes went dark, almost black. She recoiled, trying to pull the gown up again. He pushed her hands away and turned her over roughly, running his hands over her ruined back.

She waited, breathless. He stopped touching her. She felt nothing, no movement whatever from him. She turned over and sat up, pulling the cloth feebly over her breasts. He was still looking down, at the place she had been, frozen in time.

"Who did this to you?" he said. His voice was ice cold.

"He's dead. It's over."

She watched him, feeling her chest collapse, the red heat rise up her neck. There was something new in his face, something she had never seen before, something she had not thought possible.

It was hate.

"Charles—"

He was up suddenly, off the bed, striding across the room. He opened the door and went out, slamming it behind him.

Svana lay down, curled into a ball on the bed, and wept.

# 77

HE WAS STILL not there in the morning. She rose and went to the window. She could see men in the courtyard. He was not among them.

There was a tentative knock on the door.

She turned, suddenly hopeful. "Come in."

The door opened and Gera peeked around anxiously. "My dear … there is breakfast in the hall if you would like to join us." She smiled. "Gryffin is in the garden with the boys. Come down when you are ready. It's a beautiful day. Everything will be all right, you'll see."

Svana smiled, wondering at her gentle tone. What did she know? She went down to the hall to eat and sat in the garden, watching the women sew and the children play, trying to sort out her wrecked feelings. The women chatted and laughed as if her presence were nothing terribly unusual. They were making tapestries set up on large hoops on stands. Svana had never made a tapestry and had no real interest to learn. But she watched the small, delicate work, the deft fingers, with admiration.

At mid-day they went into the dining room and ate a meager dinner — provisions were tight, Gera said—and then returned to the garden, where Svana began to understand she was supposed to stay. But it was pleasant in the garden, the sun was hot and healing, and in the presence of so many silly women she could feel herself alone.

The peace was broken in the middle of the afternoon. There was a rush of opening doors and footsteps and suddenly Charles was there, flanked by Brand and Gunther, striding into the garden. The women fluttered and jumped like moths at a flame, hoops flew everywhere. Svana smiled for the first time.

He looked better, she thought. As terrifying as ever. She watched him greet Gera with a little, courtly nod, the older woman curtsying, blushing. The other women bobbed as well, red-faced and nervous. Then he turned to her.

She rose slowly as he came toward her. His eyes were clear and calm, the sky after the storm, the eyes she remembered. He smiled, and it was like the first time, as if this were the real greeting, not the nightmare of the night before.

He took her hand, turned it over and kissed the heel of her wrist, a very intimate gesture that was not lost on Gera or her ladies, who giggled.

"Come meet your son," she said softly, taking his arm. "Gryffin!"

The boy galloped in through an archway, a wooden sword in one hand, the grandsons close at his heels. He stopped when he saw Charles and stared, his face registering no recognition or surprise.

"Gryffin," Svana said, as calmly as she could. "This is your father."

There was a silence. They stared at each other. Then Charles pointed toward the sword.

"Do you want me to show you how to use that thing properly?"

Gryffin's stern face melted a little. He nodded, and Charles led him out of the garden onto the terrace. Svana watched them go, whispering her thanks. She had prayed for this, she remembered, her last prayer before dying, or nearly dying: that Charles and Gryffin would know each other, that they would have a chance to be father and son, if only for a little while. An impossible prayer come true.

The women returned to their sewing, still giggling and talking in low voices; Gunther wandered out again, trailing Charles at a distance. Brand lingered beside her.

"How is he?" she asked.

Brand shrugged. "Hard to say," he said. "I've never seen him quite so … shaken. When Lothar disappeared, none of us imagined he had gone to Saint-Emilion. To *rescue* you, no less. I would have thought he intended to kill you."

"I think it crossed his mind," Svana murmured.

He regarded her, searching her face for some answer he knew she would not give. "Well, you've come at a good time, or a bad one, depending on how you look at it."

"What's the matter?"

Brand shook his head. "The Bishop of Orléans has called a Synod."

Svana felt the blood drain from her face. "Now? Why?"

"In opposition to this war. He claims it is an illegal war, and has asked the bishops to openly oppose it. They won't contribute. Nor will many of the Neustrians and Burgundians."

"God in heaven—"

"Charles has appealed to the Pope, but there has been no answer, and the bishops have a head start. It will be months before the Pope makes a decision. It will be … too late."

"This is madness," Svana said softly.

"There is much dissension in the ranks as well. Daily fights, desertion … food is running out. Everyone's nerves are at the breaking point. There is a chance this army may not survive to meet the Arabs. It will destroy itself first."

"No, it won't. God will not let that happen."

"God?"

"He will not let Charles fail."

"I'm glad you still believe that. I want to believe it."

Svana sighed. "Brand, what about … Eudo? Is he really dead?"

"He's very much alive. He came to Paris, he swore oath to Charles. Now he is somewhere in the south, raising a new army."

Svana stared at him. Then, suddenly, she smiled. "You see, Brand? God is in control."

He chuckled. "Well, God has a bit more work to do, hasn't He?"

# 78

CHARLES INSISTED THAT she accompany him to supper that evening. She refused, claiming she did not feel well.

"You aren't sick," he said, his tone not comforting in the least. "You'll come."

She knew what he was trying to do. He wanted his captains and his sons to understand her place in his life. He wanted them to accept her as they would his wife. But she did not think she could face the baleful stares of his friends, or of his sons, who saw her as usurping their own mother. Carloman in particular—his eyes so like his father's, his gaunt face haunted by grief. She was the cause of Lothar's death. She wanted to tell Charles that such an ordeal would be as bad as anything she faced at the hands of the Arabs, but she didn't. Instead, she went with him and sat beside him and forced herself to eat the food put in front of her.

The meal passed without much incident. The men carefully ignored her, which came as a relief. The conversation centered on the war, on the Arabs, the dam, the Church, the myriad problems of keeping an army in the field. Carloman's eyes rarely left his plate, but Pipin talked and told jokes and even engaged Gryffin in an animated discussion about hunting. Gryffin, normally so shy, told Pipin about his experience with the falcon; Pipin was delighted and said that they would have to get one of those birds as soon as the war was over.

Svana listened, trying to imagine a time when the war would be over, wondering how many of those sitting around that table would live to see it. She glanced at Charles, saw him gazing at Pipin, the delicate tracery of a smile on his face. *He loves this boy*, she thought. She wondered if he would ever love Gryffin as much.

"Charles, you can't think of trying to stop their cavalry advance with a shield wall. It won't work. There are too damn many of them." Gerold spewed bits of food as he talked.

"It will work," Charles said. "There are limitations to a cavalry charge which we all know very well."

"But we are talking about ten thousand horses at least! You know very well such a number overrules all limitations—"

"Rayman is a raider by nature; he has never faced an army in pitched battle," Charles said. "He has never even *seen* a Frankish shield wall—"

They argued a long time. Svana smiled to herself. Why did they continue to doubt him, after all he had done? It was a mystery to her. She watched him patiently field their questions, so terribly calm. His self-control was legendary; she was perhaps the only one who had seen the other side of him, the side he had revealed the night before.

Carloman was the first to desert the table, mumbling his excuses under his breath. Pipin followed more reluctantly, offering to take Gryffin to the stables to visit the horses before bed. The captains, however, would not leave before Charles, so they continued to drink and talk in lowered voices. Servants came in to refill cups and clear away dishes. The candles burned lower.

Svana sat still, feeling the blackness of the previous night close in around her. She felt the scars on her body as she had never felt them before, even when the blows of the belt were falling on her skin, as if they radiated through her clothes for everyone to see. Her hands began to shake in her lap; she pressed her fingers against her knee.

At length Charles rose, offering his hand to her. She took it, rising with him unsteadily, head swimming. The men at the table stared at her, silent, unsmiling. She cast her eyes to the floor, something she had never done before. They walked silently out of the dining hall and through the garden toward the stairs leading to Charles' room.

She stood still in the middle of the room, aware of their aloneness as something once so natural now alien, awkward. He stood before her and began to undress her slowly, carefully, afraid to touch her skin as if he thought he would hurt her. When she was naked before him he ran his hands over her shoulders, her breasts, tracing the scars with his fingers. She saw the terrible, immutable pain in his eyes—he dropped to his knees and pressed his face into her belly, his mouth open against her skin. She put a hand on his head, like a mother does a child, feeling the soft, teetering tremble of his body. She waited for the moment to end and the next one to begin.

And then it did. He drew away and looked up at her, his eyes dry and peculiarly clear. She knelt before him and he took her in his arms, and the seven years of grief and courage and waiting finally ended.

Later, as they lay entwined together in the bed, she told him what had happened, the brutal assault, how Abbas had held to his oath, and that in the end it was she, not Lothar, who had killed him. She hoped this would dampen his smoldering rage, but she could see it had little effect.

"You were … very brave."

"No," she said. "I just wanted to live."

He smoothed her hair out of her face. "Did you?"

"I knew it," she said, "from the moment I heard them coming. I had always had causes I was willing to die for, but never one I wanted to live for. Do you understand? When I looked at Abbas, at the face of the enemy, I realized how much I loved them: my home, my people, my son, my life … you … I would do anything to save them." She paused, thinking. "I used to wonder … about Jesus. I could not understand why he died the way he did. Why make such a supreme sacrifice for an uncaring world? What difference did it make? I didn't understand, not until that day, what it meant to love."

He said nothing, stroking her hair, looking beyond her to something she could not see. She slid on top of him, covering him with her body as if putting herself between him and his dark thoughts.

"Charles," she said softly, "it's over. Let it go."

How strange, she thought, that I would be the one to say this to him. He looked at her blankly, his eyes soft, liquid as water. He did not answer.

# 79

PROBLEMS MOUNTED. THE Lombards did not come. Though vague assurances came from Liutprand, Frankish scouts reported no sightings of a Lombard army in the passes or on the Roman roads.

In addition to that, only half the Neustrian nobles had committed troops, the rest waylaid by Church sanctions that threatened anyone who lent support to Charles. Rations grew tighter, fish and game scarcer. The army was becoming restless and churlish. Hunger drove men to thievery and even murder. Charles had to send in his own guards to keep order, even carrying out executions to stem the tide of violence.

There was one bright spot: Rogan of Lyon showed up with six hundred men. Though it was far less then the thousand he had promised, it was better than nothing.

"I didn't expect to see you," Charles said warmly as he greeted him in the courtyard of the villa.

"My family is not speaking to me, nor is anyone else in Lyon for that matter," Rogan said with a mischievous grin, clasping Charles' arms. "I'm sorry I'm not at full strength … some men are a bit ruffled by the idea of eternal damnation."

"Not you?"

"Ha! I knew I was done for as soon as I cast my lot with you Austrasian bastards. Besides, do you think I would miss this fight? Where is that heathen Lothar, I still have a bone or two to pick with him."

Charles' expression changed. He told Rogan what happened.

"Lord, Charles, I am sorry. It does not seem possible."

"I am glad you are here. Lothar would be pleased."

Rogan shook his head. "I was hoping for one more chance at him. He was a perfect bastard. And yet—if not for his brutal lessons I would not be alive today."

"Come to the villa for dinner. I want to know what is going on in Lyon."

"You might not."

Pipin accompanied Charles on his daily rides into the camp, where he stopped often to talk with the men or share a cup of mead around a fire. Charles spoke little on these occasions; he listened. Some of the complaints were born of simple boredom and peevishness, but many, his father told him, were important. It was always the little things that determined the outcome of a battle. Food, water, shelter, these things were far more important than weapons and strategies. An unhappy army could not fight, an unhappy army would fall victim to a thousand unforeseen circumstances.

Pipin noticed that the men rarely spoke of women or of the pleasures they were missing in their beds back home. They spoke of feasting at long tables laden with trenchers of meats and breads and vegetables piled high, of pigs roasting on a spit, the licentious gorging of the Slaughterfest. They described in loving detail the preparation of a baby lamb or the proper way to cook a pig, listing the seasonings that brought out the best flavor, the accompanying vegetables and condiments most favored. When they spoke of food their eyes watered, their mouths formed loose, rounded shapes, their voices heaved with lust.

Normally so garrulous, Pipin found himself speechless most of the time, watching his father's every move, committing everything he did and said to memory. He had to remember these things, he told himself, it would be important someday. He saw how the men loved, even revered Charles, and though he was not overly friendly or sociable, his concern for them was evident. Pipin knew that this delicate combination of reserve and attention was what it took to be an effective commander.

The size of this army, and the amount of organization required to keep it together, dumfounded Pipin. He had never seen an army in the field before, had never imagined it was possible to assemble so many men in one place for so long. He bombarded Charles with questions about every detail, trying to take it all in.

"The biggest worry is disease," Charles told him. "This many men living together for so long produces a lot of waste, which can contaminate the water supply and kill a whole army before the battle has even begun."

He showed Pipin the huge trenches built for waste disposal a good way off from the river. They were narrow and quite deep and lined with rocks to prevent waste from seeping down into the water supply.

"Clay is better," Charles said. "It's denser. But there is no clay in these parts, it's all sand. It has to be refilled almost daily. Malwolfe and Arnulf have been very busy."

"How do you keep the men from dumping in the river?"

Charles laughed. "With lots of stories about the horrors of bowel sickness," he said.

Pipin made a face. "Father—what are you going to do about the bishops?" Charles glanced at him, surprised. "You don't have to protect me anymore. I am old enough to know these things."

Charles nodded ruefully. "I know. I'm sorry. I wait for news from Chrodegang."

"I want to help you."

"You do help me. More than you know."

"I want to fight, Father."

Charles shook his head. "This is no place for a first fight."

"It's the perfect place and you know it. You will need me, especially if the Neustrians don't show up. If you don't put me on the line, I will find a way to get there anyway. You know I will."

Charles sighed. "I suppose I do."

Pipin smiled broadly, his violet eyes dancing with mischief. "I will make you proud, Father. You will see."

Fridegar, the chamberlain, arrived near the end of the summer. He was the keeper of the *camera*, the royal treasure, a small, portly man who wore his clothes a little too tightly, like a vain woman. His eyes were heavily lidded, as if he were in constant danger of falling asleep. Chrodegang came with him, looking thinner and paler than usual. They had grim news: the bishops had not relented, and Charles himself was out of money.

"You cannot finance this war any longer," Fridegar said huffily, throwing the ledgers across the table. "The *camera* is empty. The palaces are empty. The treasure is gone. Your kingdom is going to starve this winter, thanks to this war of yours."

"Hugo is doing the best he can," Chrodegang added. "But he's nearly at the end of his resources as well. Many of the counts are simply defying his orders. What about Eudo? Can he help at all?"

"He has his own army to finance," Charles said, staring at the ledgers.

"Well, you cannot get blood from a stone, my lord," said the chamberlain, lacing his fingers across his ample belly. "There are no more provisions on the way. Whatever you have here now is all you will ever get."

"The Arabs are moving. We need only a few more weeks—"

"A few more weeks? The Council insists there is no war! No one is listening to your pleas!"

"Then I will make them listen."

Chrodegang sat up suddenly alert. "What do you mean?"

"I will arrest Eucher for treason and seize his properties."

Chrodegang opened his mouth and shut it again, unable to speak for a moment. "Please, my prince, do not do such a thing—"

"I have no choice. The bishop refuses to help defend this kingdom. Not only that, but he is taking an active role in assuring our defeat. He is guilty of sedition at the very least."

"What about the others?"

"They will be arrested, one by one. Their properties will be confiscated."

Chrodegang was again speechless; even Fridegar's slitted eyes had opened wide.

"Charles," the chancellor said very quietly, "if you do this, even the Pope will turn against you."

"The Pope has been no great help to me, Priest," Charles said in a low, hard voice.

"But surely God will provide what you need to see this through—"

"I cannot wait on God anymore."

"Charles, I beg you, don't do this! Perhaps we can still convince him ... if there were more evidence—"

"Is not the destruction of Bordeaux enough?"

"Not enough to prove the Arabs are a real threat to us. There must be something—"

"Should I wait until we are overrun? They are closing their eyes to this invasion, that is all there is to it. They see what they want to see. They have pushed me too far this time."

"But—"

"There is nothing more to talk about," Charles said, and, to prove his point, he got up and left the room.

# 80

SVANA SPENT HER days in the garden, listening to Gera and her women gossip, watching the boys play, the sun's rays make their languid way across the tiled floor, the flowers bloom and fade.

She was bored. Charles would not let her out of the villa. Gera had offered to show her how to sew, and she had tried, out of sheer despondency, but failed ignobly. The work was too finely detailed for her—she would get frustrated with the minuscule stitching and put it all aside angrily. *I should have been born a man,* she thought, not for the first time.

Her mind travelled to her vineyards, to Freddy and Erik and sweet Mattheus, though she was afraid to think of what happened to them. She wanted desperately to be there with them, to feel useful and wanted and free once again, instead of locked up in a remote villa with nothing to do, awaiting the advance of an unseen enemy. But she did not say this to anyone, especially not to Charles. He had enough problems already.

She saw little of him, except at night, and even then he seemed removed from her. He used her body for solace and release, but beyond that he would barely speak. She could feel a weight upon him, within him, a weight that grew daily. When she tried to talk to him he brushed her aside with one-word answers that were not answers at all.

She knew she would have to leave him, once the war was over, if the Franks succeeded. She could not stay in his world; she did not belong there, as much as she loved him. She would return to her vineyard, to her own people, if they would have her back. If that place even existed anymore. And Gryffin … Gryffin would learn to live without a father, as he had always done.

It was easier, once she had decided. She would not tell him, of course, not until all this was over. Assuming there would be an end. Assuming he survived. But she couldn't imagine the prospect of living in a world that did not contain him. Even if it had to be that she never saw him again.

One night she rose from the dining table and followed him to the terrace, where he often went in the evenings to clear his head after the long days in the camps. The terrace was a walled portico that looked out over the city of tents and paddocks and storehouses and piles and piles of weapons and the men, the growing army moving restlessly below them, the Confederation of the Armies of Gaul. She stood beside him, half-expecting him to send her away. He did not look at her. She gazed in wonder over the scene, seeing what he was seeing, the awesome responsibility he had assumed.

"Your brother is here. Do you want to see him?"

She glanced at him, surprised to hear his voice. "Has he asked to see me?"

"He has asked *about* you. He was surprised to learn you were here. And that you were still alive."

She smiled a little. "I am rather surprised that *he* is still alive. How does he seem to you?"

"Older … wiser, perhaps. Sober, at least. He has managed to keep Bavaria under control."

"That is due to your counsel," Svana said.

"I put him in a position for which he was ill-equipped," Charles said. "I did that for my own convenience. Not his."

"You did what you had to do."

"Perhaps." She heard the doubt in his voice, which seemed strange to her. "Does it ever feel to you as if everything you are doing is … madness?"

She felt a shiver at the words, thinking of that winter day in Saint-Emillion, with the Arabs at her door. "Yes," she said softly.

He glanced at her. "I suppose that was a stupid question."

"You told me to leave at the first sign of trouble. But I didn't do that. I stayed. I paid a price for that. I will never know if I made the right decision. And you have never rebuked me for it."

"I did rebuke you. A thousand times as I lay awake nights thinking about what might have happened to you and the boy. Wondering if you were alive. Wondering why you had made that choice. You took a terrible chance."

"And you would have done the same," she said. "You know you would."

"Yes. But that does not make it right."

She felt chilled by his tone, understanding for the first time the agony she had put him through, which was, perhaps, as bad as the agony she herself had faced. "I'm sorry," she said. "I could not surrender all I had built. I would rather have died there, defending it."

Charles did not answer. She saw his jaw clench, as if he were thinking of saying something he did not want to say. She thought she understood.

"If not for me, Lothar would still be alive," she said. "Is that why you are … angry?"

"No." His voice was firm, but he did not look at her. "I am not angry at you."

She searched his stern profile for the truth of that. He had never lied to her. But Lothar's death was there between them, and something—someone—else as well.

As if reading her thoughts, he spoke the name.

"I meant to tell you … I received a message from Eudo … your people are safe."

She looked up, her heart skipping. "Safe?"

"The Arabs abandoned your estate not long after you left. Your girl, Freddy, told Eudo they never attacked that day. They just … went away." He paused, his eyes closing briefly. "He found Lothar's body, along with seven dead Arabs, by the river, where you said they would be. He buried him there. He set a marker there in case—" He did not finish. His eyes closed again, his head dropped.

"Seven … so many," she murmured, shivering. Her heart hurt at the memory of Lothar, the way he had given his life to save her, he who had hated her more than even the enemy he had gone to kill. The chilling look of serenity in his clear blue eyes as he rode off to his death. She would carry that to her own grave, and she would never tell Charles about it.

"I somehow thought he might still be alive," Charles said, "that he would come back any day … I never imagined he could be dead, not really." He paused, took a shallow breath. "We have been together since we were children. I have never fought without him at my side. I wonder … if I even can—"

"Yes, you can," Svana said urgently, though his admission worried her. Charles had begun to doubt himself, doubt everything he was doing. And the loss of Lothar was weighing more heavily than she had supposed. She saw that he was truly coming to the end of himself, that for the first time he was struggling under the weight of burdens that no man should have to carry alone. And he *was* carrying them alone. She felt useless to him, not for the first time.

"Why have you never told me about Eudo?" she said.

"What do you want me to tell?"

"That he gave oath to you. On his knees, no less. I would have loved to have seen that."

"It was a terrible thing to see."

"Only you would think so. You have no idea how I had prayed for it."

"Prayed? To whom?" He arched an eyebrow at her. She smiled.

"I knew he could not be dead … somehow I knew—"

"Svana—"

"Don't. Don't say it. Don't think it."

"I'm trying." He reached out to her, took her hand absently. They stood together, not speaking, a long time.

"So you are leaving tomorrow," she said finally, in a different voice, "to arrest the Bishop of Orléans."

He gave a derisive laugh. "I thought you would be pleased."

"It's a dangerous move."

"He leaves me no choice."

"You shouldn't do it. You may win the battle, but in the end you will lose the war."

Charles glanced at her. "So … do you still think I am a tool of the Church?"

She met his gaze. "Charles … you knew it would come to this."

He looked away.

"It is the nature of your power: it is ugly and evil, but that is the only way it works. You have tried to avoid it all your life, you have tried to use it only for good … but in the end, it uses you."

He sighed. "You once asked me to run away with you. To forget the world and live in peace somewhere far away. I knew it was impossible. But still I wake up every morning wondering if I made the right choice."

She turned to him, put a hand to his face, caressing the soft beard he had allowed to grow in the past weeks. He looked so different with a beard, older and softer and infinitely weary. He covered her hand with his own, pressing his lips to her palm.

"You need to sleep," she said. "Come."

She led him to their room. She watched him undress, sit heavily on the edge of the bed. She spoke softly, tenderly.

"There was word today … from Paris. Rotruda had her baby."

Charles did not comment.

"You have a daughter, Charles … her name is Chiltruda. It was a difficult birth. The baby thrives, but Rotruda is not well."

"Not well?"

"She suffered greatly. You should go and see her … it would only take a couple of weeks … put off your Orléans trip for a time—"

"Svana … you know I cannot do that."

He lay down, his head falling onto the pillow as if he did not have the strength to hold it up anymore. She pulled off her gown and slid in next to him, her head on his chest, listening to the reassuring rumble of his heart. He put a hand on her head, his fingers sliding through her short hair, and gradually his breathing became regular, and she thanked God that he was finally asleep.

# 81

SHE AWOKE IN the early dawn to find him gone. She pulled on a gown, grabbed a cloak and ran out to the courtyard, where the horses were being assembled for the three-day journey to Orléans. A cluster of men stood about talking, drinking mead from skins, while servants finished readying the horses. There were no wagons, she saw; Charles was intent on traveling fast.

She moved through the crowd toward him. Chrodegang was standing with him, still trying, she supposed, to dissuade him from his mission. She knew Charles could no longer be dissuaded.

She walked up to them. "You forgot this," she said, holding out the cloak. "You'll need it. If it rains."

He took the cloak and put it around her shoulders. "You are the one who is always cold," he said.

"Charles—"

He pulled her to him and kissed her lightly. "Stay in the villa until I return."

Then he turned away abruptly and shouted for his men to mount. Alfric brought the stamping Epone to him, and he swung into the saddle, gathering the reins.

"Be careful," she said, looking up at him.

He smiled at her. "Always."

"One moment, my prince!" Chrodegang was struggling to mount a prancing horse much taller than his usual mules. Three boys were trying to hoist him aboard. The men began to laugh as the horse continually stepped away just as the boys managed to get the fat priest in the air. Chrodegang swore in an unpriestly way, which made everyone laugh louder. Svana smiled as well. Even in the direst of circumstances, Chrodegang always managed to provide some comic relief.

"This is the final humiliation!" he snorted.

At last he was aboard, and the forward guards called out to the sentries to open the gates. But as the gates opened a rider came bursting through, several sentries chasing after him, shouting at him to stop. Gunther drew a sword, but Charles' hand shot out to stay him.

"It's Badilo," he said. The guards and the soldiers parted as the boy on the foaming horse slowed to a trot. He was breathing as heavily as the horse, but his dark eyes burned with fear.

"What is it now?" Charles asked sharply. He wondered if things could possibly get worse.

"Poitiers—" Badilo stammered.

Charles took a breath. "So they have reached Poitiers," he said.

"So, then, are we not going to Orléans?" Chrodegang said hopefully. Charles glared at him.

"There's more," Badilo said. "They've burned the church!"

There was a collective gasp.

"They burned St. Hilary's?" Chrodegang asked softly. But he did not sound horrified. He sounded almost … happy.

"You can see the smoke for miles … Hilary's is burning!"

There was dead silence for a long moment. Then Charles turned to the chancellor. "Well, Priest," he said quietly, "it would seem you have got your evidence, after all."

Chrodegang was grinning broadly. "I told you, my prince, always wait upon the Lord."

"It may be too late."

"Never doubt God's timing! No time to waste, though, send out your messengers! I will ride to Orléans myself with this news … Bishop Eucher will be most perplexed! Or will he? I'm sure you would give anything to see his face when I tell him!" Chrodegang laughed out loud. The others stared at him in disbelief. Svana, standing in the shadows, closed her eyes and said a prayer of thanks.

Chrodegang sped off with the news to Orléans, and Charles sent messengers out to every Neustrian and Burgundian stronghold with the message: Hilary's was burning, the Arabs were very close. The black smoke from the burning church filled the sky for miles in all directions; soon men and supplies began to appear, in a slow trickle and then a stream, for the kingdom, finally, came to its senses.

A week later Chrodegang sent a message to Charles, informing him that the Synod had voted to support the war after all. Bishop Eucher alone refused to relent, declaring that God would protect him from Charles' vengeance. Brand read the letter aloud, laughing when he had finished. "He will need God's protection," he said. "What are you going to do about him?"

"Nothing, not until this is over," Charles said. "We don't have much time left. I cannot waste any of it on rebellious priests. I'll deal with him later."

"He is either mad enough to think the Arabs really don't exist," Brand said, "or he is wagering that you won't be around after to seek justice for his treachery. I hope, Charles, that when you finally do deal with him, you will keep your penchant for clemency in check."

Charles smiled grimly.

"She was right, you know," Brand said after a moment. "Your lady."

"About what?"

"She has said all along that God is with you, Charles."

"We have a long way to go, Brand, before the end of this."

Charles sent Leutgar to Poitiers to get more details on the shape of the Arab army. When the scout returned, Charles held a war council in the villa's dining room.

"It's big," Leutgar told them. "Very big. The front lines are horsed, well-armored, and very experienced. They have horsed archers as well. But the foot army is mostly rabble, not very disciplined. There are many of them, too many to count. Their strength is in their numbers. My guess is, that if you survive the initial assault, which will be organized and very tough, the rest is just a matter of endurance."

"Endurance," Charles said darkly, "will be no easy matter."

"When does he plan to leave Poitiers?" asked Milo.

"Could be any time," Leutgar answered. "Once he moves, he could be in Châtellerault in a day..."

"A day for a scouting party perhaps," Charles said. "For an army that size, it will take three or four."

"Then we have time to get to the battlefield before him," Milo said. He sounded relieved.

"We must spread out, make him think we are in several places at once. We cannot move to the battlefield until they are at the bridge."

"It will be too late!" squawked Milo. "That will give us barely half a day—"

"The horses can make it," Charles said. "The foot army will follow."

"The horses are not enough—" Milo continued, but Pipin interrupted.

"It will take time for the Arabs to cross the bridge, don't you think, Father?" he said somewhat tentatively, though his expression held no such uncertainty.

Charles smiled at his son. "Yes, the bridge will slow them down. Rome never fielded an army as big as this one in this area. That will buy us some time. Leutgar, put your scouts on that bridge at Châtellerault. Set up a network. I want to know as soon as Rayman arrives." Charles began rolling up the maps, signaling that the meeting was over.

"What about Eudo?" Gerold asked suddenly. "Why is he not here?"

"He will be here," Charles said.

"And you trust him?" Gerold asked sharply. "A man who gave his own daughter to the Musselman scourge?"

There was a long silence, all the men watching Charles. He nodded slowly. "I have no choice but to trust him," he said softly. "Eudo has paid the price. He understands what is at stake."

Provisions poured into the camps: barrels of salt meat and beer, casks of wine and sacks of grain, onions and turnips. Men appeared as well, men who heard the news and came on their own, many too old or too young but willing to fight. Chrodegang had been right; the news of the burning of Hilary's had awakened the populace to the threat that loomed on the southern frontier. By the end of the month the wayward nobles began to arrive as well. And none too soon, for in early October Charles received word that Rayman was nearing Châtellerault.

As Pipin had predicted, Rayman was indeed flummoxed by the bridge at Châtellerault.

This bridge was a marvel of Roman design, a foundation of solid masonry built upon a system of piles supporting a wooden superstructure ten paces wide, enough to march a Roman column. But a Roman column was a more compact entity than an Arab horde. It would take a day or even two to get his entire army across.

Rayman had not anticipated the slow pace of this massive army; it wore on his nerves. He was already far behind schedule. Moreover, he was unprepared for the sudden change in climate—the land had bottomed out to moor and swamp, the brilliant sun had given way to white sheets of clouds. It was a soft, persistent rain that fell, a soaking rain; it chilled a man to the bone. Rayman's blood craved heat and dry air. Iberia had suited the Arabs perfectly, for its dry, hot climate resembled that of Mauritania. But Gaul was something else entirely. He had known it would get colder. But the rain, the dismal, unrelenting rain, antagonized him. He called to his captains to get the army moving over the bridge as soon as possible.

"Emir," said one of his captains tentatively. "We should wait for the scouts to return with news. The last we saw, the Franks were spread out all along the Loire. We do not know where they plan to muster—"

"It does not matter," Rayman snapped. "We will crush them like flies, wherever they are."

"But we need time to reconnoiter the land ahead ... according to the map there is another bridge—"

"Of course there is another bridge! There are far too many rivers in Gaul. It's annoying. But we have no choice. We must move forward. We will march on Tours, and we will burn it to the ground. We are the Fire of the Desert. Nothing can stop this fire. Not even this infernal rain! Now go Captain! We are leaving!"

A few miles to the west, Badilo sat in the branches of a gangling tree and stared out over the plain. It had begun as a flicker, no more than a disturbance on the horizon line, like the first breath of a sunrise. Then it grew and spread, moving over the earth with glacial languor, spreading cautious tendrils in all directions. It was not an army, it was a natural disaster, a many-limbed dragon breathing fire and white smoke and a thousand tiny voices that rose to the rhythm of its dance—a thing so vast, so incomprehensible, that for a moment he thought it better not to tell anyone, but to let it be, let it come, for it could not be stopped.

He climbed down from the tree, jumped on his horse, and rode as fast as he could to Chinon.

# 82

SHE KNEW AS soon as he came into the room that the wait was over.

He was wearing his mail shirt with armored greaves, his swords strapped to his belt. He had done this on purpose, had come to her not as the man she loved but as the warrior she had tried to destroy.

She glanced out the window. It was past dawn yet still dark as night, heavy clouds masking the sun. The gloom had settled upon them all, like a great darkness overcoming the world. She felt the stirring of evil in the air around her, ominous. She pulled the fur wraps more tightly around her.

"So it is time," she said.

He went to her, pulled her to her feet and forced her to look into his eyes. They were clear and calm, so terribly light and weirdly beautiful. He ran his hand down the side of her face, memorizing the shape of it, the smoothness of it. She clutched the hand, pressing her mouth into the calloused palm.

"Come back to me," she said, and the tears came, she did not try to stop them. She had said this once before to a different man, knowing this same sort of sinking dread. This was the only thing she had left to fear.

He folded her into him, the mail shirt biting into her skin. But he did not answer.

The Arabs had ten leagues to travel to get to the second bridge. The Franks had more than twice that distance to cover. Within a few hours of learning that Rayman had started crossing the bridge at Châtellerault, Charles' five thousand horse warriors headed to the battleground at full speed. The foot army followed immediately, but it would take them all night to get there. Horses could do it in less than five hours, though they would be exhausted when they arrived and probably not much good for fighting. Charles knew if Rayman decided to attack at once it would be a very difficult fight.

They arrived on the field late in the afternoon. Charles immediately put them into close formation along his front. The horses were blanketed in order to fill the gaps between them, to make it impossible for the enemy to know how deep their lines were. The captains raced up and down the lines, ordering the men to be still and wait.

They did not have to wait long. The drums came first, the sound rumbling across the lowland making the grasses tremble. Then the white line of Arab cavalry appeared, glowing in the fading light, a shiver on the horizon. Charles sat his horse in front of his line, keeping himself between his men and the enemy, like a shield. The captains did the same. Then they saw the ragged enemy lines stop, horses twisting in confusion, as the Arabs finally saw what was waiting for them across the plain, blocking the second bridge.

Rayman saw the Franks waiting for him, horsed and armed and prepared for a fight. He cursed, whipping his horse in circles, ignoring for a moment the chaos around him.

"Salen!"

The captain who had advised him to reconnoiter first rode up nervously. Together they looked at the black line of horsemen on the horizon.

"We can take them," Rayman said savagely. "There are not so many of them. We attack now!"

Salen looked up at the gathering dusk. He shook his head. "This Frank," he said, "has a trick of hiding his army from view. There is a river behind him, which means the ground slopes from their position. There could be many more there than we can see. You see how he blankets the horses? That is to hide the men behind. He wants you to attack! We do not have our full strength here yet. And it is getting dark, and the ground is very wet. We should wait until the morning. In the light we can see how many there are and take them more easily."

Rayman did not argue. He had not bothered to learn much about Charles and his tactics; it had never occurred to him that such knowledge was important. But he knew that he would need his foot army to drive his victory home, and his foot army was not yet on the field.

"Then we give these Franks one more night, before we destroy them forever," Rayman said, spinning his horse savagely.

Charles, seeing the Arabs were not going to advance, called his men to stand down and wait for the morning. By then his foot army should be arriving. He allowed himself a small breath of relief; miraculously, Rayman had taken the bait.

The men hobbled the horses and settled on the cool ground, wrapping themselves in their mantels for warmth, ate dried meatsticks from their packs and tried to sleep.

Rayman stayed up all night, pacing in his tent. His doubts grew about this coming battle. He did not like the ground at all. It was too wet and marshy, difficult to maneuver with horses. It was too narrow as well; his army would be forced to close ranks and fight on too small a front, making his overwhelming numbers almost useless. It was not how he wanted to meet the Franks.

When morning came, gray and rainy as the day before, he called a war council. His chieftains advised him to retreat back to the bridge, re-cross the river and continue up the west bank. The Franks would probably move as well, but at least he would have more room to maneuver—he would be on dry land rather than swamp, and he could make use of his superior numbers by spreading his line and outflanking the enemy. It would take much longer to get to Tours, of course, but the chieftains were certain they could make up the time.

Rayman assented and issued orders to return to the bridge. Stakes were pulled up, supply wagons reloaded, and the huge army that had only begun to arrive turned, ponderously, confusedly, and headed back to Châtellerault. The cavalry went first, barreling through the masses of nomads and leading the way.

But they had another surprise waiting for them at the bridge: half of it was completely missing, the entire superstructure on fire. During the night Rayman's escape route had been dismantled. The troops he had left guarding the bridgehead were dead.

And on the opposite bank stood a force of some three thousand badly outfitted men laughing and hooting delightedly, brandishing spears, slingshots, mallets, and what looked like garden tools. Among them was Eudo of Aquitaine, seated on his Andalusian stallion, his sword high in the air.

Rayman stared in rank fury at the duke, calling up every curse he could think of. Yet he could do nothing more. The tiny army on the opposite bank was not a deterrent to him, but the river was. It was too fast and deep to cross, and his desert-bred horses shied even at the approach. He realized with mounting alarm that he was trapped. He had either to turn back and attack the Franks or retreat to the south. And he could not retreat any more.

He gave orders to his chieftains—they would move north again, between the two rivers, and face the Franks.

In the late afternoon Charles saw them reappear, the massive army, moving more slowly than before. He closed his eyes and breathed again. Eudo had done it.

"What now?" said Gunther, gazing over the plain. The rain had slowed to a tender trickle on the face.

"Too late today," Charles said. "He wasted the whole day in trying to move, and now his army will be too tired to fight. He'll have to wait until tomorrow. We were lucky."

"Lucky!" said Brand, snorting. "You see what I mean?"

"We haven't won anything yet. The beast is cornered, but it isn't dead. And a cornered beast is the deadliest of all."

The Arabs did not attack in the morning. Instead, they spent the entire day setting up their camp, complete with elaborate tents and pavilions. They were settling in, recovering their strength after the long, hectic march. Charles' scouts reported that they were sending wagons loaded with treasure to the south to find a place to hide it.

"I don't think they will attack until they are sure their treasure is safe," Leutgar said. "And perhaps until the weather turns."

Charles shrugged. "Fine with me. He's the one with the schedule to keep. If he wants this war, he's going to have to start it."

The two armies, encamped less than a mile from each other on the marshy lowland of the Vienne/Creuse fork, settled down to wait each other out.

# 83

## October 9, 732

'ABD AR-RAYMAN RODE restlessly back and forth along the front line of his camp, pausing often to stare out over the plain. He was not a happy man.

Six days had passed since coming to this place, six days of pointless maneuvering but no real movement. He had tried to goad the Franks into attacking time and again, unleashing his archers, sending in bands of horsemen and skirmishers to draw them out. But nothing had happened. Charles had not taken the bait. Charles, it seemed, was going to wait for him launch a full scale attack.

Why had he not done it already? There were reasons, of course: the rain, the mud, the treasure, the bad ground. Rayman did not like any of it. He did not like being forced into a fight. So he had hesitated, and in some dark corner of his mind, he knew he had waited too long.

Yet there was no way around this army, these rivers. He could feel the eyes of his men upon him, nervous and quiet, waiting for a decision. He could feel the rain, soft and endless, as if it were seeping into his very bones. The rain was intolerable to him, a symbol of Christian wretchedness—the malevolent weakness of the god-man Jesus. He wanted to kill the rain as much as he wanted to kill the Franks.

Rayman curled his upper lip. The Franks were on dry ground, while his men slept in swamp. They had a bridge, he had nothing but raging rivers on both sides and thick forest to the south. There were no roads that way, no maps. Gaul was a big land, bigger than he had imagined— it was not like Andalusia, where the coasts were close to each other and easy to reach. Once leaving Bordeaux he had ventured into a vast, unknown and virtually uninhabited world that seemed to have no end. He had known that if he kept to the Roman Road he would make it to Tours and eventually Rheims. He had imagined himself to be unstoppable, rolling over the land with his giant army, consuming everything in his path. So why was this small army standing in his way giving him pause?

*Charles Martel.*

Rayman's face clouded with anger, with hate. He was there somewhere, the Hammer of the Franks. He had learned of Charles' spies getting close enough to his own camp to get an accurate count of men and horses. That infuriated him. His own men had managed to capture one of them, but the man—a boy really—had refused to talk even under torture and was executed. His body was sent back to the Frankish camp, headless, dragged by a wild horse, but there was no response. Some of his own scouts were captured by the Franks, but they were allowed to return to their camp alive, albeit without their clothing or weapons. It was worse than death, being forced to walk naked in front of your fellow warriors. Charles Martel knew this.

Rayman felt his blood heat once more at the memory. To defy Allah, to laugh in his face, that was the worst sin. But this Charles did not care. This Charles thought he was greater than Allah. Charles Martel thinks he can change the face of Destiny. But he cannot … no man can …

Rayman lifted suddenly in his saddle, his back springing straight. Yes, that was it! No man can challenge Destiny. Not even the Hammer of the Franks. He can conjure all the trickery he wants, he can build dams and destroy bridges and defile his soldiers and trap him between two rivers, but he cannot win. Yes, that was the truth of it. *He cannot win.*

Rayman felt suddenly jubilant. He'd been foolish to be afraid. Allah had spoken at last. Charles Martel was only a man. He was cunning and brave, but he was still a man. Rayman would beat him. Allah had ordained it. This was the hundredth year of the death of the Prophet. Nothing could stand in his way.

He wheeled his horse and shouted for his chieftains. Men roused, heads popping from tents, eyes lifting from campfires. Rayman's voice rang in the rain-sodden air. The chieftains came, some running, some riding, through the muddy, fire-lit camps.

Rayman remained on his horse, looking down on them, his figure large and proud, his expression triumphant.

"Allah has spoken," he shouted, loud enough so he hoped the Hammer himself would hear. "We are the Chosen People. The army of the Jihad. We have come all this way—have we come for nothing? No! We come to fight—to fight for Mohamet, our prophet, for Allah, our God. We are greater, not only in body, but in spirit! For that, if for no other reason, we will triumph. So we fight, Children of Allah, Brothers of Mohamet, we fight in the morning. When the sun rises we will strike them a blow that will send them hurtling into Eternal Darkness! Remember, Brothers! When Mohamet began his quest he had few men, few weapons, he had nothing! But he prevailed, because he was beloved of Allah! We, too, are beloved of Allah! And therefore we cannot fail! So be not afraid, you Chosen! We have been sent by Allah to fulfill a promise, and this we shall do! Tomorrow we fight the Franks, and we win!"

# 84

THE ROAR SWEPT through the Arab camp, rising up from the earth, a noise so great and terrible it seemed to consume the wind. Across the lowland, Charles Martel sat alone on a rock by the river and listened. *So it will be tomorrow.*

Evening had settled upon them, but even in the dimness he could see the whiteness of the other camp, the moving figures, the horses, glowing in the sprouting, dancing campfires. An army in white. White was the force for good, wasn't it? He looked around at his own army, an army of grays and blacks. He smiled to himself.

He mounted Epone and steered slowly toward the camps. Men had come out of tents to see what the noise was about. He told them as he passed. *Tomorrow. Get ready.* There would be no sleep tonight. There was still much to be done.

He stopped his horse and gazed once more at the army in white. Now they will pray to their god, to Allah. Will Allah help them? Will God help us? Is this battle nothing more than a battle of the gods, with men used as fodder to indulge the gods' jealousies, the gods' pride? Did it make any difference, then, what he did?

Why was it only in the night when the doubts came?

He moved past a group of men sitting around a campfire. Brand was among them, he was singing a rowdy song, the men laughing.

He thought of Lothar. He missed him. He hadn't realized until Lothar was gone how important he had been. Lothar had been by his side for as long as he could remember, fighting for him and often fighting *with* him, and those fights had been important—they had channeled him, forced him to face his own truth. Lothar, for all his fierce energy and rebellious temper, had been his guardian angel. Charles closed his eyes and saw him there—the consummate showman on the magnificent black horse, with his perfect beauty and cornflower eyes, bringing to birth the songs of the jongleurs. He was struck once more with a sense of hopelessness and fear; he shook it off angrily.

He heard a sound behind him and turned, saw his brother running to catch up with him, a torch lighting his face. "I saw you pass by. Do you mind?"

"Not at all." Charles dismounted.

"I wanted to give you this." Brand held out a rolled scroll. "It came earlier, but I haven't seen you. It's a letter. From Boniface."

"Read it to me."

Obediently Brand unrolled the scroll and read while Charles held the torch. The beginning was formal, announcing that he, Boniface, had been elevated to Archbishop over the expanded Holy See of Germania.

"So Chrodegang was right," Charles said. "Poor Winfrith, he's going to hate that."

Brand went on. The tone of the letter changed, became more personal. Gregory was pleased with Winfrith's progress in Hesse and was planning to give a lot of money to the new retreat in Fulda. The Pontiff was hoping, of course, that Charles would do the same.

"Of course!" said Charles, chuckling. "Does he mention the Synod?"

Brand scanned the page, squinting to make out the tiny script. "No … I suppose this letter was sent before the Pope got news of it. Or perhaps Eucher never sent it in the first place! Listen to this: 'All of Rome sends fervent blessings for your success—'"

"Hmmm. I'll bet," said Charles, smiling grimly. "If we get wiped out tomorrow, Liutprand will be in the Pope's backyard the following day. That is, no doubt, why Liutprand didn't come. He believes we will fail."

Brand sighed. "Here is the last part: 'Godspeed, Charles, Hammer of God. You cannot lose, for your cause is just, your heart is true. Winfrith.'" Brand rerolled the scroll, chuckling. "Hammer of God, eh? Rather poetic. That would make a good song."

Charles rolled his eyes. "Do me a favor and wait until I am dead before you write it."

They walked in silence, listening to the sound of the camp. Laughing, singing, drinking, the raucous telling of jokes. A happy camp, eager for a fight after months of boredom and privation, oblivious to the looming danger.

"I've been listening to them," Brand said. "They haven't been too impressed with these Arabs so far."

"That's what worries me," Charles said. "They don't yet know what they are facing."

"Well, it's your fault," Brand said. "They think you are invincible. They think that as long as they follow you, they cannot lose. And I can't really blame them. When was the last time you lost a battle?"

"Rayman has never lost a battle," Charles said quietly. "We took them off-guard six days ago, but now they are ready and there will be no surprises—well, not many. They have the advantage now. They have many advantages." He stopped walking, looking out over the camp. "How Lothar would have loved this," he said with a sigh.

Brand tried to fill the uncomfortable silence. "It's really amazing to me, how you knew everything he would do. It's almost … eerie. I've heard the men talking about it. How do you do that anyway?"

Charles shrugged. "Rayman is a man who believes in his Destiny," he said. "That makes him predictable."

Brand chuckled. "He could have surprised you."

Charles shook his head. "They never do."

They continued walking. Then Brand said, his voice faint, carried on the wind, "Are we going to win tomorrow?"

Charles did not say anything for a long time. Brand glanced at him, suddenly nervous, seeing in his brother's face an uncertainty he had never seen before.

"I used to say I would never fight a battle I was not sure I could win," Charles said. "It has always been a game to me. That's the only way I could deal with it. To lead men into battle is a terrible thing if you think too much about it. So I treated it as a game. I even train my men by playing games—" He paused. "But it is not a game anymore."

"It never was, Charles."

Charles nodded, sighed.

Brand said: "So that is why you are afraid now? Because you are not sure about tomorrow?"

Charles shrugged. "Perhaps Svana is right," he said in a lighter tone. "Perhaps, this is God's war. Not mine."

"I didn't think you cared that much about God."

"The night before a battle, every soldier cares about God."

Brand sighed. "Well, if it comes to that, you must know that God is on our side."

"They think their god is on their side," Charles said, pointing to the dim white shapes on the horizon. "Who knows but it could be the same God after all."

"Ah," Brand said, nodding, "so this is what it comes down to—a battle for the heart of God? And tomorrow it will be decided which of us was right? Is that what you are thinking?"

"Perhaps."

"I don't know much about scripture," Brand said, "but I think there is a bit about not putting the Lord to the test."

Charles smiled tiredly. "Who's testing who, is what I want to know."

Brand stopped and faced his brother. "Brother, you are ready for this. And you are—*worthy*. More than anyone else could be."

Charles was silent.

"Charles," Brand said suddenly, "do you have a chronicler?"

"A what?"

"Someone to set your life down in writing, someone to keep track of all this—"

"What would I want that for?"

"To tell your story! You cannot leave it to the priests—they'll tear you to bits! They'll turn you into a fire-breathing dragon or something!"

"Probably."

"Well, you cannot let that happen."

"How could I stop it?"

"You can make sure your side of the story is told. I want to do this. I want to be your chronicler. So that men centuries from now will know what you did."

Charles laughed. "Why should men centuries from now care what I did? What possible difference could it make?"

"Perhaps they will learn."

Charles looked at him, smiled, shook his head. "They will never learn."

They were silent again, the sounds of the camp growing louder, invading their thoughts. Charles handed the torch to Brand and mounted his horse. Then he stopped, staring into the sky.

"What is it?" Brand asked quietly, nervous.

"It stopped raining, did you notice? The stars are out. It will be clear tomorrow." He seemed about to say more but changed his mind. He looked toward the thin strip of plain that separated faith from faith, looking for the face of the man who was the enemy, wondering if, when he saw it in truth, it would not seem desperately familiar.

He turned once more and looked at his brother. "I am grateful to God for returning you to me," he said. "See that you don't get yourself killed tomorrow."

"I'll do my best. I've always been … pretty slippery, you know."

Charles nodded, smiling. "Call the captains. We meet in an hour."

Brand bowed his head slightly, as if to his lord rather than his brother. "Where are you going?"

"To check on Eudo."

# 85

CHARLES RODE ACROSS the river to Eudo's camp. The Aquitainians did not seem to notice his arrival—they were busy reinforcing the dam and stockpiling their weapons. Eudo's army was made up of farmers and peasants, but he treated them like professional soldiers and they responded in kind. There was a sharpness in their step, a straightness in their backs that was not indigenous to men who hunched over plows all their lives. Charles saw that they were enjoying themselves immensely.

Eudo, too, was having the time of his life. He was dressed plainly in braccos and leather tunic—the uniform of the Frankish army. His smile was no longer guarded, it was open and generous, it made the face oddly attractive. Charles dismounted and they clasped arms.

"It's tomorrow," Eudo said, sounding buoyant. "I was beginning to think they would not fight at all! Come all this way for nothing."

Charles inspected the towers Eudo had built for the archers and the javelin throwers, and a curious looking *ballista*, the design of which he had never seen before. It looked like a giant crossbow with a special torsion bar of twisted rope.

"I have something special in mind for this," Eudo said with relish. "It's like the *ballistae* you use to attack fortresses, but more specialized for this kind of situation. Shorter, higher arc. And capable of throwing incendiary balls. My own design. It's on wheels, did you see? Gives us a bit more flexibility."

Somehow, the sight of this small machine made Charles' heart sink. How could their paltry efforts hold back the coming flood? Yet he had chosen this ground, had chosen to not make his stand behind the walls of Tours.

"How many of these do you have?"

"Only four," Eudo said with chagrin. "Wish we'd thought of it sooner. One of my men, a farmer, not even a soldier, came up with the design. It took some doing to get it working properly. At least they are moveable, so we can use them for trouble spots. Of course, there is a problem as well. We are liable to take out our own men as well as the enemy."

Charles nodded. "I trust you to use them—wisely."

Eudo showed him the huge vats of oil that would be used for lighting river fires. If the Frankish army collapsed, they would do what they could to prevent the Arabs from crossing the river. Mountainous stockpiles of arrows and javelins lined the banks.

"There's no telling how long these will last," Eudo said. "We will restock as quickly as we can."

"And the bridge?"

"We've stacked kindling all along the pilings. It will burn quickly. That means, of course, that your own retreat will be cut off."

Charles nodded. "We will not retreat. What about your reserve troops?"

"Fifty horsemen and two thousand men."

"Good. We'll need them for the hot spots."

Eudo led Charles into his tent—very plain and square—and gave him a cup of wine. Charles smiled, sitting on a camp chair. He took a long drink.

"Is this from Saint-Emilion?"

Eudo shook his head. "I'm afraid not. We 'liberated' it from Saint-Martin's. Not nearly as good, but it will have to do." Eudo sat opposite him, taking a cup of wine for himself. He looked at Charles. "You have doubts." It was not a question.

"Yes."

"Well, that's good. Any man who goes into a battle like this without doubts is either mad or foolish."

"I agree," said Charles, but he sounded distracted.

"You know," Eudo said gently, "once you gave me back my life and I hated you for it. That was Orléans—remember? Your damned terms of peace. Your clemency. I hated you for sparing me. I set myself against you forever—I would not rest until you were destroyed. But it's funny … I feel now I would like to return the favor."

Charles looked bemused. "What do you mean?"

"I'd like to spare you—tomorrow." He paused, searching his thoughts. Charles waited. "You will think me very strange, but I look at you and I am reminded of Baldyr—you have heard his story? The son of Odin and Frigga, the golden boy, the favorite of the gods—they used to amuse themselves by taunting him and throwing things at him, because they knew they could not hurt him, he was immune from all harm. But they were wrong, for there was one thing that could hurt him, one thing only: the thorny mistletoe. And you know what happened: the god-killer Loki learned of this one weakness of Baldyr's and destroyed him with it. But he didn't do it himself, that is the irony—he let the gods do it—he induced the blind god Hodr, the most benign and stupid of all the gods, to hurl the fateful weapon that would destroy their beautiful Baldyr forever. You see, that is what is so tragic about poor Baldyr. He was so immune to evil that he could not conceive of an evil so great as the blindness and vanity of men."

They sat quietly a moment, drinking. The sounds of the camp filtered through the tent flaps, men laughing, shouting, horses snorting. There was no strangeness in the quiet between them. It was sad, Eudo thought, that only at times like this—in the face of impending death—could men truly be honest with each other. Perhaps that was why they craved war, to escape the drudgery of their plain, common lives, to brush away the veneer of their conceit, to lay bare their souls.

"Eudo," Charles said at length, "don't worry about me."

Eudo chuckled. "Good God, has it come to that? I must be getting old." He drank. "Who would have thought it? That I would be sitting here with you, drinking, talking, preparing to do battle at your side. It does make me wonder. About Destiny. Perhaps there is such a thing, after all."

Charles said nothing, gazing at the wine in his cup. Eudo took a breath.

"How is she?"

Charles looked up, smiled gently. "She is well."

"They didn't—harm her—"

He hesitated only briefly. "No."

"Thank God."

Charles stood up, setting down the cup. "I'd better be going. You seem to have things well in hand here."

Eudo rose with him. "Charles ... Godspeed," he said. He seemed unable to say more. Charles nodded and ducked out of the tent.

Pipin met him on the bridge, riding his fine bay, his violet eyes shining in the torchlight.

"Father," he said breathlessly. Charles gave him a look full of consternation. The boy was just too happy. He would be at his side tomorrow, guarding his right, along with Theodoald. He knew he would not be able to keep him from the fight. All he could do was keep him close by. "Is it true? We go tomorrow?"

"Yes," Charles said. "Do you think you are ready?"

"I've been ready forever!"

"I was afraid you'd say that. I don't suppose it would do any good to tell you to keep your head down?"

"Not a bit," Pipin said cheerfully.

"Where's your brother?"

"Oh, who knows—" Pipin shrugged. "He's still—angry. He'll never get over Lothar."

"No," said Charles, "perhaps none of us will." He gazed at his son. "Pipin—there is something I want you to know, something I need to say now because I might not have the chance again. I am proud of you, and—I love you, my son."

Pipin opened his mouth, astonished. Before he could respond, however, his father did another incredible thing. He rode forward so that their horses were abreast and pulled him into his arms. Pipin held on tightly, knowing that miracles such as this come once in a lifetime, and never again.

# 86

## October 10, 732

THE CAPTAINS GATHERED just before dawn around a sputtering fire in front of Charles' tent, while he drew the lines in the dirt with a stick, outlining his plan one last time. Gerold and Milo, Peppo and Sigebald would be on the right; Carloman, Rogan, Arnulf, Carnivius and Odo would be on the left. The rest of the provincial armies would be integrated with Charles' own men, to strengthen the lines and keep the less experienced troops from running when the fight got hot. Eudo and his Aquitainians were to hold the river and supply reinforcements wherever needed. Ragnor would be in charge of the archers. Brand would command the couriers, who would relay orders and bring Charles constant reports of what was happening all along the front.

Charles would set up his command post in the center rear, with forty bodyguards positioned on either side of him. Pipin and Theodoald were on his right, Frido and Herne on his left. They each commanded ten men, so that Charles could use them for quick mobilization to handle problems, of which there would be many.

Charles went over the plan several times. It was vitally important to him that each one of the captains understood it thoroughly, for in their hands rested the control of the armies. He knew his own role would be relatively small—there was not a lot he could do. This army was too big for one man to command. It was a body that required many heads to keep order.

"We must have a tight seal," he told them, "a solid wall. The tiniest crack and the wall will crumble. We use the Roman formation, shield to shield. The lines must be very tight. If there is a gap, the gap must be closed."

"My men are not happy," said Frodo, the Duke of Thuringia. He was short and balding with a hard-bitten face. "There is no glory in just standing still."

"We are not here for glory, we are here to stop this Musselman advance. We cannot let them get to the river. If they take the bridge, they will take Tours."

"We came here to fight, Charles! Not hide behind shields like a bunch of women!"

Charles stood up, giving the diminutive duke the full impact of his size. "If you don't like the plan," he said levelly, "you can leave this field. Now, tonight."

"I have a thousand men here!" the duke exclaimed. "You think you can afford to lose a thousand men?"

"Why don't you go and ask them who they would prefer to fight for, Duke, you or me?"

Frodo's mouth opened and closed again.

"What are the plans for retreat?" said Hucpert, staring at the dirt drawing.

"There will be no retreat," Charles said. "This is where it ends. You must make your men understand this. There is no place to run. If we lose this ground tomorrow, we will have lost everything. Tours, Rheims, the entire kingdom. There can be no running from this ground."

They stared at him in shocked silence. Charles saw their faces, their worry, their undeniable fear. For the first time, it seemed, this battle was real to them. And everything was at stake.

"We have been preparing for months, for years, for this day. This day has come. We cannot lose heart now. Everything depends on us. You must show your men that you will stand, you will hold this ground no matter what … *no matter what.* Then they will follow you."

He saw some slow nods, yet fear still lurked in their eyes.

"It would help," said Sigebald, "if you would—talk to them."

Charles sighed. "All right. Assemble the men. When they are ready, I'll address them."

The nobles dispersed. Charles turned to Gunther.

"You should be going. Are you ready?"

Gunther nodded, rising, draining the last of his mead. They clasped arms silently, then Gunther turned and disappeared into the night.

Charles sat down again, glancing at his nephew, Theodoald. "You have been quiet these days."

Theodoald shrugged. "Not much to say, is there? Today will be a—long day."

Charles laughed a little. "If only Plectruda could see you now, eh?"

"If she were not already dead this would kill her," he said with a wry laugh. "It's funny isn't it? She pushed me into becoming a warrior, then she seemed so unhappy when I finally succeeded."

"She expected you to hate me."

"I did hate you, Uncle." Theodoald looked at his uncle, his brown eyes unblinking. "I wished you dead a thousand times. I prayed for it. I'm thankful God did not answer my prayers." He paused. "Why did you give me that chance, anyway? I've always wondered."

Charles thought about this. "I didn't want to. I wasn't inclined to give Plectruda anything she asked for. But then I remembered what it is like to be born—wrong. To be judged by *what* you are rather than *who* you are. Everyone deserves a chance."

"But I was so hopeless! I would have been dead if not for your protection—"

"No, Theo. You survived on your own. Anyone can learn to wield a sword and ride a horse. But not everyone can learn what is much harder: to act in the face of fear. The kind of fear that would render any sane man witless. That is something that cannot be taught. It can only be endured."

Theodoald nodded. "I believe it. Still, you didn't have to put me in the *Truste*. I was sure you only did that so I would be killed. So you would be rid of me, once and for all."

"Theo, if I wanted to get rid of you, there are much easier ways." Charles smiled. "You earned your place."

Theodoald gazed down at the dirt. "You didn't—have my father killed, did you?"

Charles watched him a moment. "Is that what you think?"

"Yes. No. Not anymore. Once I did. My grandmother believed it. She had you jailed for it. And your own father—"

"My father and I disagreed about many things," Charles interrupted. He sighed, running a hand through his hair. "But it doesn't matter now. Go rest now. I will need you at your full strength soon."

Theodoald nodded. "Yes." He stood up. Before he turned to go he straightened, his fist over his chest, his head slightly inclined. "God knew what He was doing," he said with a small smile. Charles rose to meet him, took his fist, clasping it in both hands. Theodoald blinked, averting his gaze, then turned quickly and disappeared into the camp.

Charles sat back down again, glancing to his son. Pipin caught his expression and grinned.

"Don't be nervous Father," he said. "I feel as though I were born for this. Right now I am truly alive, for the first time."

"That brings me little comfort, my son."

In a misty dawn the army assembled in tight ranks stretching from river to river, an impossibly long front. The captains on horses rode up and down the lines, shouting for order, suppressing any early rebelliousness in the ranks. For despite the very Roman-like character of the Frankish line, this was no Roman army. The men were restive, pugnacious—they disliked the one immutable order they had been given: *Hold*. Hold, hold, hold. Do not advance, do not break the line.

Charles was well aware of their disgruntlement. But he knew as well that their natural urges to fight at will would be a fatal mistake. Sigebald had voiced what he had known in his marrow: that in order for these men to fight the way he needed them to fight, they had to hear it from him, they had to *see* him, Charles the Hammer, astride his famous horse brandishing his famous sword, in order that they should truly believe.

So he rode out to the ground before the standing lines of men in full battle dress, the black mail he always wore overlain with plate armor on his chest and arms and metal greaves on his legs. He wore no helmet, his blond hair cascading over his mail snood. He raised his sword to the sky, the sword that had come to be named, quite without his consent, *Rappenzelle*.

He was met with a roar of adulation, the men chanting his name and cheering wildly, spears waving about in the air. They had not lost their faith in him, that much was plain, though he felt a churning nest of doubt in his belly, the sense that this moment was beyond his reach. He pulled up before them, Epone snorting and pawing the ground. He lowered his sword.

They quieted, every pair of eyes fixed on him in expectation. He looked both ways; he could not see where the lines ended. He would have to move up and down the line and give this speech over and over. He took a long, shallow breath, forcing his mind to what he had to say.

"Today is the day, soldiers of Gaul," he shouted, and they responded with a deafening cheer. He waited for the noise to subside, breathing, breathing.

"Today is the day you prove to the world that it was wrong—that the great armies of Gaul did not leave with the Romans, that the greatest of all armies ever to set foot on this land did not contain a single Roman soldier. That army is you—Germans, Franks, Frisians, Aquitainians—all of you are the true and the only masters of this land!"

He had to wait a long time for the cheering to die down before continuing.

"But don't forget—this enemy we face is also great. They call themselves the Fire of the Desert—they have burned their way through Iberia and the Aquitaine, and now they intend to burn their way into Francia. If they beat us tomorrow, they will burn Tours, and they will go on burning until they reach Rheims. They will take your homes, your land, your women, your children, they will leave nothing in their wake. And you are the only thing standing in their way. Do you hear me? If you cannot stop this fire, then no force on earth can!"

Another roar. He scanned the faces he could see, searching for the rebel, the malcontent. But he saw none.

"This fight we face tomorrow is the hardest you will ever face. This enemy is strong—it outnumbers us and outsteels us. But while the Arabs say they fight for their God, in fact they are really fighting for their *gold*, the vast stores of treasure they have stolen from our land and have stashed in their camps—" The cheering became frenzied. It hadn't hurt, he saw, to mention all the treasure sitting in the enemy camp.

"Now," he shouted, "how best is it to fight this Fire? With more Fire?"

"NO! NO! NO!" they screamed back at him.

"Then how?" he asked.

"ICE! ICE! ICE!" they returned. They had learned their catechism, after all. Charles allowed himself a smile.

"Yes! Ice! That is what you will be today—a solid wall of ice, a glacier, an iceberg! You will stand and you will hold—*hold!* But remember this: one crack in the wall, and the wall comes down. Therefore, you must not let even a sliver of sunlight through the wall. You must stand firm, even when you think you can't. Because you can! You will! Or you will be dead. There is no place to run. You can stand tomorrow and live, or run and die. And when you die, your kingdom dies, your children, your future. It is in your hands now. But I have every faith that when you see the face of the enemy, you will know what to do."

They screamed jubilantly as Charles Martel, sword in the air, galloped down the line. The cheering dissolved into chanting "Ham-MER, Ham-MER" over and over, a song, a hymn, a litany, a prayer. Brand, standing at the front of the line, felt his heart seize a little as Charles tilted his sword to his screaming warriors, a gesture that seemed to him very much like a farewell.

# 87

IT BEGAN AS did all days, with the sunrise.

In the land of the Loire the sunrise was a mystical experience, simmering in a pale pink glow on the flat horizon before bursting suddenly into a riotous spangle of color, then just as quickly dissolving, aging into a wash of pure, undiluted white. The day would be fine and clear, breaking the tide of wet and gloomy weather that had marked the preceding weeks. It was as if all the gods of the heavens had heard of the decision to fight and wanted a clear view of the action, for all would be inexorably affected by the outcome.

Rayman, still riding the wave of his revelation, had decided to treat the enemy to the full force of his frontal assault: ten thousand horse warriors hurling themselves into the enemy's midst. He was somewhat surprised to see that the Frankish cavalry was not on the field. He suspected they would attack from the flanks as soon as he was engaged on the front. But he was ready for that; no army had ever managed to outflank him.

He raised his sword and shouted his attack.

The Franks watched them come, the obliterating mass of warriors in blue and white and gold on white horses, emitting a high-pitched, ghastly keen that made the air rattle. They came very fast, banners waving, swords flying. And then suddenly, halfway through the charge, the front lines began to fall, screeching, into a tangled mass of horses and men.

It took a few seconds before the Arabs realized what they had galloped into—a series of trenches running several hundred paces in both directions. Malwolfe had gotten the idea for the trenches when the men had started digging up dirt and rocks for the dam. The trenches would not stop the charge completely, they would slow it down and remove some of the horses from action.

Yet the trenches had another interesting effect: when the Franks saw those magnificent Arab horsemen fumbling and flailing about, they burst out laughing. Suddenly the mighty army did not seem so invincible after all.

In time the Arab cavalry renewed its charge, managing to skirt around or jump over the trenches. Ragnor's archers let fly a storm of arrows from the towers behind the wall of men. Normally archers were rather useless against horsemen, but these horsemen were so densely packed together that the archers could not miss. From the height of the towers the arrows fell with more deadly force and accuracy, in a straight line rather than a high curve. The shooters were instructed to aim for the horses on the front lines; dead and wounded horses made bigger obstacles, causing the ones behind to stumble and collide, impeding their momentum.

Charles stayed still on his horse, watching the first few minutes of the battle rush by. He glanced at Pipin, his handsome young face radiating such delirious rapture it was hard to look at him.

"Look at them Father! They can't hold out much longer!"

"Pipin, they have not even begun," he said. He wished he had listened to his better judgment and kept the boy out of action.

The Arabs loomed closer, their numbers cut but still overwhelming. Charles braced himself, shouting orders to the captains, who passed them down the line. This was the moment he dreaded, when all their training, all their preparation, could crumble in an instant. To face down a line of charging horses was no easy feat. No foot army had ever done it before.

But they did.

The Arabs did not seem to realize that a horse, unlike a man, will not charge headlong into a solid object. To a horse the Frankish shield wall looked like a real wall; there were no spaces between the warriors. The shields were tall as well, nearly as tall as the men themselves, designed specifically for this kind of formation. Just before impact the horses stopped dead, shying and rearing frantically. In that moment of confusion the Arab horsemen failed to notice the long deadly spears that stuck out from between the shields in hedgehog spikes, impaling horses and men who went down in sprays of blood and inhuman screams.

They were so close the Franks could see the terror in their eyes, feel the blood from the horses splatter their faces. Riderless horses spun around in eye-rolling confusion while the Arab riders, some with horrible wounds, struggled to get control of the terrified animals. The cavalry assault dissolved into mayhem. All down the Frankish line, there were cheers of triumph.

Rayman, riding in the rear with his elaborate bodyguard, could not believe what he was seeing. His cavalry was not only disabled, it was fleeing in panic. He rode in quickly, calling his horsemen back to him. He demanded to know what had gone wrong.

"The horses will not charge their line, Emir!" shouted one of the cavalry captains. Rayman scanned the field, seeing mounds of dead animals clogging his beautiful assault route. Arab grooms ran around trying to collect the frightened, wounded animals. The men still mounted were all in retreat.

"Shall we try again?" asked a chieftain, his voice quaking.

"No. Go to the flanks," Rayman ordered. "We must do this another way." He turned then to the legions of foot warriors behind him, waiting for his signal. "Let us see if they can stand for this!" he said aloud, raising his sword in the air and signaling a charge.

Charles could see the Arab leader clearly now, swathed in white and gold, with a huge gold-trimmed turban around his golden helmet, accompanied by his magnificent Bodyguard of a hundred men on foot and more than fifty on horseback. Charles, who never distinguished himself from his men so as to not make himself a target, thought this bit of vanity rather foolish. But it did not matter, for the army around him was appallingly, stupefyingly, mind-bogglingly huge. It was almost impossible to comprehend its size. There was no end to it, the sea of blue and white and glittering gold seemed to fade into the horizon, as if it extended to the very end of the earth itself.

The attack shocked the Frankish line, shook it to the core; thousands of Arab foot warriors threw themselves en masse at the "wall of ice" with astonishing force. Yet the line held, the Franks pushing back with their shields while stabbing with their spears. A sound rose up from the collision like some cosmic disturbance—grunts and screams and battle cries of many languages mixed together in one massive stew of noise. Motion seemed to stop as the two sides plowed into each other in a colossal shoving match, neither side able to gain even a foot of ground. *Hold!* came the screams of the captains. *Hold! Hold! Hold!*

All that long morning the shoving match continued. The archers and javelin throwers kept up a steady barrage, producing more corpses, which the Arabs had to spend precious manpower removing. Yet wherever an Arab warrior went down the gap was filled in immediately, as if the army itself were a vast ocean that would absorb any disturbance and continue to rush toward the shore. Charles knew his own lines, far thinner than the Arab lines, would be the first to collapse. He did what he could to keep the Arabs from using their full force against him with the aerial assault. But even that could not last forever.

The Arabs had their own archers, and soon they managed to get close enough to shoot, sitting on their horses in the middle of the sea of men. They had not much mobility, for the foot soldiers kept them from maneuvering, but they could shoot fast and accurately. They were not aiming for the wall of men, but for the archers in the towers, who had to stop shooting to take cover. They also aimed for the captains, the men on horseback at the rear of the Frankish line.

"Uncle, get back!" Theodoald shouted. Charles and his guards immediately moved backward, but not before Frido was hit in the chest. He tumbled from his horse facedown. Theodoald jumped down to help him, but he was up in an instant, pulling the arrow out of his body with a terrible growl.

"Get that hold plugged before you bleed to death," Charles said.

Frido tore a piece of his saddlecloth and stuffed it in the hole in his mail. He mounted his horse without a word.

Charles started riding up and down the lines, shouting orders and encouragements, his guards staying close to him but struggling to keep up.

Leutgar rode up to report that the right was weakening badly. Charles had expected this; the flanks were always the first to fall. But it was too soon to let that happen. He turned to Herne.

"Take your men and go help Gerold," he said. Herne nodded. Suddenly, Pipin rode up between them.

"Let me go with him," the boy said. He was looking at his father with the steel-eyed focus that Charles remembered in the forest when they were hunting. A stillness fell around them, all eyes on the two of them.

Charles sighed. "All right. Go."

"Thank you, Father!"

"Be careful, please," Charles said, adding: "And don't tell your mother."

Charles glanced at Herne. "Watch him. I want him back alive." Herne nodded his big, shaggy head. He and Pipin called to their men and turned together, kicking their horses into a gallop for the right flank.

They rode hard to the river and arrived in time to see Gerold and his men surrounded by the enemy, their lines in disarray. The horsemen lined up, they drew their swords. Pipin felt his chest tighten, his heart thrum. When Herne called for the charge he kicked his horse into a gallop, his sword waving in the air like a banner, his scream as loud as the screams of his comrades. They surged into the Arab attackers, splintering them, instantly relieving the pressure on Gerold and his men, who now had room to maneuver.

For Pipin it all happened in slow motion, as if time itself had stalled. He saw Arab warriors turn on him, their eyes barely visible above their face veils, and he charged forward, his sword slicing and slashing, his horse dancing and weaving in a hypnotic ballet. He knew exactly what to do, as if he had done this a thousand times before. He heard his father's voice in his mind, the voice he had heard on the training grounds, echoed by his captains: *Divide and destroy … keep moving … keep a man on your blind side … encircle and trap …*

He saw the others dismount and he did as well, jumping from the horse, his long sword swaying, singing, killing. He felt a heady invincibility, a savage joy as he hacked his way through the cluster of enemy warriors. His sword felt light and easy in his hands, as if it weighed no more than a feather. Herne stayed close to him, but even he could not match the boy's wicked strokes. Pipin was small, but he was very quick, even with the cumbersome long sword. Years of bow hunting had given him extraordinary strength for his size. He moved like the deer he stalked, swift and light and almost magically intuitive, protecting the man on his right as the man on his left protected him. Within a few minutes the skirmish was over, the Arabs that were not dead fled back to their own side.

The Franks bellowed their triumph. Gerold, watching the boy, shook his head in amazement. To him it was like seeing Charles himself in his younger days, the same lean, elegant style, the absolute fearlessness. But there was a difference as well, for while Charles fought with grim determination, and Lothar had fought as a hunger or a need, Pipin fought for the fun of it, the sheer, wanton, unblemished pleasure. He had the kind of battle joy that Charles never had.

"Your father know you are here?" Gerold asked gruffly.

"He sent me," Pipin answered, smiling.

"Did he now?" Gerold shook his red head and laughed out loud. "Well, you better go back and show him that you aren't dead. Not that those Mussies had a chance."

When Charles saw his son riding toward him he breathed deeply, filling his lungs for the first time in nearly an hour. Pipin's whole face seemed to be smiling; he was breathless and excited and even a little dazed.

"What happened?" Charles asked him.

"It's secure—for now. But the right needs more permanent reinforcement. Their horsemen could still gain a foothold."

Charles nodded, calling to one of his couriers. "Tell Eudo I need him on the right."

The courier ran off. Charles was still looking at Pipin, his whole body filled with some unnamed emotion that seemed about to burst inside him: pride, relief, astonishment, love.

"Is any of that blood yours?" he said, looking at the boy's bloody tunic. Pipin laughed.

Charles turned his attention back to the battle.

"They're pulling back," Theodoald said, pointing. Charles saw it was true. All along the line the Arabs were slowing their attack. He looked up at the sun. It was noon, and the heat of the day had settled on the tired and sweating bodies on the battlefield.

"Let the men rest a bit, get some food and water," he ordered. Then he turned his horse, moved back to the river, where Eudo had his hands full giving orders for restocking weapons during the respite. Charles was shocked to see how low supplies had run already. Eudo nodded to him.

"We are collecting the Arab arrows," Eudo said briskly. "We'll have plenty, I promise."

Alfric appeared and handed Charles a water skin. He had a bucket for the horse as well. Charles drained the skin, allowing some of the cool water to spill down his face and neck. The air, after a week of rain, was so thick that every movement felt slow and weighed-down. He called for men to start moving water buckets to the soldiers holding the line. The heat might soon become more dangerous than the enemy army.

Men came to give reports from all the captains. Charles listened, nodding once or twice, offering advice, giving an occasional order. Leutgar rode up, looking at him hopefully.

"Is it time?" he asked.

Charles shook his head. "Not yet."

This day was far from over.

# 88

## Chinon

SVANA PACED THE wide, shady veranda, stopping every once in a while to look out over the river, the road. The steward came in to tell her the noon meal was served.

"Tell your mistress I am not hungry," she said without stopping to look at him.

A short time later the steward returned. Gera was with him.

"My dear—"

"Thank you, but I really am not—"

"There is someone to see you."

Svana stopped, saw the anguish on the older woman's face. News? So soon? She held her breath.

"Who is it? A messenger?"

Gera shook her head and moved aside. Another woman stood in the doorway. She was small, delicate looking, with a pale face and large, violet eyes. Svana had never seen her before, but she knew instantly that this woman was Charles' wife.

"I'll leave you alone," Gera said. "If you need anything, please call me." Gera left reluctantly, motioning for the steward to follow her.

Rotruda was still wearing her traveling mantel, as if she had just stepped out of a litter and walked up the pathway to the door. She looked drained, thin, exhausted, but still beautiful, her eyes pulsing with the energy of her hatred and her fear. Svana waited, breathing slowly.

"I came to see my husband," Rotruda said finally, her voice brittle, breathless. "I brought him his daughter."

"He is not here," Svana said. "He is … at the battle."

"Oh." Rotruda lifted a hand to her face, pushing away a strand of hair. "Lothar is with him then?"

"Lothar … is dead."

The news rocked her; she started to sway. Svana moved to her.

"You are not well, you need rest. We will talk later—"

"No!" Rotruda straightened, her voice like a whip. "We will talk now."

Svana watched as she walked toward the opening of the veranda, looking out. She turned, suddenly, imperious now, the tired, frightened girl gone. "How many times I thought you were dead," she said. "Hoped. Yet here you are. Lothar is gone, but you are still alive. It is not how God would want it." She paused, gathering her strength, her voice. "You must leave. Now. Forever. Never see my husband again. I will pay you whatever it takes to make you go. You will not be here when Charles returns."

Svana waited a moment before answering. "What if he doesn't return?"

Rotruda tossed her veiled head and let out a short laugh. "Don't try to frighten me. You cannot anymore. I have been through more than you can imagine. No one will ever know the sort of suffering I have endured."

"You are wrong about that," Svana said. She moved closer, not menacingly, though Rotruda stiffened at her nearness. Then she undid the ties at her neck and pulled her gown over her shoulders. She turned around, so Rotruda could see her scars. She heard a gasp, small and stifled, she turned back, redoing her gown, gazing with a new hardness at the woman before her.

"Don't talk to me about suffering," she said. "Don't talk to me about pain. We are from different worlds, but we have this in common. We have both suffered because of him. *For* him. We are both tied to him. Neither one of us can be severed from him. I have tried. Believe me, I have tried." Svana felt her own voice falter, rebellious tears press against her eyes.

"What happened to you?" Rotruda whispered.

"The Arabs happened to me," Svana said. "Now they are happening to him. He is out there now, fighting them. That is what is important now. Not you or me."

Rotruda breathed deeply, as if taking those words into her body, like a physical blow, a knife in her heart. Svana watched her, her own breath halted, shallow, aching. With pity, perhaps. Rotruda closed her eyes, then opened them again. They contained something new, not anger now, only fear.

"Where are my sons? Where is Pipin?"

Svana hesitated. "They are with him."

Rotruda was still a moment, then she bent over, her arms clasping her stomach. "Not Pipin … oh dear God, must he take everything away from me?"

Svana went to help her, thinking she was about to faint. But Rotruda straightened, throwing her off, her cloak falling away from her, and Svana saw the glint of metal in her hand.

She had no time to think. The dagger came down within inches of her breast before she could grab her wrist, pushing it away. Rotruda resisted; she was far weaker but more determined, she grabbed Svana's hair with her free hand, shrieking, trying to loosen her grip on her arm. Gera burst in, followed by her steward who lunged at Rotruda, grabbing her around the waist and pulling her back. She seemed to lose all her strength at once; she swooned, the dagger clattering to the floor. She fell limply into the steward's arms.

Svana stared at the dagger on the floor, her heart pounding so hard she felt it in her throat, choking off her breath.

"Oh my dear … are you all right?" Gera went to her, touching her shoulder.

"Yes."

"What happened? What did—?"

"She is … not herself, I'm sure."

"Oh Lord, oh my Lord—"

"You must get her to bed, so she can rest. Where is her child?"

"With the nurse," Gera said. "She seemed so frail, I never—"

"It's all right. Who came with her?"

"Just the nurse and the litter bearers. And two guards."

"Give them food and a place to sleep. Tell them their mistress is not well and needs to rest awhile." Gera only nodded and hurried out, followed by the steward still carrying the prostrate woman. A clamor of female voices rose up outside the entry. Svana waited until the noises died, the footsteps receded. Then she sank to her knees, bent over beside the dagger. She did not move for a long time.

# 89

THE ARABS RESUMED their full offensive, and though Charles' lines were holding they were thinning noticeably, the ones in front dissolving as those from the rear stepped in to take the place of the fallen. Men were forced to pile the dead bodies in front of them as a kind of barricade—dead men joining with the living in strengthening the Frankish wall.

Then the unthinkable happened.

Rayman had pulled back in order to reorganize. He had seen that fighting along the entire front was gaining him no ground. But he realized that if he concentrated more of his foot soldiers in one place, he might be able to punch a hole in the wall, and the hole would only widen as more and more men poured through. He chose what he considered to be the weakest point in the wall, the far left. He sent in his archers to fill the air with arrows, forcing the Franks behind shields. Rogan of Lyon, on the left with Odo and Carloman, could hardly raise his head to see what was going on.

"We must do something about the archers," he said to Carloman, who was nearest to him. One of the problems with Charles' main strategy of immobility meant he could not make use of his mounted archers, who were forced to shoot from towers, where they themselves were dangerously exposed. "Can you hold this alone for awhile? I need to go and talk to your father myself."

Carloman did not respond. But he nodded, as if he understood. Rogan was never sure how to take this man. He had the likeness of his father, with his imposing height and iron-hard eyes, but there was something missing as well, some piece of humanity left out. Carloman seemed to feel nothing, not fear in battle, not elation in victory. He was the same, always, as if experience itself had no impact on him. But this made him extremely reliable in a bad fight, so Rogan had no trouble trusting him with his own men.

Rogan jumped on his horse and raced to Charles' command post. Charles was stilled on his horse, watching the battle out of range of the arrows. Rogan pushed his way through the crowd of guards and couriers.

"My lord," he said, breathless. "We are blinded on the left. We need to do something about the archers."

"What do you want to do?"

Rogan loved this about this man. Before he dictated orders, he wanted to know his opinion.

"I have an idea. Send out the mounted archers. We can make a lane for them, I think. The enemy will not be expecting it."

"A skirmish line?" Charles asked, his brow furrowed.

"If they are fast enough, they could draw off the Arab horse archers long enough for us to get our bearings."

"It would be suicide."

"Ragnor is fast enough. Without it, my lord, we are done for!"

After a moment Charles nodded and sent a messenger to Ragnor to mount up.

Within minutes fifty horse archers, led by Ragnor the Saxon, skirted through a small opening in the left flank and charged at a dead run directly into the enemy lines, shooting fast and hard, each man able to unleash twenty arrows in less than a minute's time. The Arabs were so stunned by the spectacle of these riders, with their naked torsos streaked in paint and their high-pitched wailing battle cries, that they stopped fighting altogether to stare in wonder. Ragnor's archers were able to pick off many of the enemy archers before the Arabs recovered enough to chase after them. This gave Rogan his needed respite; he called for a reformation of the lines, bowing them slightly to compress the front.

Ragnor returned to Charles, laughing.

"Are they all right?"

"I do not know. I didn't stay to watch!"

"I don't think we will get away with that again," Charles said. "Get back to the towers."

The archers had distracted them for only a few minutes, however; the Arabs continued their aerial assault of the left. Despite everything they did, Rogan and Carloman knew it would not be enough. More and more were coming, pushing deeper, with increasing ferocity, concentrated in one area. Rogan saw what was happening: the sight was not a pleasant one. Panic spread through the ranks, and men began to turn and run. He called again to the messenger, struggling to keep his voice calm.

"Tell Charles. We need help. The wall is breaking."

Theodoald could hardly keep up. No sooner had Charles received the message of the breach, then he was away, at full gallop. This had been his fear, the nightmare they all had dreamt more than once. Theodoald did not think about it now; he had no room in his panicked brain for thought at all. Except for this: *don't fail.*

It was worse than they had expected. Not only had the Arabs broken through, but the Franks were in retreat. Charles had told them there would be no retreat. But they were running anyway. To where? There was nowhere to run. Some were even jumping into the river and soon carried off in the swift current.

Charles suddenly spun his horse, facing his bodyguards. He drew his sword. "Plug this hole," he said, his voice cool and measured, yet still full of violent energy. Frido and Herne rushed in with their men, jumping from their horses to join the fight on the ground. Theodoald hesitated, gazing in rank horror at the battle line, men screaming and slashing and dying in obscene numbers. It reminded him, dimly, of his first fight, the battle that he thought would be his last, how his salvation had come only from the dead men who had piled on top of him after his tumble from his horse. The shrill terror of that day felt fresh and raw still; though he had been in countless battles since then and had learned, for the most part, to bury that terror, it never failed to haunt him.

Then his attention was caught by a strange sight: Charles racing off after the deserters, his sword drawn. He followed, drawing his own sword, more afraid of standing still now than of moving. What was he doing? Charles seemed possessed of some new passion even he probably could not control. Theodoald saw him run down one of the fleeing men—he could not tell if it were Frank or Frisian or German—and swing his sword, nearly slicing the man's head clean off. The body fell. The others stopped in their tracks, staring in shock. Charles screamed at them.

"Get back in line!"

They turned in unison and ran back to the battle, as if facing the Arabs was infinitely preferable to facing the wrath of Charles Martel.

Then he was moving again, toward the fighting, shouting more orders, calling the Truste to himself. Pipin came first, and more men joined the two of them. Theodoald gazed at Pipin a moment, saw the effortless way he drew men to him, got them to face death with something like joy in their hearts. So like his father—

Charles was too close to the fighting, to the arrows, which still flew from both sides in a deadly storm. Theodoald rode to his side.

"Uncle, we will go, you must stay back," he yelled. "You must not risk yourself—"

An arrow shot past them, appallingly close.

"Uncle!"

Charles did not seem to hear. He raised his sword in the air like a beacon.

"No!" Theodoald gasped. He suddenly understood what Charles was doing. He was making himself the target, drawing the enemy to himself, while his guards formed a cordon around him. He was the bait, they were the trap.

It worked. They saw. And they came for him, the enemy warriors in their bright mail and white robes and long, curved swords. They came.

Theodoald kicked his horse forward, moving in front of Charles, intending to force him backward, out of the deadly path of arrows and enemy swords.

"Uncle, please, this is madness! You must get back!"

"Get out of the way, Theo," Charles said with the slow burn of rage in his eyes. "Move!"

"No! You cannot stay here. You must ... "

But he could say nothing more.

"Theo?"

Theodoald tried to answer, but his mouth felt full of something warm and thick as honey, a pain like a burn that shot down his spine, leaving a trail of cold in its wake. He fell forward, thought he would fall off the horse. But Charles caught him, somehow, pulling him toward him. *My neck,* he tried to say. His mouth opened and closed again. He tried to breathe but found there was no air left in the world. Then the pain dissolved into heat and nothing, and all he could feel at the last was the hand upon his head, soft like a caress, brushing his hair out of his eyes. It seemed far away, an imagined comfort. *I'm so tired, let me sleep.* Then the words came, words he had been waiting all his life to hear, words that came now out of the gathering darkness to lift him, to carry him forward into the light.

"You're a good boy, Theo."

His heart swelled and burst into a thousand pieces. He smiled, releasing his hold on the man he had come to love, content.

# 90

THEODOALD WAS DEAD in his arms, an arrow in the back of his neck. And arrow meant for him. Charles did not move, watching the Arabs come for him, his own men close in. It wouldn't be enough. The breach was too far gone. He waited for the clash, the collision of sword and spear, the consummation of this horror, which had gone on too long already. He suddenly didn't mind, didn't care.

But then something else happened. Fire. A burning crater appeared where men had been running just moments before. With it came a sound like thunder falling out of the sky, so that the ground seemed to vibrate from the impact.

Charles twisted on his horse, enough to see Eudo's peculiar machine directly behind him, men loading another enormous ball, a cloth-wrapped rock, and setting it on fire. He heard a shout, something he had missed before.

"Fire!"

Literally, fire was launched. Fire, a burning star crashing to earth. The machine creaked and swayed as the ball was launched, much too big to fly that high, though it did. The streak of flame passed briefly through the air and landed near the first one, sending Arab and Frank alike into oblivion.

Charles screamed at his men.

"Now!"

With that his riders formed up, shield to shield, spear to spear, pushing forward in a dressed line, sweeping Arab and Frank alike in its murderous path. The captains shouted for the remaining warriors to reform the line. The hole was plugged.

Charles heard cheering, realized it was Eudo's men, pumping their fists in the air in triumph.

"Charles!"

He looked down, saw his brother, Brand, gazing up at him, holding out his arms. "Give him to me," Brand said.

He was still holding Theodoald, cradled in his arms. Reluctantly, he released the body, letting it slide down the side of the horse, into Brand's waiting grasp.

He realized he had dropped his sword, for Alfric was holding it, ready to hand it to him. He reached down to take it, then his eye was caught by a sudden movement. He straightened. There was nothing but dead bodies around him. And then a whirlwind, rising up from behind Alfric, the flash of metal, catching the sun. A sword spinning through the air.

Instinctively, he threw his shoulder down, hoping the sword would graze off his back, but he could not get low enough. The sword slashed his upper arm, near to his shoulder. An Arab, he thought fleetingly, lying there pretending to be dead.

He saw blood pouring down his sleeve into his open palm. He looked at the blood as if he did not know where it came from, then found he could not move his arm at all.

"Good God. Charles!"

Brand had dropped Theodoald's body and was pulling him from the horse. More hands, others running to help. A strange blackness came over his vision. He heard voices, shouts of alarm, Brand calling for a surgeon. He was carried, could smell the bodies of the men holding him, the sour stink of sweat and blood. His own blood.

"The wound is deep," someone said. The surgeon, perhaps. "The bone may be broken. My lord, can you feel anything?"

"No," Charles heard himself say. There was no pain. Only a shocking emptiness, like his whole arm was missing.

"All right then, hold still while I stitch the wound—"

"No time for that," Charles said brusquely. He rose up suddenly, fighting the blackness. "Burn it."

"No," said Brand. Charles opened his eyes, saw the blue of his brother's eyes swim into view. "No, it won't hold that way—it's too deep—"

"Burn it!" Charles' voice was more of a bellow, whale-deep.

The surgeon sighed. "Fine. You there, get me the iron. And quickly, before he bleeds to death."

When the servant returned the surgeon grabbed the iron and steadied himself. "Hold him down." He slapped the glowing iron on Charles' shoulder, holding it there, letting the steam rise, the flesh sizzle and blacken. Charles' body convulsed with unrepressed violence, he roared in agony. The pain of the burn had brought his whole arm to life; it throbbed horribly, the fire cascading to the tips of his fingers, radiating down his spine. He lowered his head, nauseous and faint.

"He'll be all right in a moment," the surgeon said matter-of-factly. "Keep a hold of him until I get this wrapped."

Charles sat still, forcing air into his lungs, every breath a fresh fire. Brand bent down to him, talking to him, asking him questions. He could not respond. *Give me a minute. Let me think. Let me think …*

Brand offered him water from a skin, which he drank.

"Tell the men," Charles rasped when he could speak. "Get. Back. In. Line."

Brand sighed, rose up to give the orders while the surgeon quickly wrapped the wound. Charles continued to breathe, to focus on the ground in front of him, to keep his stomach from seizing. After a long moment he lifted his head, his vision clearing, the blackness receding to the edges. He saw several faces, Brand, Alfric, Frido, Herne, Pipin.

*Pipin.*

"Are you all right, Father?" The boy's eyes were wide with worry.

"Yes. Go back now. They need you. All of you. I'm all right."

He saw the relief on their faces and was glad for it. He rose unsteadily, refusing all help. He searched the crowd for Alfric, who stood waiting with his horse.

"Please be careful," Brand said after him. "I don't want to be the one to tell your women that you got yourself killed."

Charles grabbed the reins in his left hand and flung himself into the saddle. He sat still a moment, flexing his right hand, opening and closing the fingers; they still had some strength, even if the rest of the arm was nearly useless. He put the reins in his right hand while Alfric handed him his sword. He could fight as well with his left hand as with his right; he trained all his men to do that for just this reason. Frido and Herne moved in close to him, along with the other guards, now fearful and alert. They watched him silently.

Finally, he spoke. "What's happening?" he asked Pipin, who was nearest.

"I was with Carl—they are still pushing the flanks. They will try to punch another hole—"

"Yes. Go back and stay with your brother. He will need you now."

Pipin nodded and left reluctantly. Charles tried to focus, to assess how the battle was going. It was surprisingly difficult; the pain created a fog in his head. He tried to shake it off and surveyed the damage they had sustained. The hole was plugged, that was good. But his own ranks were thinning quickly, too quickly. They had killed so many, yet so many still remained. The wall, however, resolute, would not last much longer.

He called for Leutgar, who rode up to him immediately, expectant. "It's time." Leutgar nodded, grinned, kicked his horse and spun away.

A few minutes later the Arabs, sensing victory was upon them, were stunned by an unholy sight—a burst of fire in the sky, like the explosion of a thousand suns. Many stopped fighting, staring in fear and awe. Some may have known the stories of Constantine and Clovis, they may have known that the Christian God showed his favoritism to his warriors with fiery signs in the sky. There was a moment of hushed anxiety on the Arab front. But nothing happened after that, the hand of God did not swoop down to crush them where they stood, and so they continued to fight, deciding that the fire in the sky had been nothing but a trick of the light.

A short time later they learned that they were wrong. For the God of the Christians had been watching, after all. The Frankish cavalry arrived.

# 91

RAYMAN DID NOT understand what had happened. Where had they come from? There had been so sign of them all day, but he had forgotten, in his rush for victory. It no longer mattered. The horsemen, the black horses he had seen that first day. Suddenly they were upon him, like specters from dark dreams.

Well before dawn Gunther and the cavalry had crossed the bridge and traveled along the river's western bank, well out of sight of Rayman's scouts. They had stayed to the rear of the Arab lines, hiding just over the horizon until they saw their sign—the burning arrows in the sky. Then they moved to the river. Pipin's dam had created a ford that allowed them to cross the river unseen by the Arabs, who were completely engaged on the front. Had the Arabs reconnoitered the river they would have discovered the ford for themselves. But Rayman had not been interested in the river. It was an obstacle, nothing more.

The black horses spread like molten lava over the disordered rear Arab lines, crushing and trampling. And then the wall of ice finally broke, the men surging forward, breaking ranks to fight at will. Horses, shields and men crashed and splintered. Charles could feel the impact like an earthquake under his feet, the collective scream, the shredded screeching of a thousand swords in mid-air. He saw horses falling, their sides bursting blood. He saw men fall as well, many men, white and black, they fell without energy or emotion—it had all become too familiar, too much a part of this new, ghastly world.

This was how it would end, he thought. But he had accomplished his goal—he had reduced the ratio to almost one to one. Now, at least, they had a chance.

He hacked his way through the white, foaming sea, oblivious to the grinding pain in his shoulder, to the blood pumping through the hastily cauterized wound, to the threatening blackness. He looked for Pipin—

didn't see him. But he saw Carloman, for the first time that day, fighting in perfect order, his equipment still intact, his face hardened into a mask of sheer moral resolution. Carloman, he thought, understood his mission, which was more than he could say for himself.

He felt suddenly, extraordinarily, inexorably tired. He had never been so tired. He felt Epone heaving under him, bleeding from cuts on the neck and legs, foam collecting on his chest and mouth. He called for a fresh horse, and Alfric brought him one—a horse as white as snow.

"Gunther calls him Cygnus," Alfric said with a grin.

Charles almost smiled. Cygnus. *Swan.*

They eyed each other, man and horse. Cygnus was smaller than Epone by nearly a hand, but his eyes were keen and bright, his body all quaking muscle. Alfric quickly transferred the saddle and Charles mounted, drawing up the reins, feeling the body curl under him, coiling like a snake.

"My lord!" Alfric shouted.

Charles looked up and dodged a spear just in time; he stabbed someone in the neck, watched him fall. Cygnus reared slightly, tossing his white head. Charles dodged another spear and killed another man. It had all become too easy.

He turned the horse, searching for more prey. He struggled to see through the sweat that fell into his eyes; he had no hand to wipe it away. The fighting continued, listlessly, hopelessly, more men falling by tripping over corpses than to any sword. It will never end, he realized suddenly, it will go on and on until we are all dead, all of us, until there is nothing left. He had known in his heart that it would come to this, that the only way he would win was the final attrition, mutual destruction.

Then an odd thing happened. Just as the sun drew near the horizon line in the west, a cry rose up from the Arab rear, a cry that shivered through the enemy line like rolling thunder. And suddenly, inexplicably, the fighting stopped. The Franks stared in mute astonishment as the entire Arab army ran from the field, back to their camps, screaming in their chattering language something no one understood.

Then there was silence, deep and eerie, like death. The Frankish warriors did not know what to make of it. Some tried to pursue, but the effort was not concerted. Then, as if the strings that held them upright had finally been released, they began to fall, exhausted, to the slimy, blood-engorged earth, some to give thanks, most to lie still and breathe. There was no great joy among them. They did not seem to recognize the moment as a victory. They only wanted to rest.

Charles rode forward, deeper into the field where a moment ago thousands of Mohamet's Chosen had been swarming. He gazed about him at the massive slaughter, the worst he had ever seen. But he had no particular emotion to offer it—not sorrow, not satisfaction, not pity, not joy. He wondered dimly why this was.

He searched the dead, looking for faces. There were few faces among them; he saw mostly arms and legs and torn open bodies, many no longer connected to their original owners. But the faces were gone, somehow. He wondered how many men he had lost. He wondered if he would have enough to fight again tomorrow, when the Arabs came again, as he knew they would.

He looked up, saw Eudo riding toward him, his gaunt face broken by a wicked grin.

"We had a bit of fun," he said, "managed to raise an alarm that the camps were being looted. Who knew it would work so well?"

Charles said nothing, his eyes still focused on the enemy camp.

"God in heaven, Martel! You're bleeding!"

Charles looked down and felt the pain again—a hard, dull throb, as if some huge hammer were relentlessly pounding his shoulder. He rested his sword across the saddle, breathing slowly.

"They haven't surrendered," he said.

Eudo shook his head. "They will try again tomorrow … "

Charles swung his head up suddenly. "What about Rayman? Did you see him?"

Eudo nodded, looking rueful. "We had him surrounded. But he managed to escape—"

"He's alive?"

"Probably—what in hell do you think you're doing?"

Charles galloped a short distance away, toward the Arab camp, stopped, turned.

"Don't follow me. Stay here and gather the men. Get them ready in case they have to fight tomorrow. I'm counting on you, Eudo. This is an order. Don't fail me."

"No!" Eudo said, riding up to him and grabbing hold of his horse's bridle. "You can't go in there—this is madness—"

Charles looked at him, his eyes focused, clear. "Every man has a destiny, Eudo. This is mine."

He wrenched his horse out of Eudo's grip and galloped away, headed for the Arab camp.

Eudo watched him go, breathless, closing his eyes. Presently he heard voices—Pipin, Brand, the bodyguards. They gathered around him, questioning.

"Where's my father?" Pipin asked.

Eudo looked at the boy. Such an innocent face, he thought. Angelic, almost. Yet the boy was drenched in blood, the blaze of war in his eyes like a living being. Who was this beautiful, terrible angel? This son of Charles, hardly more than a child, and already a killer? He closed his eyes, sighing to himself. *We have turned angels into killers. We have made murderers of children.* Eudo's own son was no warrior. It had been a source of shame once. Now it was a relief.

"What's the matter?" Gunther rode up, his face twisted in alarm.

Eudo took a breath. *They might kill me for this,* he thought. He looked into the eyes of Charles' son. "He's gone," he said softly, "to kill Rayman."

Pipin's mouth fell open. "No!" he screamed.

"He gave orders. Clear this field, get a count of the remaining men, restock the weapons. They'll come tomorrow, and we have to be ready."

"No!" Pipin screamed. "How could you let him go?"

Gunther moved in, grabbed hold of Eudo's mail shirt roughly.

"Why didn't you stop him, Duke?" he growled.

Eudo looked at him calmly. "I could not stop him. No one could."

There was a silence. Then Gunther let go of Eudo and swung his horse away. The others dispersed, one by one. Only Pipin remained, turned toward the enemy camp, his eyes searching, hopeless. Eudo moved alongside him.

"You are not a boy any longer," he said. "You must learn that for him—for your father—this is all he has lived for. He has to see it through. To fail would be—worse than death."

Pipin turned his purple gaze on the older man, though there was no understanding in them.

"There is no hope of him coming back then." The boy's voice was surprisingly steady.

"There is always hope," Eudo said. "Would any of us be here without hope? Would your father—" he paused, finding it suddenly difficult to speak. "Would he want you to give up on him? No, Pipin. Never give up."

Pipin nodded, his expression softening, opening. "Can he do it? By himself?"

Eudo felt a laugh in his throat. "If anyone can do it, he can."

# 92

HE RODE LIKE a storm wind through the enemy camp. Men stopped to stare at him, not seeing who he was, seeing only a blur of white and black, most too tired or wounded or distracted to care. He rode unmolested, searching.

He saw it ahead of him, the large white tent with the gold trim, bearing the banner of a red flame on a field of gold—Rayman's tent. An alarm went up, a keening call; guards poured out from the tent, rushing at him.

Charles gripped the heavy sword in his left hand, dropping the reins, guiding the horse with only his legs. He charged them, his giant sword, far longer than the Arab swords, ripped through flesh and bone as the horse thrashed and shrieked and spun crazily. He killed four of them before he heard a voice roaring a command. The other men backed away as Rayman himself, sword in hand, emerged from the tent. He limped from several bloody wounds on his legs, hastily wrapped. Charles slid from the horse.

They faced each other across the muddied space, littered with dead men. Charles looked into the dark eyes, the dark face, a face full of loathing and power, the face of Loki, the god-killer. He dropped his long sword, knowing he did not have the strength to wield it any longer. He drew the shorter scramsax. He would sacrifice distance but gain control.

Rayman moved first, charging him. The swords met and clashed—Charles felt the blow shiver down his arm and through his body. His fingers shook. He whirled as Rayman came in for another blow, this one lower and deeper, across the middle. He met it, the blades held a moment, locked—they stared at each other, both faces contorted with pain and fury. Then Charles broke free.

Rayman circled, limping slightly, looking for an opening. Charles followed his movement, blinking away the sweat, the black dots threatening his vision. Rayman hit him, connecting with his wounded shoulder—Charles threw him off. They circled. Rayman came in again, slashing—he felt the blow across his ribs, heard them crack. He realized suddenly that he couldn't breathe; he felt the air sucked from his body, replaced by a crushing pain in his chest. Rayman took the opportunity to strike again on the other side, but Charles managed to slip away in time, gulping in air as he did.

He tried to raise his weapon, found that he couldn't—his body had ceased to obey him. Rayman saw his weakness; he bellowed and smashed into Charles' good arm, dislodging the scramsax. Rayman raised his sword over his head for a final blow. With no other option, Charles threw himself at the Arab's exposed torso, dragging them both to the ground.

They rolled in the mud, grappling, Charles only able to use the weight of his body to keep his opponent contained. Rayman finally pinned him on his back, hovering over him. But his sword was useless now—he was too close and it was too long. He threw it aside and reached for the knife in his belt.

But it wasn't there. He felt along his belt, desperate, releasing his hold — it wasn't much, but it was enough. With one last, great effort, Charles threw him off. Rayman grunted, rolled, recovered himself and lunged again. He saw too late the knife in Charles' hand, *his* knife. He tried to stop his momentum but couldn't—he screamed as he fell forward onto the knife, which sank deep into his throat.

His body hung over Charles, suspended only by the blade between them, his eyes bugged with surprise, his neck spurting blood. Then Charles relaxed his hold, rolling over, letting him fall onto his back. Rayman's eyes were still open, staring up at his killer—he looked merely perplexed now. He tried to speak, to swear or spit, but only blood came forth, gurgling to his lips. His eyes fluttered, his breath shallow and ragged. His arms were flung wide on the ground; he seemed to sigh.

Charles felt his own body collapse, sinking deeper into the earth. He waited to hear the footfalls of the men who had watched the fight, sure they would be coming now to finish him off. But he heard nothing at all. He felt the wet ground seeping into his skin, mingling with his blood. He felt no pain.

He looked at the sky, streaked red as if wounded, the whole world drenched in blood. He had been right after all, he thought, about how this day would end. That there could be but one ending, that no God would allow for victory on a battleground such as this. But still it *was* a victory, in time the wounds would close, the dead would fold into the earth, the world would heal. That was a good thing, a necessary thing.

He thought of his sons, of his wife, fleetingly, not as real beings but as paper faces without dimension, without motion. His boys—they would be all right, he was sure of that. He thought of Svana with a dull, deep ache that he had lived with for so long it had become a comfort to him, something warm and familiar, a piece of his soul.

He closed his eyes. Loki loomed in his mind. Loki, his wolf's eyes dimmed, his red lips scarred. And Baldyr, mangled by the mistletoe, blood bright on his white skin. And the gods crying, the world crying. And then he remembered that Baldyr had had a chance to come back to life—if all the eyes in the world wept for him. The world did weep, but not all the world. One pair of eyes remained dry. And one pair of eyes was all it took to send him to his death.

# 93

SVANA WAS STILL on the terrace when she heard him in the atrium—his familiar voice, soft yet commanding, followed by the scurrying of a sleepy servant. She felt for a moment that she couldn't move from that place, that if she stayed there, she would be all right, she would be safe. But in the end she did go, through the garden toward the atrium. She saw him coming toward her and stopped.

She was surprised at how he looked—she had not seen him since last Christmas, a lifetime ago. He looked much older, thinner, beyond tired; he was filthy and smelled like something long dead. She had to smile, remembering his fastidious grooming habits. He threw the end of his mantel over his shoulder, a cavalier move, elegant, so like him. But she understood his expression. He spoke only to fill the space between them, he wouldn't have needed to.

"The day was a victory," he said tonelessly. "The enemy retreated. We've lost many men, but they lost more. We are expecting another attack tomorrow."

"And Charles?" She thought it better if she said the name first.

He didn't speak for a moment. "He went into the enemy camp—he went to kill Rayman." He paused, swallowing. "He hasn't returned."

She stared at him, not responding. She thought she was prepared for this, but she had been wrong. She closed her eyes, felt a wave of dizziness, of disbelief.

"Go outside," she heard herself say. "Get me a horse. I'm coming back with you."

"Where? Don't be ridiculous, you cannot go there—"

Svana started for the stairs. Gera appeared on the landing, her kind face awash in fear.

"What's happened?"

"I must go now. Will you tell Gryffin—I will be back as soon as I can." She paused, a hand on Gera's arm. "Will you make sure she is gone tomorrow?"

Gera nodded, unspeaking. Svana went to Charles' room, slipped on his old braccos and a leather tunic, a pair of sealskin boots and a heavy mantel. She went back outside where Eudo waited.

He glanced at her clothes, *his* clothes, inclined his head, then helped her onto the horse. They rode together in silence; they were like strangers now, as if the things that had happened between them had been wiped away. He didn't stop to rest and she didn't ask him to—she knew that they if did, they might never get up again.

The dawn was very misty, speckled with rain. She could not see the battlefield at first, so thick was the low-lying fog. Men appeared as ghosts, feetless, floating past her. She saw outlines of tents and canopies, smoking fires, the air redolent of roasted horse meat. She stifled a gag. She heard the sounds of the wounded, still unseen, a constant wave of moans. But generally, she heard silence—a terrible, consumptive, relentless silence.

A man approached them as they crossed the bridge—she saw that it was the hulking giant Gunther. He had several mounted guards with him. He glanced at her, his small, expressionless eyes passing through her as if she were not there at all.

"Anything?" Eudo asked.

"No." Gunther took a long breath. Silence descended again, the men staring vacantly into nothing.

*They can't fight today*, she thought. *They will lose. They can't do it without him.*

"You should not have come." It took her a moment to realize that Gunther was speaking to her. "This is no place for—a woman."

"This is no place for men either."

Gunther made a noise, turned to Eudo. "We hope they will wait until the fog lifts—"

He was interrupted by a shout from far away, deep into the mist. Svana could not make out the words, but the tone had the distinctive ring of excitement. The men around her straightened, their attention caught. The shouting continued, more voices joining in. All at once they were moving, spinning their horses and heading into the mist. Svana followed, swept up in the current. There were still many dead on the field; her horse trotted daintily between them. Ahead of her the veils of mist parted slightly, bringing the Arab camp into view.

She stopped, as did everyone, and stared in wonder. The camps were empty. Deserted. As far as she could see, not a living thing moved.

Not a single living thing.

Around her men were shouting, wild with joy, rushing forward into the camps, storming the empty tents. Amazingly, much of the Arab loot had been left behind.

What had made them leave in such a hurry? Without their treasure? What had scared them so utterly? Only one thing. She smiled to herself, despite the consuming grief of her soul.

She rode forward, ignoring the running, shrieking men, once tired beyond death, now delirious with joy. She saw that there were still some men living, the wounded left behind. The warriors killed them as they went by, looting their bodies. They did the same for the few horses that lay on the ground, moaning pathetically. The sight of the animals made her want to weep. How could she feel pity for these beasts and not for the vain, cruel and prideful men who had died before them?

The mist gathered around her, rising up from the breathless earth like steam from an open wound. She saw before her the huge white and gold tent of the Emir. Before it lay a trail of dead bodyguards and then Rayman himself, his body sprawled on the wet ground, the wound in his throat covered in flies. His eyes were open, staring, still reflecting the last thing he had seen before he died.

She closed her eyes, imaging what that was. The enormity of it—the sheer enormity of what he had done began to dawn on her. She looked around, searching for his body, knowing it was there somewhere. She had to get to it before the scavengers did.

Men came and attacked the corpses like vultures, tearing them apart to get at the treasures. Svana could not watch.

She turned her horse and walked out of the camp back toward the battlefield, searching for him in the ruined faces that dotted the earth, every step a treachery, the horse's hooves slipping on blood and bloated human tissue, coated with the colors of earth and men. He was not there. She dismounted and went forward on foot, leaving the horse behind. She did not know where she going anymore, only that she had to keep going, keep looking.

And then there was another sound—a warning of some kind. She turned back toward the Arab camp, squinting to see beyond the fog. She heard more shouts, and men began running, brushing past her as they went. She understood. The Arabs had come back. They had retreated into the mists and waited for the Franks to enter their camps, and now they would attack and destroy them all. That was why they left the loot! As bait! It was starkly clear to her suddenly—she wondered how they could have been so fooled.

Men continued to stream past her, ignoring her. She knew she should go back to the bridge. But she couldn't move from that spot. Because he was there, somewhere, and she couldn't leave him, not now. She waited for the Arabs to come crashing through the murky white curtain.

Then she saw it—the first wave materializing from the mist. She stared, sure she had missed something, the transition from earth to heaven perhaps. She saw a molten blur in the fog, sharpening as it came, assuming the shape of a white horse. She breathed, waited for more to follow, but there were no more. There was only one. She dropped her arms to her sides, puzzled, as the horse emerged from the mist.

The men continued to rush past her toward the white horse, cheering—it *was* cheering, she understood that now. She froze, feeling her breath lock in her chest, her heart race so it echoed in her ears. For the figure on the horse was not swathed in white. He wore the black mail of the Franks, and his hair was the color of the sun.

The men engulfed the horse, stopping its movement. She saw the rider bent over the animal's neck, the tawny hair spilling forward, disappearing in the mane. The horse snorted, tossed its head. She saw him pulled from the saddle, set upon his feet until he held himself upright, miraculous, his face and his clothes caked with blood so that she should not have recognized him at all. And she wouldn't have, had it not been for the color of his eyes.

Then he was walking toward her, alone, shrugging away the hands that tried to help. She walked as well, saw the distance between them close, the truth of his body and his eyes so clear now she thought that if she were dreaming it was all right, because even this dream was better than reality. She started to laugh, soundless, light as air, she opened her arms and caught him as he fell into her. She collapsed with him, into the mire of broken humanity that was his victory, still laughing, weeping. She felt his arms close around her, his face in her neck, but she was crying so hard she did not hear the words he barely spoke—that perhaps the whole world had wept for Baldyr, after all.

# EPILOGUE

## Quierzy-sur-Oise
## April, 733

SPRING CAME AGAIN to Francia.

The Oise River ambled fecklessly through the lush, green meadows of Quierzy, wrapping itself around tall reeds, spinning over rocks, dragging with it all manner of life forms on its mad rush to the Seine. Along its steep, grassy banks horses wandered, testing the footing carefully and stooping to take brief, cautious sips of the water. After a dry and dismal winter, a month of drizzly, soul-breathing rain had brought the little meadow suddenly, violently to life; it was as if Saint-Martin himself had propelled his funeral barge down the Oise's surly waters in search of yet another, more perfect paradise.

The rain had ended, finally. The clouds were still heavy and gray, occasionally parting to let in a brief, savage burst of light, bathing the earth in blinding, spinning, swirling gold. It was almost the color of Svana's gown as she knelt beside Charles under the shade of a chestnut tree, while Chrodegang pronounced the blessing of marriage.

When the blessing was done, Charles placed a small garnet ring on her finger. She felt suddenly dizzy, the world spiraling around her as she gripped his arm for support. He kissed her, and the world stilled, and she could see him clearly again.

It was a simple ceremony, accompanied only by the music of the river tumbling along the rocks and the newly budding leaves whispering in the wind. It still seemed unreal to her. That Charles was alive was miracle enough. From the moment he had fallen into her arms on the battlefield she had known that this was not how their story should have ended, that they had been saved by Grace alone, against all the rules of the world.

Chrodegang gave Charles a little bow and sniffed audibly. "My prince, my congratulations and blessings," he said. Then he bowed to her and said, "My lady." She almost laughed aloud at the absurdity of the

Chancellor of Francia bowing to her. But she smiled and inclined her head. The company cheered.

They went back to the house where a wedding supper had been laid, a simple affair of roast pork, lentils and bread. Brand, Gunther, Milo and Gerold took turns congratulating Charles and kissing the bride while Freddy and Erik, who had travelled all the way from Saint-Emilion for the ceremony, filled cups with wine and set the food on the table. Eudo had not come, but had sent a message of good wishes. Carloman didn't come either, though no one expected him to. But Pipin attended, surprising everyone and delighting Gryffin, who followed him around like a worshipful puppy. Pipin was his usual gregarious self, but his eyes were sad, the purple eyes so like his mother's.

Charles learned of his wife's death upon his return to Paris in triumph after his victory. The doctors said she had died of sheer exhaustion and a "paleness of the blood"—they had warned her not to try to travel so soon after giving birth. Gossip flew; people said that Svana poisoned Charles' wife when she went to Chinon to see her husband. Svana had been taken to Quierzy under guard for her own protection. Charles went there after the victory feasts were over, to rest for the winter and to heal of his wounds.

They lay together that night for the first time as man and wife; for Svana it was a joy almost beyond bearing. She knew in a few days he would be gone and she would be alone again, but even this did not trouble her anymore.

"I love you," he said. It was the first time he had ever said those words to her. Then he smiled. "Battle Swan."

She winced at the name, the unwanted memories.

"You once told me you would never come here," he said, holding her against him, his fingers brushing the soft curve of her shoulder. "That it would be a prison. So … will you stay?"

She heard the veiled anxiety in his voice. She had avoided this question for the whole winter of his healing. She sighed. "That estate manager of yours is a lazy toad. He is not even rotating the crops. The yield here is half of what it could be. There is no better soil in Francia … and this house is too small. Did you build it? You can't expect to run a proper estate with a house this size. It will need to be expanded, and you need to bring in more freemen … "

She looked at him and saw he was smiling.

"Yes, Charles, I will stay. I will be bored and lonely, no doubt. I will spend the rest of my life waiting for you. But I will stay. Because I love you. And love is the exception to every rule."

He leaned down and kissed her mouth, and he did not let go for a long time.

"Are you ready to go back?" she asked some time later.

He sighed, rolling onto his back. "You might as well ask me if I am ready to die," he said. "I need to get it over with."

She turned on her side, her hand on his chest, tracing the scar. "I have something to tell you."

"You're pregnant," he said, making her raise her head and look at him sharply.

"Am I so fat already?"

He laughed. "I know your body better than I know my own, my love."

"I think it will be around the time of the Slaughterfest—"

"I will be here for the birth."

"What about the Assembly?"

"The Assembly can wait. The bishops have not much to say anymore."

She smiled. The bishops had been conspicuously silent since the battle. Though she knew the Church had not given up its fight, she was glad that he would have, at long last, a measure of peace.

"I will be fine. Freddy and Erik said they would return, after the harvest."

"That's kind of them. But I will be here."

"You won't be as useful as they are," she said wryly. "But—I would like it if you came."

He gazed down at her. "I will miss you," he said with surprising feeling. The look on his face made her start to weep.

"We cannot make the world the way we want it," she said. "But God has given us this moment, this place. It's all we can ask for."

"It's still strange hearing that from you ... my Valkyrie."

She smiled ruefully. "God gave you your victory, Charles. God gave you your life back, and mine. Never forget that. To forget is ... death."

"Then I will not forget." He smiled indulgently, pulling her to him. He moved stiffly, favoring his right arm, wincing. The wound had not healed right. It would haunt him for the rest of his life. But he had survived.

He had told her that after he killed Rayman he thought he was going to die. He remembered the darkness closing in, a blessed peace. But then he had awakened to see a crowd of figures dressed all in white surrounding him. At first he thought they were the Arabs, closing in to kill him. But they were not dressed in white, they *were* white, their faces obscured by a glowing light. They did not speak, but still he heard a voice, and though he was sure he was dreaming, the voice was clear and insistent: *Get up*. He did not want to get up. He was ready to die; he had accepted it. But the voice would not stop. Then he felt something nudging him, pushing on his side, and he realized it was the horse, the damned silly horse, the horse named Swan. Somehow he managed to get up and get into the saddle, he didn't know how, though he was pretty sure that the horse had knelt down for him. After that he passed out and remembered nothing. He didn't know how long he had been out, and when he finally came to, the horse had wandered away from the camp, over to the river. It had taken him some time to figure out where he was; it was the noise in the camps that redirected him.

"Perhaps they were angels," she had murmured.

"Or Valkyries," Charles said.

She laughed. "So you killed five men with a wounded arm, and the Arab leader, and were rescued by angels. And a horse. No one will believe it."

"Don't tell Brand or he'll make a song about it."

They spent a few more days in the little house in Quierzy, enjoying the remnant of a verdant spring, the company of friends. The calm weather held, they played with the horses and sat about under trees, drinking and talking. In the years to come Svana would look back on that time as a kind of golden pause in their lives, a season suspended, bathed in sunlight. The world was right for a moment, Francia was at peace, and Charles, after so many years of wakefulness, slept.

She did not want it to end. But the clouds returned by the end of the week as the men prepared to leave, taking their lord with them, back to Kolonia, to his kingdom, away from her. Gryffin, sensing the coming departure, grew anxious and agitated. Svana worried about him, knowing he possessed a volatility his father did not, and she wondered, as she often had, what would have happened if the immense killing power of Charles Martel had been housed in a less restrictive frame.

She sat on the stone bench in the courtyard watching horses being saddled and readied for the journey. Freddy handed out bundles of food for their saddle packs as well as skins of mead and cider.

Brand sat down beside her, handing her a bouquet of flowers he had apparently picked at the water's edge. "For the fair lady. A lily among thorns."

"Have you written a new song already?"

"It is Solomon's Song. Have you not heard it? There was never a more worthy jongleur than Solomon. *For, lo, the winter is past, the rain is over and gone, the singing of birds is come, and the voice of the turtle is heard in our land.* I believe Solomon must have come to this place." He paused, gazing at her. "We will look after him, all of us."

"How does he seem to you?" she asked.

"The same," he said. "And different too."

"I am afraid for him."

"Why?"

"Because he has lost his faith."

"In what? God?"

"In himself."

Brand laughed. "How could he? After winning the greatest victory in the history of the Franks? It was the most brilliantly fought battle since the Romans walked this land; jongleurs will be singing of it for ages to come."

She smiled thinly. "The problem is, he doesn't know what to do now. He thought it would all end on that battlefield. He hadn't planned on … going on. I think there is a part of him that doesn't *want* to go on. The fight has gone out of him, Brand."

"I don't think so. The first thing he did when he got to Rheims was exile Eucher and all his minions. And stripped the Count of Vienne of all his property. Theodouin has been forced to serfdom on his own estates! That doesn't sound like a man who's lost his fight. It is just as you have always said: Charles is God's man. If God saved him, He must still need him. The war is not over. The Arabs will not give up. He has to go on."

"I don't know if he can." She could not hide the tears pooling in her eyes.

"What do you want me to do?" he asked.

"Help him," she said softly. "Because I can't. I don't want him to go back. I want him to stay here, with me. To forget about the world. He's earned it. He deserves it. He would do it if I asked him to. I think he has been waiting for me to ask."

She turned her gaze to her husband, moving among the horses. "But I cannot ask. I know it isn't what he was meant to be. So I am giving him back to you. But you have to protect him, Brand, because he cannot protect himself."

She paused, gazing now at the ground at her feet. Brand waited. "For so long we have thought of him as the earth, the fixed point around which we all moved. We measured the changes in ourselves only in relation to his constancy. But no one stays the same forever. Not even him."

Brand put his hand over hers. "Don't worry," he said. "Really. He'll be fine. He always is. I'll make sure of it, I promise you."

She smiled at him gratefully. "I wonder how different his life would have been if he hadn't found you."

"I could say the same about you, my lady."

She smiled. "His life would have been much easier without me."

"Yes. And harder, too."

They looked at each other.

"Don't blame yourself. About Rotruda. It's no one's fault. It's just—the way it is. There is much sadness in the world."

Svana nodded. "Carloman—"

"Carloman is a hard man. Harder even than his father. But he loves his brother. He and Pipin will rule together, and it will work, somehow. Whoever thought it was possible? Brothers actually getting along."

Svana laughed despite herself. Then she glanced at Charles, who was talking to both his sons. She felt a catch in her throat, a sudden, inexplicable premonition. She shook it away.

"Pipin will make a great leader someday," she said softly. "Perhaps even a king."

"You think he will be king?"

"It's inevitable, no matter what Charles says. The Merovings cannot last another generation. And the people will demand a king."

"They might make Charles king."

She shook her head. "You and I both know that Charles would never consent to that. He is perhaps the first man in history to refuse a kingship. The last as well."

Brand nodded in agreement, then said: "You know that he will not forget your son when it comes time to decide the inheritance."

Svana sighed. "In a way I wish he would. It can only lead to fighting, in the end. And Francia has had enough of that. Gryffin—he is like him in many ways, but he is like me too. He will have his courage, but lack his forbearance. He will be rash, impatient, vengeful. It will be his undoing, as it nearly was mine." She looked at Brand. "Gryffin, I'm afraid, is very aptly named."

They laughed together. Charles heard the laughter, looked at them quizzically. Brand gave her an embarrassed smile. "I'd better see if I can be of use," he said.

Men began to mount their horses. She felt her stomach tighten. Charles walked to her, stood before her a moment, staring at her, as if he needed to remember her exactly as she was at that moment.

She smiled tremulously. He reached for her, holding his palm against her cheek.

"You are so beautiful." He kissed her, fully but gently, lingering, as if he were trying to memorize the shape of her mouth, the taste of her on his tongue. He pulled away, wiped a tear from her face. She gripped his hand.

"Come back to me," she whispered.

"I will."

He turned around and mounted his horse, the white horse named Swan—Epone had finally earned his retirement. He spun the horse in a circle and signaled the men to depart. They took off at once, heading up the path to the little hill, Brand and the guards first and then Charles following behind. She stood still, her arm resting on Gryffin's shoulder, watching him as he ascended the hill, the white horse almost lost against the whiter sky. And just as he reached the top the sun burst through the clouds above her, flashing upon him, setting his body aflame, his hair trailing like liquid fire. Then the sun was caught by another cloud, and the world darkened, and he was gone.

# HISTORICAL NOTE

CHARLES MARTEL WOULD spend the rest of his life fighting Arabs. Though the tide had turned at the Battle of Tours, the Muslim armies continued to harass the Aquitaine, and it was not until late in his life that he was able to contain them once again in Septimania. He never succeeded in retaking Narbonne or in driving them out of Gaul altogether, but he did, in his famous battle and subsequent battles, secure Gaul from the threat of Islam forever. The Battle of Tours is still considered one of the most remarkable military achievements in history, and Charles himself one of the architects of modern warfare; his blending of Roman discipline and mounted shock combat would change the way wars were fought for centuries after.

Charles died at Quierzy in 741. Many years after his death the legend arose that, when his tomb was opened by Bishop Eucher—who had been directed to do so in a dream by God—a "huge, hell-born dragon" emerged from the vault, and all the interior of the chamber had been "charred by a consuming fire." The legend was recounted in the venerable bishop's biography, supposedly signifying God's final vengeance against Charles Martel for his wanton seizure of church lands. It is not likely to bear much truth, however, for Eucher died three years before Charles himself.

Charles Martel would never make himself king. But his son, Pipin, would, and Pipin's son Charles, born the year after his grandfather's death, would eventually be crowned Emperor of the Holy Roman Empire and would be known to the world forever after as Charles the Great—Charlemagne.

Made in the USA
Charleston, SC
04 December 2014